GLORY CREEK

JENNY HALEY

ISBN: 978-1-0734-1009-5

DEDICATION

For my mama and number one fan, Sherry Diane Murphy Hubbard.
Love you more.

CONTENTS

BAILEY ROSE, M.D. SERIES

Glory Creek, Book 1

Rosie's Castle, Book 2

Lada's Grove, Book 3

The Red Rose, Book 4

Green Meadow, Book 5

PART ONE

San Antonio
1876

CHAPTER ONE

Bailey Rose owned one dress. It was bright red satin, hacked from one of her mother's discarded "working" dresses and stitched together painstakingly with an intense concentration remarkable in such a young girl. She had even stolen a doily from one of Blanche's tables and fashioned it into a crooked lace collar. She had finished it last night by candlelight, crouched beneath the porch, the usual revelry commencing overhead. And now, just look! A thrill shot through her as she gazed at her reflection in her mother's full-length mirror. She actually looked like a girl!

She hesitated, reluctant to disturb the sleeping woman and the man beside her on the ornate canopy bed. The two slept as though dead, breathing thickly and steadily. Her eyes slid to the gargantuan wardrobe that lined one entire wall of the room. This dark oak monstrosity contained all of Addie's twenty-seven dresses in every imaginable shade of silk and satin; she gazed at the magnificent gowns, realizing with a sudden pang how shabby her own hand-stitched dress actually was. She had wanted to tell her mother where she was going, but now she could barely swallow the gorge that rose in her throat, and she paused as the enormity of both her love and hatred for her mother caused hot fingers to tighten her scalp. She finally slipped from the room, shouldering her heavy brown satchel, the sounds of dolorous snores and the smell of stale beer and bitter perfume following her down the stairs and into the street, until finally it was all dissipated by the fresh morning.

Once on the street she allowed a brief grin, appreciating the irony of a twelve-year-old having to sneak out of the house to go to school. She quickened her pace, not wanting to be late for her first day at the German-English school. It was the orderliness of the school that drew her: its clean, beautiful lines, so sturdy and solid-looking; its well-scrubbed, happy children who flowed in and out of the two facing buildings every day as she had watched from her hiding place. There were no screaming Madams, not one drunk cattle rustler or soldier, and not one scraggly, hungry child to be found at the school. As a matter of fact, all of the children looked strong and healthy and well-fed. *They must feed them there. If I go to school I won't have to beg Blanche for leftovers from the clients' plates anymore.* The brief grin turned into a full-blown smile, and the dark eyes sparkled for the first time in a very long time.

Military Plaza was coming to life this May morning: the vendors were busy setting up their long lines of tables laden with early spring produce. Behind these tables the farmers' wives were scurrying to set up butter, poultry and egg stands. Wagons filled with early wool, hay and grain were aligning themselves perfectly, side by side, to sell their wares. Snatches of Spanish, German and English drifted together, and Bailey caught pieces of many different conversations as she walked. She reveled in the exotic sights and sounds and wished for the hundredth time that she had more coin to spend. The incredible abundance of meat was enough to boggle the mind: fresh beef, fish, mutton, venison, buffalo, and turkey were piled high in wagons. In a nearby stall were rows of dark, sweet-smelling French candy, wrapped for customers in brightly colored paper. Next to this the Indian women had stretched out blankets in the dirt and were hawking soft, supple skins of ocelots and leopards. One of the women called to customers while the others cured the unfinished skins with the beasts' own brains. A small Mexican child manned the next booth: several tiny Chihuahua dogs in wooden cages awaited owners as the child demonstrated how easily the dog fit into a sleeve. Next to the dogs was the part of the Plaza that broke Bailey's heart: a despondent-looking Mexican woman held out wicker cages full of mockingbirds to the passerby, whistling and singing as the birds themselves sat silent and unmoving. She had always dreamed that one day she would be rich enough to come to the Plaza, buy all of the birds, and set them free.

At the far side of the Plaza squatted a group of Mexicans with a wrinkled canvas spread before them, selling wild fruit, peppers, nuts, and magnificent sweet bunches of magnolias. Here Bailey stopped to buy her breakfast with the two coins she had saved and hidden in her satchel. From a rickety food stand she carefully selected a steaming tamale dressed in a corn husk, but her eyes were drawn again and again to the beautiful magnolias. She put the tamale back, ignoring a scolding from the tiny Mexican woman whose dark face was veiled with a ragged *riboza.* She chose a slightly droopy bunch of the fragrant flowers after haggling in perfect Spanish with the woman, and with her gift for her new teacher firmly in hand and her heavy satchel slung over one thin shoulder, she made her way out of the Plaza and through the streets.

By the time she reached the district known as La Villita on South Alamo Street where the beautiful school was located, she was limping. *Why do I have to wear blasted shoes, anyway?* Addie had purchased a pair of proper black boots for her one size ago, and it was into these shoes that Bailey had squeezed her rebellious feet this morning, knowing that all of the children at the German school had shoes on their feet. As she approached, she ran a nervous hand over her crooked braid. She noticed that the German girls all had their hair neatly braided, and some braids were even twisted into flawless coronets. Bailey had done the best that she could with her unruly curls, but they seemed to spring from her negligible braid with a will of their own.

One by one the students turned to stare at the spectacle, mouths agape. A thin girl in a blood-red satin dress, ginger hair springing in crazy corkscrews, was limping toward the neat German school, one shoulder dipping with the weight of a cracked brown satchel, with one thin hand gripping a bunch of wilted magnolias. Who was this? The girls giggled behind their hands and the boys nudged each other, looking away as she caught their stares.

Bailey squelched the impulse to turn and flee and walked right up to one of the buildings, climbed the two brick steps and waltzed through the massive wooden door. Mysterious words greeted her on the stone arch above the door: *Gottes Furcht ist aller Weisheit Anfang.*

What the heck? Bailey felt tendrils of fear creep down her neck. Was everything in German here? She was fluent enough in Spanish to procure a tamale and to carry on questionable conversations with her Mexican friends from the street, but she had not one word of German. She pushed the fear aside and resolutely continued into the building.

The heavenly smell hit her senses first. So this was what school smelled like: the rich, warm smell of kerosene, the thick powdery smell of chalk, the scents of musty old books and freshly polished wooden floors and desks. Bailey felt the excitement build. She was here to learn, in this very special place with clean, brisk-moving people who could teach her to be smart, maybe even to be a doctor like she so desperately wanted to be.

"Guten Morgen, wie geht's bei euch? Guten Morgen, Otto. Guten Morgen, Minna." The strange, thick words issued forth from the most imposing woman that Bailey had ever seen. Her thick dark hair, streaked with gray, was parted down the middle and pulled severely back into a complicated bun of braids. Over her plain dress the woman wore a lace collar with a small bunch of fresh flowers pinned carefully in the middle. Her broad German face was creased with stern lines at the sides of her mouth and between sparkling blue eyes. Bailey looked closely and noticed that they shone with kind humor and an obvious and genuine love for the children she was greeting. *"Guten Morgen, Bertha. Guten Morgen..."* Her words died on her lips as she finally caught sight of the bright red flower of a child who seemed to be hiding behind a rather large boy.

"Guten Morgen," Mrs. von Donop finally recovered. The scraggly girl stared up at her with unblinking, terrified eyes. Bailey had figured out what

"Guten Morgen" meant, but she just couldn't seem to make the words form on her tongue. She opened her mouth and worked her lips, but no sound issued forth.

The students around her giggled but moved on quickly with a glare from the imposing teacher. "Otto, move to your classroom, please. You are quite blocking the hallway. Young lady, step forward at once. Do you not speak German, child?"

"No, ma'am," Bailey finally choked. Her voice sounded squeaky and strange to her own ears.

"Your name?"

"Bailey Rose, ma'am."

The teacher's eyebrows drew up at the unfamiliar name. "Are you new to the school?"

"Yes, ma'am."

"Very well. My name is Mrs. von Donop and you will address me as such. And did your parents accompany you today?" Mrs. von Donop stepped to the open door and looked around the yard, curious to see the parents of such an unlikely child. What kind of mother would dress her child thus for school?

"Uh, they ain't here today. They had work to do, being new in town."

"They *aren't* here today."

"Yes, ma'am. That's what I said."

She looked sharply at the girl for signs of cheekiness, but saw nothing but a rather poignant sincerity.

"You must be enrolled properly by your parents. Are you of German descent?" The schoolmarm perused the girl closely to see if she would lie. *She's every bit as German as I am Irish*, she thought with an inward smile.

Bailey thought for one wild moment that she would tell a little fib, but instinct warned her to be honest with this formidable woman.

"No ma'am," she finally admitted, and as an afterthought added, "I don't know what I am." She hung her head.

Mrs. von Donop felt her mighty heart squeeze at the admission and she resisted the impulse to take the girl into her matronly arms. She cleared her throat with rigid authority.

"Do not hang your head, young lady, as if you were ashamed to be the special girl God created you to be."

At the sharp words Bailey's head snapped up. Special girl? Her mind reached back, but she could not recall a time when anyone had ever called her special, yet alone a creation of God! She thought she better set this good woman straight. She may as well tell the truth from the get-go, or at least part of it.

"Excuse me ma'am, but I better tell you that I ain't—I'm *not* a special girl, and I don't think God created the likes 'o me, if you know what I mean."

She braved a smile at the woman, to show her that she wasn't offended that the teacher had been mistaken.

Mrs. von Donop seemed to expand before Bailey's eyes. Every fiber bristled as her shoulders squared and her considerable chest puffed. She bent at the waist and stuck a thick finger in Bailey's face.

"Young lady! Such blasphemy in my school! You are a child of God, and I say you are special! Now repeat it!"

Bailey stared, dumbfounded. She felt the blood drain from her face and her knees turn to liquid beneath her.

"Repeat it, young lady, with immediacy!" Mrs. von Donop issued in a quiet voice, and although Bailey didn't know what *immediacy* meant, she sure knew that this woman brooked no disobedience.

"I am a child of God, and I am special."

Mrs. von Donop straightened and nodded grimly at the mysterious words etched in stone above them. "Those words say, 'The fear of God is the beginning of all wisdom.' Do you understand that?"

"Y-yes," Bailey gulped.

"Very well. Now you have received your first lesson at our school. How old are you?"

"Twelve."

Mrs. von Donop looked her over carefully. She was so thin and somewhat short for a girl of twelve, and yet her features reflected a maturity beyond her years, convincing the teacher that the girl was being truthful.

"Can you read?"

"Yes, ma'am! I have here in my bag a big book of Shakespeare and I've read almost every story in it." Bailey's thin shoulders straightened perceptibly.

The schoolmarm gave a sudden uncharacteristic huff of delight. "Shakespeare! Why, our students who are your age have yet to work their way through *Deutsches Zweites Lesebuch*." At Bailey's baffled look, she quickly translated: "That's the German Second Reader."

"Well, like I said ma'am, I don't have German, but name a Shakespeare story and I'll tell you something about it." Bailey wasn't bragging. In a rare stretch of lucidity, her mother, Addie, had taught her to read when Bailey was only four. On her fifth birthday she had received her first and only gift: a gold-gilded book of Shakespeare's works that was so heavy she couldn't lift it. She had never ceased wondering where her mother had acquired that book. Bailey had read the book from cover to cover over the years, lending her imagination to each scene, fleshing out the characters in her mind until she understood the strange, beautiful words. Blanche and many of the other girls had helped her along and taught her letters when they had the inclination. There had even been a few years with a former schoolteacher working in the bordello—a quiet, sad young woman who had patiently read with Bailey and answered question after question. She had disappeared years ago, as many of the girls did, in the still of the night.

The schoolmarm intuitively believed her. "I certainly am impressed, Miss Rose. Proceed to your classroom now and I will have you recite for the whole class."

Bailey's heart jumped. "Are you going to be my teacher?"

"Yes, Miss Rose; that is what we may infer. Now proceed up the stairs to the first classroom on your right. You must be seated by the time the morning bells ring." Mrs. von Donop turned away suddenly to greet some more students.

Bailey hesitantly tapped on the tall woman's arm. "Mrs. von... von..." her face flushed to rival the shade of her dress. She had forgotten the woman's name!

"Mrs. von Donop. Yes, what is it?"

"These are for you." Bailey shoved the magnolias at the startled teacher and turned and sped up the stairs, embarrassed beyond words. *That's fine, Bailey. First you get in trouble, and then you forget the teacher's name. Why don't you just go back home?*

It was this thought that snapped her out of her self-pity; the thought of slinking back to Matamoras Street, where she knew she would stay until someday she earned a room and a "business" of her own. Already the big stinking men who slithered into Fort Allen were looking at her with lustful eyes, even though she had barely begun "blooming," as Blanche slyly called it. More than once she had felt a rough, dirty hand run through the long, red curls trailing down her back, and only the intervention of Blanche had stopped certain disaster. "Give 'er a couple of years, gentlemen! She's only twelve! Come back in two years and she'll be the toast 'o the town!" Fourteen was a young but acceptable age in most parlors, but Blanche and a few other high-end madams had been known to hire out twelve-year-olds if they were mature enough to pass off as older teenagers. The brothels of the worst repute trafficked children younger than that. The young girls at Fort Allen generated an incredible amount of profit for the house. *Toast of the town.* Those words were burned into Bailey's brain, woven into every fiber of her being until she had almost forgotten that she had a choice. She had once chance: school. All she needed to do was to get smart, and then she could run as far away from this city as her ambitions would take her.

She stopped cold at the door of the classroom. These kids were big! This had to be the wrong classroom. Gradually the chattering died until the room sat in utter silence. Twenty pairs of eyes turned to gawk at the amazing sight. The neat and proper German girls felt pity for the most part, noticing the girl's ridiculous shoes and the raggedy dress. The boys felt pity, too, but an odd sort of excitement as well. Here stood a girl unlike any they had ever seen. She had flawless skin browned by the sun to the color of creamed coffee. She had the most unruly red hair exploding from her head, fighting its way out of her braids. But her eyes were the thing. They were utterly black, indistinguishable from her pupils, bright, almond-shaped, and so large and wistful. The boys didn't know what to do with the sensations that this strange girl stirred up, so they began laughing and poking each other to cover their confusion. Bailey stood at the door, straight and proud. She would not run.

One boy sat silently in the back row. He felt his gut twist with sympathy as the girl stood frozen in the doorway. She was a skinny little thing, a bright red bird of a child who looked as though she wanted to melt into the floor. *Go save her*, he thought, but before he could make a move, he saw Mrs. von Donop materialize behind her.

"Pupils!" roared a familiar voice behind Bailey. Bailey jumped and felt her heart skip, and then watched in amazement as the classroom returned immediately to silence. Mrs. von Donop grasped Bailey's elbow and stomped into the room. In her other hand she held a white pitcher full of wilted magnolias. She set the flowers on her desk at the front of the room and turned slowly to face the class.

"I wish to thank you, one and all, for making our new student feel so welcome. Each and every one of you will write a five hundred-word essay, in both German and English, describing precisely the reasons for your actions just now. Your essays are due tomorrow." Not one student groaned or complained. They knew better. The rod was used freely in this school, and any child on the receiving end suffered the humiliation in front of the entire school, every student called to the courtyard between the two buildings to witness the punishment.

"Now listen closely, please. This is Miss Bailey Rose. She is only twelve, but I have reason to believe that she belongs with the fourteens and fifteens. We will see how she reads and then make a decision. In the meantime, you will make her feel welcome." Bailey stared at the class and the class stared back, incredulous. As far as they knew, no one had ever been moved to a class ahead. They didn't want this odd-looking little girl in class with them!

"Very well, now who would like to share a desk?" The desks and the seats were the two-passenger type; the front part of the unit was the seat, and back part was the desk top for the seat behind. Bailey noticed with a quick glance that girls and boys were paired off separately. She waited for a girl to volunteer, for there were three empty seats. No one spoke. Mrs. von Donop waited, giving the students a chance to redeem themselves. Finally a soft, masculine voice spoke up from the back of the room.

"She can sit with me, Mrs. von Donop." Bailey's head snapped up and nineteen other heads whipped around to the back. It was really quite comical, almost as if the boy had said, "I am the Queen of England, Mrs. von Donop." The boy waited calmly as his classmates stared at him, mouths hanging open.

"Well! This is most unusual. Since Mr. Naplava seems to be the only student with any courtesy or kindness today, we will accept his offer. Miss Rose, please take your things and move to the back. Class, copy the passage written on the blackboard, then translate and recopy it neatly in English. Carefully, now; some of your penmanship marks leave much to be desired." This served to divert the attention away from Bailey, and the students reluctantly opened their desk tops and began copying, casting furtive glances over their shoulders at this fantastic thing going on behind them. A girl sitting with a boy!

Bailey moved with watery knees toward the boy in the back of the room. She was afraid to meet his eyes, so she concentrated on his rough brown hands. She noticed a round scar on the top of one hand and wondered about it. He stood politely and reached for her bag. "My name is Jacob," he whispered. "You can sit in front of me. Lift your desk top and put your things there."

She braved a glance at him and found herself looking into the kindest, bluest eyes she had ever seen. He had a shock of black hair, carefully slicked back but so long in the front that it fell over one straight dark eyebrow as he bent to help her lift her bag. She felt her cheeks grow hot for no good reason, and looked away, embarrassed. She sat quickly before he could see her blush.

All around her students were busily copying the passage from the board into neatly bound theme books. Bailey had never even seen a theme book, let alone own one. Before she could die her fourth death of embarrassment for the day, she felt a nudge on her back. She turned and found Jacob shoving a piece of paper at her, torn from his theme book. "Here, take it. Have you a pencil?"

She shook her head dumbly. He pressed a stub of a pencil into her hand and flashed a smile at her, revealing a deep dimple in his right cheek. "Now you're set."

Bailey turned around and placed the paper reverently on the scarred wooden desk top. This was it! She was in school, getting ready for her first lesson, and she even had a friend. Well, at least someone had spoken to her. She turned her eyes to the blackboard and obediently copied the words onto her paper in perfectly formed letters.

Dem kleinen Veilchen gleich,
Das im Verborgnen bluht,
Sei immer fromm und gut,
Auch wenn dich niemand sieht.

She checked the letters three times to make sure they were perfect. Now, what the heck did they mean? She felt the familiar dread creeping up. She glanced up to find Mrs. von Donop standing beside her.

"Quite nice, Miss Rose. You may work with your partner to discover the English translation."

Bailey took a deep breath and turned around. "Have you discovered the English translation?" she whispered earnestly to Jacob.

He suppressed a smile and leaned forward, staring intently into her dark eyes. "Like a little violet, that blooms in secrecy, be pious and be good, though unseen you may be."

Bailey's lips formed an unconscious, silent O. Was he sweet on her? He must be, quoting poetry and calling her his little violet. And how had he captured her so perfectly with those beautiful words? She *was* unseen—she spent most of her time under a porch! She struggled to bring forth an equally grand reply as he looked at her, a quizzical expression growing on his face. Finally it came to her, from her favorite story in the big gold book.

"Things base and vile, holding no quality, love can transpose to form and dignity. Love looks not with the eyes, but with the mind, and therefore is wing'd Cupid painted blind." She smiled at him hesitantly, but the smile died on her lips as she saw embarrassment beginning to creep into his expression.

It was Jacob's turn to blush, the flush of scarlet starting at the base of his sturdy brown throat and streaking his cheeks with red. Only the obvious mortification of the girl allowed him to regain a sense of grace.

"That was really nice. My quote was a translation from the blackboard, but what was yours?" His voice started in a smooth masculine tone but dipped into an adolescent squeak on the last word.

"Mr. Naplava, thank you for helping our new student, but you will do well to remember that we converse in whispers while the class is working." The stern teacher smiled briefly from across the room and put her finger to her lips in a warning.

"Thank you," Bailey whispered to Jacob, too embarrassed to say more to this kind boy. What must he think of her? And how many more times was she to embarrass herself on this day?

The answer came five minutes later.

"Class, put away your theme books. We will now hear some recitation from Miss Rose, who is well-versed in the works of William Shakespeare, an example you could do well to follow." A few acidic glances were thrown her way, and although Bailey knew that Mrs. von Donop was trying to help, she wished the teacher would just let her disappear for a while. But it was not to be.

"Who has a request for Bailey? If you recall, we discussed a Shakespearean play at the beginning of this term. Who remembers it?" A short, plump girl in perfect golden braids raised her hand. "Yes, Greta?"

"Vas it *Macbeth*, Mrs. von Donop?" Her voice was heavily accented with German.

"Very good, Greta. Bailey, are you familiar with this work?"

Bailey's heart sped up a beat with excitement. With *Macbeth* she was indeed familiar; the magic and medicinal cunning of the witches drew her personally into the play each time she read it. Naturally one of those passages rose to her mind first.

"Yes, ma'am."

There was a silence and some of the students sniggered.

"Would you like to share some of it with us, or would you rather keep us in suspense?" Mrs. von Donop smiled at her, taking the sting out of the words.

Bailey drew herself up slowly and stood beside her desk. "You can do it," whispered Jacob behind her, and his voice held her up with its conviction.

"Double, double, toil and trouble; Fire burn, and cauldron bubble. Fillet of a fenny snake, In the cauldron boil and bake: eye of newt, and toe of frog, Wool of bat, and tongue of dog…" Bailey's words died on her lips as she saw the aghast expressions on the faces around her. Greta, in particular, looked as though she would bolt from the room. Bailey looked uncertainly at Mrs. von Donop as some of the boys began the interminable giggling.

"Well, that was quite perfectly quoted, Miss Rose. Can you perhaps quote us something a bit more pleasant?"

"From *Macbeth*?" asked Bailey dubiously.

"Well, yes, I see your point there. You may choose any play you wish."

The little girl took another deep breath. From behind, Jacob took a deep breath with her.

"O! Mickle is the powerful grace that lies
In herbs, plants, stones and their true qualities:
For nought so vile that on the earth doth live
But to the earth some special good doth give;
Nor aught so good, but strain'd form that friar use,
Revolts from true birth, stumbling on abuse;
Virtue itself turns vice, being misapplied,
And vice sometime's by action dignified.
Within the infant rind of this weak flower
Poison hath residence, and medicine power."

Bailey cleared her voice nervously. "Oh, that's from *Romeo and Juliet*, Act Two, Scene Three." She sat down amidst dead silence and astonished stares. Finally Mrs. von Donop collected herself enough to speak.

"That is simply amazing, my dear. How much do you have memorized from your book?"

Bailey sat perplexed. She had never thought about it before. If she wanted to remember part of a story, she just thought about the words in the book, and it came to her, like the words were painted in the air before her eyes. She shifted uncomfortably in her hard chair and groped for an answer. "Uh, pretty much all of the parts I like, I guess." Immediately a few of the students rolled their eyes at her, and there were several disbelieving snorts.

Mrs. von Donop forgot her usual discipline in her excitement.

"Do you remember everything you read?"

Bailey began to experience a dawning recognition of her own freakish intelligence, a feeling she would experience many times in her life, as she interpreted the antagonism flowering around her like a poisonous garden. She blushed violently and withered in her chair, rare tears beginning to form in depths of her onyx eyes. The schoolmarm noticed immediately and hushed the class, diverting their attention elsewhere. But the damage had been done. Bailey couldn't wait until the morning session was over so she could go crawl into a hole somewhere.

Two hours later, Mrs. von Donop snapped the arithmetic book shut and the students began putting books away and removing lunches from their desks. "*Mittagessen*," she announced authoritatively. Dinner. For the first time Bailey noticed that all the others had brought their lunches, and her stomach was growling loud enough to be heard in the classroom down the hall. So there wouldn't be a lunch served after all. The bells rang, and before anyone could make fun of her for not bringing something to eat, Bailey shot from the room, down the stairs, and into the sunny courtyard. She made her way to a lone small tree at the edge of the yard and sat leaning against the trunk, hoping that the students did not take their lunches here. She had a decision to make: stay or go? And go where?

She imagined herself going back "home" to Fort Allen, the infamous boarding house, one of the finest in the city. She would walk in and the girls would just be beginning to rouse from their rumpled beds at this noon hour. They would be straggling downstairs in various stages of dress, hair awry and their paint smudged on their faces. They would stink of the men, and the stench of clinging smoke, stale beer, and strong cologne would follow the women down the stairs and trail after them all afternoon until they bathed for the evening. They would lounge about half-dressed in the lobby on the plush red sofas, the heavy damask drapes keeping the sunlight outside and creating a feeling of perpetual dusk. Under sparkling crystal chandeliers they would smoke and nibble on biscuits and burritos and talk about the johns.

The men who had purchased a whole night would be slithering down the stairs and escaping out the door at about this time, trying to be as unobtrusive as possible. Some would look ashamed, and they would notice Bailey and their faces would drain of color, thinking of their own children at home. Bailey would stare back evenly, her opaque eyes carefully devoid of emotion. Some would kiss their girls goodbye unabashedly, promising to return soon with money and gifts. These were the very young men—men whose fathers were incredibly rich—who were infatuated, and who would ruin themselves spending their wages on Kittie or Susana or Mona. Then there were the important men; the dandies who dressed in expensive clothes and whom Bailey knew to be the politicians of the city. They would stroll down the stairs together, as if they were members of some exclusive club and had just finished with the "facilities." They would be discussing taxes or wool prices or newspapers, and they would tip their hats to Blanche, the infamous, formidable Madame of Fort Allen, handing her a thick roll of bills, ignoring the girls they had spent the night with. The girls never saw a dime in Blanche's house; it was strictly forbidden for them to take payment or tips. All money was paid to Blanche, and in return, she fed, clothed, and housed the girls and sometimes paid them a paltry percentage of their earnings.

The girls would pad back and forth like so many languorous cats across the thick carpet all day, from the well-stocked enormous kitchen and pantry, to the deep mahogany bar, to the well-polished plank tables, where they would play poker and while away the hours until nightfall. Blanche took good care of her girls. There would be fittings for new dresses and shoes; the hairdresser would come to attend to the magnificent tresses; the druggist would come to deliver the medicine: morphine, cocaine, and laudanum, which sustained many of the women throughout the wasted days. The food was plentiful and delicious, but strictly off-limits to Bailey.

She would catch hell, for sure. Addie would be up, and she'd be worried in her own fuzzily detached way. The morphine only allowed her to feel a certain number of emotions per day. She would screech at Bailey, then apologize and hug her fiercely and disappear into her bedroom. Unless Blanche ordered her to, Addie never came out until the supper hour, when business began. She sometimes sent a girl to bring Bailey to her, and those were the afternoons Bailey hated the most. Addie trying to be a mother, trying to read or play with Bailey or brush her hair, interspersed with long moments of withdrawn silence as she drifted to the window and gazed blankly into the sun, or simply fell asleep, her chin on her chest. She loved the feel of her mother's hands in her hair; she hated the feeling that the woman in front of her was just a ghost of her mother.

Bailey would have the rest of the day to herself to roam the streets with her friends Juan and Gabriella. They would beg and steal from the food vendors, sneak into the fandango halls to watch the Mexican girls rehearse their colorful, exotic dances, and nap in the sun by the slow-moving river. Many times Bailey would read to them from her golden book. She taught Juan and Gabby English, and they taught her Spanish. *That is my school,* she thought.

When darkness fell she would retreat under the porch, afraid (and rightly so) of the city at night, which was quite lawless with its prostitutes and cowboys and soldiers and gamblers preying on each other like wild dogs. As she was getting older and her "change" was imminent, she had to be very, very careful to be out of reach of the men and even younger boys at night; Gabby had taught her well. She would read by candlelight; Blanche gave her a candle and something to eat every night. Madam wouldn't feed Bailey during the day, but her evening liquor lent her an air of generosity that briefly extended to the only child of the house. She took better care of her than did Bailey's own mother. In fact, Bailey felt a misplaced kind of loyalty to Blanche. Bailey was supposed to become a high-priced flower; Blanche had told her in confidence that someday Fort Allen would be Bailey's. "I want to leave it to someone intelligent and ambitious, and that you are, m' girl. But you must pay your dues, like we all did."

Was she ready to pay her dues? It would only be a bit over two years, maybe sooner—oh God, please don't let it be sooner—until that time came to begin paying. What was it the nice boy had said? *Like a little violet, that blooms in secrecy, be pious and good, though unseen you may be.*

She was repeating that little rhyme to herself, trying to draw courage from it, when the first lump of potato hit her in the forehead.

"Hey, Jezebel, why are you dressed like a whore?" shouted one of the boys. Bailey looked up, stunned, and was confronted with five, no, *six* boys who had been in her class. And her heart fell as she saw the girls behind them, some looking shocked, some looking ashamed, but a few looking smug. Most of them hung back, sheepish, but one boy came forward with an ugly sneer twisting his face. He was tall and fat in a powerful way, blond hair carefully slicked back and dark eyes glittering in a hard, fierce face. She recognized him as Otto, the boy Mrs. von Donop had chastised before school.

"Is your mother a soiled dove, then? Does she look like you? If she does, tell us so we can go find her."

More food pelted her then: pudding, potatoes, red berries that left a bloody smear on her cheek. She tried to cower behind the tree, but it was too small to offer much protection. She told herself to run, but fear and shame froze her to the spot.

The boys snickered, but they appeared to become nervous as Otto advanced toward Bailey. They quickly retreated, boys and girls alike, calling for Otto to follow, and one of the girls broke free and ran into the school.

"You're going to catch hell, Otto, c'mon," they called, terrified of the wrath of Mrs. von Donop, but Otto moved forward, licking his horrible fat lips. Bailey soon found herself utterly alone in the courtyard with this menacing boy.

She fought to find her voice, choked for a few seconds with fear and rage. "Leave me alone! You stupid farm boy! You smell like the cows you live with!" she yelled, all of the frustration of the day boiling to the surface.

The expression on the boy's face changed. His face flattened into a rage of his own. He walked toward Bailey with a deadly calm, but she simply could not move, frozen with dread.

"So y' think I smell 'o cows, do y'? Here, pretty girl, take another whiff." He grabbed the back of her neck with one swift, powerful hand and shoved her head into his shirt. She struggled valiantly, but he was much, much stronger than she could have imagined. A detached part of her mind noticed that he did indeed smell of cows, and worse, of unwashed, stinking boy. He yanked her back up and dragged her by the collar, quickly and easily, a short distance out of the main courtyard as her legs backpedaled uselessly. She opened her mouth to scream but found that her dress, pulled tightly around her throat, was cutting off all oxygen. It all happened in the space of ten seconds. He turned a corner and dragged her another ten feet, shoving her against the brick wall, and Bailey despaired as she realized that they were out of sight of the courtyard entrance.

For she had no delusions about what was going to happen next.

He skewered her against the wall, his hand pressing her mouth with such tremendous force that her teeth cut into her own lips, and she tasted blood. His other hand hurried to unbutton his trousers, and when he had exposed himself, he grabbed the back of her neck and forced her to her knees. "My brother said this is what yer kind will do, so do it," he growled. "If you scream, I'll snap your neck."

Bailey opened her mouth to scream and he struck her across the face with his fist, stunning her into silence. She felt as though her eye would pop clean out of her head as stars swam before her.

And then she heard an outraged roar and running feet, and Otto heard it, too, because for just one tiny, blessed instant the iron grip on the back of her neck loosened. It was all that she needed: she tucked and rolled and tore away from him with all of her remaining strength, and a sickening ripping sound seemed to echo throughout the schoolyard as she left Blanche's table doily behind.

She ran as fast as she could, not daring to stop even for her beloved satchel. She ran with a knowledge that destroyed her: the unwelcome truth that she could run wherever she wanted, but she would never be able to outrun the shadow of herself, who she was, and who she was fated to be. She ran without hearing more roars of a boy with black hair and piercing blue eyes; without seeing this boy beat her attacker until he cried like a baby and begged for mercy. She never heard her name called.

She just ran.

CHAPTER TWO

Nothing had ever felt quite as pure to Jacob Naplava as did the sensation of his righteous fist connecting over and over again with the hateful fat face of Otto Bickenbach.

One of the girls had found him in the classroom; she had rushed in and whispered in his ear when the attendant's back was turned.

And the scene that he interrupted when he raced into the courtyard and rounded the corner at breakneck speed would be etched irrevocably into his brain for the remainder of his life, returning to haunt his nightmares for years to come. The big, hulking thug was standing over Bailey, and his pants were open. She was forced to her knees in front of him and her head was recoiling from a punch.

A primitive, anguished roar ripped through Jacob and echoed off the walls, and as Otto looked up, Bailey pulled away and ran. Jacob called out to her, but she didn't stop, and he didn't blame her. She was gone in an instant.

How far had Otto gotten? *Did he make her…?*

Savage adrenaline coursed through him, and without missing a step he finished his sprint, his momentum slamming him into Otto with tremendous force, knocking them both to the ground. Jacob leapt to his feet like a cat and spun on Otto.

"Get up and zip your pants," he growled. "*Now.*" Otto stared at him, terrified, and rose unsteadily to his feet.

"You're going to pay," Jacob uttered in a low, menacing voice to the bigger boy, and saw nothing but blinding red rage before his eyes.

Jacob's friend Hans finally pulled Jacob away from the screaming Otto moments later. A primal part of Jacob was quite capable of killing this boy who had defiled a girl. He shrugged away from his cousin and aimed a final, mighty blow, connecting with Otto's chin, and the fight was over. Otto lay knocked out cold, his face pulpy and covered with blood, ribs broken and one arm sticking out at an unnatural angle. Otto was still clutching Bailey's lace collar in his grubby fist, and Jacob bent to retrieve it, shoving it into his pocket before his friend could see.

"Get out of here, Naplava," pleaded Hans urgently. "We won't tell anyone it was you. He had it coming. Just get your rig and go home." The schoolmasters and schoolmarms would appear at any moment.

Jacob flexed his sore hand and sighed. What a way to end the perfect vacation. He had begged his father to let him come to San Antonio for two weeks to visit his German friend Hans, and his father had finally relented, on the condition that he attend school and that he return home in time for the shearing. The boys had been all over the city, sneaking peeks inside the plentiful saloons, patronizing the delicious chili stands and flirting inexpertly with the beautiful chili queens, walking along the river that wound its way right through the heart of the city. Jacob liked the excitement of the foreign sights and sounds, the danger of the wild nights that he and Hans observed from a safe distance, but he was longing to go back to the serenity of his father's sheep ranch in the Hill Country.

It was spring, the most critical time of the year for sheep ranchers. His father would need him soon, even with the help of his four brothers and four sisters and the shearing crews from Mexico, who made the trip twice a year for the bi-annual shearing and the quite substantial pay of five cents per sheep. The *pastores*, or sheepherders, would have already driven their flocks to the huge pen covered with brush and palmetto at his father's ranch. A few more days and they would be ready to begin the exhausting task of shearing the sheep and filling the heavy sacks with fleece, ready for the market. He had to be there, not just because his father expected him to be, but because he felt the pull, the need to smell the warm wool, to feel the struggling, bleating sheep beneath his strong hands. He could liken it only to religion; he worshipped not the sheep, but rather the goodness and purity that he found when he leaned his young muscles into the work and reaped the bounty when it was complete. Young Jacob could verbalize none of these things; he knew only that he wished to go home.

He noticed the brown leather satchel lying in the dust, and his heart pulled him in another direction. He reached for the lace in his pocket and gripped it tightly. She had no one, did that scrawny girl with a funny name; he could tell by the desperately lonely look in her eyes. She was the same age as his twin sisters Marianna and Amalie. What if they were alone in a new place and someone had treated them so roughly? Would he want someone to watch out for them, even if it wasn't their concern? What would his mother say? She was a compassionate, generous woman, always putting others before herself. All of his life she had repeated to him her favorite

Moravian proverb: *Kdo dba, ten ma.* He who cares, has. *Has what*, he had always thought as a child. Now that he was fourteen, he was pretty sure that he knew. He who cares has everything: honor, kindness and grace, like the teacher had said today.

As the plan began to form in his head, he grew excited. It was like rescuing a stray dog. Any hurt or hungry animal he had brought home over the years, his mother had welcomed and taught him to care for. Surely this would be no different!

He scooped up the satchel and unhitched and readied his rig with aching hands. Where should he look first? He was pretty sure he knew.

Bailey ran straight back to Fort Allen, just like she knew she would. The fat blond German boy had said it loud enough for everyone to hear: she was the daughter of a whore; she wore the stigma like a costume. Even when she tried to look respectful, people could tell. Good, wholesome, clean people. She didn't belong there; she had soiled their school by simply entering its sacred halls. And then to recite Shakespeare in front of everyone in a proud, boastful tone! No wonder they hated her. She clutched her stomach, reliving the scene in the courtyard, ripples of shock coursing through her body. They hated her so much that they let a boy drag her behind the school and…and…try to….

She surely hated herself, with every bit of the enormous capacity that a neglected child has to loathe herself.

Addie was nowhere to be seen when she arrived at the Fort, but Blanche descended on her like a great green falcon, her emerald Paris silk swishing and her platinum blond hair towering ten inches above her head. She was a huge woman of an undetermined age; tall, fat, and strong. Her eyes glittered green in her broad face, and her bright red lips snarled in anger. More than once had Bailey felt the sting of Blanche's hand across her face. When Bailey stole or otherwise got herself into trouble, it was Blanche who doled out the punishment while Addie cowered in a morphine malaise. Today was no different. Bailey couldn't lie to Blanche successfully; no one could. Once Blanche found out where she had been, she yanked the girl up and shook her so viciously that Bailey thought her head would pop off her shoulders. It was a hundred times worse than the usual benign smack. Blanche's words came out in a rush of anger.

"Who do you think you are? Marie Curie's daughter? School is not for you! I will teach you everything you need to know! You already know more than they do, am I right? And I wager they were horrible to you, especially the boys, am I right? You got in a fight, even, look at that eye, it's disgraceful. I think I might give you a matching shiner on the other side, to teach you a lesson. Remember your place, girl. Remember who—you—are!" Blanche accented these last three words with three strikes across Bailey's face. The last one was with a closed fist, forceful enough to lift Bailey from her feet.

After she picked herself up off the floor and slunk from the house, Bailey crawled under the porch into her comfortable little niche. There were blankets and pillows down there, room enough to stretch out and sleep. It was like a little room; a room for children who were not supposed to happen in the course of a "working girl's" life. In fact, Bailey was the only child at Fort Allen. All of the girls knew a trick to keep from getting pregnant. She had never asked her mother why she didn't know the trick.

Many, many times she wished her mother had known the trick.

Blanche had felt some remorse and brought Bailey a huge chunk of fluffy white bread and a steaming bowl of chili. As always, she stood on the porch and stomped her foot until Bailey emerged.

"Bailey, I know this is hard for you. Don't go dreaming for someone else's life, child. Just accept your own and be as happy as you can." Blanche slurred and weaved slightly, gazing at the small girl before her. Bailey remained silent. Blanche shrugged and turned, gearing up for the night's business, the child forgotten already. Bailey felt no tenderness in her heart for the cold woman. She was surprised to discover that she felt no loyalty anymore. It was as if a black veil had been pulled over her eyes this day; she felt nothing, dreamed nothing, longed for nothing but to eat the bread to fill her empty stomach and to close her eyes and drift into another world altogether. She read the stories in her mind deep into the night.

It was the meager light from this candle that Jacob spied at the end of a long night of tedious searching, just when he was about to give up the search for his stray and go home to Boerne without her. When he saw the glow from beneath the porch, he just knew it had to be her. He felt relief loosen his tired shoulders. What a night!

He had begun the day at Hans's house, saying his goodbyes and pretending, for the sake of Hans's mother, that he was going straight home to his father's ranch. He had even started to lead his rig on the proper path out of town, waving to them until he could see that they had gone back inside. Only then did he turn his rig around and head for the heart of the city. He was supremely confident that he would be able to find the distinctive-looking girl very quickly.

He began his search in Military Plaza, assuming that surely at least one soul would be able to point him in the right direction. The Plaza was bustling with activity at midday; the vendors were busy selling their wares; the sheep ranchers were clustered at one end rounding up shearing crews and supplies, the cattlemen were clustered at the other end glaring at the sheep ranchers, and the farmers were in the middle, glaring at both the "woolies" and the cattle rustlers. Jacob felt a prickle of apprehension. For as long as he could remember, this battle over grazing rights had been raging between the three factions. Many ranches had burned; many lives had been lost over this quest for the possession of grass and precious waterholes. Looking carefully, he saw that he knew several of the sheep ranchers and a few of the farmers. He decided to avoid that part of the Plaza as much as possible; the last thing he needed was another fight.

He tied up his rig at an out-of-the-way hitching post and approached a small Mexican girl standing stoically behind a steaming chili stand. "Excuse me, miss, do you know a girl named Bailey Rose? She's got red hair, and she's about this high..." he finished lamely as he leveled his hand at his chest.

The girl's sparkling brown eyes assessed him carefully. "No English, sir," she said in a thick accent. She turned to help another customer. As Jacob moved away, she gestured to a small boy who was carefully rolling tamales in corn husks beside her.

"Juan! Run to Gabriella and tell her that an Anglo boy is looking for Bailey," she ordered in perfect English. Bailey had been teaching them English for two years, and they used it among themselves whenever possible. This way, none of their elders ever knew what they were up to. Juan scampered away, looking for the fearless Gabby. She would know what to do.

Jacob moved from table to table, from wagon to wagon, asking everyone who would listen about the whereabouts of the girl. He received the same response from all of the Mexicans: "No English, sir." No one who knew Bailey was going to give her away; if she wanted to be found, she would be found. They were very protective of their little Rosa.

The soldiers lounging around the Plaza in various stages of drunkenness were a little more helpful.

"Hello, sir. Um, I was wondering if you have ever seen a girl with red hair who lives around here."

There was a ten second span of dead silence.

"Eh?" one of them finally grunted.

"Um...she's about twelve years old, and she's real skinny..." At this point Jacob dropped off as the soldiers smirked at each other.

"A little young for you lad, 'eh?" They snickered and elbowed each other in the ribs. Jacob tried to be patient as he stood steaming in the middle of the Plaza. His stomach was growling and he desperately wanted to get started for home.

"I'd be obliged if you could point me in the right direction." He stood his ground in the bright sunshine, tensed to run in case one of the cantankerous, drunken soldiers got a burst of energy.

"Why do y' talk so funny, boy? Are you German? You look more like an Irishman to me, with yer black hair and blue eyes. Black Irish, they're called."

Jacob lifted his chin a fraction of an inch. "Moravian," he said simply.

That was sufficient to confuse the soldiers long enough for Jacob to get the conversation back on track. "So do you know where I could look for this girl?"

"Why don't you try the saloons?" one of them finally suggested, and that kept them laughing well after Jacob had walked away. But they had given him an idea. What if Bailey's mother was a barmaid? He squared his shoulders and set off for the string of saloons and gambling houses around the corner off of Main and Military Plazas.

Jack Harris's Saloon, Vaudeville Theatre and Gambling House, The Green Front Saloon; he visited them all. Soon the names began to blur in his tired young mind. Had he been to the White Elephant or the Black Elephant? The Western Star, the Lone Star, or the Star and Crescent? They were all the same: cool and dark in the late afternoon, not yet geared up for the Friday night action. Soldiers, merchants, gamblers, wagon freighters, and gunfighters all congregated there, lounging around and playing quiet games of poker. He could see with his own eyes that there were ladies of questionable reputation; the "soiled doves" that the German boys had whispered about in school. They were of all ages; some were surely younger than his fourteen years, and some were sixty years old if they were a day. Oddly enough, there was something about them that made them all look alike: Jacob thought about it until he worked it out in his mind. They all had the exact same hopeless, hard expressions on their faces. They all looked at him with curiously blank eyes that stirred a memory in him of Bailey. It wasn't anger; it was heart-wrenching impassivity. Of course, some of the girls were dazzlingly beautiful, even with the dead eyes. Especially a woman in the Silver King.

It was the last saloon on the street, and his last chance to find Bailey. Nobody had been willing to help; he had been laughed at, scolded, and chased out of one establishment, but mostly he had been ignored. His homespun clothes, his distinctively European looks and his trace of accent marked him as a foreigner and a country folk. It was getting late; night had already fallen and the saloons were getting ready to serve lavish meals to the men flooding in from the cattle drives, shearing pens, fields, and military encampments. Jacob snuck into the Silver King, acting as if he were with a group of farmers. He was tall enough to fool the big man watching the door, but once he was inside, he almost lost his cool composure. The establishment was magnificent, like nothing he had ever seen. The walls were a glossy white, filled with richly-toned paintings and engravings. Chandeliers cast sparkles about the room, illuminating the bar itself, which was cut from a flawless piece of marble. The leather chairs were deep and plush, the tables polished to a warm mahogany glow. Small rooms branched from the main room, and within these Jacob spied men and women in the richest of finery dining and drinking. Behind the bar was a huge mirror running along the entire back wall, serving to make the room appear twice as large. Jacob gulped, and with a tremendous amount of self-discipline, put away the feelings of longing and resentment. Maybe someday he would dine here with a beautiful woman; he would cease to be a sheepman for just one day and revel in this luxury. But for now he had to remember why he was here. He made his way to the bar to begin the familiar questions. There he saw the most beautiful woman he had ever seen.

She must have been thirty years old or thereabouts, because she looked to be the same age as one of his aunts. She had black ringlets down to her waist, dusky brown skin and strangely colored eyes; Jacob likened her eyes to the color of rather weak tea. She was voluptuous; her breasts had been pushed up to the limits of the neck of her beautiful blue silk dress. Jacob had never seen so much skin on a grown woman. He felt his whole body flush and was thankful for the relative darkness of the huge room.

"Uh, excuse me, ma'am, I am looking for a girl." His voice was cracking terribly and he fought against the impulse to turn tail and run.

The woman's strange eyes widened momentarily as she assessed the boy's age. He was much too young, but he was tall and solid and certainly a beautiful, unusual-looking young man. She considered carefully. What a pleasant and exciting change this would be from the fat drunken apes that pawed her every night.

"How much money do you have, young gentleman?" she purred. Her voice was thick and sensuous and exotically Mexican. She leaned forward, resting one elbow on the bar, and the bodice of her dress was stretched to its reckoning point.

Jacob gulped. Money? He had to pay her before she'd give him information? "Uh, I have twelve dollars and forty-two cents, but I can only spend two more dollars." He waited expectantly, his eyes riveted where he knew they shouldn't be.

"What's your name, sweet boy?"

"Jacob, ma'am. So do you know where I can find her?"

"You can certainly find her right where you are, Jacob love." She leaned forward and traced one long finger down his jaw, his throat, across his chest, continuing on down the length of his torso, finally stopping at the point of no return as she touched him intimately.

An instant of crazy unreality passed, a beat of time in which Jacob shed a good vestige of his boyhood and innocence amid a whirling black confusion. He struck at her hand blindly and exploded from his stool, racing for the door. Behind him he heard her laughing. He felt dirty, aroused, and ashamed, in quick succession. *It's time to go home, it's time to go home, it's time to go home.* He had tried and failed and now it was time to go home where he belonged.

He ran all the way back to his rig.

"Wait, wait!" The voice behind him didn't register until he already had his horses Joey and Bella untied and one foot up on his wagon.

"Wait, sir! I will help you!" He turned cautiously, expecting to see the mysterious lady of the night pursuing him across the plaza. Do they chase you if you don't do what they want? He suppressed a nervous laugh. Wait until he told his older brother Johann about this! He, Jacob, running from a beautiful woman who desired him! He would be a man and face her, telling her firmly that he was raised to believe that what she was proposing was a sacred act meant for his wife alone. He raised his stubborn chin and squinted into the night. All he could see was a tall, raggedy Mexican girl, perhaps close to his own age.

"Excuse me, sir, but I know who you're looking for." She was out of breath as she approached, slowing from a dead run, stopping right in front of him. Her eyes were an unusual shade of blue-green, and her straight, dirty black hair hung to her waist. She bore more than a passing resemblance to the woman who had just propositioned him. Her piquant face was thin and drawn. Did all children in this city look hungry?

"Who are you?" was all he could think of to say.

She took a deep breath. "My name is Gabriella. That was my mother you were running from! She didn't mean to scare you. She did not understand what you wanted. Please forget about that." Her fingers waved in a gesture of dismissal. One bare foot crossed self-consciously over the other and she looked up him speculatively. "Why do you want to find Bailey?"

Jacob's foot came slowly off the wagon and he rested his hand on Joey's brown flank to quiet him. "I was going to take her home with me."

After a stunned pause, Gabriella let forth a surprised huff of cynical laughter. "Take her home? Like a stray *gato*, yes? Like a little pet? What will you do with her? Build her a pen and feed her from a tin pan? Does your mama let you bring home strays that you find on the street?" Gabriella's hands were firmly planted on her hips and she moved toward Jacob as she questioned him in a rapid-fire fashion in a thick, almost unintelligible Mexican accent, until the tips of her bare toes were on top of his dusty boots.

Jacob was taken aback that she had so accurately assessed his intentions, but he stubbornly stood his ground, realizing that this girl was his best chance at finding Bailey. Obviously she was Bailey's friend. Time to talk fast. "She'll eat at the table like a member of my family. I'll give her my own bed and I'll sleep with my brother Wenzel." He struggled for words under the girl's glare. "I—I'll take her to school and—and no one will ever hurt her again. She won't be my little stray *gato*."

Gabriella stood looking at the striking boy, an expression of wonder on her pretty face. "Why?" she finally breathed. "Who are you? Why do you go to so much trouble for one girl?"

Jacob opened his mouth to answer, but found no answer forthcoming. Why did he want to find her so badly? He had seen countless children on the streets today—children begging, hungry and desperate and alone. Why hadn't he taken one of them home if he felt this awesome urge to be a Good Samaritan today? Was it just the challenge of finding her now? His mother always said that he was the most stubborn of her children.

"I don't know," he finally mumbled. He studied his boots. Maybe this was a darn stupid idea after all. Here it was almost midnight, too late to travel, and he had no place to stay. And he hadn't even accomplished his goal! It was obvious that this girl was not going to help him, and he didn't blame her. It sounded too crazy, even to his own ears.

"Okay," the dark girl sighed. Jacob's head snapped up. "I'll tell you where she is because I can see that you love her."

Jacob felt his face flare. "What? I just want to help her! She's just a baby!" He glared at the girl, who giggled in the darkness.

"She's barely younger than you, I'll bet. She's just small. Will she be your sister?" she asked pointedly.

Although the idea left him with a hollow feeling, he agreed. "Yes, she'll be my sister. I already have four of them; what's another?" He thought of the two bedrooms for nine children at home and experienced a twinge of indecision. But he knew his mother would not say a word; she would gather Bailey in like a mother hen gathers all of her chicks under one small wing. Somehow they would fit her in.

"She lives at Fort Allen, you know the place?"

Jacob shook his head.

"It's on Matamoras, between Leona and Frio. It is made of thick white walls. It looks like a fort, like soldiers would be hiding in. You can't miss it. Look under the porch in the back. This is where you will find your precious Bailey." Gabriella fled before Jacob could detect the poignant jealousy in her voice. She had seen the goodness shining in this boy's eyes, like an angel, or else she would have never given him Bailey's whereabouts.

And so Jacob had untied his rig and headed resolutely to Fort Allen, which stood just as Gabriella had said it would, with thick adobe walls and a mansard roof that pitched steeply toward the ground. It looked like a fortress, but Jacob knew it was a bawdy house. Growing up with two older brothers and a slew of cousins, he had heard his fill of stories. Through the windows he caught glimpses of dandies, nicely dressed men milling about, and exotic-looking women draped over them. And the noise! Even out in the street, he could hear the music blaring from an unseen source; he could hear the women laughing and squealing and the men shouting over their card games and cigars. He caught snatches of conversation that made his ears burn.

"Sadie, get over here this very minute and plant that nicely shaped rump right here, my girl! I didn't pay you to talk to my brother!" Uproarious laughter.

"Blanche, we need more wine upstairs."

"Stop it!" A scream exploded from an upper room, followed by a thump. He tensed. What should he do? Minutes later he heard different sounds from that room, lower and rhythmic; sounds that made his scalp tighten. This was Bailey's home? She grew up listening to this, the sounds of abuse and meaningless exchanges of flesh? He felt his resolve strengthen as he left his rig tied in front, and with a few soft words to his horses, he made his way around the big fortress. At the back of the house stood a sizable wrap-around porch, and he saw a soft glow shining from what looked to be a crawl space underneath.

He leaned down and whispered furtively, not wanting to be heard through one of the many open windows in the house. "Bailey? Miss Rose?"

There was no answer.

"Bailey, it's the boy from the school. Come out and talk to me."

Bailey lay paralyzed with fear underneath the porch. The boy from the school? The one who had ripped her dress, called her a whore, and tried to force her to do an ugly thing. He had found out where she lived! Her hands shook as she reached for her knife, a gift from Gabriella. Gabby had told her to keep it close at all times, and Bailey thanked her silently now. She scooted back into the furthermost corner of the little niche, cowering from the edge of the porch. She held her knife at the ready.

"Bailey, come on out. I don't know if I can fit in there." She heard him drop to his knees as he bent to peer under the porch. Bailey squelched a scream that was building in her throat.

"Come on now, little one." A hand reached toward her and Bailey raised the knife.

"Hello?" There it was, a dim face in the candlelight, followed by two broad shoulders. He was coming in to get her, and she damn sure wasn't going to let it happen without a fight. She lunged awkwardly in the confined space, slicing through air until she felt her knife connect. There was a soft "Humph" and a few whispered words in a language she didn't understand, and the figure withdrew. There were no screams or cries like she had expected, and she felt a sudden flash of intuition. *Dios Mio!* Who had she just stabbed? Surely that dreadful Otto would have been swearing and squealing like a pig!

"Otto? You get away from here. So help me, I'll cut whatever part of your body you stick in here next!" She tried to make her voice sound brave, but it came out high-pitched and shaky.

"Bailey, it's me, Jacob." The words were gasped out through a certain measure of pain.

Bailey's breath caught in her throat. She had just stabbed that sweet boy from school! She crawled on her hands and knees from her hiding place and rushed to Jacob, who was kneeling in the grass, holding a hand over one eye.

"Oh nooooo!" The last word was a drawn-out moan. "I gouged your eye out! Oh Jacob, I'm so sorry! I thought you were Otto."

"Shh," he interrupted gently. "I don't want them to hear." He nodded at the house. "You didn't gouge my eye out, by the grace of God and about an eighth of an inch." He removed his hand to reveal a neat slice in an arc above his right eye. It was quickly covering that side of his face with blood, and he brushed at it to keep it from getting in his eye. Amazingly, he was smiling.

Bailey stared at him, mortified. Tears began to pool in her eyes and wash down her cheeks. Suddenly, she was overcome by the pain and fear of the day. "I am so, so sorry. Will you ever forgive me?" She reached out and gently bracketed his face with her small hands, then just as quickly, withdrew them.

"Forgiven." His voice cracked and he sat mesmerized for a moment, watching her cry. She wept without making a sound, the tears coursing down her cheeks in rivers, her face tired and drawn.

She swept an impatient hand across her face and reached for his hand. "Get under the porch and I'll fix your eye. I know just what to do! I have to get my medical bag from Addie's room, but I'll be right back."

She scampered away so quickly that Jacob had no time to object. It took some doing to fit his lanky limbs under the porch, but he was surprised how spacious it was once he squeezed inside. The porch had been built up to allow for storage space underneath, and he saw that half of the space was used to store construction supplies such as lumber and bricks. Her side of the "house" was simply furnished, with one fat beeswax candle, three tattered blankets, and a few flat pillows. He tucked her brown satchel into the corner and settled down into the blankets, half sitting up, and gathered his thoughts. What a truly bizarre night this had been! And now the twelve-year-old daughter of a prostitute was upstairs getting her "medical bag" so she could operate on his face that she had just slashed. Jacob grinned to himself. What a story this would make for the next family gathering! He would be telling this one to his grandchildren.

Five minutes passed and the girl returned, slipping expertly under the porch. She held a blue felt bag with twine for drawstrings and a wet rag, and Jacob felt his first twinge of apprehension.

"So, Dr. Rose, what are you proposing to do to my face?" His voice was light and teasing and concealed his trepidation. Blood flowed steadily from the cut and dripped into his cupped hands.

"Well, let's discuss my fee first. That will be five hundred dollars to stitch you up." She smiled delightedly, and he noticed that her face was transformed when she did so, like a flower blooming. Then her words registered in his tired brain.

"Stitch me up?" Jacob sat up, truly alarmed now. Bailey noticed and tried to put him at ease.

"Don't worry, young man, I have been in practice now for two years. When I was eight, I splinted Gabriella's broken finger. Last year I put stitches in Maria's hand when she sliced it open cutting potatoes, and there was more blood than this, let me tell you! And just last week I helped Midwife Martinez deliver a baby on the east side." She smiled proudly as she rummaged in her bag for her supplies.

"I'm not having a baby." Jacob made to move past her to make his escape.

"Oh no you don't! You must be a brave man to not even cry when you get slashed. This won't hurt, honestly, Jacob. I'll be real careful and it'll only take me three minutes. I don't think it's going to stop bleeding without a few stitches. And while I'm working, you can tell me what you're doing here in the middle of the night." She tugged gently on his arm, feeling steely resistance.

"Please, Jake?" This got his attention. Nobody ever called him that, not since he was ten and his older brother Anton had spent an entire week swinging a snake skin at his face and calling him "Jake the Snake," enthralled with his cleverness. He had only stopped when Jacob had bloodied his lip. He hadn't been "Jake" since. He looked at her somber expression and the appealing tilt of her head, and he thought he finally understood what his older brother meant when he warned him about "feminine wiles." He guessed that little girls had them, too. At times it was hard to remember that she was only a bit over two years his junior—she was so small—but at other times her maturity revealed her age plainly.

"Okay, okay. But only if you promise not to call me 'Jake'." He realized as soon as he said it that he didn't mean it.

"It's a deal. Now lean back here in the blankets, just like you were before. There, that's right. Now close your eyes and tell me why you're here." She gave him a cloth for his hands and then maneuvered herself until she was supporting his head in the crook of her arm. He relaxed and let himself enjoy the sound of her musical voice as she smoothed the warm wet rag across his brow.

"Well, I beat up Otto, that jackass." He opened one eye to gauge her expression, but her face was carefully neutral. "Bailey, did he…?"

"No," she said quickly, her face red. He believed her, and his shoulders sagged in relief.

There was a pause. "I decided to find you and take you home for a visit. I think you'd like my mother, and I have little sisters your age," he said abruptly. His words sounded preposterous, even to him.

Her hand stilled. She was prepared to hear just about anything but this!

"Did I hear you right? You want to take me to your home?"

Jacob opened his eyes. "Yes. Now before you say—"

"That's the dumbest thing I ever heard," she interrupted. She began sponging his face again, forcing him to lie back. "Why would you want to take me to your house? You don't even know me!"

Jacob felt his way carefully, not wanting to hurt her feelings. How could he tell her that she lived in a cesspit? "Well, I live on a sheep ranch. It's shearing time, and Mama could use some extra help in the house with the extra chores."

"A sheep ranch?" she giggled. "What do I know about sheep? And why do you go to the German school if you live in the country?"

She's quick, he thought with an inward smile. "I was just visiting my friend for a couple of weeks."

"You don't sound German."

"I'm not German. Look, we're getting off the subject here. I saw that you had a bad day, and I thought you may like a change for a while. And like I said, Mama could use the help. She told me to hire someone." This last lie slipped out so easily that it was out before he could stop it.

"So you came looking for me to hire me? To work on your sheep ranch?" She was looking at him with a bemused expression on her face. This was one of the craziest stories she had ever heard.

"Well, when you put it that way, it sounds a little strange. I thought you were nice, and I'm inviting you to our ranch for a little break from this place. It's really pretty. It's up in the Hill Country, two days' ride from here. We could leave at dawn. What do you say?"

Bailey finished cleaning his face and put the rag down slowly. What could she say? Addie wouldn't care two cents if she went. She'd probably be relieved, if she noticed at all. Blanche was another story, but at the moment, she didn't care a whit what Blanche thought. The prospect appealed to Bailey's sense of adventure.

"Okay!" she said so suddenly that Jacob was startled. She was going with him! He hadn't expected to win the argument so easily, and he was at a loss for words. "So how come you can run around in the city by yourself? How old are you anyway?"

Her quicksilver change in conversation left Jacob a little dazed. "I'm fourteen."

"That's it? I would have guessed seventeen or eighteen. But then I guess you wouldn't have been in that class if you were that old. You sure are big."

Jacob smiled self-consciously. "Ya, that's what my mama says. I'm going to be big like my father." He watched her dig around in her bag. "Look, I'm really glad you're coming with me." He felt his cheeks warm and he looked down to avoid her quick glance.

"How much do I get paid?"

"Get paid? For wha—?" Jacob stopped and gulped. How quickly a lie catches up! He cleared his throat nervously. "Uh, well, it's not exactly a job." He snuck a peek at her and found her gazing at him, and he was suddenly reminded of her intelligence. "I wasn't really supposed to hire anyone. I kind of told a fib, and I apologize. I just wanted you to come home with me." He stared steadfastly at the blankets, chagrined.

"Oh." There was an uncomfortable silence until Bailey finally found the words. "You mean you lied? And now you're sorry?"

"Yes," he said simply. He looked at her quickly and she saw the same goodness in his bright blue eyes that Gabriella had seen. She suddenly felt very, very glad that she had gone to school that day. Here was the big brother that she had always wanted: a protector, someone who cared that she was hungry and unhappy. Some whisper of doubt still lingered, though. Men of any age and size were not to be trusted.

To better see him she leaned forward until her face was inches from his. "Why do you want to take me with you? I don't understand."

"I don't either," he finally whispered after a long pause. Bailey felt a queer sensation in her stomach and waited for him to speak again, but he remained silent. Time seemed to stop, bind them, and then begin again, haltingly. His cut had begun to bleed freely again, but he sat still as a stone.

"Hey! Now stop that. I'm going to clean you up and make pretty little stitches, and I want you to just relax and not talk after all." Jacob sat back, relieved, and she sponged his eye again. Minutes later he detected the unmistakable smell of grain alcohol.

"What are you doing, Doc? I don't want any of that." Bailey smirked and Jacob watched, puzzled, as she doused the rag with alcohol and applied it to his cut.

"Ouch! That stings! What in blazes are you up to?"

"Midwife Martinez always puts spirits on her patient's wounds. She says it keeps the wounds from getting sick. She learned it from her mother, who learned it from her mother, who learned it from—"

"Okay, okay, I get the point. Get to the stitching."

"Bossy! You better talk nice to the one with the big needle. No, keep your eyes closed," she ordered. A pungent smell assaulted his nostrils.

"What are you putting on me now? Are you preparing a soup up there, Doc?"

"This will numb the area so you won't feel a thing. I learned it from—"

"Let me guess; Midwife Martinez," Jacob grinned. "Yes, smarty, she taught me this, too. She's better than the doctors because she knows ancient Mexican magic, things they don't teach in those fancy schools." Bailey carefully cleaned the needle with the alcohol and threaded it with strong silk thread stolen from Addie's sewing box. "So do you want to be a midwife when you grow up?" Jacob relaxed in the crook of her surprisingly strong arm.

"No!" Bailey said emphatically. She squeezed the edge of the cut together at one end and steadily made the first stitch, drawing the skin together. Jacob tensed for a moment, but then relaxed as he realized the pain was quite tolerable. Ma had stitched him up many times in the past.

"A nurse? I bet you'd be good at that."

"Maybe. I want to move away from this city, no matter what." Bailey spoke distractedly as she centered all of her concentration on her task.

"I love this city," Jacob murmured. Bailey made no reply.

"I think you should forget about being a nurse and become a doctor. Doctor Rose. Don't you like the sound of that?"

Bailey paused for the first time. "A doctor? Girls can't be doctors, silly!" She shook her head and bent again to her task.

"Oh yes they can. My older sister Rosalie took a trip to New York last year and there was a woman doctor there. She had just finished medical school." Jacob opened one eye expectantly.

"Close your eye." Bailey paused and felt her heart race with excitement. "You say she was a real doctor, and had gone to school with the men?" She finished the stitches and clipped the thread and tied it off, carefully cleaning the area with alcohol again.

"Yes, ma'am. So now you don't have any excuses. You're going to be a doctor." Jacob sat up and touched a finger to his tender eye. "You're finished? It didn't even hurt! Let me get my money bag and I will pay you your five hundred dollars."

"That's okay. I'll stitch you for free any time."

There was an awkward silence as the two looked at each other, somewhat at a loss.

"Well, are we going to the sheep ranch?" Bailey made a move as if to gather her things together.

"We can't go now! Are you crazy? I'm not traveling at night with all of those bandits and wolves out there waiting to pounce." He expected her to be frightened, but she looked at him evenly.

"I guess we'll spend the night here, then." She began matter-of-factly arranging the blankets in the meager space. He looked at her, a little frightened himself. Sleep under a porch with a girl?

"My rig is out there. I'll just sleep in the back of my rig and I'll come get you at dawn."

"I wouldn't do that if I were you," Bailey said carefully. She looked out from under the porch nervously.

"Why not?"

"If you don't put your horses in the stable, someone will steal them, if they haven't already. We have a stable boy with a gun; they'll be safe in there. And if you sleep in the stable, a john will see you when they leave. The men leave at all hours of the night. They'll tell Blanche and I'll catch hell."

"Oh." The explanation sounded a little patchy to him. "Why don't I just hide under some blankets in my wagon?"

There was a pause as Bailey shifted around to face him again. "Could you stay with me?" One of her hands fluttered halfway to her face, then back down again to clutch the other. Jacob began to form a suspicion, and for the first time he picked up the candle and shined it fully in her face. Both of her eyes were bruised and purple.

"What the heck?" He cupped her chin to turn her face more toward the light. "I'm going to *kill* Otto," he growled. "I'm going to finish him off."

She shrugged away. "It wasn't all Otto. Blanche was mad that I went to school. She let me have one. She said I needed a matching shiner on the other side." Bailey shrugged and looked at him levelly, and Jacob stared back, gaping in disbelief.

"Usually she doesn't use her fists, but she was plenty mad. She's still mad. If I get in any more trouble, she'll tan my hide."

"What if she finds me under here?"

"She's too fat to get under here. She doesn't even bother to bend over. She just stands on the porch and stomps her foot when she wants something. I'm always afraid the whole thing will collapse and crush me." Bailey allowed the tiniest of grins. "She's drunk by now, anyway. She never comes out this late."

Jacob smiled with her and buried his misgivings. "Okay. Let me stable the horses and I'll be right back."

Moments later she heard his boots in the dry dirt and grass. She had carefully arranged the blankets and pillows to give him as much privacy as possible. She found her satchel, and the thought of him lugging it around the city in search of her warmed her to him considerably. Gabriella and Juan had slept here a few times, and she liked having someone share her little space. She spent so much time alone that the novelty of having company was always a delicious thing.

Jacob crawled in, stuffing arms and legs in as quickly as he could. "A few more months and I wouldn't have been able to fit," he teased, trying to lighten an awkward moment. "And I got some ice from the icehouse. For your face, I mean."

He held out his cupped hands, and she stared at him, pleased beyond words at his thoughtfulness. She adjusted her view of boys. Not all boys were bad. Not all men were lechers, she supposed. She smiled, pulled up a corner of her dress and bundled the ice, placing it on her eyes and feeling immediate relief.

After a few moments of companionable silence she lowered the ice and gestured. "Here. This is your side. Go ahead and lie down and stretch out. I'll sleep where you aren't." She smiled, watching his long frame fill the tiny space.

"I'm afraid there's not much room for you," Jacob answered. "I'll sleep sitting up."

"No, I can fit." He lay down obediently and she lowered herself beside him, trying not to let any part of her touch any part of him. She put the ice back on her face and hoped that her eyes would not be black tomorrow. She noticed that he smelled good, like fresh air, earth, clean laundry, warm boy, and something else; something a little sweet and spicy.

"You know, it's gonna take two full days to get there," he reminded her.

Bailey sat up again. "Two days? Really? It's that far?"

"Yep. All the way to Boerne."

She snickered. "I've always liked the sound of that town. *Bernie.* Like a grizzled old man with a long beard."

He grinned in return. "We'll stay tomorrow evening along Leon Creek. My folks have friends there; we always stay there when we're making wool runs."

"Wool runs?"

"You know—bringing wool to market, and then—well—going back home again." Bailey lay back down and tried to imagine what bringing wool to market entailed.

"What's it like where we're going to stay?"

"Oh! The Milans are friends of ours—my pa emigrated with Mr. Milan. They aren't ranchers—they have a big orchard. They grow peaches. We kids always sleep in the barn; they have a special room all made up for us. They'll be expecting me—I stayed with them a few weeks ago when I traveled to the city."

"You mean you came to the city all by yourself? From your home, two days away?" Bailey was flabbergasted. He seemed to her more and more like a young man rather than a boy just a few years her senior.

"Ya, it was my first time. It was fun!" He shrugged and smiled, elaborating no further, and then gave a huge yawn. He was clearly exhausted, and Bailey decided there would be plenty of time for questions during their long trip.

"Goodnight," she said meekly.

"Well, good night, then. We'll leave at dawn." Jacob rolled onto his side, but changed his mind quickly as his back came in contact with her arm.

So they both lay stiffly on their backs, and they finally slept as the endless party raged on all night above them.

CHAPTER THREE

Jacob awoke reluctantly at the first hint of light in the eastern sky, obeying his inner clock. All of his life he had been called at dawn by his mother to begin the day's chores, and for a moment he was confused. Where was he? Why didn't he hear Johann, Anton, Wenzel, and baby Joseph stirring in their beds? He felt a warm weight on his chest, and he looked down, remembering. The girl was curled up next to him like a puppy, her face buried in his neck and her arm flung across his chest. Each of her exhalations sent a tiny whirlwind down his shirt. He felt curious sensations build within him; above all, a fierce desire to protect her from women like Blanche and pigs like Otto. These last two weeks had been an awakening for him; his world was composed of a warm, loving family, plenty to eat, and boundless possibilities for his life. He had never conceived of a world where children were perpetually hungry and raised themselves amid squalor and immorality and abuse. He studied the bruises staining her face and wondered how she had grown into the compassionate girl that he perceived her to be.

I should wake her, he thought, and wondered why he didn't move. He lay quietly, unwilling to forsake the peaceful moment to the long journey that lay ahead. He shifted ever so slightly, and the girl awoke immediately, her dark eyes snapping open as she tilted her head to look up at him.

"Oh! Good morning." She sat up, her impossibly tangled hair falling to her waist in disheveled waves. She stretched mightily and yawned. "Is it time to go to the sheep ranch?"

Jacob smiled. He wasn't so sure she was going to like the sheep; they were stinky, loud animals who possessed an alarming lack of motivation to do anything but graze and grow wool. "Get your things together and meet me in the stables. We need to be heading out so we can get to the Milans in time for supper." His stomach rumbled painfully, reminding him that he hadn't eaten since yesterday noon. He had some hard biscuits and apples in the wagon, and that was going to have to hold them all day. He didn't want to ask the girl for food; it was obvious that she didn't have any under the porch.

"How does my face look? Is it horrible?" she asked anxiously. He was happy to see that the ice had prevented swelling.

"It looks pretty," he said without thinking, and reddened. "I mean, it's not puffy or anything. Just kinda purplish-reddish, under your eyes. It's not as bad as I thought it would be," he yammered, trying to cover up his slip.

She nodded mutely, staring at him for a few beats, and turned away suddenly, inching her way out from under the porch.

Within the hour they were on the path out of the sleeping city, heading northwest to his beloved ranch. Bailey slumbered almost as soon as Joey and Bella began their brisk, rhythmic pace, her head lolling on Jacob's shoulder. Jacob felt his own eyes grow heavy, and he tried to keep himself awake by figuring out a way to introduce Bailey to his family.

Hi, Ma. This is a girl I picked up in San Antonio. She lives in a whore house, so I thought I'd bring her home so we could save her soul. He grinned. Although his Ma appreciated a direct approach, that wouldn't do at all.

Hi, Ma. I brought someone home to help you with the chores during shearing. I met her at school. Her mother said she thought it would be good for her little girl to have a holiday out in the country. Can she stay for a while? This was better, but it involved a lie, and Jacob had never been able to lie successfully to his mother. She could tell, just by looking at him.

Hi, Ma. This is Miss Bailey Rose. She lives in San Antonio and I met her at the German school. She's never been to the country, so I invited her to stay with us for a bit. This was better, but the truth was that Jacob planned for Bailey never to leave once he got her home. How could he ask his mother to adopt another child when she already had nine of her own? Well, at least Bailey would make an even ten. And how would he ask Bailey to stay if his mother said yes?

Bailey, would you like to stay here for good? You can be a member of our family and go to school with me. You'd like our school: it only has one room and a really nice teacher. You'd learn to speak Moravian, and after you were done with school, we'd send you to New York to become a doctor. And you could be my sister. That was the part that stuck in his throat. *You could be my friend.* That was better.

Jacob dozed, exhausted, and the horses made their way along the well-worn trail, needing no guidance to find their way on a trip they had made countless times. Not until the morning burned into a searing noon did Jacob wake with a start. He looked at Bailey and burst out laughing. She had taken the reins from his lax hands and was confidently leading the rig along. Or at least she thought she was.

"Oh! Good morning, sleepyhead. I woke up to find you snoring away, so I thought I'd better grab the reins before we ended up in Dallas." She smiled, delighted at her prowess.

"You're doing just fine. It's a good thing you woke up." Jacob leaned back and pulled his misshapen dark brown hat over his eyes, planning to sleep a few more winks.

"Oh, no you don't! Sit up and tell me about all of these flowers. I've never seen them before." Bailey grabbed his hat and smashed it down on her own head.

"You're interested in flowers? I thought you were much too tough for that."

"Well, I'm a girl, aren't I? I can appreciate pretty things." She glanced at him, ready to play angry until she saw the teasing smile on his face. "What are those climbing things that look like yellow beards?"

"Well, you almost got it right. They're called Old Man's Beard. Just wait until July; they get really pretty." His voice petered out as she glanced at him sharply. Careful!

"And which of these flowers smell so sweet? They smell good enough to eat!"

He pointed to small white flowers with purplish-red anthers growing along the trail. "You're probably smelling the Wild Honeysuckle. They'll turn pink later on in the summer."

Bailey gazed out over the sea of bluebonnets, buttercups, daisies, and brown-eyed Susans that covered the gently rolling hills like a colorful patchwork quilt. She threw her head back and sucked in a succession of deep breaths. Already she felt different, better. Hordes of butterflies fluttered and fat bumblebees droned around the lavender-blue flowers growing from the Texas mountain laurel. Pecan and cottonwood trees outlined the clear, spring-fed streams that crisscrossed the hills, and grey-green live oak trees, gigantic and crooked, spread their arms to provide shade to the meadowlarks with their bright yellow breasts. *See-you, tee-year* they whistled clearly, and Bailey whistled back. Red-tailed hawks wheeled lazily in the sky above them, and Bailey watched longingly, wishing she could fly.

Soon Jacob commandeered the reins and directed the horses to the side of the road under the shade of a huge live oak. "Time to eat," he said simply, and helped Bailey down from the wagon. They settled against the tree and gnawed contentedly on the biscuits, pausing now and then to cup water from the clear stream to quench their thirst.

"These are good. What do you call them?" Bailey asked politely, digging in the basket for another.

"Biscuits."

"Oh." There was a silence as she tried to think of a better question. Jacob seemed to be a little out of sorts just after waking. "So where did you say you were from?" She peered at him from beneath the brim of the floppy hat.

"Near to Boerne. Our ranch is near Cibola Creek."

"No, I mean where did your parents come from? Aren't you from a far-away place, like Germany?"

"No, but you're close. My parents came from Moravia. Do you know where that is?"

She shook her head. "I'm not too smart yet."

"That's okay. It lies next to Bohemia..." his voice faded as he noticed the blank look on her face. "It's in Europe."

"Oh. I know where England and Ireland are, but I don't know where Europe is." She stared at her biscuit.

"When we get home, I'll show you a map, okay?" He waited for her nod. "Why don't I teach you some Moravian words? You're pretty good at memorizing."

"Okay!" She sat up eagerly and faced him. "What are you going to teach me?"

"Well, what's the first thing that you'll want to ask my mother?" He smiled at the look of intense concentration that puckered her elfish face. She suddenly snapped her fingers.

"I want to ask her where all of that good food is that you keep talking about!" She rubbed her stomach, and Jacob was suddenly reminded of how young she was and how hungry she must be. When was the last time she had eaten a good meal?

"Okay. Mama's specialty is roast pork with dumplings and potatoes and gravy. She's probably serving it tomorrow, on Sunday. Roast pork is *veprova pecene*. Now you say it."

"*Veprova pecene*," she mimicked expertly.

"Perfect! Now say *knedliky*. That's dumplings."

"*Knedliky,*" she said obediently. "*Veprova pecene* and *knedliky*, please." She pronounced the words with a flawless imitation of his accent. "Teach me another one!" She scooted on two knees closer to him.

"Do you like sweets?"

"I would die for them!" She sighed dramatically with the back of her hand to her forehead, and fell over backward in a graceful faint.

"Sit up, silly." Jacob laughed and whacked at her playfully. "You will love *kolac*. It's a pastry—you know; a tart—and its middle is filled with sweet fruit." He watched as she sat up to pay attention.

"*Kolac*." She licked her lips, hunger pains settling low in her belly.

The two stared at each other, thinking of mounds of delicious food waiting for them at the end of the trail. Jacob rose and offered her his hand. "That's enough talk of food already!" They clambered back into the wagon, spending the next four hours chatting about food, unable to help themselves, starting with traditional Moravian dishes and ending with delicious San Antonio chili.

By the time they reached Selma at sunset they were both famished again, but Bailey was distracted from her hunger by the picturesque Leon Creek, a sparkling stream that flowed steadily through deep canyons and rocky flats, at one point forming a lovely waterfall. A few minutes further, rounding a bend, they came upon a quaint stone house with a deeply pitched roof and an inviting porch. Behind the house was a small barn, a green pasture with a few horses and goats munching contentedly, and a newly-planted vegetable garden. And behind the garden was a spectacular orchard of peach trees, lined up in precise rows. Bailey gasped at the beauty of it: the trees' gray branches were wide-flung, in full bloom, their blossoms rosy pink and delicate. "They look like butterflies! Can we take a walk in the orchard later?"

"Sure we can."

A woman was taking down laundry from a line strung between two trees, a baby playing at her feet, and she turned to look over her shoulder as Jacob approached. She waved and gathered the baby up, hurrying into the house, and by the time Jacob had pulled his rig up to the house, half a dozen noisy children spilled from it, flanked by the woman and her smiling husband.

"Jacob Naplava!" She greeted, gathering him into a hug as he jumped down from the rig. "We didn't expect you for another week or so!"

"Ah, time to get home and help with the wool," he murmured, returning her hug and shaking the hand of the older man. "This is Bailey Rose, a friend of mine who will be helping us out this summer. She's going to get a taste of the ranch!"

The woman chortled and clapped her hands together. "Oh, my dear! You may find that you wish you had stayed in the city! Gacenka Naplava will keep you busy!" They all laughed, and Bailey was bustled into the house while Jacob and Mr. Milan tended the horses.

After a dinner of turkey, gravy, and freshly-baked bread, they played a few lively rounds of Skat—a card game Bailey had never played but picked up with ease, beating Jacob handily and causing the children to cheer loudly. When Bailey began to yawn, Mrs. Milan showed them to their quarters in the barn. "I hope you don't mind sleeping out here," she worried, a line forming between her brows. "We just are plumb out of room in the house; all we have is the floor, and this so much more comfortable."

"Oh, no, I don't mind!" Bailey exclaimed, and she meant it. The hay looked inviting, and there were mounds of soft quilts and pillows. "This is better than my porch!" This last comment drew a puzzled look from the kindly woman, and Jacob scrambled to bridge the awkward moment.

"Ah, every place looks better than home, just 'cause it's different," he laughed.

After Mrs. Milan took her leave, Jacob sank to the hay, pulling a blanket over his chest. "I'm beat," he admitted. He grinned at her and closed his eyes, and Bailey could tell by his breathing that he was immediately asleep. She had never seen anyone fall asleep so fast in her life! She watched him awhile, fascinated, before her cheeks grew warm from the intimacy of the moment, and she made herself turn away.

He woke her at dawn, softly calling her name and tugging on a piece of her long hair. "Bailey! Bailey!"

"What?" she grouched. She was finding that she did not care too much for rising early.

"I have to show you something." He pulled her up, helping her to brush the hay from her dress. "Follow me."

She stumbled after him, comically groggy, making her way through the barn, around the house, and past the vegetable garden. The sight that met her took her breath away. The rising sun had touched each peach blossom with a sparkling, golden hue, the dew making them glow all the brighter. It was impossible, magical. *Enchanted.*

Without a word, Jacob took her hand and they walked silently through the orchard, up one row and down the next, through each and every row, Bailey's head turning this way and that to absorb the majesty of the moment. As they approached the very last tree, Jacob reached up and broke off a pink blossom, then leaned forward to tuck it in her hair behind her ear. He was so close that Bailey could make out faint freckles on his cheek; she saw, up close for the first time, the truly monochromatic bottomless crystal of his eyes.

"There! Now you have been properly inducted into the Milan peach orchard," he laughed.

She laughed, too, finding her mouth to be a bit dry.

A short time later, they were bidding the Milans goodbye. "Get back in the wagon and I'll tell you a scary story about Vodnik," Jacob smirked.

"Vod-who?"

Jacob smiled and helped her into the wagon. Once on their way, he began to tell her about the mysterious creature, sneaking peeks at her to make sure she wasn't too scared. "Vodnik is a water sprite that lives in these hills. You have to watch out for open wells and rivers and creeks because Vodnik will catch you and drag you down into the water."

Bailey snorted unbelievingly. "Come on, Jacob. There is no such thing." She gave him a disdainful look and gazed off into the hills, but Jacob could tell by her tense posture that she was still listening.

"Oh yes, I should tell you what he looks like. He wears red, yellow and green, and he has a long white beard, long green hair, and a wreath of seaweed on his head. His hands and feet are webbed like a duck, but watch out, because he has sharp cat claws."

"How could he wear clothes if he lives under water?" asked Bailey, yawning hugely. She wasn't easily impressed.

"The clothes never get wet. They protect him from drowning, but they won't protect you if he drags you down. Oh, and you might not recognize him, because he can transform into a wolf or a white horse. And it doesn't have to be a boy; Vodnik can be a girl. Mama says they are real back in the Old Country. She's seen one." Jacob paused and looked at his small charge to see if she believed him. She was fast asleep.

They rode peacefully all day, stopping once to enjoy Mrs. Milan's packed luncheon of turkey sandwiches and fresh peaches, talking easily about a dizzying variety of subjects: dogs versus cats, how much they wanted to ride that new-fangled contraption called a bicycle, whether or not man would travel to the moon someday (Jacob said yes and that his children would live to see it, but Bailey scoffed), the theatre, figs versus peaches, the color of Bailey's hair (she said ugly orange; Jacob said a sunrise), Jacob's nose, which was slightly bent from one of many rambunctious fights with one brother or another, which Bailey said saved him from being too pretty of a boy, and a lively debate about which bleeds more, an eyelid or a lip. As the wagon bumped along, Bailey slipped in and out of a pleasant doze, dreaming of pastry, roast pork, sheep, and scary creatures.

At some point she awoke, confused and disoriented. She stretched hugely and opened her eyes, and was surprised to find that dusk had almost relinquished itself to night. How long had she been sleeping? She sat up straight, looking around for Jacob. She was apparently alone, and even more strangely, the wagon had stopped.

"Jacob?" she ventured. Her voice sounded hollow and tiny. She felt tendrils of fear raise the small, fine hairs on the back of her neck. The enormity of her journey struck her: she had left home with a virtual stranger, traveled with him for two days without permission, and everything was suddenly sinister and unfamiliar. Strange sounds surrounded her; it sounded like children wailing; *hundreds* of children. And underneath this baleful clamor was another sound. Were the children ringing little bells? There was an overpowering stench that she could not identify, but it burned her eyes until she felt tears beginning to form. And then the unearthly howling began.

I have died and gone to hell. Up to this point she wasn't sure she believed in such a place, but what else could explain this? Children crying, bells ringing, a putrid smell, howling. She felt a scream beginning to build. Suddenly the wagon gave a sickening lurch. Gathering her last bit of courage, she peered over the side of the rig. There stood a massive, ghostly white, dog-like shape, eyes glowing. Its huge front paws were propped up on the side of the wagon, as if it were readying to jump up. Its eyes locked with hers, and Bailey felt a palpable evil emanating from the creature, almost like a stench. *It has come for me personally.* The inane thought popped into her head, followed quickly by another that she understood with much more clarity. *Run!*

Over the side of the wagon she went, falling to her knees as she hit the ground. She swore and struggled to her feet and began running into the darkness. Behind her she could hear the steady cadence of the creature, gaining on her gradually, biding its time, knowing she would tire eventually. The wailing was all around her now. She thought she heard someone calling her name, but the sound was lost in the din. The earth suddenly shifted and became a pit of slime, and her feet flew out from underneath her. She lay on her back, not daring to breathe or move. The deafening noise closed in, and amid the wails and tinkling bells, she covered her face with her hands and screamed, over and over.

"Bailey! Bailey!" Finally the voice registered, and Bailey struggled up to a sitting position and looked around. In the distance six or seven dots of light were becoming bigger and bigger, until finally a blessed path of light illuminated the darkness. Bailey covered her eyes again, not wanting to see the terrible creature that she knew must be upon her. Hadn't Jacob warned her about Vodnik? Why hadn't she listened more closely?

"Bailey." Two strong arms pulled her into a tight embrace. "What in God's name are you doing?" She buried her face in Jacob's familiar soft shirt.

"Where am I? Is this Hell?" Bailey's tremulous question was met with several deep-throated chuckles.

"You could say that again, missy," drawled a man's voice in a thick Mexican drawl.

"Okay, Gonzalez, back to your cards and liquor." This was issued with a no-nonsense tone in a voice that reminded her of Jacob's, only deeper and more thickly accented.

Jacob finally pushed her back at arm's length. "Open your eyes. See where you are."

One by one Bailey removed the fingers covering her eyes. She looked around her, dumbfounded. She saw no devils or tortured children or fallen angels ringing bells. She saw no gargantuan wolf-like creature ready to consume her. She saw five thousand sheep staring dumbly back at her. Behind Jacob stood what could only be his family: a seemingly endless row of siblings, some with his bright blue eyes, others with his jet black hair, all with his wide smile. And boy, were they smiling now! A very pretty woman pushed her way through and gathered Bailey in her arms, nudging Jacob aside.

"Oh! You poor child! Jacob! Who is this lovely child, and why is she sitting with Papa's sheep?" The younger children giggled and the older ones covered their mouths with their hands.

"Ma, this is Bailey Rose," Jacob said simply, and found that despite all of his careful planning, he couldn't think of a darn thing to say next. His brothers and sisters gaped at him, and his father regarded him silently, an unreadable expression in his eyes.

Gacenka Naplava gave her son a quick, keen glance and assessed the situation in an instant. "Well hello, Miss Bailey Rose. Papa, look! A good friend of Jacob's has come to visit us." She smiled widely at her husband and shot a warning glance to her children as they took in Bailey's outlandish dress and ragged appearance. "You know, now that I think about it, the rooster did crow on my porch this morning. Miss Bailey, that is a Moravian sign that visitors will come this day!" She beamed at her, as if this explained everything.

"See, Mama, I thought—"

"Enough thinking for one night, young man," she interrupted, and pulled Bailey to her feet. "Miss Rose does not wish to linger in the sheep pit while Jacob does his thinking." The brood laughed again and Bailey couldn't resist a grin herself, even though she was truly mortified.

"Ah! Miss Rose has a delightful smile. Come, child, we will get you all cleaned up and you will eat until you groan for mercy. Are you hungry?"

"*Veprova pecene* and *knedliky*, please," Bailey said shakily. The plump woman gave a whoop of delight, her warm eyes sparkling.

"You speak Moravian! Papa, this girl is from the homeland!" Jacob grinned and tried to keep from rolling his eyes.

"Uh, no, ma'am, Jacob just taught me some words."

"Well! You must be very brilliant. We shall teach you some more very soon. But first, inside you go." She took her by the hand and pulled her briskly toward the large ranch house, the rest of the family following, incredulous. The sight of the immaculate Gacenka leading a strange small girl covered in sheep slime into their home struck them speechless, an unusual state for the lively family. Jacob's older brother Anton nudged him from behind.

"Jacob, I know how you like to bring home stray dogs, but stray girls?" He ruffled Jacob's hair and the boy pulled away angrily.

"Don't call her a stray," he growled. Anton backed off, surprised.

"Sorry, little brother. I didn't mean anything by it." He gave him a friendly shove, wondering at Jacob's rare display of temper.

The family filed into the large, rambling ranch house and the boys scattered at Mrs. Naplava's orders. "Yes, you too, Jacob. We'll take care of your girl." *Yakoob*, she pronounced his name, and the boy blushed.

"She's not my girl," he mumbled, and then flushed to an even brighter shade as his sisters giggled.

"Shoo! In a little bit of a while we will eat, and we will all meet your friend properly." Jacob left the room reluctantly with one more backward glance at the girl. She stared back at him, bashful to be left in the company of strangers, and still dazed from her dream-like experience. For the first time she dared to take a good look at Mrs. Naplava. Her face was startlingly beautiful and wore an expectant grin as if she were waiting to hear a good joke. The hazel eyes were the kindest Bailey had ever seen. The woman was wearing a full blue and white skirt of at least eight widths, and it was gathered at a fitted Basque waist. A beautiful embroidered apron was tied behind her in a large white bow. Her honey-golden hair was parted carefully in the middle and braided back into two plaits wrapped tightly around her head. She was removing a large, diagonally-folded kerchief from her head when she noticed Bailey staring at her. Bailey blushed and looked away.

"You look all that you want, little Bailey. No doubt we dress very different from your family. We are all in our Sunday best today; tomorrow, not quite so fancy as this. Now, let me tell you about my girls." She beamed at the girls standing shyly behind her and waved the tallest forward.

"This is Rosalie, my oldest." A lovely girl of about twenty with the same smooth honey-colored hair smiled widely at Bailey. "And these are my twins, Marianna and Amalie. They are twelve years old, about your age, is that right?" Two girls with black pigtails and big blue eyes grinned at Bailey. They were identical twins, she could see, although one of them was chubbier than the other. They bore a strong resemblance to Jacob, and Bailey was immediately charmed.

"We'll give you some of our clothes, Bailey. Can we, Ma?" They seemed to speak in unison, and Bailey stared, entranced. She had never seen twins before.

"Yes, girls, run and get a nice thick gown for nighttime."

"Can I get my brush, Ma? Bailey can use my brush." This was issued from a little girl of about six, with light brown curls and dimples.

"Yes indeed, Annie. This is Annie, my very best helper." She stroked her daughter's hair and then shooed her off to fetch the brush.

A small boy suddenly materialized from the shadows and crawled onto Bailey's lap, as if it were the most natural place in the world for him to be. He stuck one thumb in his mouth and twisted to get a better look at Bailey.

"And this is Joseph, my baby. As you can see, he dearly loves girls already." Bailey smiled, delighted with her new admirer.

"Joseph, now you run along and find the boys." The toddler crawled down again and ran off on pudgy legs. "I'll introduce you to my other boys while you and Jacob eat dinner." Mrs. Naplava bustled around the large room, building the fire in the stove and warming a huge cast-iron kettle of water. "As soon as it is warm, you'll have a lovely bath and we can forget about the sheep!" She gave a motherly smile to Bailey.

Without warning, tears began to form in Bailey's eyes. Had her own mother ever given her a bath? She must have, when Bailey was a baby, but Bailey had no memory of it. She felt so safe in this large room and this big comfortable chair. She felt safe from everything but the wolf that waited for her outside.

"Whatever is wrong?" Mrs. Naplava came and gathered the child in her arms quite naturally. She felt the girl shaking, and her heart broke for the sharpness of the shoulder blades she felt through the bright satin dress.

"I g-guess I sh-should tell you s-so it doesn't g-get the sheep," the girl sobbed out.

"So what doesn't get the sheep? What scared you so and made you run from the wagon?" Mrs. Naplava stroked the girl's hair with the healing touch only a mother can provide. "You're safe now and you can tell me."

"I think I saw a w-wolf. I've never seen one before, but I've heard ranchers talk about them. It was big and it chased me into the pen." Bailey felt her tears subside, but she stayed where she was.

"You probably *did* see a wolf, my dear. Where there are sheep, there are wolves, although it's unusual that it would be this close to camp with all the noise from the shearers. But I believe you, of course. Why, one year we lost fifteen sheep in one night, right under the men's noses! I will tell Papa to send some men around the ranch to scout. Don't worry, we will take care of the wolf, little one." Bailey smiled into the kind eyes and felt immeasurably better already. "Now let me tell you all about the little village I grew up in. It was Bordovice, in Moravia." Her gentle voice wove story after story and put Bailey at ease. Marianna, one of the twins, came to listen and even held Bailey's hand.

An hour later she was clean and cozy in a thick white nightgown. Amazingly, Mrs. Naplava had managed to wash and comb Bailey's tangled hair and smooth the whole mass into a perfect fat braid that hung past her waist. Mrs. Naplava had been taken aback by the bruises on her face—Bailey could tell by a soft indrawn breath—but she had not questioned her. Bailey felt immaculate and more than a little awed as she and Jacob were seated ceremoniously at the end of an immense plank table and served steaming plates of roast pork and dumplings. Various members of the family sat around the table, having eaten hours ago but wanting to hear about Jacob's adventures in the city. Of course, they wanted to get a better look at Bailey, too, but only with very discreet glances under the watchful eye of Gacenka. They all noticed the purple bruises under her eyes and tried heroically not to stare.

"So, Jacob, what trouble did you manage to get into with Hans? Did you get into a tangle with a chili queen?" The oldest boy teased as he gestured toward Jacob's prominent blue stitches. That had been the only color of thread that Bailey had. The two of them together looked as though they had been in a bar fight. The others giggled and leaned forward, expecting to hear a good story. Jacob scowled and shrugged.

"Just for that, I'm not going to tell you," he returned, trying to wriggle out of the question.

Gacenka noticed his unusual reticence. Usually he was so eager to tell a story! She decided to rescue him, and shot him a look that said, "I will hear about this later."

She moved around the table to Johann. "This is my oldest boy, Johann. Already twenty-one years old, and no wife, but he finds time to learn about chili queens, whatever they are," sighed Gacenka.

"Ma, I am fixing that minor problem," Johann smiled. His smile was much like Jacob's, wide and infectious, although he had his mother's thick brown hair. He had a rather longish nose and twinkling brown eyes. "I am getting married in two months' time to a wonderful girl named Melinda. Lindy and I would be delighted to have you attend our wedding." The girls giggled and Bailey blushed.

"Okay, enough noise from you, Johann." Gacenka walked around the table and placed her hands on the wide shoulders of another big boy. "This is another boy of mine, can you believe it, Bailey? Anton is eighteen, ready to marry, and no girl who will look at him for miles and miles." This produced another round of laughter, and Bailey joined in. Anton was a stunning young man, with Rosalie's honey brown hair and strangely amber eyes, his face beautifully featured. He looked more like a prince than a sheep rancher.

"I've had more than a few offers, Mother," he boasted. Although he was teasing, Bailey was uncomfortable, reminded of the dandies who strolled with such confidence in and out of Fort Allen. Anton smiled engagingly at her, and she could feel the charm emanate in palpable waves. She felt repelled and intrigued at the same time.

"And of course little Joseph you've met already," continued Gacenka, stroking the baby's curls. He had attached himself to Gacenka's leg and was taking the ride with her around the table as she introduced her brood.

"I believe the only one you haven't met is Wenzel." She stopped at the chair of a serious-looking boy, a younger and pudgier version of Jacob. He had the ebony hair, but his blue eyes were pale and sprinkled with brown. Whereas Jacob's chiseled face always seemed to be on the verge of a grin, this boy had a dreamy, somewhat somber expression. Bailey found herself wanting to make him laugh.

"Hello," he said at last, with much aforethought, and Bailey answered back, echoing his greeting. She tried to think of a joke to tell him, but nothing came to mind. There was a brief uncomfortable silence until Gacenka finally seated herself beside Bailey, baby Joseph on her lap.

"Tell us a little about yourself, Bailey. Do you have brothers and sisters?" She was smiling gently, not prying, but expressing a genuine, friendly interest. The others smiled encouragingly toward her, waiting for her to speak. She felt surrounded by a warm, encompassing emotion she could not identify. Nevertheless, she froze. What should she say? *No, Mrs. Naplava, I haven't any brothers and sisters. As a matter of fact, I haven't a father. My mother sleeps with men for money.* The words echoed in her head, and for a moment Bailey was terrified they would slip past her lips. For some reason, she wanted to tell this wonderful, warm lady with the strange accent everything that was in her heart. *I don't have much of a family, so could I stay here?* Automatically her eyes were drawn to Jacob for help. Her look of panic was reflected on his face.

His heart went out to her, seeing her sitting there looking very small and vulnerable at the end of the huge table, all eyes on her. His well-meaning mother couldn't possibly imagine the answers to the questions she was asking the little girl.

"Uh, Bailey is really shy, Ma. She doesn't have any brothers or sisters." He paused and swallowed thickly. Now was the time to explain Bailey's presence here; his mother had been patient enough. Still, the words wouldn't come.

Gacenka filled the silence quickly, seeing the distress of the little girl and her son. "Well, we can understand that, sweetheart. You just eat and ignore all of these nosy Naplavas. I haven't finished my introductions yet, anyway." She sprang from the table with a lightning energy that dazzled the little girl and moved around to stand behind Jacob. "And of course, this is Jacob! You haven't properly met Father yet, but Jacob is the image of my Franticek. First Jacob, then Wenzel, then the twins, all the image of my beloved husband." She placed her hand over her heart in a comical fashion, and the children laughed again. She was a talented entertainer. "Now Jacob is special, Bailey, as I'm sure you know." Bailey blushed for no good reason.

"Who has a good story about our Jacob?" She asked, looking around the room expectantly as Jacob groaned. Bailey was charmed all over again with Gacenka's pronunciation of his name. *Yakoob.*

"Mother, Bailey doesn't want to hear—" he was immediately shouted down.

One voice rose above the others. Not surprisingly, it was Johann, the obvious clown of the family. "Rosalie, remember the time we put Jacob in the chicken coop? He was in his little baby dress and he was squatting down to pet a hen, and you wouldn't believe what got pecked!"

Jacob was around the table faster than Bailey believed possible. He was readying for a full-body tackle when Gacenka grabbed him around the waist, laughing.

"Okay, Johann, perhaps we should save that story for Jacob to tell Bailey himself." Johann conceded and Jacob took his chair again amidst much mirth.

Marianna shot up from the table, eyes shining. "Do you know what we call Jacob?"

Jacob groaned audibly and Bailey shook her head.

"Blue Boy!" The siblings all snickered.

"Why?" Bailey ventured, sneaking a look at Jacob, whose face was red and brows were drawn down. She would have guessed it was because of the remarkable color of his eyes, but she wasn't going to say that out loud.

"Mama always dressed him in blue when he was little," Rosalie explained with a wide smile. "She dressed him to match his eyes. Every piece of clothing he owned was blue, and everyone just started calling him 'Blue Boy.' It still slips out from time to time."

"Not everyone, just you sorry lot," growled Jacob, and the snickers grew louder.

Bailey looked at him, delighted. "Can I call you that?" she whispered.

"No." He was frowning fiercely, but there was a glimmer in his eye.

"Who else has a story about our Blue Boy?" laughed Gacenka.

"Jacob saved me from a snake," piped up Annie, and Jacob shot her a grateful look.

"Yes, Annie, that's a much better story. Tell us," encouraged Gacenka.

"I just did," said the shy little girl, sticking a finger in her mouth and retreating behind her mother's skirts as the others laughed.

"I have a story," Wenzel said very formally. The table grew quiet as the family seemed surprised. Jacob looked at his brother with a gentle expression in his eyes.

"Go ahead, Wen." His voice was encouraging.

"One time Jacob took me to the creek, and we went fishing. I caught the biggest fish." His voice was slow and deliberate, and his face remained perfectly impassive. Bailey stared, incredulous. Why was he talking that way?

"I remember that, too, Wen. Your fish was bigger and we ate it for supper that night." Wenzel nodded solemnly and looked down at his folded hands.

Is he slow? Bailey wondered, and her heart gave a tug.

"I've never fished before, Wenzel. Do you think you could teach me how?" The others glanced at her, surprised. This was the most she had said all evening. Wenzel looked up and smiled and nodded, and Bailey felt rewarded. Her gaze collided with Jacob's and she met an expression of intense emotion.

"Plenty of time for fishing after a good night's sleep, you two," admonished Gacenka, delighted with the little girl's kindness to her Wenzel. "Now that we have made introductions and embarrassed Jacob, let's allow the weary travelers to eat in peace. Girls, the dishes are not yet clean. We must get everything ready for tomorrow's meals. Johann, Anton, fetch your guns and walk around a bit. Lots of sheep to protect, you remember, and the *pastores* are already too drunk to hit the side of the barn. I believe I may have seen some wolf tracks earlier today." Gacenka did not give away Bailey's secret, and she was grateful. "Wenzel, you may put Joseph to bed, please." The boy picked up the baby obediently and carried him gently from the room, with a quick backward smile at Bailey.

Quite suddenly the room was empty save for Bailey and Jacob. They looked at each other and laughed a little self-consciously.

"I love your family," Bailey said, and meant it.

"They like you, too." Jacob smiled back at her, shoving food in his mouth as fast as he could. "You're not eating much. Don't you like it?"

"This is the most delicious meal I've ever had," she admitted, and dug in, relieved to be out of the spotlight so she could relax and relish the sumptuous fare. In between bites, Jacob stole glances at her, entranced. She ate with a peculiar delicacy, almost like an aristocrat. Her utensils were managed with perfect grace, and she blotted at her mouth delicately with the napkin, displaying flawless manners. Where had she learned that? His own mother insisted on exemplary manners, but it seemed as though Bailey's mother was not in the picture enough to teach her daughter proper etiquette. It was on the tip of his tongue to ask her, but he didn't know how to phrase it without hurting her feelings. He contented himself with watching her, until she caught him staring. He searched his brain for something to say.

"Um, you look really nice in Amalie's gown." It was the first thing that popped into his head, and he was relieved to see he hadn't embarrassed her. Sometimes girls could be funny that way, he had found in his many years of experience with sisters.

"It's Marianna's, and thank you." Bailey grinned at him, and he relaxed.

"I see Mama's got you into Moravian braids already."

"I told her how I loved the girls' braids, especially Rosalie's, and so she braided mine. She said she had never seen such curly hair." Bailey put her fork down and touched her braid self-consciously. "I wish my hair was smooth and straight and yellow like Rosalie's."

"I like it just the way it was. I like it when it's down and flying all over the place." It was out of his mouth before he could stop it, and he flushed a deep shade of red. What had possessed him to say that? He dug resolutely back into his meal, face flaming. Bailey stared at him, bewildered, and picked up her own fork. They finished their supper in silence.

Thirty minutes later Gacenka had her bundled into Jacob's bed, which had been moved into the girls' room at Jacob's insistence. "Wen and I can sleep on the floor," he had explained to a proud Gacenka. Such compassion she was seeing from her boy! He set up the bed himself, arranging his own blankets that he had used from the time he was a baby into a comfortable nest for the sleepy little waif.

Bailey lay in the dark room, with the twins and Annie already fast asleep in a huge bed beside her. Rosalie hadn't come to bed yet, and Bailey found herself listening to the soft hum of conversation from the older children in the parlor. She thought she could hear Jacob and Anton arguing softly, good-naturedly, and Rosalie and Johann chiming in from time to time. She wondered at all that had happened to her today. Had it been only a few days ago that she had awakened curled next to a big, warm boy under the porch of Fort Allen? She giggled to herself as she remembered the look on Jacob's face when she had pulled out her needle and thread to stitch up his eye. She had to admit to herself that he had taken the stitches without as much as a flinch. She relived the trip they had taken through the beautiful hills, carefully omitting the part about the wolf and her humiliating race into a sheep pen. She thought of Mrs. Naplava and all of the children, of the wonderful food and the soft warm bed, but most of all she thought about Jacob. Why had he brought her to this fairy-tale place? The question troubled her deeply. Anything that she could not immediately grasp was a source of frustration, even fear. She slumbered, the thoughts slipping from her consciousness into her dreams.

She was running, and the wolf was chasing her. It was dark and silent; the sound of bleating sheep absent because she wasn't afraid of that sound anymore. She was afraid of the wolf. The wolf was big and white with glowing eyes. Bailey tried to run with all of her might, but it was a dream run, her muscles constricted. She looked back and she could see the wolf advancing. The wolf opened its mouth and spoke. It said "Time to eat!" Amazingly, it was Jacob's voice that emerged from this vicious creature. Bailey was enraged. It was a liberating, empowering anger. Suddenly she wasn't afraid anymore. "You're not Jacob!" she said calmly to the wolf. The wolf smiled. "No. But I'm going to eat him when I find him." Bailey screamed a warning.

She was still screaming his name when Jacob arrived at a dead sprint, followed by a cluster of brothers and sisters and a concerned Gacenka. He knelt and obeyed an instinct not to shake her; instead, he enveloped her in his strong arms for the second time that day. "Bailey," he said in low, calm voice, trying to ease her terror. He was accustomed to comforting small children in the dark of night, having performed this service for his little siblings. She opened her eyes and stopped wailing.

"Oh," she whispered. She looked around at the crowd of concerned faces and buried her face in his shirt, abashed. "I've brought everybody running again, haven't I?"

"It's okay. It was just a bad dream." He rose from his knees and plunked down on the bed next to her. Gacenka settled the twins and Annie back into bed and bustled the others from the room, seeing at a glance that Bailey needed Jacob alone. She saw something else, too, with the keen eye of a mother. Her boy was infatuated with this girl, already connected to her in ways he himself probably didn't yet understand. She had seen it all evening, this growing fascination. She knew he would come to her and explain where the sad child had come from, and she would wait patiently until then.

"Do you want to tell me about your dream?" Jacob whispered as he guided Bailey back under the covers.

"Well," she hesitated, not sure how to explain. She didn't want to sound like a coward. "You were there, and a great big white wolf. But I wasn't afraid of it. It was after both of us, but I wasn't afraid. I was trying to warn you."

Jacob found her hand under the covers and gripped it tightly. "Good for you! If the wolf comes back while you sleep, you take care of it for me. You know, this is all my fault. I'm the one who told you all of those scary stories about Vodnik. You forget about all that. Tomorrow I'll show you the ranch, and I'll teach you how to shear a sheep. You can even do one yourself. Would you like that?"

"You mean you'll let me shave the wool off? Won't the sheep get cold?" Her brows puckered with concern.

"No, no; they stay nice and warm until they grow a new coat of wool. They are very strong, even though they seem helpless." He searched for a change of subject as Bailey looked unconvinced. God help him if she asked about the mutton stew they would no doubt enjoy tomorrow. "Tomorrow I'll show you a secret meadow that no one else has ever been to."

Her eyes shone with the mystery of that. "How did you find it?"

"No more questions tonight! Now close your eyes and I'll sing you a lullaby like Mama sings to Annie."

Bailey's huge dark eyes remained wide open, staring into Jacob's blue ones. He was going to sing to her? She tried to remember if anyone had ever sung her a lullaby or tucked her in with this degree of care, but no memories came to mind. Tears threatened, and she pulled the blankets over her face before he could see.

"Are your eyes closed under there?"

"Yes." The answer came back muffled and a little shaky.

"Now I'm not as good as Mama, but I'll give it a try if you promise not to laugh.

> *Spi, detatko, spi,*
> *Zavri ocka suy,*
> *Andelicek bude spati,*
> *A maticka kolebati,*
> *Spi, detatko,spi."*

Jacob sang softly, and although his young man's voice was still trying to decide between tenor and baritone, his pitch was true and beautiful. The rich foreign sounds enchanted her, the Slavic words clicking and rolling and bringing to mind a strange and distant world. Bailey ventured from under her covers with a look of wonderment.

"You should sing in the Silver King in the city! You would be famous!"

Jacob gave a self-conscious snort of laughter. "No, I'm just a rancher, not a performer for the stage. I only sing for little girls who won't go to sleep."

"I'm not a little girl! I'm almost as old as you." Bailey's lower lip protruded in a pout. Jacob reached out with a finger and pushed her lip back in.

"Time to get some sleep. I'll see at you at breakfast, okay?"

"Jake?"

He tried not to smile. "You promised not to call me that, remember?"

"What did the lullaby mean?" She gazed at him steadily, and he resisted an impulse to smooth back a straying curl that was wandering across her cheek.

"Something about little angels sleeping. I promise to sing it again someday if you close your eyes."

She obediently closed them, and he backed out of the room quietly, wishing he could stay and watch her sleep so she would feel safe.

CHAPTER FOUR

The next morning Jacob awoke in somewhat of a fog. Where was he? Why wasn't his cousin asleep beside him? His second thought was *I'm home*! His third thought was of the girl who slept in his bed, and he propelled himself from his bedroll and padded silently across the sleeping house with a great anticipation. He couldn't wait to show her the ranch and the secret meadow. He wanted her to see how the world could be beautiful and good, and he wanted to erase the blank look from her great dark eyes.

Convincing his mother to let Bailey stay had been easy, although he knew he owed Gacenka a great deal of explanation. He had talked with his mother long into the night, his father drifting in and out of the parlor with the usual inscrutable expression on his face. Gacenka's expressions betrayed every emotion, just as Jacob's did. She had heard Jacob singing to the little girl, and when he had returned to the parlor and sat by the cozy fire, the older children were sent to bed and the questioning began.

"So, my son, your gentle heart has earned you another friend." She smiled as she said it, but her eyes were concerned.

"Mama, I'm sorry I didn't tell you. I left her sleeping in the wagon so I could come in and explain, but you know what a disaster that was." Gacenka nodded and waited silently for him to continue.

"She came to school. Nobody wanted her to sit with them, so I asked her sit with me. She's so smart, Mama! She was reciting from Shakespeare!" He paused to shake his head in disbelief, remembering Bailey's flawless performance and searching for a way to describe the enormous intelligence buried within the despondent child. "Then at lunch I stayed to talk with the teacher. I told her that they should let Bailey stay in school, even though her parents didn't come with her and nobody paid. Then I walked outside and they were torturing her in the courtyard, Mama!" His face flushed and his fists clenched at the infuriating memory.

"She was sitting all by herself under a tree, and then they started throwing food at her. Then some big oaf dragged her behind the school and was trying to make her—he had her on her knees…" here he stopped, quite unable to make himself repeat what Otto had been about to do. "So I ran down there and I...." He looked at his mother and tried to gauge her reaction so far. She looked as angry and shocked as he had felt at the time.

"I beat him, Mama. I could have killed him. I *wanted* to kill him." He bowed his head and the anger left him. He stared at his young, strong hands, knowing in his heart that he had come close to killing another human being with those hands. Tears welled in his eyes as the residual anger was replaced with shame.

Gacenka moved to sit beside him and pulled him to her gently. "You did the right thing, beating the boy. He was abusing a defenseless girl, so you taught him to feel her pain. There is no shame in that." They sat quietly for a spell, mother and son, adjusting to the first grown-up conversation that had ever passed between them. She rose again eventually, picked up the fireplace poker and stirred the dying embers. She gave her son a chance to wipe his tears away and present a man's face.

"Well, she left her satchel behind with her book of Shakespeare, and I figured that was about the only thing she owned, so I decided to go look for her." Gacenka seated herself again and stared back at him, one eyebrow raised.

"You searched for her just to return a satchel? You could have given it to the school teacher, no?"

Jacob reddened. "Yes ma'am. I could have. I looked for her because I decided to bring her home for a while so you could..." He stopped, not sure of the word he was looking for. What did he want his mother to do for Bailey? So many things! "So you could love her," he finished miserably.

Gacenka stared for a long moment into the fire. There were questions she was going to have to ask; things that her son could not bring himself to say. She cast about for the words that would force her son to tell her the full story, one which she was convinced was sordid and that he was embarrassed for her to hear. If he wanted to be involved in this child's life, he must be prepared to deal with it honestly. Finally she spoke with an air of forced disdain. "What kind of parents would let a child dress so gaudily for a long trip to the country?"

The injustice of it struck Jacob with a surge of righteous, youthful anger. "Her dress? That's the least she has to worry about!" He lunged to his feet and ran both hands through thick black hair. He would give anything not to have to say these next words. "She has no father that I know of. Her mother is a—a lady of the evening."

Gacenka pinned him with a direct gaze.

"Her mother's a prostitute," he amended, and was amazed to see no reaction from the mother he imagined as perfect, pure, and naive. He gulped and continued, each word taking him another step away from an innocent boyhood. "She lives in a brothel where her mother works. She sleeps under a porch and the madam of the house beats her. When I found her two nights ago, it was already midnight. She can hear everything from where she sleeps, Mama. Everything that goes on in the rooms."

Gacenka could maintain her blank expression no longer, and she whispered softly, "Oh, poor child," and shook her head, eyes squeezed tightly shut against the tears. "Jacob, you're old enough to know about the sins of the flesh that go on in the city. Some say that it's harmless, but they don't see the children hiding under the porches, do they?"

Her words brought forth a flash of memory, not of Bailey curled under the porch, but of the exotic woman in the Silver King. He remembered the arousal that coursed through his body when she touched him. What had he thought of at that very moment, the moment before childish fear propelled him? Not of the evils of the bordellos! He had thought of one thing only; he had wanted to touch her; he had wanted to see what the next step would have been, and had he not been made of such a strong moral fiber, he would have let her lead him to her boudoir. The private admission was devastating, and he sank back into his chair, defeated.

"I don't know why I brought her. I'm no good for her, but she needs you, Mama. You already have so many; couldn't you make room for one more? She can have my bed just like she does now. I'll do extra chores to pay for her food." He stopped abruptly at his mother's sudden snort of laughter.

"Oh, Jacob! You think you're no good for her? You are the best thing that has ever happened to that little girl!" She gazed at her son, her finest child, intelligent and sensitive and mature beyond his years, and admired the man he was going to be someday.

"I can see that you love her. No, don't deny it, Jacob. We will all love her soon, no doubt." She smiled at her son's flushed face. She had embarrassed him, but he looked her in the eye as she spoke. "Let's do it this way. You go with Father to find the girl's mother. He's going into the city the day after tomorrow to take the first load of wool, and you and he will take the girl with you. Father will ask humble permission for Bailey to stay with us for the summer, and Bailey can say goodbye to her mother."

She had barely spoken the last word before Jacob gave a whoop of delight. She shushed him and continued. "Now listen, son. If her mother refuses, Bailey must stay there. We have no right to take her away, can you see that?"

Jacob's delight fell away, replaced with a slow-growing anger. "No right? She's treated no better than a dog, and we have no right to give her a good family?"

"That's correct, young man. Her mother is still her mother, and you must never forget that. No matter who she is, she still has a daughter, and perhaps she loves her very much." She paused a moment to allow Jacob to analyze this injustice, rebel against it, and finally accept it.

"Okay, Mama. But if her mother gives permission, can Bailey stay forever?"

Gacenka was momentarily speechless, amazed at her son's temerity. What spell had the fiery-haired waif cast over her usually level-headed son? The look on his face was so intense, so wistful, that Gacenka felt a chill pass over her heart.

"Slow down! You are racing ahead like a thoroughbred. Let's take things one day at a time." She leaned forward and squeezed his hand, and he surprised her by lunging into her arms, not wanting her to see the expression of joy and fear in his eyes.

And so it had been decided; Bailey was to stay for one day and two nights, and then make the trip with Jacob and his father into San Antonio to ask her mother permission to stay with the Naplavas through the spring and summer. The only thing left to do now was to tell Bailey the good news and introduce her to his home.

Jacob reached the other end of the house and pushed the girl's bedroom door open silently. Although Annie and the twins slept soundly, Jacob's bed stood empty, the blankets neatly pulled up and tucked in. Jacob felt a queer prickling sensation over his scalp. Where could she be at this hour? It was still an hour before dawn on this spring day; surely she must have been exhausted last night. He turned to leave, but something held him there, and he obeyed the instinct. He checked his sisters' beds, but there was no Bailey there curled up with them. And then he saw it: a fat, bright braid sneaking from under his bed. He knelt and stared in wonderment at the girl curled up under the bed, shivering from the cold.

It struck him then; how unusual this girl's life had been, and how different from his own. Of course she was sleeping on the floor; she probably couldn't remember a time when she had ever slept in a bed. He couldn't begin to fathom the things she must have seen and heard on a daily basis. He began to feel the same unease he had read on his mother's face the night before, and it made him pause and consider the ramifications of inviting this strange person into his precious family. But as surely as he stood there, he knew that she was already a part of his life, and this realization filled him with a sense of peace and purpose.

As gently as he could he gathered her up and tucked her under the blankets on the bed, but just as he was about to turn to go, she awoke. She gazed at him, confused, and then suddenly the confusion seemed to clear.

"Are we ready to shave the sheep?" she piped, and Jacob threw back his head and laughed, unable to help himself, and before long four girls were following him to the breakfast table to join the rest of the early risers.

After a feast of a strange, thick stew that remained nameless and delicious hot tea, Gacenka began issuing orders. "Jacob, your brothers have already been shearing for well over an hour. Time for you to leave your guest with the womenfolk and go on to the pen and help your Papa. We'll teach Miss Rose how to run a big Moravian household!" She beamed at Bailey and somehow missed the crestfallen look on the girl's thin face.

Bailey's hopes for a day outdoors with the sheep seemed to be crushed before she even drew one breath of crisp, clean air. Gacenka had no way of knowing how many countless hours of the little girl's life had been spent inside Fort Allen, scrubbing the place from top to bottom, emptying wash basins that made her retch to look at, scrubbing vegetables, baking bread, dusting the thousands of expensive knick-knacks, and the most hateful job of all, doing the laundry. Years of being immersed in lye and steaming water had left her small hands raw and her nails ragged. How she longed to be outdoors, surrounded by the beautiful hills and flowers! Her lower lip trembled and she bit it savagely, ashamed that she could even think about feeling sorry for herself after everything this wonderful woman had done for her. She forced a bright smile in Gacenka's direction and rose quickly from the table. "What can I do to help you, ma'am?"

Jacob saw her dismay before she masked it and quickly intervened. "Mama, I promised Bailey that she could help shear sheep today. Could she come outside with me for a while?" He gave his mother his best beseeching look.

"What? Is this true, Bailey? You'd rather spend the day sweating in that wretched pen with those stinky sheep?"

Bailey felt the blood rise to her face. What should she say? Jacob put a brotherly arm around her shoulder and grinned. "Ma! When you put it that way, what is she supposed to say? Come on, let's break her in right."

Gacenka finally relented. "Okay, but you keep an eye on her. Get her some of your trousers and an old shirt, and Mari, fetch her a hat to tuck that hair up into. Remember what a time we had washing that hair last night, Bailey? No tea parties with the sheep today, young lady!"

Bailey giggled, relieved that Mrs. Naplava was not angry. How different from her own mother! With the thought came a flash of guilt. Was her mother worried about her now?

Within a few moments the small girl disappeared and a small boy stood in her place. Jacob stared at her as they walked to the pen. "I'm going to have to give you a boy's name today!" he laughed. This earned a glare from Bailey, who sulked until they rounded the far end of the barn and were greeted by an unparalleled pandemonium.

Bailey had flashbacks of the previous night's disaster as the sound of two thousand nervous sheep assaulted them. Never had she heard such a ruckus, not even in the streets of San Antonio during *Fiesta*! Everywhere there were men and boys yelling. Long, wicked-looking shears flashed, and gray-black crusty sheep moved in all chaotic directions. The pace was intense; in no corner of the colossal pen was there stillness. Bailey's mouth dropped open in disbelief.

Jacob grinned. "Are you sure you don't want to go inside with the women? I think they're making pastry today."

Bailey gathered her composure and whipped around. "I'd like to try this, please, but you needn't make fun."

Jacob cleared his throat uncomfortably and was reminded once again that Bailey was twelve years old, and he knew from experience with his sisters that twelve-year-old girls could be *very* touchy and unpredictable. "I was only joking with you, Bailey. Sure you can try. Let me explain what everyone's doing, and then we'll pick a job for you, okay?"

Bailey looked back at the pen dubiously. "It looks like no one knows what they are doing! How do they keep everything straight?"

Jacob plopped down on the grass on a little hill that overlooked the pen and pulled her down with him. He patiently began to explain the whole operation, with a precision and know-how that belied his years. "Let's just watch one sheep all the way through the process, and then you'll understand."

Behind the shearing pen was a huge corral. Two ranch hands, both thin and deeply tanned from months on the range, crowded twenty sheep at a time into the shearing pen. This accomplished, they balanced themselves once again on the white fence of the corral and sipped coffee from tin cups, watching carefully to see when the next twenty sheep would be needed. In the shearing pen were twenty Mexican workers: dark, handsome swarthy men with muscular arms and shoulders. With amazing prowess, each man grabbed a sheep by a hind leg and hauled it to a platform. The sheep were forced to hop backwards, and this ludicrous ballet was performed to the accompaniment of an ungodly bleating.

Once the platform was reached, the shearer showed his true brawn by lifting the sheep bodily and placing it unceremoniously on its back. From a shelf under the platform he grabbed two lengths of twine and tied the forelegs with one and the hind legs with another. This was done with amazing speed, the hands moving so quickly that Bailey found the movements impossible to follow, even after Jacob explained the knots three times. From another shelf under the platform the shearer reached for his tool, a pair of bright, sharp-edged shears, and the clipping began.

To Bailey, it seemed as though the sheep were being undressed rather than sheared. The shearer used a combination of long, smooth, lightning-quick strokes and shorter, painstaking strokes for the critically sensitive parts of the animal. Underneath the superficial layer of crusty gray wool was a smooth, creamy whiteness as the wool fell to the platform. In less than five minutes the process was completed, and the shearer slipped the blade under the platform and yelled "*Tecolero!*" at the top of his lungs. Bailey was surprised to see Wenzel come running, carrying a can. He arrived at the platform and ran his hands carefully over the sheep, stopping every now and again to blot black goop onto the sheep's skin. "That's *tecolé*," explained Jacob. "If a blowfly sees any blood on the sheep, she'll lay her eggs in the wound, and a few days later there will be a heap of little worms that feed on the flesh of the sheep." He glanced at her to see if he was making her queasy. She was listening intently, watching the process with an eagle eye.

"Go on," she said, and Jacob smiled to himself. No weak stomach here! He'd never known a girl like this one.

After the *tecolé* was applied, the shearer lifted the animal from the table and shoved her through a chute that led to the second corral. Now a white, naked animal with black, gloopy polka-dots, she looked like a different creature altogether. Meanwhile, the shearer rested briefly until the ranch hands saw that most of the men had finished, and the next twenty sheep were pushed into the pen. Another boy, the *lanero*, folded the wool white-side out and rushed it to a collection of wooden frames. From these frames were hanging three huge bags, at least seven feet long, with an iron hoop at one end to hold them open. Bailey watched, amazed, as the bags seemed to move with a life of their own. "There's a man in each bag," laughed Jacob. "His job is to pack the wool down and get as much wool as he can into each bag." A head emerged from one bag, and Bailey recognized Anton's handsome features, now covered with grease and dirt. He jumped out nimbly and retrieved a needle and twine from his pocket and proceeded to sew the bag shut. Johann and Franticek moved in to lift the heavy bag directly onto the wagon.

Meanwhile, a tall, important-looking man with a brightly colored handkerchief around his neck inspected the shearer's sheep carefully and approached the weary shearer with a smile. He handed him a metal disc, which the shearer quickly put in his pocket before turning to capture his next sheep. Each disc meant five cents, and if a man worked hard, he could shear 100 sheep in a day.

Bailey watched the cycle over and over, fascinated with the precision and perfect order that emerged only after she understand the pattern. Jacob broke into her thoughts. "Well, which job would you like to try? You could be *tecolero* with Wenzel for a while, or you could help me fold wool and inspect sheep."

Bailey's stubborn jaw was set. "I want to *shear* a sheep, Jacob. You promised." A sharp, piercing whistle from the pen interrupted them.

"Jacob! Get down here! Anton needs a break." Jacob groaned as he heard his father's words.

"Packing wool is the worst," he muttered. "Stay here while I ask Pa what you can do."

He ran down the hill, jumped into the pen and navigated his way to his father. Bailey saw Franticek lean in to hear his son's words, then take off his hat to wipe the sweat and grease from his brow. Jacob pointed up to her and Mr. Naplava looked her way, lifting a hand in greeting. Bailey felt a surge of guilt, knowing how hard he was working and how tired he must be. He didn't have time to entertain a city brat the likes of her! She rose, meaning to wave goodbye and make her way to the house, but was surprised to see Jacob waving her down to the corral. She ran down the hill, excited. He was going to let her do it!

Jacob met her at the corral's fence with a smile. "Pa says you can have a small sheep to shear, but once I get you started on him, I have to go pack. Okay?"

Bailey stared back at him with wide eyes. "You mean I'm going to shear one by myself? With *them*?" She pointed anxiously back into the pen.

"No, not exactly. I'm going to set you up in the barn in an old stall, so you'll have more room."

"You mean, so I'll be out of the way!" Bailey laughed to show she wasn't offended.

"Okay, but you said it, I didn't!" With that, Jacob searched for a small sheep, and finding one, picked it up effortlessly and walked to the gate. "Follow me." Neither of them noticed the chuckles behind them. The shearers and ranch hands couldn't wait to see what the poor sheep looked like when it came out of that barn!

Inside the cool, roomy barn, the noise and stench from the outside was lessened to a great degree. Bailey followed Jacob to a big stall filled with fresh hay on the far side of the barn. A window let in streams of sunlight, dust motes spiraling along the rays. It was strangely beautiful, and Bailey closed her eyes and took a moment to appreciate the tranquility.

"You're not having second thoughts, are you?" Jacob teased as he lifted the animal and laid it on its back.

"Oh, no! It's just so beautiful in here! I wish I could live in here," she answered wistfully. He looked at her, amazed, and was reminded yet again of her impoverishment.

"Now do you remember how I told you to tie the legs together?" He held the twine out to her, and she took it hesitantly.

"Um....I'll try." She made a few attempts, but even though she would not admit it, she was deathly afraid of those sharp hooves that Jacob had told her cut like knives.

"Here, why don't you let me tie him up, and then you can clip him, okay?" He took the twine and deftly tied the legs without one wasted motion.

"Wow! How long did it take you to learn that?"

Jacob smiled, gratified. "After the first time a sheep stepped on me and split my hand open, I got real fast at tying the legs." He held out one hand, palm down, and Bailey looked at it, remembering the curious round scar and the first time she had seen it back at the German school. Her hand reached out, seemingly of its own volition, and one rough little finger traced the scar tenderly. He stared at her, speechless, and she snatched her hand away, flushing. *Why on earth did I do that?* She berated herself silently. He must think she was crazy in the head after all of her antics.

Jacob gulped a couple of times, cleared his throat, and silently began to show her how to begin the clipping along the back before handing her the shears. He noticed the steadiness of her hands and the precise motions that imitated his own so well.

"That's great! You've really got a knack for this! Look, I've got to go pack for a while. You take your time, and I'll send Wenzel back in about twenty minutes with the *tecolé*, okay? He can help you finish the parts you weren't sure about." She nodded absently, her hand moving faster and faster, and he allowed himself a couple more seconds to watch her progress. She was all seriousness, the picture of intense concentration. He felt a surge of pride.

It couldn't have been more than ten minutes later. Jacob was deep in a wool bag, drenched in sweat and packing the wool tightly, cursing every bit of it, when he noticed something strange. The noise level outside was gradually getting lower and lower, until finally there was only an occasional bleating. He felt his skin crawl. What was bringing everything to a standstill? He made a few comical attempts to jump to the top of the bag, but the wool wasn't high enough yet. "Anton! Get me out of here! What's going on?"

Anton reached down a strong arm and pulled Jacob up. "Come take a look at your beautiful little protégé," he murmured, and before Jacob could object—he wasn't sure what protégé meant, but it didn't sound good—he caught sight of Bailey standing by the second corral. The sheep was standing beside her, crowding against her legs as sheep will sometimes do, completely and perfectly shorn. Even from this distance Jacob could see that no *tecolé* would be needed. Over one small arm was fluffy white wool, folded neatly. One bright red braid crept from beneath the filthy hat. Every eye in the pen and corral was fixed on the girl. Finally one shearer gave a blood-curdling whoop.

"Sign her on, *el capitan*! She shears faster than Garcia!" Suddenly all the men were whooping and hollering, offering their congratulations, exploiting the brief respite from the sweltering work. Wenzel approached at his father's command and inspected the sheep, then stepped back and shook his head.

"No cuts, Pa." Mr. Naplava approached the beaming girl with Jacob on his heels.

"Well, now, little one. You gave us quite a surprise. I believe you sheared that dirty little sheep faster than Jacob could have."

Jacob nodded his head quickly. "Lots faster, Pa. Maybe we should set her up at a platform. I could tie the sheep for her."

Mr. Naplava snorted. "You're just trying to find a way out of those packing bags, son." He affectionately ruffled the boy's hair. "Miss Rose, we'd love to have you shear for us, but shearing is the livelihood of these men. This is how they eat. Do you understand? Every sheep you shear would be five cents taken from their pocket."

Bailey was disappointed, but she hid it well. She had felt so skillful with those clippers in her hand; her fingers seemed to have a mind of their own as they guided the sharp instrument across the sheep. She had been most concerned with not hurting the frightened little animal, and she hadn't nicked him, not even once.

"That's okay, Mr. Naplava. I'm kinda scared of those hooves, anyway. I only untied him because we made friends."

Franticek took her small hands in his own huge paws. "You have a gift in these hands, my girl. I don't think you're destined to be a sheep shearer, but there's some magic here that you would do well not to ignore." She blushed under his close scrutiny, sensing Jacob in the background listening to every word. "Well, you can help Wenzel with the *tecolé* for a while; he'll show you what to do." Abruptly, he turned to go. "Follow close, Jacob. You're still packing."

Jacob gave Bailey one last delighted smile, dimple flashing, before he turned to go. Bailey basked in the glow, storing that smile away to pull out and examine later. Then she went to find Wenzel and the tin can of black goop.

The day flew by, and Bailey was sure that she had never worked so hard in her life. She was given her own can of *tecolé*, and soon she became as fast as Wenzel at examining the smooth skins for nicks. She was no sooner finished with one sheep when a shearer was yodeling the familiar call, *"Tecolerita! Hurry, over here!"* Her body was bathed in sweat, and despite the brief break at noon for a huge plate of beans, thick crusty bread, a peach, and a tin cup of iced water, her stomach growled so loudly she was sure the men would hear it over the bleating of the sheep. Finally she heard *el capitan* give the cry for the men to clean up, and they scattered soon after to retire to their dinner and gambling. She sagged to the ground in relief, black medicine covering her hands and a great deal of her shirtfront, not to mention the streaks on her face. She heard a chuckle and looked up to see Jacob standing over her.

"What are you laughing at?" she snarled. Her buoyant mood of the morning had melted in the heat of the Texas sun.

"You should see yourself. You put more on yourself than you did on the sheep!" His exhaustion lent itself to giddiness and he began to roar with laughter. "T-Tar ba-baby! You look like a tar baby!" He leaned against the fence and held his stomach as the tears of mirth leaked from his eyes.

Bailey looked at him stoically. How dare he make fun when she had worked all day without complaint! And she was good at it, too! She'd show him!

Jacob didn't notice as Bailey knelt to pick up the last full *tecolé* tin. She carefully inserted three fingers into the black medicine, cupping as much as she could in her hand. "Blue Boy," she said sweetly. "Hold still. I think I see a nick in your skin." With that, she reached up and smeared the black goop all over his smirking face, tenaciously pursuing him as he tried to shrink against the fence and protect his face with his hands. When she was finished, his entire face was covered.

Two bright blue eyes stared out at her in astonishment from the sticky mess. She sensed a strange gleam in their depths that she had never noticed before. She read his intentions too late; before she could run, one of his hands darted out and snagged her braid firmly, holding her in place. As neatly as if he was handling a squalling sheep, he flipped her gently on her back, and amidst ear-splitting screams, proceeded to apply the remaining *tecolé* to every square inch of her face until she begged for mercy. By this time they were both in hysterics, laughing so hard they were gasping for air. The black tar-like substance flew through the air as they plastered each other, rolling on the ground, each trying to get the upper hand.

A deep masculine roar put an abrupt halt to their mirth. "Jacob!"

It was his father, and he was not amused. "What in the name of God are you doing?" He was standing over them, hands on hips, a ferocious glower on his face.

Jacob could only swallow and stare while Bailey hid her face in his soft cotton shirt. His arm crept around her shoulders. Franticek opened his mouth to bellow again, but stopped when he realized that the little girl was frightened. He got a grip on his anger and pulled Jacob roughly to his feet. He tugged him a few feet away from Bailey, who cowered on the ground, staring at the empty tin can in her hands.

"Boy, you are in a heap of trouble. You have wasted *tecolé*, and that means we'll have to make more tonight. More work for Benito. You'll pay him out of your own pocket." He paused for effect and looked wearily at his son.

"Yes sir," answered Jacob promptly, looking his father straight in the eye. He attempted no explanation. He knew better than to explain before he was asked to.

"Now what in God's..." Franticek drifted off as he realized he had been that route already. "What were you thinking, son? Did it start as a fight?"

"No sir." Jacob held his gaze.

"Well suppose you explain it to me."

"I made a joke that Bailey got more *tecolé* on herself than she did on the sheep, and she smeared a little on me, just to get even. And I deserved it.

Then I smeared some back on her to get the last word in, and that's how it happened. I guess we're just tired and silly." Jacob's usual storytelling skills were absent as he gave his father a brief, to-the-point summary, no embellishment.

Franticek sighed. "Okay. Well, that's the end of that. You two wait out here. I'll get some fresh clothes and rags from the house, and you take Bailey down to the creek and take a bath. You won't be tracking that mess into your mother's house. Then come straight home and you'll take the money to the *tecolé* mixer explain to him why he's making an extra batch tonight. Understand?"

"Yes, sir! And I'm really sorry." Jacob bowed his head for the first time, and Franticek suppressed an urge to laugh. His son looked like a different creature entirely, his hair standing up in spikes with the stiffness of the black medicine. And the girl was ludicrous, staring at him now with big black eyes, one finger inserted deep into her ear, trying to dig the gunk out. She opened her mouth and a big black bubble formed. She closed it quickly, abashed. Franticek barely had time to turn away before the smile broke over his face. Wait until Gacenka heard this! She'd laugh until she cried.

Several minutes later the entire Naplava clan stood on the porch to get a look at Jacob and Bailey before they headed to the creek. "Hey, *tecolero* twins," taunted Johann, holding the clothes and rags just out of Jacob's reach. "Do you think you can take a bath without getting into another fight? Or shall we all wait to see you come back from the creek covered with mud?" The children giggled and Gacenka remained silent, wanting to see how the girl would handle a little healthy poke of fun. She didn't have to wait long.

"Hey Johann! We saved some just for you! I'd sleep with one eye open tonight," Bailey shot back. Jacob used the moment of distraction to grab the clothes from his older brother.

"Come on, Bailey. Let's not get into more trouble than we already are." His tone was sullen, but Bailey saw the humor in his eyes.

Gacenka stopped them with an unusually stern warning. "Don't forget the song, Jacob."

Jacob nodded and turned to go, Bailey following on his heels.

"What song?" she asked breathlessly, trying to keep up with his long strides.

"It's nothing," he reassured her with a smile.

"What song?" she repeated insistently, and his smile grew wider.

"It's *nothing*."

There was silence as they made their way down the path.

"Jake?"

"Mmmm?"

"What song was your Ma talking about?"

Jacob let forth with an exasperated laugh. "You get a hold of something and don't let go! Like a dog with a rabbit!"

She swatted at him.

"Well?"

He sighed, knowing he was beaten. He'd have to sing the song that his mother had been making all of them sing for as long as he could remember. "It's a song Ma has us sing to protect us against the Vodnik when we go in the water."

Bailey froze in place on the path, and Jacob took quite a few steps before he realized his young charge was no longer following.

"There's a Vodnik in the river? I mean, in Cibola Creek?"

He jogged back to her and tugged on her hand. "Nah. Ma is just—you know—she still believes in a lot of that Old Country lore."

She refused to move, her feet planted. "Sing it."

"Bailey!"

"Sing it. Please?"

He sighed deeply and hung his head, and without looking at her, softly sang in his sweet baritone.

Hastrmane, tatrmane, vylez z vody ven.
Dej nam kozich na buben.
Budeme ti bubnovati až vylezeš zi vody ven.

She gazed at him, quite enthralled. "What does it mean?" she breathed.

"It's stupid," he said dismissively, feeling rebellious. That was *twice* now he had sung for her; what was wrong with him?

She remained planted, crossing her arms. She looked so ridiculous, caked with *tecolé*, but he squelched a grin and sighed again.

"If I tell you, will you come? We need to get washed up. Ma's plenty mad."

She nodded.

"*Hastrman, buffoon, come out of the water. Give us a head for a drum. We will beat on the drum until you come out of the water.* Hastrman is just another name for Vodnik."

She frowned at him, clearly having expected something much better than this. "That doesn't make sense," she finally said.

"I know. I told you it's stupid. As if a powerful creature would just throw up a head of one of his victims for us so we could beat on it!"

Her eyes grew wider, but she began walking again, as promised. He looked back at her, noticing that she had become quiet.

"Don't worry, Bailey. It's just stories. It's not real." He chatted on, telling her all about the big creek and the various floods and droughts; stories of sheep being rescued as they floated away like cottonseed on the water, and she began to relax.

Fifteen minutes later, standing before the swiftly moving Cibola, Bailey was struck with an unaccustomed shyness. She had never bathed with a boy in close vicinity, even if he was out of sight! And although she didn't want to admit it, she couldn't swim. The creek looked deep and swift, even by the shore.

"Um, where will you bathe, Jacob?" He failed to notice the quiver in her voice in his preoccupation with scraping the dried *tecolé* from his neck.

"I'll be just around this bend, on the other side of the tree." He handed her a chunk of strong-smelling soap, scooped up his clothes and headed for the tree.

"Jacob?"

"Yes?"

"I should tell you something. I really can't swim very good." She felt her face growing red. Thank God he couldn't see it under all the black goop! Now he'd surely think she was a city pansy!

"How well is not too good?" he frowned.

"Well...toss me in and I'd probably sink like a rock," she admitted miserably. "Unless I drowned right away and began to float."

"That's okay," he assured her. "Just stay on the shore and scoop some water onto your face and arms. That'll get most of it off. You can take another bath up at the house later on to get the rest. But don't go all the way in, okay? It gets deep really fast, and the current's pretty strong right now with all the flooding. If you fall in and get scared, yell for me." He squeezed her arm reassuringly. "Promise?"

She nodded her head silently and watched him disappear around the tree. Was he real? She had never known a nicer boy! Any other boy would have lost patience with her by now, but Jacob never made fun or yelled or criticized. An intense desire to stay in this place, with this boy, began to ripen inside her. How could she make that happen? She wasn't sure she had the audacity to tell Jacob that she wanted, no—she *needed* to stay with him and his family. She couldn't even verbalize the feeling; it was just a lump of longing lodged in her heart, with no words attached to clarify it.

All of these thoughts rolled around in her busy, tired brain as she stripped off the muddy, stinking, sticky clothes. Not until she was sitting by the creek without a stitch of clothing, her legs plopped into the cool, refreshing water did she fully remember where she was. Her head snapped around to the tree, but Jacob was nowhere in sight. She glanced down at her thin body and considered the two hard little apricot-sized bumps on her chest. These were new, and she didn't like them. She dreaded the day when her breasts would be full and heavy like her mother's and like most of the girls at Fort Allen. She was an intensely modest child, loathing the display of wantonness that she had to witness every day. The girls thought nothing of walking around the huge parlor in open robes, bouncing freely for everyone to see. Bailey had dressed herself since she was four years old, and never let anyone, even Gabriella, see her without her clothes. Anything less would be an admission that she was one of *them*, and that soon she would be sprawling on the lap of a man in one of those deep leather chairs.

She'd never forget the first time Blanche had ordered her into the parlor during business hours. She was supposed to be cleaning tables and sweeping the floors, but she knew Blanche wanted her to watch the girls in action. She was nine years old. Liza, a ravishing sixteen-year-old blonde with enormous blue eyes, was the toast of Fort Allen that year. She had since vanished, rumored to have died from a bungled abortion, although Bailey preferred to think she had run away and married a nice gentleman, like she always said she would. Many infatuated, handsome young men had loved her, and she was waiting for a rich one who would be willing to marry her and take care of her forever, so she'd never have to give it away again. Liza was balanced on the lap of a young, rich man that evening; a dandy with expensive clothes and a proprietary, arrogant manner. He must have been a city official—probably an insignificant councilman with delusions of grandeur—because everyone called him Senator. He was exceedingly drunk. As Bailey worked around them with a constant stream of orders from Blanche, Liza guided one of his hands into her bodice. The man had looked straight into Bailey's eyes, his glazed gray eyes sending her a message that she could not decipher. She had watched, her stomach twisting, until Senator had swept up Liza in his arms and mounted the staircase. These were the lessons Blanche expected her to be learning, and these were the visions that haunted her dreams.

She shook the image away. She wasn't Liza, and she never would be, and Jacob was a good, sweet boy who was surely just as shy as she. Slowly her embarrassment was replaced by the glorious, invigorating feel of the silky smooth water on her hot skin. She splashed her face and neck and chest and got to work with the big chunky soap, lathering until every bit of the horrible *tecolé* was gone. Now, what about her hair? She stood on her knees and tried bending over, her hair hanging in the water, but try as she might, she just couldn't get all of the black tar-like substance out of the thick curls without losing her balance. A steady pounding began behind her eyes as the blood rushed to her head, and she sat up quickly. She didn't want to bother Mrs. Naplava with washing all of this hair again!

Finally she hit on a solution. She lay on her back and immersed her head into the creek, the water just covering her ears, carefully leaving her face out of the water. She worked the soap leisurely through her mass of hair until she felt the last chunk of *tecolé* slip away with the current. She stretched her arms out beside her and felt a gradual, delicious lethargy descend as the swiftly-moving water massaged her scalp and cooled her while the sun warmed her from above.

She was a few seconds away from sleep when she heard it. *"Bailey,"* an androgynous voice ordered. *"Come in the water. It's so cool."*

The words were spoken directly into her ear, not whispered, but commanded in a slightly menacing and yet charming tone. The voice was both man and woman, adult and child; all of them, or none of them. Bailey had never felt a fear so deep and true. She was completely vulnerable, naked, her head floating in water, and apparently there was a strange person sitting right beside her—a stranger whose voice held a thread of something inexplicably malevolent.

She was frozen with a sense of dread. She could not lift her head from the water; she dared not turn to see the face of this thing that was talking to her. Could Jacob have been telling the truth about Vodnik after all?

"Are you coming in, Bailey Rose?" This time the voice seemed to be coming from the water directly behind her head. Bailey's scalp tightened and her hands curled into fists with the effort of trying to move or speak. *Yell for Jacob*, her mind screamed, but her vocal chords were paralyzed, useless.

The pull came with such unexpected force that Bailey had no time to react, even if she could have. She felt a tremendous, painful yank on her hair, rendered with such strength that she felt some of the strands tear away from her scalp. Her body slid backward into the water without so much as a struggle, and once she was immersed, the current picked her up and carried her away like an ethereal feather on the wind.

CHAPTER FIVE

Bailey was drowning slowly, in fits and starts. Every so often the force of the creek would push her head above water, and she would suck in a great breath of life-sustaining oxygen before being pushed under again. Then the whole process would begin again: her lungs began to starve, her brain screamed for air, panic rolled her body wildly in sharp, mindless waves, and the blackness began to creep around the edges of her vision. One thought managed to make its way to her consciousness. *Scream for Jacob.*

The thought fueled her and she struggled to the surface again, her arms and legs beating at the water. Only her face emerged, but it was enough. She opened her mouth and put all of her remaining life into a piercing cry that seemed to shatter the air around her. She screamed his name, and it was the scream of an animal in the last desperate moments of life.

She finally relinquished herself to the churning Cibola Creek after a fierce battle, and a total, painless black descended quickly this time, perhaps as a blessing.

She never felt the strong young arm that encircled her across her chest and beneath her lifeless arms; she couldn't feel the pounding heart against her back as he kicked her to shore, his body under hers; she never heard the heart-rending sobs of a young boy as he knelt over her on the soft grass, and she was spared the embarrassment of being cradled against skin as bare as her own.

She wasn't breathing. She was dying in his arms; her beautiful skin was a deathly pale marble and her pink lips were turning blue. Jacob was wild-eyed with panic and grief. What should he do? It was five minutes to the house at a dead run. He had to do something now! He lifted his face to the cloudless sky. *Help me, God,* he pleaded.

At that moment a story popped into his mind, a tale from his childhood. His mother never tired of telling old Moravian folk tales, and she especially liked the ones in which love saved the day. This one was about a beautiful young girl who fell from a fishing boat into the sea. A merman fell in love with her at first sight, but she was drowning, so he put his mouth on hers and gave her the kiss of life; he breathed for her. Jacob couldn't remember the whole story, and it wasn't even one of his favorites, but that part about the kiss of life had been locked away in his memory.

He brushed away the strands of red hair that were clinging to her face and leaned down, touching his warm lips to her cold sealed ones. Nothing happened, and the panic threatened again. He pushed it away and concentrated. He had to breathe, not just kiss. He pushed up on her jaw to tilt her face toward his, and gently parted her lips. He bent to her again and opened his mouth on hers, and blew gently, dismayed to feel the air coming right back out of her nose and stirring his cheek. He pinched her nose carefully, having no idea if he was doing the right thing but acting purely from instinct, and breathed again. Then again and again, praying that he wasn't hurting her or doing something sinful.

Nothing was happening. Panic began to set in. "Breathe, dammit, Bailey! Breathe!" he croaked. He pushed on her chest a few times, willing it to start moving on its own. Nothing. It occurred to him that she was full of creek water. How could he get the water out of her lungs? How? *Please, God.* Again, an image popped into his head, an answer to desperate prayer. When they were younger, he and his brothers used to fill pig bladders with water and use them as weapons, shooting fantastic streams of water at each other as they ran screaming around the ranch. The best way to force the water out was by squeezing the bladder in the middle, with a good deal of force. He yanked her to a standing position and squeezed her roughly from behind with both of his arms, again and again, and at last her body convulsed. She turned her head and expelled a fountain of water from her lungs, coughed and gasped a few times, and turned her head to look at her rescuer. She opened her mouth but no sound came forth; she just stared at him, blinking back tears of shock. Then she leaned over and vomited, her thin body heaving with terrifying force, every rib visible on her spine. Jacob held onto her tightly, feeling her stomach muscles contracting against his arms. Finally, she was still, and she straightened and turned again, giving him a tremulous smile. "All right, I think I'm done," she whispered.

Jacob gave a whoop and hugged her to him fiercely as both of them sank to the ground, the strength gone from their legs. "Bailey," he finally whispered, not really believing she was alive. "I thought you were gone. I'm so sorry." He began to weep softly, to the girl's amazement. She had never seen a big boy cry. Tears coursed down his cheeks, and he finally buried his face in his hands, shoulders jerking.

"It's okay. It's not your fault." Her voice was weak and raspy, but she stroked his wet hair, and they clung to each other, bound by the awesome knowledge that somehow she was alive, even after there had been no breath left within her. Bailey clearly remembered drowning, the very moment that the black had come for her, a ceasing of all sound and sensation, a soft floating toward an incredibly bright and desirable and loving light. Surely a miracle had occurred, and Jacob had performed it.

Long moments passed while the two recovered, heartbeats and breaths slowing, panic and shock subsiding amidst the peacefulness of the creek. Meadowlarks serenaded from the trees, a warm breeze stirred and began to take the chill away, and the creek that moments ago had swallowed a little girl now gurgled harmlessly, adding its melody to the symphony of the late spring afternoon.

As the crisis abated and rational thought returned, Bailey's hand stilled in Jacob's hair. A moment innocent and good shifted into one of growing awareness. For the first time she felt his bare legs beneath her own; her bare chest pressed to his, the thump of his heart on her chest, his cheek on hers. She tensed in his arms, and an instant later, Jacob quickly shifted her to the soft earth. She curled up, covering herself with her arms as Jacob stood and turned away. "I'll go get our clothes. I'll be right back," he croaked over his shoulder, and his voice wasn't his own. Bailey couldn't help herself; she stared at his retreating form: strong, muscular back, wide shoulders tapering to slim hips, and legs and backside knotted with muscle formed from years of hard, physical labor. She wasn't as scandalized as she thought she'd be, but finally her own sense of decency overtook her curiosity and she buried her face in her arms. That was the body of a young man, and she was more than a little shocked. She had thought of Jacob as a boy, her contemporary, and now that she saw him for who he was, she realized that he must see her for who she was: a skinny little girl. She groaned to herself as she realized that he had seen her apricots, those negligible little things growing on her chest! What had he thought of her? Was he so busy saving her life that he hadn't noticed? She hoped so, and she hoped not.

Jacob was experiencing mortification of his own as he half-ran, half-walked back to his clothes beyond the tree. It had happened again, that thing that had been happening for the past two years or so. At times he thought he had it under control, but at other times, the feelings surging through his body didn't even seem to belong to him. He knew it was normal because his brothers and friends laughed and teased each other about it all the time: the dreams, the times when a pretty girl smiles and a hardness forms down below, refusing to go away for what seems like an eternity. He could be holding a girl's hand or raking manure; it didn't seem to matter. The damn thing had a mind of its own! And at the worst possible time, it had happened again. A girl had almost died in his arms, and his body turned traitor.

His face flushed scarlet as he thought about it. Had she noticed it? Did she know what it was? And what if, God forbid, she thought he was trying to.... He banished the thought, cursing, and dressed quickly. They had done nothing wrong; she needed help, and he rescued her. When had the simplicity and unadulterated sentiments of childhood been replaced with this sense of shame? What was it about their own natural, God-given bodies that caused them such discomfiture? Jacob had grown up with an honest, forthright mother who had often voiced these very thoughts on the occasions when the children screeched if one's bath was interrupted by another member of the family. "When you children were little you would run naked through the house without a second thought. If it was hot outside, you'd strip down. Now look at you, cringing in your tub!" As near as he could figure it, that freedom disappeared when his body began to change from a boy to a man. He assumed it was the same way for girls; kind of a pay-off for growing up and wanting to do more with the opposite sex than play hide-and-go-seek in the dark. *And while I spend time on my selfish thoughts, a scared, cold little girl huddles down by the creek, waiting for her clothes.*

Not a little girl. The image of her body came back to him, unbidden. He hadn't given it a second thought when he went splashing into the creek after her, even when he pulled her to shore and held her in his arms in the most intimate pose he had ever been in. He had been thinking of saving her, the child who trusted him so implicitly. But now the picture of her was right before his eyes: the slimness of a neglected child, the smooth brownness of her skin, the perfect bones of her face, the legs that promised to be willowy someday, and the shadow of a young woman beginning to pass over her, to sculpt her. She was *beautiful*, like Anton had said; still a child, but a stunning young woman waiting just a few years down the road. He was abashed as he felt another surge of desire.

And she was shy and insecure, Jacob reminded himself. Would she ever be able to forget that they had seen each other like this? Would he? How could they live together as brother and sister in the same house now? Jacob had never seen his sisters naked, only when they were babies and toddlers. What would his brothers say if they knew what happened today? Johann, his favorite brother and confidant, would be embarrassed but would find some way to make Jacob feel better, but Anton would ask him for *all* of the details, and he would ask with a leer on his perfect, handsome face. Anton had already been flirting with Bailey all day, making Jacob clench his fists every time. And his sisters! Gentle Rosalie would be shocked, certainly still a virgin at twenty-one. The twins, the same age as Bailey—he couldn't even think about that. Were their bodies going through these changes as well? They must be. And his father....

That decided it. His father would be even more embarrassed than Jacob himself. No one could know about this; it would be their secret, nobody else's business.

As he approached her, a quick glance told him she was sitting in the exact same pose, unmoving like a perfect sculpture, a work of art. Her long hair covered most of her body, and her face was buried in her arms. He steadfastly looked at the ground. "Here's your clothes," he called out, voice cracking terribly. "I'll meet you by the tree in few minutes."

Bailey looked up and was gratified to see that his eyes were trained on the ground, and he was already turning away. He was gone before she had a chance to thank him.

A few minutes later both stood beside the tree in an awkward silence.

"You okay?" Jacob finally asked.

"Yes."

Silence.

"Are you warm enough?" he ventured. She was wearing one of Marianna's hand-me-down summer dresses, a sleeveless, faded white cotton with tiny red and blue flowers. It hung barely past her knees.

"Yes."

Jacob cleared his throat. "Um, I don't think we should say anything to anyone about this. You're okay now, and it was my fault that you fell in. I should have kept an eye on you." He flushed at the implication. "What I mean is, I was responsible for you."

This broke the ice. "No! It wasn't your fault! You saved my life. I was dunking my head and it felt like someone pulled my hair, and I slid right in." She searched his face for a sign of understanding. She didn't want to say anything about the strange voice; she didn't want him to think she was crazy! But maybe he would suggest that Vodnik had played a role...

"It was probably the current, or maybe even a fish biting on your hair," he suggested. "There's some pretty big fish in this creek."

Bailey automatically reached back and felt the sore spot where the hair had been ripped from her scalp. She didn't think the current or a fish could do that. The voice, or whomever or whatever belonged to it, had pulled her in, tried to kill her. How silly that story sounded, even to herself! Perhaps she had fallen asleep, dreamed the voice and the tug, and had fallen into the creek. She would never breathe a word about it to anyone, as long as she lived. She would just have to learn how to swim.

"Maybe you're right. I won't tell anyone about today, even though it wasn't your fault," she emphasized. Jacob stood with his head hung low, staring at the ground, still in the throes of embarrassment about seeing her bare.

"Jacob?"

He finally lifted his head, blue eyes refusing to meet hers.

"Thank you so much. I hope I can save you someday like you saved me from Otto and the creek." She took a step forward, stood on her bare tiptoes, and brushed her lips across his cheek before stepping quickly back.

Jacob took a step forward of his own, thought better of it, and grabbed her hand instead. "Come on. We don't want to go back already. I'll show you the secret meadow I told you about."

They walked for a mile in a companionable silence, achieving that sense of ease that had been threatened earlier. The narrow path suddenly widened and opened up into a large, breathtaking clearing. Surrounded by sprawling live oaks, pecan trees, cypress and sumac, the clearing was layered with wildflowers of every color imaginable. Daisies, firewheels, prickly poppies, and sunflowers carpeted the little valley.

But oh, the hill! The hill was awash with bluish-purple flowers that bobbed their heads merrily in the breeze, creating waves and ripples that made her gasp with the beauty of it. Bailey thought she had never seen a sight more glorious; it was as if a blue ocean surged above them. And birds, everywhere! She took off at a sprint, running up the hill, laughing in sheer delight. She sank down into the soft grass and closed her eyes, breathing in a fresh, clean floral fragrance.

"Oh, Jake. This is now my favorite flower ever! What are they? Do you know the name? Why are there so many? Are they here all of the time?"

Jacob snickered at her exuberance. "Well open your eyes, sleepyhead."

She opened them to find a cluster of bright royal-blue flowers resembling sweet peas held in front of her face. She accepted them and buried her nose in, breathing deeply.

"They're bluebonnets. And up here on this hill is where the house is; that's why I picked this hill; for the bluebonnets and the birds. The birds flock here like crazy; I don't know why. You'd have to ask Ma."

Bailey's head snapped around. A house? How had she missed seeing a house? "You mean somebody lives here? Where?" She stood and peered in all directions.

Jacob turned her around until she was facing a small mound of round, white stones piled three feet in front of her by the laurel. "Here, silly. Can't you see a house?"

Bailey thought he had lost his mind. "Jacob, are you sure you didn't swallow too much water?" She turned to give him a worried stare. He took her firmly by the shoulders and turned her around again.

"Now look. Imagine that the pile of stones is much bigger, say as big as that tree over there. Now imagine the stones are arranging themselves into a cottage: a really big two-story house with lots of windows, a deep front porch right there, and a tall chimney over there. Can't you see it? Isn't it beautiful?" His soft voice wove around her and through the small pile of stones, increasing them and rearranging them until a lovely, rather large house stood before them, bordered with fluffy green laurel bushes covered with fragrant blue flowers.

"I see it now!" she gasped. "The house is covered with ivy, and the windows are deep and have pretty wooden shutters that open out." She paused, searching her imagination for the house she had always dreamed of. "There are rocking chairs on the porch, and a woman feeding her baby and her husband whittling a toy and smoking a pipe." She walked forward dreamily, stepped up the steps of the porch, and opened the door.

"Come on! Come inside and see what it looks like!" She invited. Jacob felt a little silly, but he had started this, after all. He followed her as she wandered across the top of the hill.

"Look! Over here is a gigantic kitchen, and a long plank table with high-back chairs." She sat in one elegantly and sampled the fare on her plate. "Delicious!"

"Upstairs are four bedrooms, each with a bed I've made myself!" yelled Jacob from the other side of the hill. He was beginning to enjoy himself. "And the largest bedroom has its own fireplace!" Bailey joined him and plopped down on her back on the soft grass.

"This is the most comfortable bed I've ever had the pleasure to sleep in," she sighed, and closed her eyes, pretending to sleep. Jacob nudged her with his foot.

"So what do you think of my house?"

Bailey sat up. "Oh Jacob, it's perfect. Only now it's my house, too. What shall we name it?"

"Name it?"

"Of course! It's too beautiful not to have a name."

They considered that for a few minutes. "Do you have any ideas?" Jacob finally asked.

"Well, let's start this way: for your ranch—your family's whole big ranch, I would say Bluebonnet Ranch."

"There's prickly poppies, too. How about Prickly Poppy Ranch?"

Bailey rolled her eyes and shoved him.

Jacob shrugged. "Okay! I'll think about it." He was secretly pleased that she cared so much about the ranch to want to name it, although he wasn't so sure about naming it after a flower. "But what about the house—*this* place? I'm really going to build it one day. I've only got a few stones now, but in a few years, this place will be mine. Pa already gave me the land."

Bailey stared at him, astonished, jealousy beginning to creep up on her. "This is yours already? You're so lucky! I'd give anything to have a secret place like this." She slowly turned in a full circle, memorizing every detail, and Jacob could see that it affected her deeply, the same way it did him. It was a genuinely enchanted place; he had sensed the protection and nurturing of good magic here, but had never told anyone about it.

He jumped up, inspired. "Close your eyes again, and hold out your hands when I say," he ordered.

She obeyed, and a few moments later, she felt the weight in her palms, somehow soft and prickly at once. Her eyes flew open and she gasped.

"What is it? Oh, is it a bird? No, it's a nest! Made of feathers! Oh, it's beautiful!"

He shrugged, suddenly shy. "With all the birds here, there's always feathers everywhere. I found that nest a while ago and I've been sticking feathers in it. I thought maybe the birds would like it, but I haven't seen any eggs in it yet. I guess I'll try a different tree."

She stared at it for long moments, enthralled, imaging him carefully constructing a soft nest for baby birds.

"Feather Hill," she whispered. "This is Feather Hill."

He nodded, feeling an appreciative chill. This moment seemed to be, in chorus, the most real and magic of his short life.

"You can come here any time you want," he blurted, and bit his tongue as she turned to stare at him.

"What do you mean? That'd be a long walk from San Antonio!" She sat perfectly still, waiting for him to answer.

"Well, it's like this..." he faded, not knowing how to begin. He hadn't planned on asking her like this, but what better time and place could there be?

"I asked Mama if you could stay for the spring and summer, and she wants you to. No, wait!" Bailey began to object and get to her feet.

"Sit! Now listen to reason, Bailey." He pulled her down and took her hands in his, brushing the pads of his thumbs over her knuckles. She shivered. "There's nothing but trouble and heat in the city during the summer. You can stay here and learn about the house stuff with Mama and the girls, and about the farm stuff with me. It'll be fun! I'll introduce you to my friends and cousins, and you can go to church with us, and to parties and dances. Doesn't that sound good?" he finished lamely, reading the disbelief in her eyes.

She knew she should object; she should get up and run down the path back to the house, find her red dress, and wait for the ride back to the city where she belonged. She would never fit in with this family! They were good and strong and smart and wholesome, and she was the daughter of a whore. She had already caused more trouble to this fine young man than she cared to remember. And after a summer in paradise, would she be able to bear going back to Fort Allen, knowing that in scarcely more than two years, she would be fitted for gorgeous dresses, hair curled, skin painted, and offered to the men of San Antonio like a dish of candy? Would she be able to live knowing that the day she turned fourteen—Jacob's age—she would let a stranger slip his hand inside her dress like Liza did, then take her upstairs?

She had snuck into St. Mark's Episcopal Church more than a few times over the last couple of years, first drawn out of curiosity, and then falling in love with the cool, sacred, quiet interior of the sanctuary and the kindness of the Reverend Thomas Eckles. The nice man had read with her from a big black bible, sensing a child in desperate need of some moral guidance. From Reverend Eckles and the big black book she had learned that what her mother and other Fort Allen girls did was a sin. The part of themselves that they sold was meant to be shared by a husband and wife only. She had asked Reverend Eckles if that meant that she was a sin, since she had no father. "No, my dear," he had said gravely, in his preacher voice. "You had nothing to do with that. But you are responsible for what you do now. Do you understand?" She had nodded, and then she had run away from the church, never to return, because she knew that she couldn't make any promises to the gentle man of God. What choice did she have? Live on the streets and starve? Run away and be abused by a stinking cowboy or a lecherous bandit? As far as she could see, and she looked at it from every possible angle, there were certain people who weren't born with choices. She had no other family to live with, no other place to go, and no money. At least at Fort Allen she had security, all the delicious food she could eat, dazzling dresses, and pampered days. All she had to do was lie with men, only five or six a night if she was lucky, ten if she wasn't; just lie down on the soft bed, slip out of her dress, and remove herself from her body, and take herself to Feather Hill. She could listen to the birds and smell the flowers in her mind, and have long talks with a dark-haired boy with laughing eyes the color of the bluest sky.

"Bailey? What do you think? You haven't said anything." She snapped back and met his eyes, then dropped hers to look at their clasped hands. She wasn't born with choices, but one just dropped in her lap, perhaps sent from the Almighty God that Reverend Eckles prayed to. And by God, she'd take it, even if it was only for a while. It would give her more to remember later on, at the moments when she needed to slip away to a majestic place in her mind.

She looked back up at him. "Okay," she whispered, and knew there was no going back.

CHAPTER SIX

They were all up long before the sun the next morning, the boys loading the last of yesterday's wool into the wagons. Bailey rose early, too, and reluctantly donned her red dress again, eating a quick breakfast of flapjacks and warm syrup with the girls in the kitchen as Mrs. Naplava bustled in and out, chattering happily. As Bailey was licking the last bit of syrup from her fingers, Wenzel shuffled in, arms laden with fishing sticks and a bucket filled with dirt and worms. Gacenka laughed and tried to shoo him from the long plank table where mounds of food were waiting to be packed for the men.

"Wenzel! What on earth? Outside with your fishing gear, my boy!" she scolded gently.

"Yes, mother. But I came for Bailey," he mumbled, sneaking a shy glance at the girl in question. She froze, her syrupy finger in her mouth.

"For me?"

Wenzel just nodded and smiled, and Bailey noticed that his front teeth overlapped, making him look vulnerable and adorable at the same time. His shoes were on the wrong feet and a raggedy straw hat, three sizes too large, was pinned under one arm. It was impossible not to return his smile.

"Oh! You came to fetch me for fishing! I'm so glad you remembered!" she said warmly, and rose immediately. Wenzel shifted the bucket to his other hand, precariously juggling everything for an awkward moment, and Gacenka and her daughters were astounded to see him reach for Bailey's hand; he was deathly afraid of anyone outside of the family and almost never showed affection. He led her through the house without a word, fingers entwined, right out the front door, past the men and boys loading the wagon. Bailey caught Jacob's eye and noticed his dumbfounded expression, and as they passed by and made their way to the creek path, she twisted around to look at him again, smiling uncertainly.

"Hey!" he called. "Wait!" He dropped the bag he had been about to load, causing Anton to swear loudly, and jogged toward them, wiping his hands on his trousers. Wenzel stopped obediently. "You goin' fishin'?" he smiled at Wenzel.

Wenzel nodded. "Yep. I'm gonna teach her."

Jacob nodded. "You want me to come?" This was directed at Bailey.

"Jacob! Leave your girlfriend alone and get your ass back over here!" Anton yelled from the wagon, much to the amusement of the others. Jacob flushed as they guffawed at his expense, but stood his ground.

"Where you taking her, Wen?" Jacob asked kindly, never taking his eyes from Bailey.

"To the creek. To my spot." Bailey felt herself grow pale. The creek? Her heart began to hammer. The Vodnik was there.

"I'll go if you want me to," Jacob said softly, his eyes probing hers. Bailey gulped. She didn't want to disappoint Wenzel, and Jacob was clearly needed at the wagons.

"No, that's okay, Jake. I'll be fine." She tried to smile. He regarded her silently for a long moment, finally nodding curtly.

"Take care of her, Wenzel," he said, his voice low and serious. His eyes flickered once down to Wenzel's and Bailey's linked hands and a muscle in his jaw jumped. He turned and made his way back to the wagon, Wenzel gazing after him with confusion. Suddenly his expression cleared. He turned to Bailey.

"You're scared," he said softly, his voice slow and careful. "Don't be scared. I'll always protect you." He smiled at her, squeezed her hand, and they proceeded down the path, Bailey's heart still pounding. She had no idea what he meant by that, but as odd as his proclamation was, she found that it comforted her.

They reached a spot much closer to the ranch and shallower than the bathing spot she and Jacob had used the day before, and Bailey felt herself relaxing. The sun was already warm, bright and crisp as it reflected off the water of Cibola Creek and turned the leaves of the trees golden.

Wenzel patiently showed her how to bait her hook with a wiggly worm, a task she finally confessed she just could not bring herself to do. "I feel so sorry for the worm," she laughed. Wenzel laughed, too, and baited her hook for her. Once they had their lines in the water, they sat in companionable silence, their backs against a Honey Locust tree.

"I may not know how to bait a hook, but I can make a flower garland," Bailey suddenly announced. Wenzel turned to look at her.

"Will you make one for me now, please?" he finally asked.

Bailey nodded happily, handed him her pole, and wandered up the bank a bit to gather flowers: she found a nice patch of yellow primrose, and just a few steps farther, cheerful pink winecups bobbed their heads from sturdy stems. She sat again with a pile of them in her lap and began knotting them together, wholly content.

"I like to fish," Wenzel said. Bailey glanced at him, sure there was more, but not wanting to rush him. There was a long silence that stretched into minutes.

"It's nice to be here with the trees and water and animals," he said in his slow, measured speech. There was another pause. "I can hear them talk sometimes."

"What do they say?" she finally asked, not sure what the proper thing to say was. She remembered that Jacob always asked Wenzel questions and never treated him like he was slow.

Wenzel considered that question for a few moments. "Well, lots of things. The birds are easiest. They tell each other where to find food, and when to beware, and who gets what space, and where to fly next. They're busy all day. And they all have names, so they tell each other their names if they're just meeting up for the first time. And they have meetings, lots of meetings, about different things, like who's in charge, and news from other places." Bailey stared him, her hands stilled now, the garland forgotten in her lap. Was he crazy, and not just slow? Or did he just have a rich imagination, like a very young child? She decided it must be the latter.

"The trees are sometimes hard to understand. They sound—really old. Their voices are croaky and gritty and deep. They talk mostly to each other about—I don't know—things I don't understand. About stars and people who live up there, with the stars I mean, and about things deep under the earth and about creatures I've never heard of. Like humans, but before there were people like us. Little ones. And great big ones." Bailey felt a chill begin to creep along her spine. "They try to talk to me sometimes, but when I answer, they get real quiet, like they're thinking."

Bailey cleared her throat and tried to think of what to say. "What do they say when they talk to you?"

Wenzel considered that for so long that Bailey thought he must be ignoring her. Finally he spoke. "They ask me how I understand them. You know, because they don't speak my language. They say 'Who are you? Do you know about the Master?' I tell them I'm just Wenzel, and I don't know about the Master. Then they get real quiet."

Bailey's mind was reeling.

"But the water is bad," Wenzel said softly. "I mean, what's in the water. I can't really hear the actual *water* talk good, because it moves so fast. I only hear bits and pieces; mostly it whispers about where it's been and where it's going. And the trees thank the water for the drink, and the water answers back. But mostly I hear something *in* the water. It's a bad thing. It calls my name and invites me in. It sounds like—like a woman and man at the same time. Isn't that funny? But I always say no."

If Bailey had doubted his sanity before, she now had no doubt that Wenzel was completely sane. What he had just described was identical to the voice she had heard in the creek, only it had not given her a choice to come in. It had come for her.

Wenzel looked at her then and noticed her terrified expression. "I heard it, too, Wen," she whispered. "Yesterday. It pulled me into the creek and Jake just barely saved me." What a relief it was to tell someone.

He nodded, unsurprised. "I thought so. Don't you worry, Bailey. I won't let it get you, ever." He anchored his fishing pole under a protruding root, scooted over on his rump and held her hand clumsily. She suddenly felt as though she were in a sanctuary, utterly safe. She felt another chill, but not of fear or apprehension. It was dawning on her that Wenzel was someone truly extraordinary; that he wasn't slow at all, as she first had thought. He may *speak* slowly, but he was gifted in a way she couldn't begin to fathom. They sat for a long, long while in silence, Bailey finishing her garland and draping it around Wenzel's neck, then waiting for a fish while Wenzel patiently held her hand, guarding her against all unseen fears.

"Hey, you two! Catch anything yet?" Jacob's cheerful voice called a long while later, and Bailey whipped her head around, startled. She had been dozing, her hand still linked loosely with Wenzel's, who was wide awake and clearly taking his role of her guardian seriously. Jacob jumped down to the bank of the creek stood in front of them, a wide smile on his sweat-streaked face. He hopped on one foot and stripped off a boot and sock, then repeated it with the other foot, turning and walking few yards to stand in the rushing water and cool his feet. Bailey watched, mesmerized, as he stripped off his faded blue shirt and leaned down to splash his chest, arms, and head. He had a remarkable drawing on his chest! It appeared to be a dragon's wing or some such thing. She felt a funny tingly sensation while she watched him. He dunked the whole shirt in the water, wrung it out, and shrugged back into it, buttoning up as he approached them again. "We finally got the stinking wagons loaded. Thanks for your help, Wen," he teased. He snatched the straw hat from Wenzel's head and jammed it down low on his own wet, spiky black hair, so low she couldn't see his eyes. Rivulets of water dripped down his cheeks.

"I didn't help, Jacob," Wenzel said solemnly. "I was fishing with Bailey. I still am."

Jacob laughed and nudged Wenzel's backside gently with his boot. "Make room, buddy," he ordered with a smile, and Wenzel dutifully released Bailey's hand and moved back to his original spot. Jacob plopped himself right between the two of them, his wet arm brushing up against hers and setting goose bumps up and down it. "Where's all the fish? You two have been down here for an hour! What have you been up to?" He leaned hard into

Bailey, pushing her until she lost her balance. She fell to the side, laughing, righted herself and pushed him back, feeling herself growing warm. She had zero experience with this sort of thing, but she could swear that Jacob was *flirting.*

"I wasn't fishing," said Wenzel in his methodical, unhurried voice. "I was talking to Bailey and guarding her. And holding her hand." Jacob glanced at Bailey and she blushed to her roots.

Jacob grinned at his boots and nodded a few times, his elbows propped on his up-drawn knees. "Thanks, Wenzel. You did a good job," he said finally, and clasped his brother affectionately on the shoulder, winning a beaming smile from Wenzel.

Bailey cleared her throat, curious yet shy. "What is the drawing on your—chest?" she managed.

"You tell her, Wen."

Wen gazed at the water. "Jacob lets me put henna tattoos on him sometimes. Our grandmother taught me. He asked for a dragon wing this time."

Suddenly the pole jerked in Bailey's hand, and she jumped to her feet and squealed.

"You've got one!" yelled Jacob. "Pull 'er in!" Bailey wasn't sure just *what* she had—who knew what lived in that creek?—so she tossed the pole in a panic to Wenzel, who pulled in the line with practiced ease and proudly displayed a large, squirming, silver trout.

"Look what you caught, Bailey! You did it!" yelled Wenzel. Bailey laughed and raised her fists in triumph, then executed a remarkable little victory jig, grabbing Jacob's hands and making him dance a waltz with her. They laughed and twirled until one spin knocked her off-balance, and he reached for her, his hand tightening around her waist, drawing her close. Their gazes collided for a beat, and she pulled away quickly, her breath catching.

She turned and held out her hand to Wenzel, who was looking at them with a wistful expression, and he threw the fish back into the water and offered his fishy, wet hand, making her laugh. She turned and recaptured Jacob's warm hand, and Jacob grabbed Wenzel's hand to complete the circle. The three danced and spun in wild circles, faster and faster, until they were staggering, finally collapsing to the ground in a giggling heap. They watched the trees spin crazily above them, and Bailey wondered if the trees were talking to Wenzel right at this moment, and if so, what they were saying. She rolled her head to look at him, and marveled to see his look of utter concentration. Of *listening.* She rolled her head to her other side to look at Jacob and found he had turned to look at her, his face inches from hers. They allowed it for twenty breathless seconds or so, this silent, unsmiling regard, until the earth finally stood still. Her eyes drifted to his lips and back again to his cerulean eyes, and she wished for something she knew she could never, ever have. A normal life with brothers and sisters, with fishing and silly dancing and laughing, and with this boy, this boy beside her.

Jacob reached over and traced her lips ever so softly with one finger, ending the journey at the dent in her full lower lip, and something exploded into a million luminous pieces within her. "Rosie…" he whispered.

And then Franticek whistled shrilly to call them home, and the spell was broken.

"Wait," said Jacob sternly, as they all stood and readied for the walk home. "Wen, did you know that Bailey has named two places since she's been here? One's a secret, but I can tell you the other one: 'Bluebonnet Ranch.' That's what she named our ranch. What do you think?"

Wenzel grinned and nodded in approval.

"So I was thinking," Jacob continued, bending to find a smooth stone rounded by the water, "let's let her name this place."

"It already has a name. Cibola Creek, right? Big as a river." Bailey snatched at his hand, trying to get the stone, but he was too quick for her.

"Well yeah, but let's name just *this* part of it. Cibola is a hundred miles long, all the way from Turkey Knob here near Boerne to meet up with the San Antonio River. But this is our special part." He chucked the stone into the creek, and they all watched, still dazed from spinning, as the ripples expanded into nothingness.

"Glory is like a circle in the water, which never ceaseth to enlarge itself, till by broad spreading it disperse to nought." Bailey uttered the words wistfully, willing the stone back out of the water and into Jacob's hand, so he could throw it again, and the moment could enlarge itself without end.

Jacob found her hand and squeezed. She heard him take a breath and release it slowly. "That's it, by golly. You did it again. Picked the perfect name. Glory Creek. So it shall be."

They beamed at each other, the three of them. Bailey felt the horror of her near-drowning slip away, to be replaced by this tender moment. Now she could visit Feather Hill and Glory Creek during the dull endless moments of her life at Fort Allen. Nobody could take that away.

Bailey walked between them all the way home, holding both their hands tightly, swinging their arms high and bumping them off-balance, making them laugh. They swung her high into the air between them, her red dress flouncing like a flamenco dancer, and she shrieked with glee. She couldn't think of a time when she had ever been so utterly, blissfully happy.

When they returned, Jacob and Wenzel left Bailey at the house and headed for the barn to finish chores. The two brothers worked in silence, Wenzel mucking out a stall but feeling exultant. But he noticed that Jacob was quieter than he usually was, and he thought he knew why. He noticed more—much more—than most folks realized.

He noticed the way Jacob looked at Bailey sometimes, like the way his Pa looked at his Ma when he didn't know Wenzel was watching. Like Jacob wanted to put his arms around Bailey and never let her go. Wenzel flushed thinking about it. He didn't feel that way about Bailey. He kind of felt that way about a girl named Bonnie, a girl who came to the Naplava barn dances, but he would never tell anyone about that. Bonnie was all moony over someone else, anyway. That was okay with Wenzel. He was pretty happy with the way things were and he didn't cotton to change too well.

He didn't want Jacob to be mad at him. He loved Jacob more than anyone on this earth. Jacob always took the time to listen to him. It took him a long, long time to get out what he wanted to say. Most folks couldn't wait that long.

Wenzel cleared his throat. "Jacob?" he ventured. Jacob looked up from the cow he had been milking, resting his cheek for a moment on her warm hide and gazing at Wenzel, giving him his undivided attention, as always.

"Ya, Wen?"

Wenzel frowned and removed his hat, scratching his head for an interminable moment. Jacob waited patiently as Wenzel shuffled his feet, replaced his hat, took it off again, examined it, and stared at Jacob. The whole process took a solid three minutes. The cow shifted impatiently; a horse nickered from her stall. Dust specks were diamond dancers in a ray of early morning sun slanting through the partially-open barn door. Wenzel finally cleared his throat to speak.

"Jacob, I love Bailey," he said bluntly. He watched as Jacob gulped repeatedly, his Adam's apple working furiously as his face colored and a look of amazement and dismay crossed his face.

"You do?" Jacob finally asked, forcing himself to keep his voice neutral.

"Yes. But Jacob, I want to be her brother, not—the—the other kind of love, where you—you *want*." Wenzel struggled to express himself. How he wished he could talk like other people. He always, without fail, knew what he *wanted* to say. He simply could not get the words past his lips. He noticed, however, that Jacob's face was changing now: he looked relieved. He must have said it right after all.

"That's great, Wen. I think she loves you like a sister loves a brother, too. She had a lot of fun with you today." Jacob ordered his heart to resume beating normally.

"So can I hold her hand? And you won't get mad?" Wenzel asked slowly. Jacob flushed again. These feelings he was having for that girl must be waving around in the air like a flag. No wonder his older brothers were teasing him! And now he had made Wenzel feel badly about a simple show of affection, which was a huge, huge deal for Wenzel. Time to get this under control.

"Gosh, no, Wen, I won't be mad," he smiled. The two grinned at each other and then went back to work, Jacob's heart thumping and his neck unnaturally hot.

The girls were buzzing around the kitchen, preparing meals for the shearers and the men who would haul the wool to market. Bailey helped to mix and shape the bread, the girls teaching her Moravian words for this and that, delighting in her memory that absorbed like a sponge. She and Marianna—a smart, merry girl with round cheeks and a sweet smile—whispered for two hours straight, giggling and poking each other.

By the time Jacob, his father, and a half dozen of the workers were ready to leave, Bailey knew upwards of fifty words and phrases, including how to say goodbye. That one stuck in her throat as she faced Gacenka.

"Thank you for your hospitality," she began formally, trying to get it right, and was abashed when she burst into tears. She threw herself into the plump woman's arms.

"Oh, child, hush now. You'll be back tomorrow! You tell your mama that I'll take good care of you." She gave the child one last squeeze and gently pushed her away. "Now the boys are waiting for you. Hop in the wagon." She made a shooing motion with her hand and bit the insides of her cheeks as she watched the girl walk away. She had a bad feeling about this, and she sent a prayer heavenward.

Jacob led Bailey by the hand to the lead wagon—if Wen could do it, so, by God, could he—and settled her in back with himself while Franticek and Wenzel sat up front, much to the amusement of Anton and Johann, who shouted at them from the middle wagon the entire first five miles. "Hands off, Jacob!" "What's going on up there, kiddies?" "No funny business, children!" Jacob had never been so embarrassed in his entire life, and he could see at a glance that Bailey looked like she wanted to crawl in the straw and disappear. He finally stood and hurled a well-aimed sandwich, bellowing "Shut the hell up, you sons of bitches!" Anton was left with a smear of something brown and gooey on his handsome face; Johann scooped some off and ate it, a comical expression on his face. Bailey laughed until her sides hurt. Franticek finally roared for them all to shut their fool mouths, and the two settled in for the long trip. Bailey took a quiet opportunity to ask Jacob about Wenzel.

"Jake?"

"Ya?" he smiled at her. He had given up correcting her. He was growing quite accustomed to the sound of it.

She paused and wondered how to begin. "When I was at the creek with Wenzel, he told me something. Something, well, *fantastic*." She picked up a piece of straw and shredded it with her fingernail.

Jacob nodded at her. "I already know what you're going to say. He told you he talks to the trees, and animals, and the water, and God knows what else!"

Bailey smiled with relief. "He told you?"

"He tells me everything."

"And you believe him?"

Jacob leaned back against the side of the wagon and looked up, considering the trees for a long, thoughtful moment. "Bailey, I'm going to tell you something I've never told anyone else. Everyone thinks Wenzel is an imbecile. He's not. He talks slow because he's—he's got the whole world in his head, you know what I mean?" He looked at Bailey with intensity. "You know what I think? I think he's a genius. It's just that nobody ever stops their busy lives long enough to listen. I mean, Wenzel's world is slower than ours. You have to slow down to step into it." He chuckled and shook his head. "And once you do—wow!"

Bailey regarded him with wonder. "You know what I think? I think Wenzel is the luckiest boy in the world to have you as a brother. And I think *you're* the genius." Jacob flushed, embarrassed, and threw a piece of sandwich at her. She caught it neatly and popped it into her mouth, making them both laugh.

The rest of the day was spent dozing, snacking, stopping for "necessaries," and exchanging very loud insults with Johann and Anton in the wagon behind them. As the afternoon waned, Wenzel joined them in the back of their wagon and Bailey entertained them both with stories of her adventures with Gabby in the city: fights with the Italian gangs, snitching food from the stands in the Plaza—Juan had a wonderful distraction technique involving a dramatic seizure, complete with a frothing mouth—and hitching rides on the stagecoach by hiding in the baggage compartments. Bailey admitted they had made it all the way to New Braunfels one time and didn't return for four days.

"How did you fix that with your Ma?" asked Jacob, amazed.

Bailey shrugged. "We just pulled the switcheroo. You know—I told her I'd be with Gabby's family for the week, and Gabby told the same lie." Jacob continued to stare at her, trying to imagine telling a lie like that to his mother. It would never fly.

They exchanged middle names as if they were secret codes. Jacob's was Franticek. "Because you look just like your Pa!" Bailey laughed. "So can I call you 'Jake Frank?' Or how about 'Jakey Frankey'? That's perfect!"

"Just try it," he threatened, pushing her off-balance into Wenzel.

Wenzel was Wenzel Kouzelný, and it took her a few tries to get it right. "It means *magic*," Jacob explained, and Bailey clapped her hands in appreciation.

"Your turn," Jacob nudged her again. "Out with it. Is it something horrible like *Mildred* or *Fanny*?" He smiled. She melted.

She shook her head shyly. "It's *Faith*. Bailey Faith. Isn't that weird? It doesn't really chime together well, does it?"

"It suits you," Jacob offered. "It's solid and, well, beautiful."

The three of them fell silent, Jacob and Bailey embarrassed and shy, Wenzel gazing off into the trees.

They spent the night at the Milan orchard again, Mrs. Milan inviting Bailey to sleep in the house this time. Bailey's eyes skittered to Jacob. She preferred the barn, but found that she was too bashful to say so.

"Ah, let us have her in the barn," Jacob finally laughed, coloring as Anton poked him meaningfully in the back and made kissy sounds. "We were going to scare her with ghost stories."

Mrs. Milan agreed, and Bailey spent the next two hours playing hide and seek in the dark orchard with four rowdy Naplava boys and the Milan children, Wenzel sticking extra close to her. She found her blankets mysteriously placed by Jacob's that night, and long after the boys were fast asleep—finally having given up trying to scare Bailey with scary stories—she inched closer and linked her fingers ever so carefully with Jacob's, pressing her lips ever so briefly and softly to the very tip of his longest finger after checking to be sure he was asleep. She relaxed immediately and slept.

Only he *wasn't* asleep, and he stayed awake for hours, holding her hand and listening to her breathe.

They were up again and traveling at dawn, and Bailey was bright-eyed and bushy-tailed the entire trip, taking in everything she could see and smell and hear. She spent long moments studying Jacob as he slept, exhausted. She would never forget his face: his wide, infectious smile with a deep dimple on the right side; his soft, thick black hair that he would rake back impatiently with his fingers when a hunk escaped over his eye; his high, distinctive cheekbones that marked him as new to this country; and his muscular brown hands, bigger in proportion to the rest of him, waiting for him to grow. He liked to hold her hand, to drape his arm across her shoulders protectively; she had seen him similarly affectionate with his little sisters. The whole family was affectionate in a way that Bailey had never known before: a giving, loving, touching family. How she was looking forward to that! To being tucked in at night, kissed, cuddled. She was an affectionate person by nature, but only with her friend, Gabby. She loved to hold Gabby's hand and hug her every chance she got; she had spent hours braiding and brushing Gabby's long, black hair.

She suddenly followed an urge to reach out a hand and run it softly through the long front of Jacob's hair, smoothing it back across the top of his head like he did, wanting to discover if it was as soft as it appeared to be. It was *softer*. She shifted closer, and his eyes opened suddenly and gazed into hers, serious and not grinning for once, looking through her as if he could read her thoughts.

"Hello," he said simply.

"Hello," she returned. She struggled with her emotions, so near the surface, and decided that she had better ask now, just in case she never had the chance again.

"Jacob?"

He lifted his eyebrows in a silent question.

But she just couldn't make herself ask for what she really wanted. She settled for the next best thing.

"How did you make me come to back to life?" She waited as the most amazing collection of expressions passed across his face. He gulped and looked down into the soft blankets.

"I mean, I know you pulled me out of the water, but I think I wasn't breathing, right? I've seen people stop breathing when I've helped Mrs. Martinez. She won't touch them after that. She says their spirit has already left." She stopped and waited, knowing him well enough already to know that he would deliberate before he answered. There was a long silence as he emerged from his groggy state and then seemed to struggle with something. Finally he looked up into her eyes.

"My mother told me a story about a girl who fell out of a boat. A merman saved her from drowning by kissing her. I mean, not kissing! He breathed into her, and she came back to life." The truth was out, and his face was scarlet. What must she think!

Bailey gaped in amazement. He had *breathed* for her? She had never heard of such a thing! How magnificent to be able to save someone by taking one's own breath and putting it into a dying person's lungs! Her natural curiosity for anything that involved doctoring overtook her shyness.

"Oh, Jacob! That's wonderful! You've got to show me how you did it. You may have invented something new! Come on, show me now." She flipped onto her back, closed her eyes, and held her breath.

Jacob's mouth hung open. He thought she would be mortified! Any other girl would have burst into tears or slapped his face, he was sure. And she wanted him to do it again!

"Uh, Bailey, I can't." He sat up and backed away from her, his shoulder blades pressed against the side of the wagon. Her eyes snapped open.

"You can't? Why not?"

"Well, you're not hurt. If I do it while you're okay, I might hurt you." He groped for any excuse he could think of. "And the whole breathing thing really didn't work. I pulled you up and squeezed you really hard, like a pig's bladder, over and over, and that's when you threw up all that water," he stammered.

She gave him a skeptical look. "Okay, you don't have to do the actual breathing, just show me how you did it; how you positioned me, where your hands were, you know." She sat up impatiently.

She was crazy! Where was the bashful little girl beside the creek? She had the tone of schoolmarm now.

"Pa might see!" he glanced nervously towards the front of the wagon. She followed his glance and rolled her eyes.

"Oh, Jake, your father can't see us! Don't be a baby." She was right, of course. They were nestled down in a soft bed of blankets, surrounded by supplies and separated from the front of the wagon by a high wall of tightly secured wool bags and a sturdy, wooden partition. He could only see the tops of Wenzel's and his father's hats. He looked back at her with resignation. If he refused to show her, she'd see how uncomfortable he was and she'd get embarrassed, too. Besides, what was the big fuss? It was a medical procedure, after all!

"Okay, Okay. Act like you're passed out." She promptly fell back on the hay, limp, and he pulled her partially onto his lap.

"First, I supported your head like this. Ma had always called the story "The Kiss of Life," so I thought you just had too—well—" He cursed his stammering as he looked down into her expectant face. If she could be bold, then so could he!

He took a deep breath and jumped in. "This is what I tried first." He leaned down and pressed his lips briefly to hers, and was gratified to see her flush. She wasn't as grown up as she thought she was!

He sat up again and resumed talking in a distinctly professorial tone, beginning to enjoy himself now. "When that didn't work, I had to find a way to open your mouth, so I pressed on your chin like this. Then I tried again." He pressed under her full lower lip, and her mouth opened. She gazed up at him with huge eyes, a much less confident look on her face now that the process had actually started. This was much more like kissing than she had expected. She had never been kissed.

"Once your mouth was open, I was sure I could get you to breathe." He leaned down again and placed his open mouth on hers, and gave a puff of air. She jumped and yelped.

"Jacob! I thought you said you could hurt me if I was already breathing!"

"Oh, don't be such a baby. What's a little air going to hurt?" He grabbed her again and repositioned her. Her dark eyes were as huge as saucers.

"Well, that didn't work, because the air came right back out of your nose. So I pinched your nose and tried again." He started to pinch her nose and lean toward her, but she was too quick and lurched out of his arms.

"Okay! I get it. I mean, thank you for showing me." She inched as far away from him as she could get and crossed her arms over her chest. Her face was a perfect match for the color of her dress.

Jacob laughed his contagious laugh until he saw her relax and smile. "Oh, Bailey. You think you're so grown up. I'll bet you've never even been kissed." He smiled at her gently, eyes twinkling and warm.

"A lot you know! I may be twelve, but I'm very mature for my age." The truthfulness of her words hit home and he was silent again. Who was he to tease her about these things? She had no doubt seen and heard more sexual things in her young life than he ever would.

"I'm sorry, Bailey. I really am. I was just teasing." He reached out and captured one of her small hands in his brown rough one. The wagon rolled. Jacob grew quiet and reflective, a look of worry causing a single vertical line to appear between his eyebrows. He fought a battle with himself, wondering if he should ask, afraid to ask, and afraid not to.

"Bailey? Can I ask you something kind of—personal?"

Bailey frowned and withdrew her hand, and the peaceful moment shifted into something uncertain. "Okay, I guess you can."

Jacob took a deep breath. "I was just wondering if you had ever—if you—are you one of the working girls?" There. The burning question was out, taking up all of the fine space between them and shaping it into something cynical and sad.

Bailey flushed and swallowed convulsively. How could he think that? Did she look and act like one of those girls? She glanced at him, mightily self-conscious and confused, and he immediately cursed his decision to pry.

"I'm sorry. Forget I asked. That was so *stupid*," he ground out, smacking himself on his forehead with his open palm. "I don't even care what the answer is—so I don't know why I asked you that. *Dammit!*" He flung himself face-forward into the hay.

Bailey was surprised to find that she wasn't angry. "It's okay, Jacob. I don't mind—honest. I'm not a working girl, unless you count working in the kitchen or doing laundry." He peeked up from the hay to see her smiling, and he felt his whole body wilt with relief. She wasn't a soiled dove, and she wasn't mad! He sat up and felt the tension leave his body.

A long silence passed comfortably, as Bailey considered the question she was dying to ask. If he could be bold, so could she. If he laughed at her, she'd die. But what if she never saw him again? And she knew they were only a few miles from the city. Time was running out.

"Jake?"

"Mm?"

"You were right. I mean, about me never having—well, I've never been kissed." She felt her face flush and their gazes ran into each other again, full of something sweet and wholly good.

"Would you kiss me? I mean, for real?" She held her breath as his own caught in his throat. His stomach seemed to flip. Kiss her? Like a boy kisses a girl? His eyes locked with hers and he gulped audibly. How could he do that, when he intended to make her his sister, and he had already been having some very un-sisterly feelings about her? How could he not, when she looked at him with tears beginning to form in her eyes? She already thought so little of herself. It would crush her if he said no. Anton and Johann were fast asleep in the wagon behind them, and the man at the reins was a tightlipped fellow named Gomez who minded his own business. He suddenly found that he didn't care if Gomez was witness to this.

He thought long and hard, gazing at her. Oh, he *wanted* to. He had wanted to kiss her by Glory Creek this morning, when the three of them were flat on their backs under the trees, the world spinning, her dark eyes sparkling with laughter, her fiery hair coming loose from its braid. He had wanted to so badly. He sent up a prayer, hoping that if he was doing the wrong thing he could undo it later, and if he was doing the right thing, that he would do it right, not too deep and lingering like he had kissed other girls behind the barn after a dance. "Okay," he whispered. *Just once.*

He sat up and inched toward her slowly, and then surprised them both when he pulled Marianna's crisp red ribbon from her hair and unbraided it with hands that were shaking ever so slightly. He combed his fingers through the mass of waves, lifting it from her shoulders again and again and cherishing the soft feel of it in his hands. She stared at him, enthralled. And then he finally took her face in his hands and meant to keep them there, but they were quite helplessly drawn back through those bright curls. He leaned in and gently laid his lips on hers, intending to keep it brief and simple, but as if by their own accord, both mouths opened ever so slightly and the kiss became deeper, sweeter. Heads moved to taste more, and they drank from each other like nectar. Bailey's arms crept around his waist and pulled him closer, and he moved to her obligingly, compressing the space between them. He felt himself blending into her, as if he had shifted from his own body and stepped right into hers; they were a magnificent, blooming flower, expanding toward the sun. The kiss unfolded layer by layer. It was peculiar and unsettling, and then, peaceful. And then *exhilarating.* It seemed to stretch on and on, and he never, ever wanted it to end.

"Wake up! Rise and shine, sleepyheads!" bellowed Mr. Naplava, and the cry was echoed two wagons back. "Get stretched and ready to unload this god-awful stinking wool," he called cheerfully.

And the moment was over. Their heads jerked apart and they stared at each other, lips parted in amazement, breaths coming fast, his hands still buried in her hair and her arms still around his waist gripping his shirt, until the wagon lurched to a halt a few seconds later.

It was late afternoon, and they were in the Plaza already. Five whole days had come and gone, and Bailey longed to start over and experience them one more time. She felt the tears pooling in her eyes again, and for reasons she did not understand, a deep and profound depression pressed onto her.

"Hey," Jacob whispered, not wanting his father to hear. "I'm so sorry. Did I scare you? I shouldn't have kissed you like that."

She shook her head and attempted a smile. "It was perfect! You did it just right, just like I imagined." She removed her arms from his waist and gazed down at her lap, suddenly unspeakably shy. It had been the best moment of her life.

He paused, unwilling to end it, then finally, reluctantly, withdrew his hands from her hair, pausing to graze his knuckles gently across her cheek. He pulled her up, helping her brush the hay and stray wool from her dress. "Come on. Let's get out of here and stretch!" He vaulted out of the wagon, glad to hide his own confusion, and turned to help her down. They must never, *ever*, do that again! His knees were wobbly and his heart was pounding triple time, and he knew the symptoms. If this "adoption" was going to work, they had to start being brother and sister now. He decided to tease her like he would his sisters back home.

"Why are you wearing that again? Are you going to a dance?"

She grinned, recognizing what he was doing. She had insisted on wearing the red satin again, not wanting to appear before Blanche and her mother in country clothes. She wasn't even going to tell them that she had been gone. It would be easy to explain away the last five days; she had been gone for longer than that before, staying with Gabriella at her aunt's shanty as long as the kind, harried woman with seven children could feed them. She would take a beating from Blanche, but nothing like what she would get if Blanche knew she had traveled with a boy alone. The crass old woman would assume that Bailey had relations with the boy—sex was always Blanche's frame of reference—thus meaning that she would not be able to get the incredibly high fee that she was already planning for Bailey's first night and the lucky man who would have a virgin for dessert.

Bailey had it all planned out: she would go straight to Fort Allen alone, deal with Blanche and take her licks, and then corner her mother, who would be semi-conscious in her bed, trying to pull herself out of a morphine haze. Permission would be easy. And she would write her a letter to make sure that Addie remembered where her daughter had gone. Then she would gather her things and sneak out while Blanche was supervising the dinner preparations.

The other wagons lurched to a halt and the men jumped out, stretching and preparing to unload. Franticek turned to Bailey. "Just as soon as we get this first wagon unloaded, I'll take you to your Mama's," he smiled, wondering at the worried expression on the little girl's face.

"Um, Mr. Naplava, sir, that won't be necessary. I need to talk to her by myself, and then I'll come back here. It won't even take an hour. Is that okay?" Her brow puckered as Franticek looked dubious.

"Now Missy, that's not what the missus explained to me. I was supposed to ask your mother for permission and introduce myself properly, so she knows you're in good hands." He smiled and turned away as if the manner were finished. Jacob looked on, anxiety beginning to show in his face.

"No, sir. I know my Mama, and she won't want to see you. Please, sir, just let me take care of it." She looked at his boots, dreading that he would be stubborn like his son and refuse her wish. She was so bashful around Mr. Naplava: Jacob's resemblance to him was remarkable, and she found herself tongue-tied around this big handsome rancher who spoke little but was clearly a wise and strong leader. She had just never encountered such a seemingly perfect father figure, and she was quite at a loss about how to communicate with him. A long moment passed.

"Well, I guess there is a lot of work to do here. You go on and get things straight with your Ma, and be back here directly," he admonished, and turned away to begin bellowing orders to his men.

Jacob stepped forward. "Bailey, I don't think this is a good idea. Let me go with you."

"No, this is something I have to do on my own. I know how to handle her."

"I don't know." He frowned and reached out to trace the fading bruise on her cheek. "What about Big Bully Blanche?" Bailey let out a huff of laughter, imagining what Blanche would do if she ever called her that.

"I know how to handle her, too. She'll be so busy she won't have time to argue much. Besides, she's not my mother."

They stood and stared at each other. Bailey felt the strange foreboding again, an immovable, oppressive weight on her heart, and she longed for the next hour to pass so she could be safe in the Plaza again, working beside Jacob.

"Okay, I guess you know best," he finally relented. "Good luck."

He offered his hand and she gave it, but then he changed his mind and pulled her roughly into his arms. He was downright alarmed to realize how much he wanted to kiss her again. As her arms encircled his neck, he held on to her tightly, even lifting her off her feet a bit, she was so light, inhaling the scent of her warm skin and hair. Memorizing it. "Come back, Rosie," he whispered. She nodded mutely, her cheek pressed to his.

His head dipped and she felt him kiss her neck, hard, and she thought she would die of happiness.

They pulled apart and she thought she saw tears in his eyes.

She never knew for sure, because then he let her go and turned away, willing himself not to look back.

CHAPTER SEVEN

Bailey walked right up to the front door and entered, expecting the great room to be empty at this time of the late afternoon. She was not disappointed. She could hear the girls upstairs getting ready for the night's work. Not a soul was downstairs, not even Blanche, and Bailey breathed a sigh of relief. She must be in the kitchen at the back of the house. This was going to be easier than she thought!

A moment later she stood in her mother's room, staring at the empty bed. It was made up neatly, meaning that the maid had been in here at her usual time around noon and Addie hadn't been here since. Bailey felt a chill of apprehension. If nothing else, her mother was a creature of habit. She was *always* in her room at this time. At noon, she would meet in the kitchen for a light lunch, waiting for the pharmacist, looking nervously out the window, listening for his footsteps on the back porch. When he arrived she would remove the leather bag attached to a thong from around her neck, carefully set the syringe and needle aside, and he would fill it with morphine sulfate tablets. This was as much as Bailey ever saw, because she would be ordered from the room by her mother, a guilt-stricken look in her pretty eyes. Twenty minutes later she would crawl upstairs and drift for hours until it was time to eat dinner and get ready.

Bailey backed out of the room and ventured down the hall. She'd ask Lola, a buxom, thick-lipped brunette from the east who never ceased to talk, even when she was with a john. Chatty Lola knew everyone's business. Bailey had thought many times that Lola should quit the business and work for the newspaper. She knocked on the door tentatively.

"Come in!" bellowed Lola from the other side. "Oh, hello Bailey. Haven't seen you around for a couple of days. Stay out of Blanche's way, my dearie, or you'll catch *hell*. She's in the kitchen. Come over here and help me with these buttons. Damn this dress! I always said, why do we have to wear these fancy things? On and off, on and off, all night long. Why don't we just walk around in robes like the girls at Triple Star? You'd move a lot more men through in one night, if you know what I mean. Well, you'll know soon enough, anyway." She paused to take a breath as Bailey struggled with the tiny buttons.

"Say, you're getting mighty pretty, little one. I'll tell you, if you were just one year older, Blanche would put you on the floor and you could start making the big bucks." Bailey's hands froze.

"One year? I thought you had to be fourteen." Her voice was trembling and she struggled to sound nonchalant.

"Well, usually so, yes, but they're starting earlier now, you know. Why wait? You've got the equipment, or you will have," she amended with a glance at Bailey's chest. "We'd start you on the old men, no rough stuff. Besides, Blanche is spittin' mad. She's mad enough to make you start turning your tricks tonight, my girl." Bailey finished the buttons, her body cold to the core.

"My mother would never let that happen," she said calmly, turning away to hide her disgust.

"Well, my dear, your mother is not here." For once, Lola was tightlipped. Bailey tried to wait her out, but was forced to ask.

"Where is she?"

Lola sat her bulk down in front of her vanity and began opening jar after jar. There must have been over two dozen. She picked up a stick of black kohl and carefully began applying it under one eye. "You remember Senator, that big, mean fancy dresser who used to sniff around after Liza? Well, he was always after Addie, at first, wanting to buy her off the floor just to *talk* to her. Would bring her lilies and treated her so gentle. He cornered her one night and they were chattin' all intense-like, then I'll never forget it, your mother's face went white and she passed clean out. We all thought she was dead. Senator got down on his knees and took real sweet care of her, tried to revive her and all; you would have thought that he loved her. But Blanche had Mack throw him out, thinkin' he did somethin' awful to Addie, and he didn't come back for a long time, not 'til the next time he was in town. He didn't come back 'til a couple of years ago, you might not remember. He tried to talk to Addie again but she wouldn't have anything to do with him, and he finally gave up. You could tell he was real sad, and then by gum, *real* pissed off, like a switch had been flipped in his mind. Crazy, he was; we all saw it. Anyway, that man loved girls, the younger the better. He's mighty young himself, only mid-thirties, they say. Liza was the youngest we had at the time, sixteen she was, and he'd buy her off the floor three or four times a week, spending all night up there with her. Lucky her! Only one man a lot of the time." Lola paused to apply a perfect circle of pink paint to her pudgy cheek. Bailey looked away, dread beginning to grow. What did any of this have to do with her mother?

"Well, you won't believe it, but Senator showed up here two nights ago. He hadn't shown his face around here since Liza left; I guess he didn't want any of us old bags and he gave up on your mother, although you could still see him look at her with those haunted eyes. What a doper." Lola snorted and began applying a thick black gunk to her sparse eyelashes. It reminded Bailey of *tecolé*, and she experienced a pang of homesickness for the sheep ranch and the Naplavas, and most of all, for Jacob.

She cleared her throat. Lola seemed to have lost the thread of her story. "So what did he want?" she prompted.

Lola swiveled around to face Bailey. She had transformed herself in the course of a few moments from a pale, sad woman who looked younger than her twenty-nine years to a garish clown. She smiled hideously, showing red lipstick on her teeth.

"Why, my dear, he wanted *you*." She paused to let the words sink in, watching closely for a reaction from the child. She didn't mind Bailey too much—she was all right to have around—and she suddenly felt sorry for her. Bailey sank down into the chair behind her, her face draining of all color. She could only shake her head dumbly.

"If he can't have Mama, he'll take Daughter. That happens, you know. I saw him meet with Blanche in her office. He pulled out a huge roll of money that would make your eyes pop clean out of your head. Later on she told me all about it. She told him that you were still a little girl, and in two years he could be the first, but he would pay the price all right! But he convinced her to put you to work early, like *now*. He left with a big smile on his face, no mistake." Lola paused to pat Bailey's hand, then turned to the mirror again to wipe off the smeared lip paint from her mouth and teeth, and started over, drawing a bright red mouth where her own thin lips had been.

Bailey was calm now, and numb. Everything had cleared; suddenly her life shone before her like a beacon. She had to get out of here, forever. She would tell her mother goodbye and turn her back on this place for the last time. She wasn't sure where she would end up; maybe the Naplavas would keep her, or another family in the hills. But one thing she was sure of: if Senator, that huge, wicked man, took her to bed, he'd kill her, and if he didn't, she'd finish the job herself.

"Where is my mother?" she said clearly, determined to be done with this woman and out the door.

"Well, now, I'm getting to that part. Be patient! Anyway, like I was saying, Senator and Blanche struck a deal because he was back two nights ago. All day Blanche had been looking for you, getting madder and madder. She had everybody looking for you; she even dragged your mother out of bed."

"My mother knew?" Bailey interrupted.

"Naw, she didn't know at that time; she was stumbling around like she was sleepwalking. I hate to be crass, my dear, but the pharmacist makes more money off of Addie than the rest of the house combined!"

Bailey stared at her, a stony expression on her thin face.

Lola turned back around to face the mirror. "When Senator got here, Blanche had to tell him you weren't here, and seeing that he was as drunk as a skunk, and who knows what else, he threw a fit. He broke three of Cook's best crystal goblets, kicked over chairs, and pounded his fists on the walls until I thought the windows would break. 'You better give me something, you old bitch,' he kept screaming at Blanche. I swear, he went plumb crazy. It was like he turned into a monster, he did. Well, now comes the funny part. Blanche runs upstairs and yanks Nadine out of a working room, you understand? Nadine was already engaged, and Blanche yanks her downstairs, stark naked! You've never heard such hootin' and hollerin' in your life, from the customers, I mean. It was the best show in town." Lola paused to giggle and powder her chest. She dabbed perfume behind her ears and between her breasts.

Bailey closed her eyes then, appalled at the disgrace Nadine must have taken in her stead. Nadine was the youngest of the house, only fifteen, a shy girl with dark, wavy hair and big despondent eyes. Bailey had spoken to her on a few occasions, finding her to be sad and uncommunicative. Nobody knew where she had come from; she had just shown up on Blanche's doorstep one day about six months ago, and announced that she needed a job. She had wanted a job in the kitchen, but within a week Blanche had her turning tricks. All the girls whispered about her because she was so mysterious, never saying a word about herself. And now this quiet girl had suffered the humiliation of being dragged down the stairs naked, to be thrown into the arms of a raging drunken beast.

"What happened to Nadine?" questioned Bailey, barely above a whisper.

"Huh? Oh, nothing. She took his hand, cool as a cucumber, and led him upstairs. She's fine, I don't think he hurt her at all." Lola seemed to lose interest in the story now that the good part was over with.

"And my mother?"

"Oh! Well, Addie was none too happy with Blanche, once the dope wore off and I told her what had happened. I was in her room just thirty minutes ago, thereabouts. She went to see Senator, is my guess."

Bailey felt cold tendrils of fear reaching up her back. "Addie is with Senator? Where?" She rose from the chair and was already headed for the door.

"He's holed up at the Gaslight; where else would a senator stay?" chortled Lola.

Bailey stopped dead in her tracks. "He's a *senator*? You mean like from where the President is?"

"Why else would we call him Senator, my dear?" Lola turned back to her mirror, dismissing Bailey. The girl stood dumbly in the hall. She had always thought that 'Senator' was just a nickname to boost the man's ego. To find out he was a powerful, important man made her skin crawl. A man like that, in charge of making rules for the whole great country, had desired a girl of twelve. Another piece of innocence slipped away, and it was a wiser and infinitely sadder Bailey who ran down the stairs and out the front door of Fort Allen for the last time.

Bailey had never been inside the brand new Gaslight Hotel. San Antonio, though growing every day, was still somewhat of a cowpoke Southwestern city, dotted with saloons and bawdy houses and restaurants and other numerous thriving businesses of every kind. The Gaslight was, to Bailey, the pinnacle of wealth. In front was a great wide plaza with tropical trees and flowers of every kind sprinkled alongside the wide walkways. Hidden cleverly were the famous gaslights, just beginning to gain popularity, and of course the Gaslight Hotel had them first. At night the gaslights were ceremoniously lit by a man in a red jacket, and the plaza brightened with an unearthly, breathtaking glow. In the middle was a dancing fountain, and the water sparkled like diamonds during the day and like fire at night. Dandified ladies and gentlemen strolled along, the women protecting delicate skin with brightly colored parasols, the men swinging canes. The hotel itself rose before her, giant, white, forbidding columns seeming to bar the likes of her from entering its hallowed halls. She couldn't imagine what the inside must look like!

This was no time to be having second thoughts. Somewhere in that hotel her mother was meeting with Senator trying to protect Bailey, and she simply meant to tell her where she was going, and to say goodbye. She couldn't leave without doing that; she owed her that much. And she wanted to look Senator in the eye and tell him that he would never, not if he lived to be one hundred years old, touch one hair on her head. She didn't know if she would have the courage to do this last thing.

Bravely she sauntered up the steps, trying to act like she entered magnificent hotels every day. She swung open a massive white door and stepped inside, stopping momentarily, speechless at the grandeur around her, unable to take it all in. Above her hung an enormous, many-tiered chandelier, and she was mesmerized by its beauty. Lovely wicker furniture with wide, colorful cushions was tucked charmingly into corners by deep bay windows. And plants! There were flowers and plants everywhere, in vases and in huge native earthenware pots. One entire wall was covered with an intricate mural of San Antonio, with every aspect painted in minute detail. Bailey felt as if she could crawl into that painting and be right at home. Thick, exotic Mexican rugs covered the floor, and she had an insane desire to shed her painful shoes and proceed barefoot across the lobby.

Her dazed delight was interrupted by a polite clearing of the throat. Bailey looked up into the face of a short, handsome black man, maybe the age of Mr. Naplava. He looked to be a servant of some sort, maybe one to carry people's parcels or tend to the door, although Bailey didn't know the right word.

"May I help you, ma'am?" he drawled politely. Bailey was encouraged by his kindness. He hadn't even asked her if her parents were staying here, or yelled at her get out, which is what she had expected. She obviously didn't belong, and he was trying to spare her feelings.

She lifted her chin and tried to speak with authority, the kind of arrogance and command that she knew came with money. "I need to know which room the senator is staying in, please." She tapped her foot a little, for effect.

The man's eyes widened. "You mean Senator Hawk?" he asked, disbelief tingeing his voice that a street urchin would demand to see a senator.

Bailey tried to keep herself from smirking. Hawk! What a perfect name for that predatory man! Well, that hawk was not going to get his clutches into this little mouse.

She nodded her head imperially. "Yes, that's the one. Which room?"

The servant leaned back from the waist, resting one elbow in the other hand, and stroked his neatly trimmed black whiskers tinged with gray. His rich brown eyes sparkled. Finally, he spoke. "May I ask why the young lady wishes to see the senator?'

"It's a private affair," she retorted haughtily, but she began to falter as she saw the laughter in his eyes.

"My little one, you'll have to do better than that." He regarded her sternly.

Bailey thought quickly and could come up with nothing plausible. *Think*, she shouted to herself. All of the stories she knew, stored neatly in her head, and she could not think of one excuse to give this man. Well, then, she would give him no excuses. She'd let him have the truth, all at once, and hope that the shock value would loosen his tongue.

"Okay. My name is Bailey Rose. My mother is a working girl, and she's up there with Senator right now. She's up there working. And I'm going to go away for a long time, and I need to tell her and say goodbye so she doesn't worry." She finished in a rush and braved a glance at the man's face.

All trace of humor was gone, replaced with an expression of shock, then one of sadness. He knew the truth when he heard it. "Did you say your name was Rose?"

This was the last thing she expected him to ask! "Yes," she answered, a puzzled look on her face.

"Your mother must be Adele." He nodded and smiled, seemingly recalling a fond memory as he gazed off into space.

"Adele? No, her name is just Addie. Addie Rose," Bailey corrected.

"Oh yes, I knew her long ago when she first came to San Antonio. I always wondered what happened to her." He stopped, seeing the look of amazement on the girl's face. "Well, I'll say no more. It's not for me to say." He gave a quick jerk of his head. "Follow me."

She did as he asked, longing to ask him questions about when he first knew her mother. But was that really important now? Jacob and Mr. Naplava must be getting worried; she'd already been twice as long as she had promised. She hurried after the servant, running every couple of steps to keep up with his quick pace.

He led her down a long narrow hall to a flight of steep steps. "These are the back stairs, Miss Rose. Climb them and turn to your right at the top. The senator's room is the last one at the end of the hall, number 226. Be careful, now. That one runs with a wild bunch."

Bailey looked at the steps doubtfully. Could she really do this? Was it wise to put herself in the presence of a man who was seeking her out just the night before? But what could he do in a fancy hotel? If she kept the door open, she could always scream and run. And he wouldn't dare touch her in front of her mother. Lola had mentioned that he had a fondness for her mother. Maybe she should ask this nice man to go with her. "Uh, Mr..."

Her voice faded as she turned to find that she was alone.

She took a deep breath. Night was falling already and she had to get this over with. The longer she stood here, the more her chances slipped away. The Naplavas wouldn't wait forever, or worse yet, they would come looking for her, starting at Fort Allen and ending up here to witness her mother's shame, and her own. The decision made, she mounted the stairs quickly and entered a great wide hall with plush red carpeting and a golden mosaic on the walls. She felt as if she were in a fairy tale! She had never dreamed that a place like this really existed; not right here where she lived. She walked silently down the hall, her nerves strung to the breaking point, until she stood before his door. "Gaslight #226" was inscribed on a golden plate, and the heavy door stared back at her, as if issuing a challenge.

She took a last deep breath and knocked five times. There was absolutely no sound from within. What if they weren't there anymore? Had she gone through all of this for nothing? Tears welled in her eyes as she thought of leaving without seeing her mother again. She still loved her, no matter what, and she knew that on some level, perhaps buried beneath the sordid, hazy layers of her convoluted life, Addie loved her, too. But if her mother had already been here and gone, chances were that Senator was gone, too. She'd make one last swing by Fort Allen, leave her mother a note, and begin her new life. The decision made, she began to turn her back.

Without warning the door swung open, and Senator Hawk stood

glowering down upon her. He was swaying ever so slightly, and his face was ruddy with drink. That face registered three emotions in quick succession: utter shock, then an almost comic look of buffoonish confusion, which was rapidly replaced with a curiously blank look. His eyes were utterly glazed over and his gaze jerked from side to side in what seemed to be an uncontrollable spasm.

Bailey was shaking from her very core, but she opened her mouth to ask for her mother. "Where's my m—"

She never finished. A hand reached out, grabbed a fistful of hair, and hauled her through the door, flinging her viciously to the floor. He slammed the door behind him and leaned against it, smiling wretchedly down upon the girl. She lay still, stunned beyond words. Never in her wildest imagination had she expected him to do this! She thought she'd have the chance to run, or at least scream, before she ever stepped foot in his room. There were people in the other rooms! A senator couldn't act this way!

"How nice of you to pay me a visit, Miss Rose. Your mother, you know, has already visited. I only hope that our visit will be just as pleasant."

His voice was silky smooth and cultured, but the words were slurred together. Bailey stared up at him, mesmerized. Automatically she reached back and felt the sore spot on her scalp, the place where her hair had been ripped away as she was pulled into the creek just the day before. She rose and forced herself to look at him.

She had never really seen his face; she didn't pay attention to him two years ago in the parlor with Liza. She suspected that since he was a monster, he would look like one: sharp, green teeth, big red eyes, maybe even a tail hidden under his fancy clothes! And certainly he must be very old to be a senator. But she was shocked to find herself looking at a young man, just like Lola said. He may have been five years older than her mother at the most. And he was handsome! He was tall and solidly built, with a neatly combed coif of sandy hair. His lips were nicely shaped, and his face was smoothly shaven and aristocratic, the bones perfectly placed. But the remarkable feature was his eyes. Never had Bailey seen eyes as completely devoid of any flicker of human emotion as these. They were the color of the sky on a day when it is neither sunny nor cloudy, but a haze somewhere in between gray and white. When he looked at her, he looked right through her, as if in a trance. Senator Hawk didn't seem to be present in his own body, as if he was possessed. And his eyes seemed to glow, just like she knew they would. They glowed like a wolf in the night. *Just like a wolf…*

"Miss Rose," he said, almost conversationally, no hint of malice in his voice. "Have you ever seen a gun?" The words, slurred, emerged *Havyouverseenagun?*

She stared up at him blankly.

"Well have you, then? Answer me."

Finally she managed to shake her head. This simply could not be happening. He must be mad.

"No? Well, I'm surprised, because your mother owned a gun. In fact, if you turn around, you can say hello to Mother." He smiled on her benevolently, and Bailey knew, in some deep intuitive part of her soul, what she would see if she turned around. She felt her entire body turn cold. She was paralyzed. *Your mother owned a gun. Your mother owned a gun. Say hello to Mother.*

"Miss Rose, I said to turn around. Now, we're not going to misbehave, are we? You won't like what happens if you misbehave." He grinned, devilishly handsome, and took a step toward her, but Bailey sat unmoving, pinned by the glow of his colorless eyes and his flashing white teeth.

He sighed as if bored and rolled his eyes, clicking his tongue. One hand reached down to caress her cheek, and before she could pull away, he pulled the hand back and delivered a powerful smack that rocked her head back onto her shoulders and knocked her to the floor. She lay on her back, stunned, her black shoes pointing at the ceiling as her dress fell around her. She saw points of light float before her eyes. *This isn't happening. It's another bad dream. If I yell for Jacob, he'll rescue me.*

For a split second she thought she saw an expression of shock and horror on Senator's face, but it was gone in an instant, and she knew with his next words she must have imagined it. "Now, you will turn around, please." The deep, pleasant voice brought her back to reality.

She sat up slowly and turned around, and found herself looking at a huge canopied bed.

"Stand up so you can see," he ordered. He nudged her backside with one black boot.

She stood up and looked, blind with panic and dread. At first she didn't understand what she was seeing. All she could see was red. The bed itself was covered with red. With blood, she admitted to herself numbly. *It's blood, stupid.* Blood everywhere, soaking the bed. Puddles of blood on the carpet leading to the bed. And in the middle of the ocean lay her mother, face up, a red stain covering her chest. That's where the ocean came from. Her mother's heart. So much blood in one small person. It was incredible, really.

Bailey sank again to the floor, closed her eyes, and let the blackness come.

She awoke because her hands were tingling. She was in a deep, cushiony chair, and her hands were being stabbed with a million tiny little pins. She looked down dazedly and saw that they were tied clumsily together with the sash from her own dress. Her dress was laid neatly on the bed; she sat shivering in her white shift. Her legs were tied to the legs of the chair with what looked to be torn strips of sheets. She saw something else, too. Against the wall sprawled Senator, a gun held loosely in his hand.

Bailey tried to think. She glanced at the window: it was black outside, and the night felt old; she intuitively knew that several hours had passed. He must have tied her up and passed out before he could do anything else. His chest was bare, the first three buttons of his pants gaped open, and his boots had been flung in the corner with an empty whiskey bottle. She wished she could thank that bottle personally.

She looked again at the bed. Addie stared at the ceiling, looking to be deep in thought. She was beautiful. She was dead, and she had died trying to protect her daughter. She had come here with a gun, to kill Senator, so he wouldn't hurt her little girl. A great wave of grief and love surged inside the girl, squeezing her heart and forcing its way up her throat. She sobbed twice before she saw Senator shift. She must be quiet! Her mother had started something here, and she was going to finish it. She wouldn't let herself sit and blubber until the sleeping monster awoke. There was no Jacob to rescue her. She would rescue herself.

She worked her hands free easily, blessing his drunken stupor again. She quickly untied her legs, took a deep breath, and bent down and took the gun from his hand. It was too simple! She now had all the choices in the world; she could walk out or she could kill him first.

Or she could turn the gun on herself.

She rose and suddenly rocked on her feet. She sat back in the chair and tried to control her breathing, feeling the room spin wildly. Sweat beaded on her forehead and nausea rolled over her in a sickening tidal wave. She bent forward and vomited, unable to help herself. What was wrong? Had he drugged her? How? She felt something more trickle out of her mouth and wiped her hand across her lips. Her hand came away white and foamy, with a sweet, sickening familiar smell. She had grown up knowing this smell. It was morphine, her mother's drug of choice. She smelled it on Addie every day, every time she allowed herself to get near enough. And now it was in her, a part of her, put there by the monster who wanted to crawl into her body and destroy her.

She looked down at the crook of her elbow, already knowing what she would see. A puncture was there, and a dried bead of blood with a spreading bruise. No doubt he had injected her with her mother's own drugs.

That decided it. She couldn't walk away without killing him first. He'd hunt her down; she was sure of it. She's be running from Senator for the rest of her life if she left him sleeping on the floor. He was desperate, he was crazy, and he was sick in a way that Bailey couldn't give voice to, sick enough to have to drug a little girl to have his way. Why, why?

The truth suddenly crashed its way into her consciousness, taking her breath away and numbing her mind with fear. She knew without a doubt now that he was, incredibly, a Vodnik. It was his hand that had pulled her into the creek, it was he in the form of a wolf who had chased her into the sheep pit; she was as sure of it as she had never been sure of anything else in her life.

Something closed within her. She felt as though she were outside of her body, watching the scene unfold. She had no control over her actions anymore; she was a passive bystander, interested and curious. She raised the gun slowly, aimed it at his head, and tried to squeeze the trigger. Nothing happened. An eternity seemed to pass.

Then something *did* happen. The Senator opened his glowing, colorless eyes, only they weren't glowing now. They were sad and tired. He tried to sit up, but his arms wouldn't hold his weight. For the first time Bailey noticed his arms. There were hundreds of scars and bruises covering them, in the same place the drop of blood laid on her arm. Finally he pushed enough to prop himself in a sitting position against the wall, his head lolling against his shoulder.

"What did you give me?" Bailey tried to say, but her words were so slurred she was sure that he wouldn't understand her.

He gazed at her, tears welling in his gray eyes and finally coursing down his face. "Your mother's morphine and heroin." He suddenly took a deep, shuddering breath. "I don't know what I'm doing. I don't know what I'm doing." He hung his head and wept.

Bailey looked at him impassively, no change of expression on her thin face. She was sure this was Vodnik trickery.

"I'm so, so, sorry. I know you can never forgive me. But I'm asking anyway." He buried his face in his hands, shoulders heaving.

Still she stared, unmoving, the gun leveled at his head. She didn't know how to pray, but she shot a message up anyway. *Help me, God. Help me do the right thing.*

Moments passed, and he wept.

Suddenly the vision of the secret meadow flashed through her racing mind. She was sitting in sweet clover, holding Jacob's hands. They were knee-to-knee, chatting away, teasing each other, filling the meadow with their laughter; and then they were silent, reflective, contemplating their house-to-be, soaking in the mysterious and ancient magic of that enchanted place. Now they were gazing at each other; she was lost in his bottomless blue eyes. *Forgive him*, he whispered.

"Mr. Hawk?" She finally said. Her voice was steadier now.

He raised his head, grief etched on his once handsome face.

"I forgive you." The words came out all by themselves, pulled from her as if on a magic string, flowing toward the wretch in the corner on wings of mercy and grace that she knew did not, could not, have originated from her own heart.

For a long moment they stared at each other. Outside the lovely window the torch lights lit up the fountain. Addie contemplated the ceiling, Bailey felt a little girl fade away as the young woman inside her began to gain strength, and the pathetic being on the floor began to yearn for his needle and for the shelter of a young girl's body.

Finally he spoke, barely in a whisper. "I wrote you a letter today. After she came. I sent it. I told you to stay away. *Why didn't you stay away*?" The last words were a sob.

Long seconds passed.

Finally he opened his eyes again. He smiled gently at her. "You have to pull back on the hammer all the way until you hear two clicks."

She did it automatically, never questioning why he was telling her this. She knew. Her heart pounded.

"Your mother's death was an accident. She charged into the room and tried to shoot me, and the gun went off when I tried to get it away from her. She was my—my friend." His voice broke on the word and he heaved a sob. "I never meant for it to happen. She was the only one who *knewwwww*." The last word was a long, loud wail, followed by more sobbing. Finally he fell silent. His chest heaved with the effort to breathe. Bailey sat immobilized, the world whirling on around her. "I didn't touch you," he finally said softly. "But I can't stop myself. If you walk out, a needle will be in my vein as soon as I can get up, and I will come for you, child, just like they came for me."

They continued to stare at each other, Bailey's confidence beginning to falter as she saw at last the miserable human being trapped inside the monster on the floor. She began to lower the gun. She couldn't do this. Could she? If she killed the Vodnik, would the human survive? Had he ever *been* human? He seemed to be saying just that: 'just like they came for me.' He admitted he couldn't stop himself; was he saying that he, the man, could not stop the Vodnik beast that possessed him? She was so utterly confused and terrified.

"Who came for you? The monsters?" she whispered. Would he tell her?

He nodded miserably. "Yes, the monsters. And now I'm one."

Well. There it was, as clear as it could be. He was a Vodnik.

"I don't want to kill myself," he choked out, and he suddenly sounded like a young boy. "I want to go to heaven. Oh please, God, forgive me." He dropped his head and prayed, his lips moving soundlessly for several moments. His shoulders relaxed and a strange sense of peace seemed to enter the room. It came to her that he knew what to do—he knew how to escape the monster—and that she must listen to him.

Finally he looked up again, his gray eyes locking with Bailey's dark ones, and something indescribably profound passed between them. "*You* can be forgiven," he whispered. "Please, please, help me. Please end it," he begged, and she raised the gun.

She was running, and as she ran, she had a curious sense of *deja vu*, as if she had already been through this scene in her life. *Now it will rain,* she thought, and the sky opened and the rain poured, mixing with her wild, hysterical tears. She had never in her life cried like this before, as if the world was coming to an end, the story of her life being concluded. She tripped and fell face-down in a puddle, and only with a push from some unseen force did she find the strength to rise again, and to run.

She had killed a United States senator. There had been no doubt about it. After she lowered the gun, an ocean of his blood began to flow, just like her mother's, as the bullet had pierced his heart. She had sat and waited with him, praying aloud the only prayer she knew, the one about the valley of death and fearing no evil. She had knelt beside him and held his hand, their eyes locked. He had smiled at her, and that's when she knew she had vanquished the monster within. She waited until he drew his last gurgling breath and a measure of peace settled on his face, and only then did she close his eyes and stumble from the red room, flinging the gun away from her into the hallway in a blind panic. When the door closed, a dam closed in her mind, too, sealing the scarlet ocean behind it.

Her first thought had been of Jacob. They had to be looking for her, probably desperate now, and there was no telling if they would find Lola and get the name of the Gaslight Hotel from her. Blanche most likely would not even let them in the door. Bailey cringed to think of those fine people seeing where she came from, coming face to face with Blanche and the half-naked girls who were no doubt sprawled around the great room. She couldn't go back to them. She was a *killer* now. She had cocked a gun and deliberately pulled the trigger and watched a man die, and even if it was what he had wanted, even if it was to save her own life, even if it had been an evil Vodnik, it didn't change anything. There would be a public outcry: an important senator killed by a whore's daughter! She'd be thrown in jail or into an asylum. She would never let the Naplavas become tainted by that. She couldn't imagine the look of shock and disgust that would come over Gacenka's sweet face.

So she ran on as the streets began to flood and the lightning struck all around her. *It's the hand of God. I'll be struck down like the murderer I am.* She had no destination; she simply wished to run until her legs could no longer carry her, and then she would lie down and let nature take its course.

But she found herself in the Plaza looking for Jacob after all, her heart full of desperate hope. The Plaza was deserted in the storm, and as she stumbled through it, she reminded herself once again that she was not worthy of his family anyway. She wept for the loss of that boy, wanting to die, willing it to come for her as it had in Cibola Creek. But as the lightning reached out a fiery hand and split a tree ten yards in front of her, a flicker of determination was born, motivated by years of steely survival instinct. She struggled through driving sheets of rain, running blocks and blocks, to what looked to be a large building on her left; she could see candles burning from within and a great overhang over the door under which to take shelter.

She reached the door and collapsed against it, and with the last of her strength looked up to see the words etched into the beautiful stone. *St. Ursuline's Convent.*

She closed her eyes and gave in to the familiar blackness, and it embraced her as a mother comforts a lost child who has been found.

CHAPTER EIGHT

Jacob was frantic. All evening they had waited, his father working calmly while Jacob's stomach twisted in agony. Something was horribly wrong. It shouldn't have taken her three hours to collect her things and say goodbye.

He finally convinced his father to let him walk over to Fort Allen. "But I'm coming with you," Mr. Naplava had added. "You're not going into a place like that alone."

So the two of them covered the short distance in silence, and reached the entrance of Fort Allen fifteen minutes later. Jacob knocked tentatively and the door swung open, and a huge woman with platinum blond hair and sticky red lips stood before them. She took one amazed look and a wide, sardonic smile broke forth, exposing small, yellow, feral teeth. "*Gentlemen,*" she began, her booming voice heavy with sarcasm, "I believe you have the wrong establishment here. We cater to military officers and important officials. If you would just proceed on down the block, you will find a house more to your own liking. And perhaps you may want to take advantage of the city bathing facilities first." Her nose wrinkled, distorting her already loathsome face.

Jacob felt his face flame. They had been working all day unloading stinking wool in the hot sun; good, honest work, while she sat inside and grew fatter. He wanted to smash the face of this wicked woman who had blackened Bailey's eye; this woman who meant to sell Bailey as a cut of butcher's meat. He took a step forward and his father restrained him with a firm hand on his shoulder.

"Thank you for the suggestion, Ma'am," he said pleasantly. His voice was heavily accented, but his English was faultless. "My name is Franticek Naplava, and this is my son Jacob. We are not interested in sampling your wares. We are looking for a young girl named Bailey Rose. She was to spend the summer on our ranch, and she came today to ask her mother's permission. It has been several hours, and still she does not come back to us. Would you happen to know her whereabouts? And if she is here, could you bring her to us?" He smiled as both his son and the madam stared at him, incredulous. Jacob had never heard his father use such polite, perfect words! And the madam was thrown off guard by his good manners, handsome visage, and gentle voice.

After the initial shock had worn off, however, she was enraged. So that's what that little bitch had been doing for the past five days, while her entire establishment was threatened by a madman! If she thought she would run away while other girls had to take up her slack, she'd have to think again.

She smiled hugely at the tired rancher and his remarkable-looking son. No wonder Bailey had wanted to run away. She had probably already bedded this young swain and had romantic notions in her foolish, empty head. She'd fix her, for good.

"Bailey isn't here," she began, uttering the first and only truthful words she would give this man. "But she left you a letter. Let me fetch it for you." She hurried from the front room through the parlor and kitchen back to her tiny office, on the way whispering to Clarabelle, one of the few girls not with a customer, and setting her on a task. Clarabelle began to circulate among the few remaining women in the parlor, bar, and ballroom, whispering briefly in each ear. Blanche reached her office and pulled a piece of stationary and a quill from her drawer. She herself had taught that brat her letters; she knew her handwriting well. She set to her task, sealing the child's fate.

After she left in a great swish, leaving a trail of clinging perfume behind, Jacob looked at his father in apprehension. "Why wouldn't she be here, Pa? She wouldn't just leave a letter."

"Could she write?"

"Well, yes, sir, she could."

"Then she may have very well left a letter. Be patient and we'll see."

They didn't have long to wait. The madam was back in five minutes with a folded piece of paper. She handed it to them and watched smugly as Jacob read it, accurately guessing that the father was illiterate.

Dear Jacob and the family Naplava,

By the time you read this I will be gone. My mother does not wish me to spend the summer with you. She has taken me away for a better life with a nice man she met. Thank you for every kindness you have shown me. Best wishes for your future.

Yours sincerely,

Bailey Rose

Jacob felt his face drain of color. She went away with a man? What did this mean?

"Is it her writing, son?" his father asked bluntly, and Blanche huffed indignantly.

"It looks like it, Pa." As a matter of fact, it looked exactly like her writing. Even the distinctive, ornate capital letters were identical to the ones he remembered from her slate at school.

"What does it say, then?'

"It says she can't come with us, and that her mother took her away with a man. What does that mean?" He directed this last question at the smirking woman.

"Well, young man, there's a lot you don't know about our Miss Rose. How old did she tell you she was?"

"Twelve." Jacob frowned at the odd question. What had this to do with anything?

"That, then, was the first lie. She is fourteen, small indeed, but sickly as a child and never growing as she ought. And she has been working for me for a year. Do you understand, young man? *Working,* with the customers, upstairs. She and her mother are on, shall we say, a special extended assignment." She watched in satisfaction as the boy's initial anger was replaced with a devastated, crumbling expression. He believed her! And why shouldn't he? It would be true soon enough, anyway. There were many pretty girls twelve years of age already working in the competing bordellos and bringing in a hefty profit.

It was the father who intervened. "How do we know this is the truth?"

"Mr. Naplava! You may step inside and search the premises! Ask anyone about Bailey! Here, Lynda, come over here, please. Tell these fine gentlemen about Bailey and her mother."

Lynda had been well prepared. "Bailey has been working the floor for the better part of a year now, that's the sad truth for the rest of us. All the men want her."

"Stop it!" Jacob pushed at her blindly and ran out the door, followed closely by his father. They could hear the mocking laughter before the door was slammed.

Franticek sighed and ran both hands through his hair. He looked at his despondent son and dreaded the words he must say. "Son, this is too much. There are things here that are not a part of us, and I will not have it in my family. Come now." He pulled him firmly toward the street and back toward the market.

"But Pa! What if they're lying?"

"I'll do this for you: I'll check again the next time we bring wool, in about six or seven days. I'll even go inside and look everywhere, okay?"

"Do it now, Pa, please. She may be in trouble." The boy was frantic, and his father regarded him for a long, silent moment.

"Okay. I'll do it now, and then that's the end of it. If she's not there, and her mother is not there, then we know the big woman is telling the truth. I'll even ask everyone I see. But that'll be the end of it, Jacob. Understand?"

The miserable boy nodded, and the father turned around and entered the establishment again. He was gone for well over thirty minutes, and Jacob began to feel hope blossom. Maybe he had found her and was helping her get her things.

But when his father emerged from the house without her, he knew the truth instinctively, even before his father reported to him. He had searched under the porch and most of the house; of course, he was barred from the locked bedrooms upstairs, and neither Bailey nor her mother was there. And every woman he had asked, even outside of Blanche's presence, had answered him the same way, with an undeniable conviction. Bailey had been a boarder in this house for almost a year, and she had gone away with her mother today.

Jacob turned to look at Fort Allen one last time through a haze of bitter tears, and when he finally turned his back on it, he turned his back on a child he thought he knew so well. His face flared at her seemingly innocent request for a kiss. He had even teased her about never being kissed before! How many men had she kissed? She must have been laughing at him when he kissed her! She probably knew a dozen better ways to kiss, and to do other things that he wasn't even sure about. He had thought she was a child, maybe even *his girl*, and now she was suddenly his own age, and yet much older.

And the realization that she had never been his, and never would be, sealed off a part of his young heart that he didn't even know existed, not until now, now that it was breaking.

PART TWO

San Antonio
1891

CHAPTER NINE

Dr. B. Rose was in agony. She had been for the last three days; an unrelenting, exquisite agony of which even she, with all of her newly acquired medical know-how, was not permitted to relieve. She felt a shooting pain begin above her ears and travel to the back of her head, tightening like a medieval torture device. She had finally reached the breaking point, and with a resolve born of sheer desperation, she lifted both shaking hands to take action.

She plucked the hat from her head with a savage yank and commenced to pull ninety-three pins from her hair; she knew how many because she counted them all, rejoicing as each one liberated a bright, heavy tress from the tightly wound bun at the top of her head. Her travel companions seated in the compartment across from her gaped in disbelief. Mrs. Scheihagen glared in equal parts of scandalous outrage and self-satisfaction, a smirk on her beefy face. She could hardly refrain from turning to her husband with an "I told you so." She had told him all about the women who traveled alone, and maybe now he would believe her! Mr. Scheihagen's reaction was easier to discern: an unconcealed fascination as the professional-looking woman whom he had judged to be in her early twenties quickly transformed into a strikingly beautiful maiden of surely no more than eighteen. He had never seen any woman except his wife take her hair down, and he was mesmerized by the way her uplifted arms tightened her jacket; by the way her previously hidden hair caught the sun and turned to fire as it fell to her waist in riotous curls. Only a sharp elbow in his ribs directed his attention elsewhere.

Bailey sighed as the last pin dropped unheeded to the empty seat beside her. How wonderful it felt, after three days of ungodly pain! She cursed the conventions that put the ugly bun in her hair and the even uglier hat on her head. The grey felt hat with a black band looked like a man's, except for the ludicrous black and gray feathers attached to the front. And the rest of her costume! She was sure that she looked like a man in a skirt! Her black tailored jacket with long lapels and puffy sleeves gathered at her shoulders was stifling in the Texas sun, even on this first day of March, and they had been traveling through Texas for over eleven hours in this stuffy compartment. And to complete the ghastly ensemble, a pale grey satin waistcoat with a pattern of dark red dots, complete with a man's wing collar and dark red knotted tie and stiff shirt front! When Lizbeth had delivered the outfit to the hospital for her, Bailey had thrown a fit. She had wasted good money, and she certainly didn't want to look like a man! But Lizbeth had assured her that it was the going fashion; that all the women of class were wearing this get-up, and if she wanted to fit in and be a doctor, she better look the professional part. The flared gray tweed skirt was the only item that Bailey could ever see herself possibly wearing again, once she was freed from this wretched locomotive. How she longed to be back in her soft white cotton blouse and skirt, her hair loosely braided and coiled under her cap. And how she longed to be back in New York.

For the tenth time in as many minutes she asked herself if she was doing the right thing. How very few people pursue a dream to its fullness! And she had done exactly that. A doctor! She still couldn't quite comprehend the enormity of her new title. *A long way for a dirty street urchin to travel, my girl. Thank God, thank God for Sister Anna.*

The name popped into her mind and sent her reeling back, crossing fifteen years as if they were but a shallow creek instead of a great ocean of time. She was twelve again, traumatized, experiencing the end of her world and waiting to die. Again she was propped against a door of a great building, the words "Ursuline Academy" shining down on her protectively from a huge arch in the dark sky. There had been rain; torrents of cold rain, and she had slept for what seemed like days. But a silence had awakened her, and she was bitterly disappointed to discover that death had cheated her after all, and she was to live this wretched life for one more day. She had been so weak! She considered crossing the small stony courtyard and moving on, but to where? There was no home to go to, only prison or a children's asylum, where they tied the children's hands to rusty pipes and let them sit in their own filth until they starved, if not for food then for love and human contact. Or so she had been threatened by Blanche on occasions too numerous to count.

On that day she had turned her weary body and noticed a long chain beside the entrance door. It was a pull-bell, and it was within reach. She wouldn't even have to rise. *If I pull it, will I become Catholic?* She pulled, slumping back down beside the door.

"Good day? Good day? Is anyone there?" The gentle feminine voice was coming from a small grating high in the door. Bailey was warmed by the voice. It sounded so motherly!

"It's me," she said softly, and then cursed herself for such a stupid answer. What would the nice voice think? She wanted to say more but found to her dismay that she was breathless with the effort of speaking. For the first time she noticed that she was burning; every part of her body was burning with fever, and she was hot and cold at the same miserable time.

The door opened and she was scooped up in strong arms. "Oh, you poor dear! Have you been out here all night?" The sister was dressed in black with a simple white covering on her head. She smiled down on Bailey as she carried her through a vestibule. On each side was a parlor, and she hurried the girl through the parlor on the left to a couch in the corner.

"Yes, ma'am," answered Bailey dreamily, fighting an intense urge to close her eyes. How she wanted to see everything in this elegant room!

"That's right, you sleep, little one. I'll bring you some hot tea and blankets and some cold rags for that fever. Then we'll talk to Mother Superior."

I'm to have a superior mother, Bailey thought happily, and that was her last thought for a long, long time. Later Sister Anna told her she had slept for two days and two nights, only half-waking to take tea and soup. She had hovered close to death; she had conversations with her mother, who was now clear-eyed and beautiful and happy, standing with a handsome young red-headed, dark-eyed soldier Bailey didn't know, one who always held her mother's hand and couldn't keep his eyes off of Addie. She had so wanted to stay with them, but when she asked, they just looked at her and smiled and shook their heads gently. "It's not time, but we'll be here when you're ready," they just kept saying. Bailey knew in her soul that these were not dreams. And then finally she woke up for good.

It had been so incredibly easy to fall into a life at St. Ursuline's Academy. She had told the nuns the truth; well, part of it, anyway. She was an orphan with no place to go, and an abusive woman wanted her to work in a house of ill repute. She knew the nuns read the papers carefully and made discreet inquiries to discover if she was a runaway, but Bailey wasn't worried. Blanche would never report her missing, and the Naplavas had probably just assumed she had decided to stay with her mother. The nuns had taken her in as part of their family, never questioning her too much about her past. The trick, Sister Anna taught her, was to live in the present and plan for the future, and to have ultimate faith in God's plan.

The murder of Senator Hawk had not caused the scandal that Bailey thought it would. The young senator was evidently well known for imbibing heavily in drink, drugs, and whores, although all accounts in the papers made no mention of drugs of any kind. Neither was there mention of a third party in Room 226 that night; only a woman of an unknown identity who had shot the senator and then turned the gun on herself. A neat trick, Bailey thought numbly, since she herself had left the gun on the floor in the hallway. Only much later did she realize that the police had undoubtedly been paid off by the very wealthy and prominent Hawk family to cast the senator in a favorable light, and having no third suspect, they had probably shuffled bodies and gun to suit their version of the truth.

She didn't care anymore. It was all behind her now. She was a convent girl, dressed in a black skirt and a white waist. For six years she sought refuge behind the sturdy stone walls, playing in the nuns' garden, praying in the cool chapel filled with candles and incense and large colored statues on altars. Meals were taken in the refectory, served by two silent nuns, and she slept in a dormitory with four other girls whose faces changed over the years. Each narrow, comfortable bed was equipped with a tall frame and a white curtain on hooks, giving Bailey her first taste of privacy.

She leaned back in her seat now, twisted a curl around her finger and gazed out of the train's tiny window. She had learned to accept her mother's death and the sacrifice she had made, and she was comforted beyond measure by the memory of her "visit" with her mother and the mysterious soldier. Addie was in Paradise now, perhaps reunited with some long-lost love. The truth was, the only thing that marred the carefully-structured serenity of her life at St. Ursuline's was grief over the loss of a boy with the bluest of eyes. For weeks after her recovery, every night she would pull her curtain and curl herself into a tight ball on her bed, clutching her stomach, rife with the physical pain of losing him and the family she could have had. As the years passed the pain subsided, but she found herself lapsing more and more into daydreams of the meadow. *Oh, the meadow!* Jacob was always there, proffering fragrant flowers, flashing his wide grin with that dimple he despised and she loved, holding her hands, stroking her hair, building their house stone by stone with his magical words. And then the bells would ring and usher her back to her new life at the convent.

Never would she forget the sound of the bells! The wonderful bells were rung to wake the sleepy children, to call to worship, to eat, to class, to retire for the evening. Much later, far from home in New York, when she was in a desperate moment in the hospital or feeling lonely and lost at night, she would close her eyes and listen for the bells, and they would comfort her.

The sisters had recognized her intelligence immediately, and a first-rate education was hers for the taking. By her fifteenth birthday she had read every book in the sizable library, and the nuns had sent for more, especially medical texts. They nurtured her love for learning, and she blossomed under their tutelage, many of them very learned women. Finally, at the age of seventeen, they realized that they had taken her as far as they could, and they arranged to send her to Ithaca, New York, to the esteemed Cornell University, boasting the best medical preparatory course in the country, enrolling her under her own name but giving no indication of her sex. "The rest is up to you, my love," Sister Anna had whispered through uncharacteristic tears on that fateful day when Bailey boarded the train.

She would never forget that trip, that terrifying train ride that took a frightened young teenager in the opposite direction of where she was headed now. She had cried for the first three hours, face buried in her hands, not wanting to look out the window to see Texas disappear. The train had been full, and her seatmate and the passengers across from her were extremely distressed, not knowing what should be done for this distraught young woman who was all alone. Finally her seatmate, a gnarled old cowman named Joe Blank, had ordered her a whiskey. She had spent the next three days in a state of mild intoxication and general hilarity as Joe recalled his life on the range in the funniest collection of stories Bailey had ever heard. When she confided in him that she was going off to college to become a doctor, he hadn't even batted an eye. She had admitted that she was terrified of failing, and he had nodded wisely. "Well, of course ya are, Miss Rose. Yes ma'am, and you just go and get it done, simple as that. I been scared a'plenty in my life, but there's no use in hesitatin'. Just go on ahead and do it, and the fear will go away when it's time."

She had given him a fierce hug at the end of her journey and told him that she loved him, which brought a tear to his eye, and she had never seen him again. But she had never forgotten those words of advice. They bore her through many spirit-breaking days, the first of which was the day she stepped through the doors of Cornell to register and was told in no uncertain terms that she would *not* pursue a degree in medicine unless she was to be a nurse. "I would like to see the rule in the handbook that bars me the choice of my course of study," she had said sweetly, and the next week she had begun her educational career in medicine.

All of her life she had been surrounded by and raised by women; first by the women of Fort Allen, then by the nuns at St. Ursuline's. The only man she had ever really known was Mr. Naplava, and she never had the chance to know him well. The first day she walked into the lecture hall, ready to delve into Anatomy 100, seventy-five young men turned around to stare. They had not risen to their feet, booed, or clapped; they had simply given her a collective icy stare. She felt her face flame, not just with anger and embarrassment, but with a crushing disappointment that this was the way things were to be.

Of course things did not stay that way. She met their disdain with frankness and a friendly challenge, giving as good as she got. In six weeks she had won them over, and she had seventy-five champions ready to meet her every need. And if they had doubted that this beautiful young girl, a member of the sex which obviously possessed an inferior brain, could complete the rigorous medical course, their prejudices were quickly destroyed as Bailey outstripped them all, finishing the four year course of study in three years, at the very top of her class.

As difficult as that time had been, in retrospect, it had been the easy part.

For now came the real test: was she just an academic, accomplished in memorizing pages of text, or could she apply what she had learned to an actual human body? The three years at the Woman's Medical College of the New York Infirmary for Women and Children were an utter blur to Bailey. The pace was unbelievably hectic. At night, if she was lucky, she could collapse for two or three hours on her cot in the small room she shared with two other women doctors. More often than not, they were awakened by a fierce pounding on the door in the wee hours of the morning to attend to the latest emergency. Bailey assisted in splinting broken bones, stitching wounds, and delivering babies on the good days and tended to terminal patients in their last throes of illness on the bad days. And besides this there was the grueling coursework, which put a halt to the careers of many of her peers. At the end of four years she emerged exhausted and triumphant, Dr. B. Rose.

One by one her women colleagues, few that there were, took internship positions in the various women's hospitals across the east, and urged her to do the same. Bailey would have none of it. The two year internship was crucial to any doctor, and she wanted nothing but the best of instruction that a general hospital could give. She applied to six hospitals and was categorically refused by all of them. In desperation she appealed to Bellevue; it was here that she had done bedside training. Couldn't they consider her for an internship? The head of the board, Mr. James Thomas, had a daughter who was interested in the field of medicine, and he took pity on the young woman whose chances of securing an internship were disappearing with each passing day. She sat for the admissions quiz and finished in first place, and Mr. Thomas appointed her to Gouverneur Hospital, an emergency branch of Bellevue located in the most populous part of the teeming city. Only Gouverneur had an extra room in which she could sleep; Bellevue refused to provide such an accommodation.

Thus began the worst, and the best, two years of her life thus far. The nurses resented working under a woman and refused to acknowledge her as a doctor. Any orders that she gave a nurse were either ignored or carried out with scathing remarks. The interns who were her immediate superiors set out at once to discredit and embarrass her. She would never, for the rest of her life, forget her first day at Gouverneur.

The day began pleasantly enough; she sat through a breakfast meeting with the other four new interns—all male, of course—the hospital board, and the chief of staff, Dr. Harvey Brickle. After a sumptuous fare the men were introduced first, Dr. Brickle praising their efforts in medical school and their performance on the admissions quiz. And then there was a silence as his eyes roamed over Bailey, very slowly and with deliberation.

"And here we have Dr. Bailey Rose, our, eh, fifth new intern this year. I will have it understood that Dr. Rose will be subject to every standard that we expect from our male doctors. She will not be coddled or given any extra assistance in any form whatsoever, is that understood?" No mention of her superior performance on the admissions quiz, of her college and medical school marks which far outpaced the other interns. There was a heavy silence as he stared icily at her, and she began to burn with a clean, hot anger as the silence stretched on. Was he expecting her to say 'yes sir' like a meek little Polly? How dare he lecture her on standards while his eyes could barely make it above the level of her chest!

"I would like the other interns to know that *I* would be glad to assist *them* at any time they need." Three of the four interns glanced knowingly at each other and grinned. They had been classmates at Cornell and had spent many nights in the library being instructed by the brilliant young woman.

Dr. Brickle flushed a deep red, cleared his throat, and moved quickly on to the rules of the hospital and the duties to which they would be assigned. Mr. Thomas had given her a reassuring wink, but Bailey knew that her fate had been sealed. When would she learn to keep her big mouth shut? She had made a powerful enemy today, and she was sure that she would pay.

And pay she did. For the first three months of her first precious year, the one year she had to learn general medicine, she emptied bedpans, cleaned up vomit, and bathed drug addicts, most of whom were men who seemed to have ten hands. She was called every foul name imaginable; she was groped every time a desperate hand managed to get free. Every intern was responsible for the condition of the patients and rooms of which he or she was in charge, and since the nurses for the most part refused to carry out their duties for her, she was left to do the nursing as well as her own duties as the doctor. While her four peers learned crucial diagnosis and treatment skills of a wide variety of illness and injury, she was given every drug addict who darkened the door. As she became a master at restraining patients during withdrawal and cleaning up the ungodly, inevitable mess, the other interns lunched with their superiors and discussed the latest fascinating case in pediatrics, obstetrics, and especially the growing acceptance of Lister's theory of antisepsis. While her fellow doctors reveled in the gratification of healing a patient, she often sent an addict out the door clean, only to tend to him or her the very next week. It was disheartening and debasing, but she tended to her patients with the utmost of respect and loving care, uncomplainingly doing both the nurses' jobs and her own. She began to counsel her patients, candidly recalling her own memories of her mother, boosting their self-confidence, even helping them to find little jobs around the city. Once in a great while a former patient would visit her, clean and sober and reformed, and her resolve would strengthen. If these were the patients they would give her, she would give them the best medical care in the city!

But her resolve began to crumble one dark dreary day. Ben Sardi, a fellow intern, had invited her to dinner on a rare free evening for both of them, and she had accepted despite the great risk. If she was caught keeping company with *any* man, not to mention a fellow intern, she would be summarily dismissed. But she was lonely and attracted to Ben, a thin, witty, intellectual type with curly blond hair, sparkling eyes and thick spectacles that somehow added to his appeal. He had taken her to Twelve Nights, an expensive yet unpretentious dining establishment on the east side, and once they were comfortably fed, the discussion turned inevitably to the hospital and medicine in general. Ben enthusiastically launched into a story of a five-year-old boy who had come into the hospital with difficulty in breathing, and as he delved deeper into the details, Bailey found herself growing intensely jealous. Never had she had a challenging diagnosis, let alone being able to work in pediatrics!

"So what would you have done, Bail?" He finished the description and waited expectantly for what he supposed would be a brilliant answer. Instead, his companion burst into tears.

"Oh, Ben! I'm so sorry. I don't mean to complain, but the only patients I've had have been addicts and drunks. They're cheating me, Ben. I'm not learning the things I need to learn to be a doc-doctor." This last was gasped out in a sob.

Ben hurried around the table and offered a handkerchief, wanting very much to gather her in his arms, but knowing better. "Here, Bail, dry up, old girl. Listen. You've got to go to Dr. Brickle and put it on the line. Or better yet, go to James Thomas. He seems to be on your side."

"I can't go to Mr. Thomas. He expects me to fight my own battles, and I don't want Dr. Brickle to think I'm running like a helpless female to the board director because I can't handle my job."

"It's not that way at all!"

"I know that. You know that. But that's what Brickle will say, and I'll be dismissed. I've got to talk to Brickle myself." She straightened and handed back the soggy handkerchief.

"Maybe you could reason with him. Just tell him what you told me and appeal to his decency." Ben moved back to his side of the table reluctantly.

"Decency? That's a good one, Ben. That man has no decency when it comes to me. But I'll make him see reason, all right. I've just got to negotiate from a position of strength, not weakness. That's the only way I'll win."

Ben stared at her blankly. "You lost me."

She managed a bright smile. "I can't ask him for anything. I've got to put him in a position in which he'll be forced to be fair." The young man looked skeptical and opened his mouth to argue. Bailey held up one hand. "Don't worry. Are you finished? Come on, let's go for a walk before I have to return to my lovely charges."

It took her two weeks, but she practiced her speech in front of her tiny mirror every night until she could say it without sounding pleading or vindictive or angry. She made a visit to *The New York Sun* and struck a deal with an eager young reporter hungry for a story. It took another two weeks for Brickle to agree to see her, although with the other interns he seemed to have an open door policy.

No sooner was she seated in front of his massive desk than he began the staring routine. No words; just an unbroken, hostile stare, with a repugnant sexual undertone as his gaze drifted south. Bailey smiled back distantly, reigning in her anger. She knew that he assumed she would remain silent until asked to speak, but it just wasn't in her nature. She took a deep breath and began.

"Good morning, Dr. Brickle. Thank you for taking time in your busy schedule to see me." She paused, giving him one last chance to redeem himself as a polite professional. He continued to stare. She sighed inwardly, determined to proceed without giving him any more opportunities to open his fool mouth to speak.

"My reason for requesting this meeting is twofold. Firstly, I would like to thank you for the wonderful opportunity you have given me to learn from the amazing doctors in this institution. As you know, the city is watching to see if the lady doctor will emerge from this internship victorious or beaten. And it couldn't have been possible without you." *You pompous bastard. It could be very possible if it* wasn't *for you.*

She sat up straighter and continued without pause. "Secondly, as a tribute to this hospital and to you and your staff, and in appreciation for the fine opportunity you have given me, I have contracted to write a series of articles for *The New York Sun* describing in detail the experiences I am having. I will be describing the type of patients that I am assigned, what my duties are with these patients, and in general, everything I am learning under your tutelage. The public, including others in the medical profession as well as our own board and trustees, will be able to see for themselves how an intern is trained and how I am being given no inferior or superior special treatment. And for your fine institution, as much free publicity as you can imagine!" At last Bailey paused, satisfied to see the red blotches streaking Brickle's neck. He appeared to have quit breathing and was now staring at her with an entirely different expression: one of fear, and perhaps a little loathing before he disguised it carefully under an icy smile. It was Bailey's turn to stare as she waited for his response, and she did so magnificently, unblinking. Minutes passed.

Brickle finally leaned back in his chair, fighting for composure, stalling for time until he could figure out how to respond to this brilliant sneak attack cloaked in false gratitude. "Well, Miss—er—Dr. Rose. Thank you for the kind words and for the opportunity to show the city what a fine medical establishment I am running here." He choked to a stop, unable now to meet her eyes. It was for the best, for a huge smile was spreading over Bailey's face. She had done it!

She waited a few more seconds as Brickle gazed at his desk, and then she stood and offered her hand. "You're quite welcome, Dr. Brickle. You can't imagine how pleasurable it was to be able to do this for Gouvernour."

He rose and shook her hand quickly and wetly, abruptly turning his back to her to shuffle through some charts. He quite conspicuously wiped his hand on his trousers, as if to rid himself of all traces of her.

Everything changed from that day forward. She became an intern that day instead of a glorified nurse, and thrived with the challenge and the camaraderie of her fellow interns. One year of general medicine, one year of general surgery, and three months of ambulance duty flew by, one month blending into the next, seasons turning without her noticing. Her column in the *Sun* was hugely popular, and she was gratified to see more females applying to medical schools and internships than ever before. And the icing on the cake: at the end of her internship, Mr. Thomas asked her personally to stay on at Gouverneur, to be a permanent doctor, in charge of training interns. And she had turned it down.

She had turned it down! Regret weighed heavily upon her as San Antonio drew closer, with all of its haunting memories, replete with pain and neglect. Why on earth was she coming back here? She couldn't explain it to herself; it was just a certainty that this was where she belonged. In the city, *her* city, where her mother died trying to save her daughter from becoming the shell of a woman that her mother was. Where fatherless, unwanted children like Gabriella and Bailey herself roamed the streets while their mothers worked themselves to exhaustion, then drugged themselves to forget the pain. As far as she knew, there was no medical care for these lost souls, no Gouverneur Hospital even to go to when ill or pregnant or injured. Had any of the girls at Fort Allen ever gone to a doctor? The St. Rosa Hospital was near to the Red Light District, operated by the Sisters of Charity of the Incarnate Word, but as far as she knew, no working girl ever stepped foot into that place. Only the pharmacist with his false promises and murderous drugs and alcohol sold as "medicine" was available to the women, even when they had been beaten or were sick with syphilis or other occupational hazards. And how was she to survive caring for those who couldn't pay? And would they come to her anyway, a woman who still looked to be eighteen despite her old-maidish twenty-six years? Would they remember her, the daughter of a whore who had disappeared? Would anyone rent her a few rooms in which to live and set up her practice? Would she make friends; would she have someone to confide in now that she left her best friends behind?

With the thought of her friends, a fresh new wave of longing and self-pity washed over her. Ben had asked her to marry him. He had proposed sweetly, taking her in his arms and kissing her with all of the passion of youth, and she could not return his desire. His brown eyes, as dear as they were,

were not the color of a pristine, sparkling, summer sky and did not look directly into the middle of her being; his blond hair was lacking in color and did not flop over one eye; his nose was straight and perfect, with no slight bump to give it charm. It had been painful to turn him down, and she had done so with the utmost of gentleness and sincerity, but she did not love him. She was not sure she was capable of that emotion. She had felt it once, as a child, but that child was gone now, and the object of her childhood crush and her first kiss had grown up too; probably married to a perfect Moravian wife with five little Naplavas running around.

Jacob would be twenty-eight or twenty-nine now. *Jake.* How she had tried to forget his name, his face, his strong arms around her as they lay shivering by the creek. Almost unbearable was the bitterness of knowing that had events been otherwise, had she made different choices, she may have grown up as a member of that family: a daughter, a sister. She would have had big brothers to protect her, sisters to confide in. She would have helped Jacob build his house on the hill. She would have stood up with the bride at Jacob's wedding; she would have delivered Jacob's babies and been their godmother. A fine Moravian man would have asked her to marry him, maybe a cousin or a neighbor of the Naplavas, and the wedding would have been joyous. Jacob would have given her away, standing in for the father she had never known. *Or maybe, just maybe, she and Jacob…*but she never let the daydream wander too far in that direction, because true pain lay there, and utter regret.

She bit her lip and turned her face sharply toward the windows as the tears welled and escaped down her cheeks. To think of these things, to have regrets, would make her life miserable. She had to live for the present, just like Sister Anna had said.

With the thought of that name came the ringing of the bells, and Bailey knew just where she would go to begin her future as Dr. B. Rose.

CHAPTER TEN

"I'm sorry, my dear, but we just don't have the resources to help you. Have you tried securing a loan from a bank?" Sister Anna's lovingly familiar face was puckered in distress, two worry lines added to the host of other new wrinkles. They were seated in the convent garden to catch the coolness of the late evening breeze blowing in from the great river which flowed around the garden, separating the convent from the city, until it meandered west along the south side of the higher convent grounds to Convent Bridge at Augusta Street. Bailey had slipped off her hated shoes and jacket and was reveling in the sights and sounds and smells she had missed so dearly, especially the comforting rush of the river and the long pealing of the bells. Her head lolled lazily to the side to listen to Sister Anna, and she felt a stab of guilt for causing such consternation in her dearest friend.

"Oh, Sister! I'm not asking for money. Of course I'll seek a loan from the bank, but I'm not getting my hopes up too high. A bank lending money to a young single woman with no collateral, who has no home address?" She smiled at the thought and dug her toes into the soft grass.

"Well, whatever will you do? You can use this address as home, of course. Perhaps you should get a job for a few months until you have the money to get started." Sister Anna rose and paced in front of Bailey, wringing her hands.

"Sister, please, you're always trying to solve things for me. Everything will work out all right in the end. For now I just want to rest. Tomorrow is soon enough to begin my life!"

"I've got it!" Bailey jumped as Sister Anna threw up her hands and hooted with glee. "I know exactly who you should go to for help! Do you remember a man named Thomas Eckles? He's the reverend at St. Mark's

Episcopal. He was here more than a few times over the years, but I don't know that you ever met him."

Bailey experienced a sense of unreality. How she remembered him! He had been the only person, except for Jacob, who had tried to intervene in a little girl's life and make it better. And she had treated him shabbily, running away from him when he had tried to lead her away from a life of debasement. She hadn't thought of that gentle man in years.

"Um, no Sister, I never met him here, although I knew him once when I was a little girl, before St. Ursuline's." She elaborated no more, knowing that Sister would not question her about her past. In all her years at the convent, she had never confided the details of her childhood to anyone. All the nuns and Mother Superior knew was that she was raised in one of the high-class parlors and that she had run away to escape it.

"Well, what you probably don't know is that Reverend Eckles is a great humanitarian now, and a genius at fundraising. He takes in unwed mothers and is running a home for them—Harding House, it's called, after Candace Harding, a great benefactor—near to the church. I know that he would help you! Please let me send for him so you can talk with him tomorrow."

And so it was; the next morning Bailey found herself waiting in the dim, cool parlor to meet with a man she hadn't seen in almost twenty years. What would she say? How could she ask for help from a virtual stranger? He knew more about her past than did her precious Anna; would he be insulted that a woman like her would ask for help from a man of the cloth? She sat up straighter and fussed with her jacket, wondering again if she had managed to remove all of the travel dust and smell from her only professional costume. What did it matter? She would have to admit to him just how poor she was; all she owned were the clothes on her back, some simple working skirts and blouses from New York that had been bleached to get out ugly stains, and her medical books and supplies. And these were pathetically scarce! Whoever agreed to give her a start would have to stock her office if she was to be of any use to her patients. Perhaps Anna was right; she should get a job for a few years and save her money instead of begging for it from total strangers. But already she missed the healing process; the wonder she felt when she knew she was helping her patients and even saving lives. How much would she forget in two years?

She was startled by the two sets of footsteps in the vestibule. That would be Anna and Reverend Eckles. She couldn't do this! Damn this impossible situation! She just couldn't make herself beg for help. She rose and made for the door, hoping against hope that she could sneak out the front before they saw her.

"Oh, Bailey, sit down, child. This is Reverend Thomas Eckles, but then I believe you've already met. Reverend, this is Dr. Bailey Rose, our prize pupil and just come home from New York." Sister Anna beamed, utterly pleased with herself for introducing the two for more than just the reason she had given Bailey.

Thomas Eckles felt a fluttering sensation in his stomach as he stared at the pensive young woman standing in front of him. Here she was. Ever since Sister Anna had sent for him, he had been wondering what manner of adult the lost child from so many years ago had turned into. Of course he knew she was a doctor, certainly remarkable, but what had she experienced before being rescued by St. Ursuline? Did she fall to the same fate as her mother? Would she be rough and coarse and cynical, the story of her life written on the lines of her face, or the same elfin girl he remembered?

And here was the answer in front of him, a stunning young woman of average height—not the tiny young thing he remembered—with flawless skin and great dark eyes, a heavy twist of ginger hair gathered into a bun, curls springing from it, her full lips rounded into a surprised "O." She looked every bit the smart young professional, with no trace of the child he knew, at least none that he could detect in his first breathless assessment.

Bailey had expected a much older man, probably overweight with heavy jowls like all men of the cloth seemed to be. She imagined him to be stern and tall, with a disapproving eyebrow cocked at her. She had pictured a white-haired, righteous, imposing man of sixty, but now she could barely suppress a nervous giggle. What had she been thinking? The perspective of a child had placed him to be forty when she knew him, and now she could see that he must have been very young indeed when he had treated her so kindly so long ago. The man in front of her was just past forty in her estimation, and no bushy eyebrows or white hair was in evidence. He *was* very tall—she had gotten that much right—but his brown hair was only lightly touched with a distinguishing gray, and it curled boyishly over his collar in the back, as if he had no time for a haircut. He had the kindest eyes she had ever seen, brown and warm and tender, crinkled pleasantly at the corners. A pleasingly attractive man with a boyish grin, and he was looking at her with a healthy, respectful admiration on his handsome face. She felt a flutter of her own.

There was a long silence as the two assessed each other, adjusting the faulty pictures in their wondering minds, and tried to think of something to say. Thomas stood with a great silly smile and Bailey was frozen with the surprised "O" upon her lips.

Anna cleared her throat purposefully. "Reverend, Bailey, please take a seat. I'll go to fetch some tea while you two get acquainted all over again." She bustled them efficiently into the straight chairs sitting against the wall, and hurried out just as quickly, a satisfied smile upon her face.

Bailey groped for proper words. How on earth was she going to begin? "Well then, thank you so much for seeing me, Reverend Eckles."

"Thomas." He smiled at her cultured tones. She was so different from the girl he remembered!

"Oh! Well, Thomas, thank you for agreeing to see me. And you must call me Bailey."

"Oh no, after all of the years of hard work you've put in, nothing will do but Dr. Rose."

Bailey grinned appreciatively. "I must admit, that sounds wonderful." She stopped again, not knowing quite how to continue. Thomas helped her.

"Sister Anna tells me that you wish to set up a practice right here in the city."

"Yes! I really want to administer to those who have no other access to medical care. To be honest with you, I just don't know how to begin."

"Were you thinking of any district in particular?" Thomas felt acutely uncomfortable. How could he ask this fine young woman if she wanted to set up a practice for prostitutes and street children? Would she be offended with reference to a place with which she must be very familiar?

Bailey tipped back her head and laughed unaffectedly, although Thomas found himself very much affected. "Reverend Eckles, let's not pretend that I am a precious flower born and bred behind these beautiful walls. You and I both know where I come from. And that is precisely where I wish to return." He stared at her, entranced by her frankness and her approachability. "I want to set up right in the Red Light District, right in the middle where the women and any children or indigents can have easy access. The only trouble is, I don't have the resources to set up business, and I can't imagine how I'll stay in business once I begin. I know that those girls usually don't see a dime of the money they earn, and a madam will rarely send for a doctor, if ever." She paused to take a deep breath, realizing that she was babbling but unable to censure her words before this attentive, serious man. He really looked to be listening to her! Maybe Anna was right; since he was interested in much the same cause, perhaps he would find a way to help her.

But Thomas had a deeply concerned expression on his face. "Dr. Rose, you've been away for how many years? Eight or nine? Your city has changed much in the last decade. I'm sure you saw the changes for yourself on your journey from the train. It has grown *incredibly.*" He was interrupted by her forceful nod.

"Oh, I quite agree! I simply can't believe how big and sprawling San Antonio is now. It must be three times the size that I left it!"

"Well, *all* parts of the city have grown. Businesses, residential, market areas, and, um, entertainment." He cleared his throat uncomfortably and reached up to pull his right earlobe, a nervous habit he had developed as a child. Bailey found it endearing and tried to keep the smile from her face.

"What exactly are you trying to tell me, Reverend?"

"When you were here as a child, most of the vice activity was centered around Main and Military Plazas. The bawdy houses, around fifteen or so, were mostly located northeast of the Alamo, around Elm and Starr, to use Fort Allen as an example." He glanced at her, red in the face, and found her coolly nodding.

"I remember it well."

"That has all changed, Dr. Rose. Two years ago Mayor O'Malley convinced the city officials to lay out a new Red Light District, a *legal* one sanctioned by the very laws of this city. It was supposed to be very hush-hush, but word got around quickly. It's common knowledge now."

Bailey looked at him cynically, disbelief etched on her face. "You expect me to believe that the whorehouses are legal now? And that they are run by the city officials? I won't believe it!" She stopped to laugh at the very idea. "Surely you must be mistaken or you must be overstating. Officials have always patronized the houses, but that doesn't mean that they built them and legalized them!" She remembered the raids of her childhood well; she would invariably be well-hidden underneath the porch when the police arrived. Rather than being frightening, the raids were always comforting to her; at least *someone* knew what was going on in this house, and she couldn't help but to harbor the false hope that Fort Allen would be permanently closed and she and her mother would move on to a normal life. But after the heavy boots thumped into the house, the customers were chased away, and the women were dragged off to jail, the silence of the house was foreboding, waiting. It would only be a few hours before they all came back, and they were always back in business the very next evening, as if nothing had transpired at all. And even though every time a raid happened she knew it was only temporary, she was still relieved. There was a right and a wrong to the world, and it gave her some direction.

The reverend looked at her gravely until the smile died from her face. "That's exactly what I expect you to believe. Like I said, it's common knowledge. The public has remained amazingly quiet about it, the predominant justification being that as long as the city is controlling and regulating the district, it will be cleaner and safer. Even the churches remain quiet about it, although my own parishioners have been up in arms." He rose from the chair and stepped to the window, his back to her. The next part would be difficult to say. "The sad aspect of this, Dr. Rose, is the size of the district now. It covers no less than fifteen city blocks, south of Market Square at Dolorosa to Durango, from South Santa Rosa five blocks west to Frio, more or less. Have you heard of the Blue Book?" He turned to look at her then.

"No," she said numbly.

"It's a guide *printed by the city officials* with the names of all the houses, madams, and prostitutes. There are now ninety-eight houses."

She gasped then, the numbness replaced by a rapidly growing fury. She opened her mouth and shut it again, not knowing what to say. This couldn't be true!

Thomas returned to his chair and turned it to face her. "Can you imagine the decay this has wrought? The notion that the local government has fixed the problem by controlling it could be nothing further from the truth. My dear Dr. Rose, you thought to have to beg for patients; you will be turning them away! The rates of syphilis, gonorrhea, morphine, cocaine, alcohol, and opium addiction, suicide, homicide, and unwanted pregnancies, to name a few, are astronomical!" He sat back and rubbed both hands across his face in a gesture speaking of frustration, his face no longer gentle, but passionate and angry. "Sister Anna mentioned that my parish is operating a home for wayward girls. Not one of the girls we care for is free from one or more of the afflictions I have just mentioned. And we have eight babies in our nursery, all unwanted pregnancies, abandoned around the city or on our doorstep." He was pulling his earlobe again, a profoundly sad expression on his kind face.

The room was oppressively quiet, both the inhabitants deep in thought. Bailey was crushed. How foolish she was to have thought she could single-handedly change the squalid part of the city, of her own childhood. She had harbored fantasies of ministering to women like her mother, weaning them from the drugs and degradation of their lives, perhaps helping them to find honest, decent work. She had actually imagined that she could be the catalyst for a new era in this gorgeous city; a time of clean, industrious living, free from the abuses of the flesh. No more bawdy-houses, all thanks to Dr. Rose! And now to find that the district had grown like a cancer, spreading disease and filth across the city, fed by the sanctimonious city officials who sat in church with their families on Sundays, wearing their pious faces. The same officials who had lain with whores the night before, girls as young as the daughters sitting beside them in braids and bows, resplendent in their youth and wealth and innocence.

Her thoughts were interrupted by Sister Anna, who quietly entered bearing a tea tray. She took one look at the down-turned faces and knew where the conversation had led. "So he's told you, then. I'm so sorry, little Bailey. In many ways our city has grown wicked since you left."

"That much I could handle, Sister. But the fact that the men who govern our city are the very ones who work to destroy it! How is it that no one is outraged? How can no one be standing up and screaming against this *travesty*?" Her voice rose in anger and she thrust herself from the chair and began to pace. Thomas and Anna shared dubious glances. Bailey looked to be a woman on a mission, and they knew exactly where this was headed.

She stopped pacing suddenly and faced them. "I know what must be done. I will set up my practice just as I planned, with the Reverend's help, of course." Here she paused anxiously and looked at Thomas. "Oh, I beg your pardon! We didn't even discuss that yet!"

Thomas took in her determined stance, her flashing eyes, and her expressive face, and wondered if he would ever be able to tell her no, even if he wanted to. "Of course I'll help you, Dr. Rose. There is a druggist in our congregation who has extra rooms near his shop that would be the perfect size, and in the perfect location, too. And I'll propose an offertory to help you get stocked, and if my church disagrees, we'll go together to secure a loan. I know many bank officers around town." He basked in the glow of gratitude radiating from her face.

"Oh, thank you so much!" She came to him and gripped his hand tightly, pumping it like a man. He was surprised at the strength in her grip. He rather hoped that she would keep shaking his hand a while longer, but she twirled away as suddenly as she had approached him. She seemed energized by some brilliant force unknown to him.

"But just my practicing in the district is simply not enough. It's putting a small bandage on a great, gaping wound. The disease must be treated, not just the symptoms. We must go after these officials who pander to greed and their own sick perversions!" She stopped to take a breath and noticed that Anna was sadly shaking her head. "What? Why do you have that look on your face?"

Anna finished pouring and handed a fragrant cup to Thomas. "Bailey, as soon as you told me what kind of practice you wanted to have, I knew that you would want to get involved in the politics of the whole thing. But it's so much more complicated than that. You can't just waltz into city hall and challenge the mayor! These are powerful men, my dear. You wouldn't get halfway to the mayor's door before they'd show you out. It's been tried, by *men*, and nothing has changed! Why just last year a minister from—"

"Politics?" Bailey interrupted, feeling an uncharacteristic flash of impatience toward her friend. "This is not just politics! There are lives at stake here, *children's* lives!"

Anna put up both hands, palms out, in a defensive gesture. "I'm just trying to warn you. You had better think long and hard how you can best help those you say you wish to help. If you make the wrong enemies, you won't be practicing medicine anywhere in this city, and then where will those women and children be?" She picked up the tray and left the room abruptly, clicking her tongue, and Bailey couldn't help but smile through her frustration. Sister Anna was kind and gentle, but she had a temper much the same as Bailey herself. They had clashed many times over the years, but Bailey had never doubted her love.

She turned to Thomas and sat down again, disconsolate. "Well, what's your advice, Reverend? Am I being unreasonable?"

He smiled. "No, not at all. I would be worried if you weren't so adamant about this. It's a lot to digest all at one time, isn't it?" He rose and straightened his coat as if making to leave. "Why don't you concentrate on getting your practice up and running, and the rest will fall into place later if the good Lord so wills. Make a list of the supplies you'll need and I'll call again tomorrow afternoon and show you the rooms. Agreed?"

Bailey couldn't believe her luck and felt a tremendous rush of gratitude and affection for this man from her past. "Agreed! I don't know how to thank you!" She took his arm happily and walked him through the vestibule to the door.

"Don't thank me yet, Dr. Rose. You have had many rewarding experiences in New York, and I have no doubt that you left behind some golden opportunities. I venture to say that by the end of two weeks' time, you may be packing your bags and heading right back to that train."

Gabriella Flores picked up the brown paper packet of chalky pills and considered, certainly not for the first time, killing herself. The weight of the packet felt good in her hand; it was a comfort; an absolute, irrevocable answer to the utter misery of her life. She spilled a few of the pills into her open palm, imagining the bitterness in her throat, and then the sweetness of drifting off into an everlasting sleep.

Who would miss her? Her mother Maria was dead two years ago now, her beautiful body and sharp mind wasted away by syphilis. She had been utterly crazy in those last two months, drooling and wetting herself and crying and laughing uncontrollably. Her beloved brother Juan had been in prison for three years for the knifing death of a cowboy during a drunken bar room brawl. Her aunt and cousins had fled back to Mexico over twelve years ago, never to be heard from again. How she had wished at the time that they would have taken her, but she would have been one too many mouths to feed. She had no friends to weep over her body. The other girls would shake their heads sadly and fight over her room, the biggest and best boudoir in the Purple Pansy.

She used to have a friend. She popped two pills in her mouth and thought of Bailey Rose. She had loved and looked up to that fiercely brilliant little white girl from Fort Allen, who had a whore for a mother, just like Gabby did. They had lived on the streets together, sharing secrets and stolen food and teaching each other their languages. They had made a pact; they would get out of the city together, and they would never work in the bordellos. Gabriella snorted aloud at the memory and popped two more pills, washing them down with a glass of lukewarm water. Bailey had disappeared the night her mother had killed herself at the Gaslight Hotel. Nobody had ever claimed Addie's body, but everybody from the district knew who the slain woman was. And everybody knew that she had killed

Senator so he wouldn't prey on Bailey. The rumor was that Lola had sworn she had spoken to Bailey that night, and told her that Addie was at the hotel. What had happened to the little girl? It was as if she had been swallowed whole by that fancy hotel. Gabriella thought this over and popped another pill. She feared the worst. The girl had probably found a bloody scene and run away. Everyone knew what happened to little girls like that who tried to run away. She was most likely dead, or doing exactly what Gabriella was doing to survive, but in much worse conditions.

After Bailey had disappeared, Gabby's life had become a mundane blur. For three years she worked at odd jobs around the city: housekeeping at a dumpy "hotel," which had actually been nothing more than a ramshackle old house with a few rooms to rent. She had mucked out stables, operated a chili stand, and even sold newspapers with her little brother. The money she made was barely enough to feed the two of them, and even though Maria had always made sure they had a tiny room to sleep in at night, she had stopped regularly feeding them long ago. She was lucky to hang onto her job with two small children, two signs of her carelessness. Gabby, of course, had no idea who her father was. She assumed he had been white because Gabby's skin was a few shades lighter than her mother's and her eyes were blue-green, although her features were classically Mexican; her sensuous lips and the very shape of her face spoke of her heritage. Juan was much darker than she was, with kinky black hair, and she had often wondered if his father was Negro. But it really didn't matter; it did no good to speculate. Maria had no way of knowing who had fathered her children. The women at the Purple Pansy, on the average, turned over five customers a night, unless the men paid for extra time. Only the most desirable of the ladies were bought for extra time, and sometimes she spent the whole evening with only one or two men, a luxury indeed.

The night she was inducted into the ranks of the Pansy would burn in her memory for all time. Her mother was no fool; she knew if she talked to Gabriella about it before-hand, the girl would run away or kill herself, being the melodramatic and emotional young woman she was. It had been her fifteenth birthday, traditionally the biggest and most important day in the life of a Mexican girl. She should have been having her *quincañera* on this day, a coming of age party for Latin girls. She should have begun the day with a church service, in which the officials formally presented her to the adult members of the community. After a grand feast, the *baile* should have taken place, a dance in which her father danced with her first, thereby introducing her to her peers as an adult. The dance and party should have lasted all night, far into the morning, and she should have been showered with gifts and money and familial love. It should have been the happiest day of her life. *Should have been.*

Instead, she had worked all day in a chili stand, finally turning it over to the next chili queen for the night shift, and dragged herself home. It had been a terrible day; she had earned next to nothing. She hoped Juan had done better, because she'd never be able to feed him on her paltry coins, let alone herself. All she wanted to do was to lie down and sleep. But it was not to be; her mother had met her at the door, an unusual event to say the least, and had led her up the stairs to a large room with a four poster bed with a dark red velvet canopy, a chair, a washstand, and pretty lace at the windows.

"This room will be yours, my love, starting tonight. It's time that you learned your trade and earned a living." And her mother had begun brushing Gabby's hair lovingly, and had brought forth a gown to be tried on. It was quite lovely, the color of buttercup yellow. Her favorite color. Gabriella had sat stiffly, numbly, fighting a hysterical laugh. She had known this day would come, and today of all days, she had realized that she'd never be able to survive on the odd jobs that she worked at. And wasn't this who she was? There was nothing else for her to do. She was uneducated, never having gone to school a day in her life. She knew no skilled trade; there was no one who would teach her. She was not white. Here she would be taken care of; every need would be met by Madame Kendra, a basically kind woman compared to some of the others. She would be fed and clothed and housed, and although she would never see a dime of the money she earned (unless the johns tipped her privately), the food was famously delicious and plentiful. She would have no trouble feeding Juan, now eleven years old and growing like a weed. If she kept odd little jobs, maybe a good housekeeping job for a wealthy family, she could make enough to send Juan to school or to be apprenticed.

And so it was with only half of her brain did she listen to her mother's instructions. Ask the man what he likes. If he doesn't speak Spanish, sit him on the bed and stand before him and undress provocatively. Did she know how the sex worked? Gabby finally had to laugh at this point. She lived in a whore house and her mother wondered if she knew about sex? Was she a virgin? She stopped laughing. She was, and how she wished that she had let her cousin's friend Diego make love to her last year. He had been in love with her, sick in love, and she had held him at arm's length. Now everyone would know she was a virgin, because she would bring a huge price tonight. Yes, she would be introduced to her peers as an adult. For sale.

That night she had been instructed to wait in her room. For this first time only, the man would be hand-picked, probably by her mother. For the rest of her career she'd have to find her own johns in the parlor below. She sat on the bed, her hair a beautiful nest of curls, her buttercup dress arranged just so. She let herself imagine, for just one magical moment, that she was waiting for her father to come escort her to her *quinciñera* dance. She would dance all night, and maybe receive her first kiss from a handsome young Mexican man. She had never been kissed.

Her stomach churned. Her palms began to sweat. She suppressed great, heaving sobs that wanted so badly to surface and give voice to her pain. *I'm still a little girl!* She wanted to scream it out the window. She bowed her head and said a quick prayer, even though she didn't know how. *Please, God, don't let it hurt. Make something wonderful happen so I don't have to.*

That's when the door opened. She didn't want to look up, didn't want this life to begin, but her head snapped up anyway. Maybe it was the miracle she had just prayed for.

It was no miracle. It was a tall white man dressed like a dandy, and he brought the smell of his importance in with him: sickening, powerful cologne. He was about thirty or so, with dark brown hair and whiskers and shifty, close-set eyes. He was powerful looking, and not a nice young man, like she had hoped. Not a dashing young man that would say, "Come with me, beautiful child. Let's get married and we'll live in my mansion." This man said nothing. He sat on the chair in the corner and made gestures telling her to get undressed, and then crossed his arms and watched her speculatively, as if judging a cow at an auction.

She rose, shaking, and reached behind her to unbutton her dress. The tears began to flow. She couldn't help it; she tried so hard to hold them back. How ridiculous and wrong she felt! Here she was, undressing in front of a *stranger*; she, who had never let any man see or touch her body. It was beyond comprehension to think that in a few moments, this man would shed his clothes, too, and they would lie on this bed, and his hands would be all over her, and maybe he would want her hands on him, and then he would push himself inside her. Her stomach recoiled and she felt as if she was going to retch.

She stood before him in her shift, and he came toward her. She ordered her legs to run, her mouth to open and her throat to scream, but she was paralyzed. He pulled the shift over her head, and she was naked.

And so it began. He had kept her for two hours, unusual on a normal night, but for the price of a virgin, extra time came with it. When he first touched her, she bit her lip savagely to keep from screaming. He had bedded her quickly, fallen asleep for thirty minutes with her pinned underneath, and then woken up and started the whole process again.

In retrospect, the man was gentle and quite harmless compared to some of the monsters she had spent moments with. He had expected only the basic deed, with a minimum of touching and no kissing at all. But that night, after the man had left and she had bathed like her mother told her, she gathered the sheets and was mesmerized by the blood. Amazingly, the tears were gone, the fear was gone, and something that couldn't be named was gone, and in its stead was a void, a vast blankness. She knew where it had gone; it was in the blood on those white sheets, and so she crumpled them up and shoved them under the bed. Later she burnt them, and after that, everything was easier, automatic. She never, never allowed a john to kiss her. She was twenty-eight years old, and had never been kissed.

She was so unspeakably tired. Twelve years ago was a lifetime, and she barely remembered the girl in the buttercup dress who had lived before the shell that she was now. Her reasons for wanting to leave now were different, not inspired by fear or even revulsion. She was simply exhausted.

She removed her filthy apron with a groan. She had been working for twenty-two hours straight; first at the Purple Pansy, then at the shabby little dining establishment on the south edge of town as a cook for fourteen hours. She had to tell many lies to explain to Kendra why she was gone so much, but for a while it had been worth it. She really was saving a lot of money, and for one or two glorious moments out of each day, she actually thought she'd be able to earn her way out of the Pansy. She even had a plan; she was headed for the east coast, maybe Boston, the land of ladies and gentlemen and cool ocean breezes. She was going to open a restaurant of her own, serving genuine Mexican fare, which would surely be a novelty there.

But those plans were all for naught; she had been fired from the restaurant today, her first offense being thirty minutes late. Her last john at the Pansy was voracious; stone cold sober and insatiable, and had not wanted to leave her, and since he had paid Kendra for three hours, Gabby couldn't make him go. And he had been rough. It had taken a while for her to clean up, and by the time she got to Benvito's, she was used up, besides being late. She had been up all night, and the thought of facing fourteen more hours made her sluggish and grouchy. She had made it through the day, but as she was getting ready to leave, Benvito had slapped her pay for the day in her hand and told her never to come back. She was too tired to argue.

She had spent a few precious coins on the pills in her hand. How many had she taken now? Four or five? What was stopping her from taking the rest? What could she possibly care so much about in her miserable life that she couldn't just swallow the packet and lay back and rest?

She remembered then, through a drugged haze of fatigue. She lay on the bed, on the crisp, clean sheets that she scrupulously washed and bleached every day, and stroked her belly, once flat and firm, now beginning to puff a little. *My baby...*

CHAPTER ELEVEN

Time, it seemed, had come to a standstill. Bailey sat immobilized in a stiff wooden waiting room chair, a white-knuckled death grip on the seat, staring at the clock. *Tick, tick, tick, tick.* 12:13 pm on the opening day of her new clinic. She had chosen a Tuesday in mid-March to open the clinic, and now she was wondering if she should have aimed for a Saturday instead. Exactly thirteen minutes past the opening hour! Where were the patients? She had taken out advertisements in the newspapers, handed out flyers, and with Thomas' help, spread the word in the Red Light District. She thought that patients would be stampeding the door, but here she and Thomas sat in a tense silence, punctuated only by the clicking knitting needles of Rachel, a kindly old lady from Thomas's congregation who had volunteered to be the receptionist.

Thomas—they were on a first-name basis now—had been extraordinary as Bailey struggled to open the Rose Clinic for Women and Children. He had begun with a collection taken at his church, one that yielded an amazing amount of money; he was able to fully furnish and stock the clinic. Chairs for the waiting room, two tables for the examination room, cabinets full of medicinal supplies and equipment. Bailey had cried with relief after she and Thomas had finished stocking the office and arranging the furniture; she couldn't believe that her dream of being a doctor in the Red Light District was about to come true. The funding was a little *too* amazing, and Bailey recalled their conversation with a mix of exasperation and affection.

"Thomas, you know how grateful I am, and I honestly don't mean to pry…"

"Then don't, and just thank the good Lord for these blessings that are allowing you to open your clinic."

"Thomas?"

"Hmmm?"

"Where did the money come from?"

"Are you sure the exam table wouldn't better fit over here against this wall? That way you'll get the light from the window…"

She had finally given up, realizing that Thomas, for all of his gentle, sweet, and seemingly innocent qualities, was not a nut that was easily cracked.

Although at this moment, Thomas did indeed look as though he was ready to crack. "I'm going to check the street," he muttered inanely, and slid his six foot four inch frame from his chair with exaggerated nonchalance. He exited and Bailey watched him stroll one way down the street and then retrace his steps to patrol the other way, glancing nervously left and right. She exchanged a wry glance with Rachel.

"My dear, you may have to administer a sedative to our beloved reverend," Rachel murmured. "He looks as though he will jump out of his skin."

Bailey forced a laugh and gripped her chair more tightly. "Yes, I wish he would just relax," she squeaked. Her eyes followed Thomas as he re-entered the clinic, triggering the bright new brass bell hung above the door.

"I see no patients as of yet," he reported solemnly, and this time Bailey's laugh was genuine.

"Oh, Thomas, sit down and read a book or work a puzzle or write a sermon or something!"

Thomas took his seat with an apologetic grin and the silent waiting resumed. Ten more long moments passed before a young dark-haired woman approached the clinic and opened the door. Bailey and Thomas shot to their feet in unison as the bell chimed, both rushing toward the door.

"Good afternoon! We are glad to see you today!" Bailey tripped and just managed to regain her footing inches away from the shrinking woman.

"Come in, my good woman! Let me show you to our reception desk! Right this way!" Thomas shook the woman's hand as though he were priming a pump.

The startled woman took two cautious steps back, glancing at the door speculatively. She was ready to bolt. Rachel put her knitting aside calmly and cleared her throat.

"Dr. Bailey, why don't you ready the examination room? Reverend Eckles, I believe that your Bible Study group is scheduled to begin in fifteen minutes; perhaps you ought to start for the church?" Bailey hesitated a beat, then nodded woodenly and headed for the examination room, heart pounding with anticipation. Thomas opened his mouth and stammered, then bid the ladies good day and headed for the door, looking nervously back over his shoulder.

Bailey closed the door softly behind her and danced a wild, exuberant jig around the small room. Her first patient! It was going to happen: after years and years of dreaming, of back-breaking work, of sacrifice and self-doubts, she was finally Dr. Rose, with her very own practice! She barely restrained a joyful *whoop* before Rachel slid open the small peek-a-boo panel between the waiting room and the examination room and gave her a reassuring smile. "Are you ready?" she asked quietly. Bailey nodded and Rachel slid the panel shut again. She took a deep breath, smoothed her white smock, and opened the door. She accepted the chart from Rachel and smiled at the patient.

"Hello, welcome. My name is Dr. Rose. Won't you sit down?"

The homely young woman nervously took a seat in one of the two chairs.

"So you are Lizzy Carter?"

The woman nodded miserably.

"Well, Lizzy, let's start with some basics…" Bailey began to take a thorough medical history, her hands shaking a bit with excitement as she made detailed notes in the chart. Lizzy tapped her foot nervously on the floor and chewed her fingernails to the pink. She was a pale, unattractive young woman with limp brown hair, slightly-crossed eyes that never stopped darting, and a mournful countenance.

"Now, what brings you here today?" Bailey finally asked.

"Well, this is a private matter…" the nervous woman hedged.

Bailey leaned forward with a smile. "I assure you that all information that you give me will be kept in the strictest confidence, Mrs. Carter."

Lizzy smirked at the formal address. "Oh, it ain't no missus, Doctor."

Bailey waited patiently.

"Well, I've been having a problem after I conduct my business," the patient finally blurted.

Bailey's pen paused over the chart. Her business? Was she talking about the business of sex, or the business of using the restroom? She was horrified to discover that a nervous giggle was building.

"Go on," she managed.

"Yes, well, I bleed after business."

Bailey waited, hoping and praying the woman would clarify her statement, but no further information was forthcoming.

"Ms. Carter, by 'business' are you referring to sexual relations?" Bailey finally said.

Lizzy stared incredulously at Bailey. "Well, I ain't talkin' about *banking*."

Bailey turned and pretended to cough, hiding a huff of laughter. What on earth was wrong with her? She was acting as though she had never seen a patient before! She gave herself a mental shake and turned to the patient again. Time to start acting like a doctor! "So you are experiencing bleeding after intercourse?"

The woman nodded.

"Any other symptoms?"

"Well, I seem to spend the better part of the day runnin' to the toilet, you know, making water, and it burns."

Bailey made some more notes on the chart, rose from her chair, and straightened the sheet on the examination table. "Ms. Carter, I will need to perform a pelvic examination at this point to confirm a diagnosis. Please remove your clothing from the waist down and cover yourself with this blanket, and I will return momentarily to conduct the exam." Bailey moved to wait in her tiny private office that was connected to the examination room, but was stopped by Lizzy's indignant huff.

"What? You mean you want to look at my privates?" The young woman was scowling but looked strangely vulnerable at the same time, her hands nervously working a handkerchief with a pink embroidered "L." Bailey felt a surge of compassion for her. To Lizzy, exposing herself to strange men every evening had become routine; normalized by the setting and by the circumstances of her life. To expose herself in a doctor's office, however, was almost incomprehensible.

Bailey turned, summoning her patience and remembering lessons from her residency. This scenario was familiar; patients had often expressed fear upon being examined for a sexually-transmitted disease, especially by a woman doctor, and they often refused outright. "Ms. Carter, please understand that your condition is serious, and I cannot possibly make a diagnosis without examining you. Surely you do not wish to keep suffering?" She smiled gently and let that sink in a moment, then turned and entered her office, shutting her door behind her with a soft click.

Twenty minutes later the examination was complete. Lizzy Carter had early-stage gonorrhea, a common ailment among prostitutes, and Bailey carefully gathered the prescriptions. "Now Ms. Carter, I am prescribing one ounce each of the liquids in these bottles: spirits of nitric ether, balsam copaiba and camphor tincture opii, and one draught of veratrum viride. Mix these together in a spoon and drink it four times a day, for the next ten days. Please avoid meats of all kinds, fats, tea, coffee, and absolutely no alcohol or tobacco. Take a hip-bath two or three times a day. And Ms. Carter, there is to be no *business* for the next ten days, until I see you again and give you the all-clear. I have written these instructions down for you. Is everything clear?"

Lizzy stared at Bailey, mouth agape. There was an uncomfortable silence. Finally the woman rose. "Did you say no business for ten days?"

"Yes, I did, and I need to see you again at that time. If you are not cured, we will commence with a different treatment plan, possibly injections. Please stop by the receptionist as you take your leave, and she will arrange the appointment."

Lizzy stood open-mouthed for a few more seconds, finally shuffling toward the door. She turned before opening it. "You know, Dr. Rose, I heard that you grew up at Fort Allen."

Bailey smiled guardedly. "Yes, that is correct. My mother worked there."

"Then you must know the rules of the house. The madam won't take kindly to a girl off work for ten days. Isn't there something else to be done?" Tears began to form in her narrowed eyes, and for the first time, Bailey wondered if her listed age of twenty-two was an exaggeration. If she was a well-established girl in her house, one who regularly brought in a handsome amount of cash, the madam would not blink an eye at a ten-day hiatus, recognizing the importance of the house maintaining a disease-free reputation. On the other hand, if Lizzy worked in a derelict cat house, she could very well find herself on the street, and judging by her appearance and clothing, this was most likely the case.

"Ms. Carter, you must stick to this treatment plan. If you are put out of your house, please come back here and I will introduce you to Revered Thomas Eckles. He has established a house of refuge for working girls who are ready to make a new start."

For a moment there looked to be a glimmer of hope in Lizzy's eyes, but it was quickly replaced by a cynical sneer. "I don't need a new start—I make plenty of money as it is. I'll be back in ten days." She left abruptly without a thank-you, and Bailey's scalp tightened with anger. Why wouldn't someone trapped in such a life jump at the opportunity to escape it? She washed up thoroughly, carefully changing the sheets and sanitizing equipment while mulling that over. She fell back on the one thought that had kept her going as a resident: at least she had helped to cure this one woman today, perhaps making her life a bit more tolerable. She sighed; the way business had begun today (she chuckled at the word "business" and wondered if she would ever be able to use the word again in polite conversation), this may have been her only patient. She headed into the waiting room to chat with Rachel, and stopped dead in her tracks, dumbfounded.

Every one of the ten chairs was full, and three women were standing against the wall. Rachel smiled at her. "Dr. Rose? Are you ready to see the next patient?"

The next two weeks passed by in a blur. Bailey was thrilled with the success of her clinic; word had spread rapidly among the working women of San Antonio's famed Red Light District: there was a new doctor in town, a *woman* doctor, and her free clinic was exclusively for the women and children who populated the bawdy houses. Bailey had treated patients for sexually-transmitted disease, infections of all kinds, burns, cuts, and other injuries, drug addictions, influenza, breast cancer, uterine cancer, and pregnancy.

The women who presented with pregnancies were the most heartbreaking patients of all: they often assumed that the cessation of their menstrual cycle was caused by a disease of some sort, hoping against hope that they were not with child. Inevitably they requested an abortion, a procedure Bailey was unwilling to perform. She urged the patients to consider Harding House.

Nineteen women currently lived together there, supporting each other throughout their pregnancies and learning various trades and crafts from the womenfolk of St. Mark's Episcopal. The home was partially funded by the congregation but largely sustained by the efforts of the women themselves, who took on laundry, sewing, catering, tutoring, typing, and many other jobs, and shared cleaning and cooking chores. The home was a brilliant success so far, and Thomas was working feverishly with a lawyer to match families with the women who wished to have their babies adopted. Bailey had been successful in referring three of the seven women she had counseled; the remaining four flatly refused and threatened to visit one of the many notorious abortionists in the city. Bailey sent these women to Dr. Arnold Thorndike, a man she had gone out of her way to find and interview, a careful old doctor willing and qualified to perform abortions. These referrals left her with a heavy heart and made her more determined than ever to educate her patients about proper forms of birth control.

Bailey became an expert in black-market procurement of birth control devices. The Comstock Law prevented birth control from being sold on the open market, but Dr. Thorndike provided Bailey with contacts who kept her in good supply. She provided all of her patients with a hearty supply of condoms, urging them to require their clients to use them to prevent disease, but she was largely met with derision. *Have you lost your senses, Dr. Rose? No john is going to wear this thing.* She was more successful in teaching the women to use the womb veils, devices designed to cover the cervix. Her patients seemed to be much more invested in preventing pregnancy than disease.

The workday was exhausting: seven hours non-stop, with only Rachel and another woman from the church volunteering receptionist duties. Certain exams and procedures were nearly impossible to conduct without a nurse's help, and Bailey began to search for a full-time nurse. She had taken out an advertisement in the local newspaper, but this attempt had been a dismal failure; no one had applied, although she did receive a few pieces of hate mail. Dr. Thorndike advised her to hire a young girl and train her as an assistant, as he was in serious doubt that any trained nurses would take a position in the clinic, especially at the low wage that Bailey could offer, drawn from the contributions of Thomas's church.

It was the nagging thought of hiring a nurse and an overwhelming fatigue that followed Bailey home to St. Ursuline's on Friday evening of her fourth week. She forced the thought from her mind and thought of Thomas instead, smiling at the memory of him in church the past Sunday, urging the congregation to loosen their purse strings to continue funding of the Harding House and Rose Clinic. Bailey had been delighted with the name of her clinic, suggested by Thomas, and even allowed him to put up a sign, which featured a deep red rose between "Rose Clinic" and "For Women and Children." He had been such a friend to her, and had asked her two weeks ago to accompany him to dinner that evening. It didn't take much convincing; Bailey had grown to like Thomas more and more each day, appreciating his serious, gentle nature and his lanky, boyish features.

After Thomas had issued his invitation, she had reluctantly taken a small amount of clinic money, at Thomas's insistence, to buy one outfit suitable for going about the town. She had received the distinct impression that Thomas wanted her to dress like a proper lady in public, which simultaneously pleased and irritated her. For all of Thomas's kindness, he had an undeniable conservatism and heightened sense of Victorian propriety. The shopping trip had been a disaster, and not for the first time had she wished for a friend or a sister who could advise her about fashion. There were only a handful of dressmakers who had gowns ready-to-wear, and in every store she encountered the same thing: dresses consisting of incredibly tight bodices that required severe corseting, a practice that she loathed. "You must wear the corset to achieve the hourglass figure, Madam," the frowning shopkeepers had repeated as she squirmed during the fittings.

And the sleeves! How they aggravated and constricted her arms! Without fail, every dress she encountered featured sleeves that were tight around the arm, and even worse, at the top of the shoulder they had a small, vertical, puff. She tried a few on and had laughed out loud at her image in the store mirror—she looked like a pastry.

She had all but despaired when she happened upon a "sports dress" in a small mercantile store that sold everything from bicycles—which she eyed speculatively—to fishing rods. The dress was a pleasant indigo blue and featured ample, nicely draping skirts with hidden trousers and a belted blouse. When she tried it on, she had breathed an audible sigh of relief. It was attractive enough, she supposed, and certainly modest.

But back home at St. Ursuline's that afternoon, *sans* corset, she had experienced a twinge of apprehension as she gazed critically at her reflection in her bedroom mirror. What would Thomas think? It certainly wasn't dressy or smart, but she could breathe and fling her arms over her head if the occasion called for it. One never knew when one may need to fling up one's arms.

And then a bit of chaos ensued as she descended the staircase and paraded in front of Sister Anna.

"Well, how do you like it? Will it do?" she had asked anxiously, twirling around at the foot of the stairs leading up from the main foyer as Anna bit her lip and looked vaguely worried. Bailey's hair was a-fright, springing wildly from a hastily-structured bun at the nape of her neck and trailing down her back in incorrigible fiery curls.

"Well, dear, you *do* look comfortable, and that color is simply beautiful on you, but…"

And at that moment, Sister Margaret let Thomas into the foyer. Bailey swung around at his familiar voice and froze. Thomas was regarding her with a big smile. "Oh, hello, Bailey! I'm sorry to call on you without prior notice. I was just stopping by to see how the shopping trip went. It looks as though you found something serviceable for work; I'm so glad!"

Bailey felt the smile slide from her face. He wasn't going to like this, but he would be so painfully nice about it.

"Actually, this is the dress you asked me to purchase." Thomas cocked his head to the side and frowned a bit, the smile faltering.

"The dress? You mean for formal occasions?" His voice was somewhat strained, the smile pasted on his face.

There was a silence, and then the swishing sound of Sister Anna's and Sister Margaret's habits as they quietly left the room.

"Why, yes, for formal occasions. Do you not like it?" Bailey decided to play innocent and twirled a few times in front of him. "And look! It has trousers underneath!" She lifted the skirts to prove her point and Thomas looked quickly away, reddening.

He cleared his throat and tugged at his earlobe, a sure sign of distress. There was an awkward pause. "Yes, I like it, but—well, you see—I was hoping that you would perhaps purchase a formal gown with all of the—accompaniments that go with it." Thomas managed to look everywhere but at Bailey. Accompaniments? Was he referring to a *corset*? She bit her cheeks to keep from laughing.

Thomas rushed his next words. "You see, I was planning a bit of a special dinner, somewhat formal, and had hoped that you would accompany me there. I would be most honored," he finished miserably.

Bailey was embarrassed and began to regret her decision to buck the Victorian expectations of formal wear. Poor, kind, Thomas—he was really suffering, and she was being a brat, disappointing and confusing him to satisfy her own nonconformist bent.

"Oh, Thomas, I was just kidding with you. Of course this is for work. But I really don't know where to look for a nice gown, or what to buy. I really did try today." She tried to feel as contrite as she sounded, but it all felt a bit forced.

"I can help you with that! Mrs. Hannah Birchwood is a dear friend of the church, about your age, and I just know she would be delighted to help you find the perfect thing."

And so it was: Bailey closed the clinic early the next day and set forth with the chatterbox Mrs. Hannah Birchwood to find the perfect frock for her evening with San Antonio's elite. It had been an exhausting afternoon, Hannah whisking her into shop after shop, Bailey pretending to be fascinated with all of the styles while she secretly longed to dip her feet into the river and then go have lunch at the chili stands. Pointed corsages, butterfly sleeves, gold and pearl beads embroidered on velvet and satin, fitted darts, laces up the back…the dresses swam before her eyes in a confusing array. When Hannah asked for her opinion, she could only stammer and shrug, not wanting to hurt the nice woman's feelings, until dear Mrs. Hannah Birchwood took the hint and began to take charge.

Finally they arrived at a dressmaker who offered beautiful and exclusive enough fabrics and patterns to satisfy Mrs. Birchwood's lavishly correct taste. Bailey was aghast at the prices, but she allowed herself to be measured and the dress and shoes were ordered, and at last she arrived home with painful feet and the dreaded corset.

And here it was, two weeks later, and Bailey was trussed up like a turkey before Thanksgiving dinner. The corset, which Hannah laced up the back for her with disconcerting strength, was biting into her flesh, shaping her naturally trim and toned figure into an improbably-proportioned hourglass. Hannah went on and on about the beautiful bronze sateen cotton with a spoon busk and steel supports; the buff-colored casings embroidered with terracotta; the yellow and cream twisted silk flowers across the top and bottom. The top of the corset was trimmed with a machine-made braid, earning more praise from Hannah. "My, oh, my! I've never laid eyes on such a beautiful corset! Isn't it lovely?" The jolly Hannah clucked her tongue and shook her head in appreciation.

Bailey bit her tongue to keep from cursing the contraption. "Yes," she gasped. "But could you maybe loosen those lacings just a little bit, please?" Hannah had ordered her to hold her breath while she laced her up, a directive of which Bailey was only now beginning to understand the consequences. "I'm having trouble breathing," she added weakly. Hannah took one look at her face and quickly unlaced her.

Bailey gasped for air and the room stopped spinning. "Really, Hannah, would anyone notice if I didn't wear it?" Bailey pleaded. Hannah looked justifiably scandalized.

"You *must* wear a corset, my dear. Here. Breathe *out* this time and I promise I'll lace it more loosely. You're so thin anyway, you lucky girl. I'm just so used to lacing mine tightly because I'm a bit more—generously proportioned, you know, after having my girls." Bailey groaned and allowed herself to be trussed again. She expelled every bit of air from her lungs and pushed out her abdomen to buy another inch. Then it was time to don the gown, which had just been completed and delivered to St. Ursuline's that very day.

Bailey had to admit, the dress was dazzling. Hannah had minded Bailey's request to avoid huge mutton sleeves and an excess of bows, ribbons, scarves and lace, and the resulting gown was lovely and understated in a shade of Nile-green silk with handsome embroidery. The round, un-darted corsage was trimmed around the low neck with three strands of green and golden-brown beads, and below that over the breast was a drapery of silk embroidered with white silk and small, fine beads. Rows of beads matching the top were repeated around the waist, and triple rows of embroidered beads began at the waist and traveled down the skirt. The skirt was edged at the foot with a row of beads and very richly embroidered all around in points of white silk and beads. The point in the middle of the front of the skirt was higher than the others, and each point was bordered with a row of beads. Bailey slid into the dress and Hannah heaved a great sigh of approval. She ceremoniously handed Bailey long white suede gloves, and Bailey drew them over her arms to the elbows. Next came the shoes: French kid beaded one-strap Grecian slippers, Hannah informed her, dyed to match her dress. Bailey gingerly stepped into them and found, to her surprise, that they were quite comfortable.

"Now for your hair," Hannah muttered, biting her lip.

"Can I look at myself?" Bailey asked, craning her neck to catch a glimpse in the mirror.

"No! Not yet! I want you see the finished product, my dear." Hannah led her to the vanity and Bailey sat facing her, dreading this next step. Her hair was long, thick, frizzy, and tangled, and Hannah was sure to have met her match at last. But Hannah cheerfully gathered her large collection of brushes and combs and hot curling irons and set to work brushing Bailey's hair, with the practiced gentleness of a mother. "Do you mind if I cut you some bangs, my dear?" she murmured. "All of the women wear bangs now." Bailey gazed at Hannah's curly forehead fringe and found that she did not care for the look at all.

"I'd rather not have bangs, if it doesn't ruin your plans too much," she said as kindly as possible.

"Oh that's, fine!" Hannah chirped, merry as ever. She deftly arranged Bailey's hair in large loose waves and formed the bangless front into a soft Pompadour. She fluffed the back of the hair out at the neck and then rolled three horizontal puffs across the back, with three tiny ringlet puffs at the sides. She placed three shell combs, two close to the puffs at the sides and one at the back, and secured a perfect small green bow embroidered with beads toward the side at the top. She stood back and clapped her hands with joy. "Beautiful!"

She quieted then, gazing at Bailey, and then stared at her own clasped hands. She opened and closed her mouth a few times, her brows crinkling.

"What is it?" Bailey asked, alarmed.

"Oh, nothing! Nothing at all of consequence. I just wanted to ask you a question about your clinic. Can I do that? We haven't really talked about it, and I'm just so fascinated and envious of you, Bailey! Why, you're a *doctor*!"

Bailey laughed, surprised. She had thought that Hannah must be disapproving of her chosen profession—quiet and kind, but perhaps silently condemning. She saw now that she had misjudged her. "Of course you can ask anything you want," Bailey managed, more pleased than she wanted to admit.

Hannah nodded and licked her lips nervously. "Well, it's just that I was wondering if other—ladies—ever come to your clinic? Ladies other than—" she stopped, embarrassed.

"Other than ladies of the evening?" Bailey gently provided.

Hannah released a breath and nodded, relieved.

"No, I have no patients who don't work in the District. Why do you ask?"

Hannah's face had achieved the hue of a tomato. "Well, Bailey, I'm willing to bet that other ladies—even some of my friends from my own social circle—would appreciate a woman doctor for their...*womanly* questions! I know I hate having Dr. Evans examine me when I'm pregnant! It's horrible! He doesn't even look at what's he's doing, as if it's too disgusting for him to take a peek." Her hands flew to her mouth as she realized what she had just said.

Bailey nodded knowingly. "It's a common problem, Hannah. I saw it all the time in New York. But unfortunately, I'm so busy with my patients now, I couldn't possibly invite others. I can't even accommodate the women I aimed to help."

"Oh." Hannah seemed deflated. "It's something to think about, anyway, if you'd ever want a change of pace. There's really no doctor for women or girls to turn to in hard times, you know. None at all." Bailey thought the choice of words was strange, and she was about to question her when Hannah suddenly transformed again into a cheerful, giddy friend.

She swung to the window and pinched off a petal on one of the red geranium plants she had arrived with earlier. "Here!" she thrust the petal at Bailey. "Lick your lips and press this petal between them." Bailey tried not to roll her eyes as she obeyed. Hannah then struck a match and blew it out, then carefully stroked it onto Bailey's eyelashes. "Be sure not to rub your eyes, or cry," she ordered, with a hint of a smile.

"Oh wait!" Hannah cried as Bailey attempted to move toward the mirror. She rummaged in the dressmaker's box and emerged with a sizable fan constructed of white ostrich feathers. "You simply *must* carry this! Oh, won't Lydia Middleworth *die* of envy?" She handed it to Bailey, beaming, and Bailey blinked a few times in disbelief.

"What do I—how do I—" she found she was at a loss for words, and hysterical laughter was threatening again.

"Oh, you simply carry it with you, dear, and when you enter a room you may unfold it and hold it thus." Hannah grabbed the fan and unfolded it, her arm bending up and out as if she were holding a tray, and one tip of the fan resting behind her shoulder. "Or you can hold it down across your dress as well." She demonstrated this pose next, and Bailey tried to picture herself displaying her fan without dissolving into the dreaded nervous laughter. Hannah noted the look of despair and took pity. "Don't worry about it—it will feel natural. Now go look."

Bailey took the fan and made her way to the full-length mirror, wondering who she would find there. How long had it been since she'd been dressed this fine? *Never*, she realized. The girls at Ft. Allen had dressed like this every night, her mother included, but Bailey the child had lived in rags, and Bailey the medical student had lived in simple white dresses.

But the Bailey in the mirror was no child: she gasped as she beheld the visage of a shapely, elegant, richly-attired woman. Her lips were a pleasing shade of red, her eyelashes longer and darker, giving the effect of making her eyes appear even larger and darker. She moved in a slow circle and the dress whispered with her, the green shades accentuating her hair, which somehow looked auburn now instead of the usual orange-red. She was physically uncomfortable, but she supposed this must be the price of dressing like a lady.

"Oh, Hannah, how can I ever thank you?" she murmured with sincerity to the beaming woman. "Thomas will be so pleased."

Hannah rose and joined her in the front of the mirror. "And are you pleased, Bailey?" she asked, tilting her head and pinning Bailey with a direct gaze that belied her cheerful, carefree nature.

"Yes," Bailey said after a pause, but the response sounded more like a question. Hannah smiled and caught one of Bailey's hands and squeezed it.

"Is it possible you are feeling a bit ambivalent about dressing this way, and maybe even about our good pastor himself?" Hannah continued to gaze at Bailey, and Bailey found herself quite unable to lie. There were many more layers to Hannah Birchwood than Bailey had first judged.

There was a long pause. "Yes," Bailey said, and dropped her eyes to share at her shoes.

"Never mind that. It's natural. Don't try to figure everything out at once, Dr. Rose," Hannah quietly advised. They sat in silence for a beat, and Bailey realized the friend that Hannah could be. She squeezed Bailey's hand and suddenly spun away, her voice once again bright and cheerful. "You are ready! The princess may now descend the stairs, but let me go first, and wait a few moments before you follow, okay?" She was gone before Bailey could even form an answer.

A few minutes later a very nervous Bailey descended the stairs, her hands shaking ever so slightly as she clutched her oversized ostrich fan. She saw, much to her chagrin, that a full cadre of spectators was waiting to receive her at the bottom of the stairs: Thomas, who was beaming and pulling double-time on his earlobe; Sister Anna, who looked incredulous and somewhat wistful; Hannah, who was not looking at Bailey at all, but instead, covertly checking Thomas's reaction; and an unidentified man, blond, blue-eyed, slightly portly, and handsome in a dimpled, jolly, rakish manner. It was this man that Bailey fixed her gaze upon, hoping to calm her nerves by focusing on an unthreatening stranger.

She finally arrived at the foot of the stairs, relieved, and Thomas took her hands in his own. "Bailey, how wonderful you look," he said simply. He bestowed upon her his gentle smile, and Bailey felt her anxiousness slipping away. This was just Thomas, after all; her kind, caring, and quite handsome friend Thomas. She turned as Hannah tugged her arm.

"Dr. Bailey Rose, allow me to introduce George Lucas Birchwood, my husband." Bailey extended her hand for handshake, prompting a slight frown and shake of the head from Hannah, and she hastily withdrew it. George covered the awkward moment and chased her retreating hand, gently taking it and leaning his blond head over her to kiss the air above it. Bailey blushed as she realized that she was ignorant of a simple proper social action as this, and she wondered how many more times this evening she would commit a *faux paux*. She didn't want to embarrass or disappoint Thomas, and she glanced at him in apology.

"Dr. Rose, how pleasant to finally meet you," boomed George Birchwood. "Hannah has been going on and on about Bailey this, and Bailey that. You certainly have made an impression, yes, yes indeed," he laughed jovially. Bailey glanced at Hannah, surprised, and they exchanged smiles.

"We should be moving along," Thomas recommended suddenly, with a bit of nervous wiggle to his knee. He glanced at the grandfather clock in the corner and extended his elbow toward Bailey. "Are you ready?" he smiled nervously, pulling on an earlobe, and Bailey was charmed by this unassuming man all over again. He was a delightful mixture of a benevolent, calming presence interspersed with moments of jittery energy, and she experienced a sudden revelation that Thomas also had many undiscovered layers.

The party of four made their way outside and walked along the lovely path to the front gate. They walked in pairs, in silence: Bailey was struggling with the unaccustomed heaviness of the beaded dress and was desperately trying to refrain from rubbing her eyes or licking her lips, while Thomas was suddenly bashful and tongue-tied in her presence. He had been quite overcome when she descended the stairs: she was a vision, more beautiful than any woman he had ever seen. *The transformation was miraculous*, he raved to himself silently; he wondered if he should thank God for it, then gave himself a bit of a mental shake. As he had come to know Bailey better, he had reached the conclusion that she was, well, a bit *lax* with her appearance, preferring simple clothes and coiffure, but he assumed that this was due to the rigorous demands of her profession more than anything else. He was relieved and delighted to finally see her in proper attire. His palms were sweaty and he had to force himself to quit pulling on that infernal earlobe. He had gingerly taken her elbow and escorted her from the convent, but found that he could think of not one word to say. Behind them strolled Hannah and George, poking and nudging each other and shaking with restrained laughter as they watch the awkward procession of the couple.

They meandered through the main garden and around the stunning angel fountain, past the two-storied dormitory and lovely limestone chapel, and under a myriad of shady live oaks. The grounds were serene as always, even if the couples were not. They strolled around the last bend and Bailey stopped dead in her tracks, finally distracted from her discomfort. "Thomas!" she gasped. Waiting there was a beautiful barouche, complete with a driver and four pure-white horses. The wheels and body of the carriage were a deep wine red, and the black collapsible top was drawn up to enclose the passengers within the cab, with two small windows on each side. Visible through the windows were two bench seats facing each other, elegantly padded with festive red and yellow cushions and boasting plenty of room for the four travelers. The horses stood placidly, their manes and tails braided with red ribbons to match the carriage. The driver was in coat and tails, and upon the approach of the couples, offered his hand in assistance to Bailey with a slight bow. Bailey chanced a quick look at Hannah, who gave her a reassuring wink, and she boarded the fine carriage. She had assumed she and Thomas would be traveling in Thomas's customary one-horse shay, a fine, well-appointed two-seater in its own right. *Thomas likes his horses and carriages*, Bailey mused to herself, adding another piece of information to her expanding catalog of Reverend Eckles.

Once the four were seated, Bailey turned to Thomas and murmured, "Oh, Thomas, it's just beautiful! And the horses! I had no idea you owned this. Oh—is it yours?"

Thomas opened his mouth to respond but Hannah snickered and beat him to the punch. "Oh, sweetie, you haven't seen anything yet. It's a well-kept secret, but Thomas has another carriage that is quite a controversy, don't you, sneaky?" Thomas laughed and shook his head modestly.

"Well, it's not a well-kept secret anymore, blabbermouth," George broke in, smacking his wife playfully on the arm. She ignored him and went on.

"Bailey, you should see his spider phaeton. It's wickedly dangerous and fast—he just flies! You'll never get me in it, though, but it's a sight to see."

Thomas finally cut in. He glanced at Bailey, his brown eyes twinkling. "This barouche is actually owned collectively by St. Mark's. We use it a lot for funerals," he added sheepishly. The four of them had a good laugh at that. "But Bailey doesn't want to hear a boring description of my spider."

"Yes, Bailey does," Bailey corrected him. "What *is* a spider phaeton, and when can I ride in it?"

"Oh, no, you won't be riding in it," laughed Thomas, causing a brief prickle of annoyance in Bailey. He went on to explain why the phaeton that was "much too perilous" for a lady. When he said "lady," he smiled into

Bailey's eyes and squeezed her hand and held it for a beat, and she felt a bit of a flutter in spite of herself. Thomas was flirting with her! She was simultaneously flattered and amused.

The ride through town was pleasant, albeit much too rushed for Bailey's taste. She longed to order the carriage top down so she could take in the sights, smells, and sounds of the city, but she caught only fleeting glimpses of the beloved chili stands and a dizzying array of humanity: fine soldiers in blue uniforms, dandified Beau Brummel gamblers, cowboys decked out in tight-fitting dungarees and brightly colored shirts and neckerchiefs, soubrettes and dance hall girls in short, lacy bright skirts and low-cut blouses, and Mexican and Gypsy children forever navigating through the throng, which brought a special pang to her heart. But the horses clipped along at a very rapid pace, and the four passengers remained properly shielded from the teeming life in the streets.

Bailey mused that she was stepping out with a man who was at the helm of a large, established church with many wealthy and powerful parishioners; hadn't they come together to stock her clinic? She wondered for the first time if she would be meeting some of those influential citizens tonight, and realized that she had been so preoccupied with the clinic and the ridiculous preparations for the evening that she had no idea where they were going. When she said as much, Thomas finally enlightened her.

"I have made reservations at Scholz's Palm Garden and Restaurant," he announced a bit nervously. Bailey felt a tendril of dread; she had suspected as much. Scholz's was a popular gathering place of the elite and powerful of San Antonio, and she had a natural-born aversion to places such as these. No doubt the patrons would know of her background—there were no secrets among the tightly-knit clique at the top echelon of the city's movers and shakers—and they would be scandalized to see a prostitute's daughter dining with an esteemed reverend. The fact that she was a doctor would make matters worse, not better. For the first time, Bailey considered the risk Thomas was taking tonight by bringing her here—the risk to his reputation as well as his funding.

"That sounds wonderful," she replied with a forced cheerfulness, and Hannah reached over and patted her hand comfortingly.

The ride seemed to be over almost before it had begun, and the carriage rolled to a gentle stop on the west side of Losoya Street, right on the river front. The ladies were handed down from the carriage ceremoniously. Bailey paused a moment at the threshold of Scholz's to marvel: the two-story brick building boasted broad galleries along its length, creating delightful, cool shady outdoor seating for evening dining and socializing. A fashionable promenade ran in front of the building, and fine gentlemen and ladies strolled by slowly, the gentlemen tipping their hats at Thomas and George and the ladies nodding their heads ever so slightly at Hannah and openly ogling

Bailey. Huge potted palms created the tropical ambience that gave the restaurant and beer garden its name, and music filtered from the second floor, creating a festive atmosphere.

Bailey took a deep breath, feeling rather faint, and took her first step forward into San Antonio society.

CHAPTER TWELVE

Bailey took Thomas's arm and they made their way through the entrance, following a waiter through the lobby and traversing around an enchanting, enormous patio filled with every imaginable tropical plant, tree and flower: rich, giant green king palms, light green Mediterranean fan palms with finely-textured fronds, sago palms with their distinctive spiky, horizontal shoots, abundant, richly-colored African violets nestled in floor pots and hanging pots of every size, exotic Gypsy orchids with peach, purple, orange and pink hues, and one of Bailey's favorite, the delicate bird of paradise flowers, with their orange and violet petals that bloomed in the shape of a bird's head. The effect was one of a tropical paradise, right in the middle of a restaurant! She stopped abruptly and gazed at the garden, her mouth a perfect "O." Without making a conscious decision to do so, Bailey wandered from her party and stepped onto a quaint stone path, making her way through the garden, pausing to breathe in the heavenly scents and touch a delicate petal here or there. What a brilliant idea for a restaurant! Bailey determined that she would ask to meet Mr. Scholz and have a grand conversation about how he had conceptualized and acquired these tropical beauties; how Sister Anna would love a garden like this at St. Ursuline's! Many of the young boarders there would delight in creating something so magical…

Her thoughts were interrupted with a gentle poke on her backside. Startled, she turned to find Hannah nudging her with her fan. "Bailey! People are staring!" She giggled. Bailey snapped out of her reverie and looked around; indeed, she had attracted the attention of those patrons seated on the first floor around the patio: the women were covertly stealing glances and talking behind their hands while the men were openly staring in appreciation. Thomas, standing with George and the waiter at the foot of the stairs to the mezzanine, appeared to be flustered.

Bailey groaned. "Oh nuts, I've messed up already," she muttered, and followed Hannah with as much dignity as she could muster. They rejoined their party and Thomas gave his earlobe a few quick pulls.

"It's beautiful, isn't it, Bailey?" he said kindly. "I'll never forget the first time I saw it. Quite a shock to enter a restaurant and find yourself in a tropical rain forest." Bailey smiled at him appreciatively, her cheeks stained pink, and the four of them followed the waiter up the stairs to the mezzanine above, the tension somewhat lessened. They arrived at their table and Bailey found that they had the best seat in the house: she could gaze down at the patio to her heart's content. Meanwhile, Hannah and George had the perfect view of most of the other patrons and could commence to gossiping, which they did at once, and Thomas had the perfect view of Bailey, which he enjoyed greatly. The evening passed by in a blur: after a delicious meal of grilled marinated fish with tropical salsa and coconut rice, Thomas and George moved to the bar to socialize with the men, as was customary. The women remained seated, and after pleasant conversation with Hannah about her four daughters and Bailey's medical school experiences, Bailey found her attention wandering.

"When can we get up and socialize with the women?" Bailey finally asked. Hannah smiled with delight.

"Oh good," she said. "I was hoping you were up for that. Shall we go?" She stood gracefully in one fluid movement while Bailey struggled to her feet, becoming a bit entangled in her long gown.

"Have I smudged my eyes yet?" she asked anxiously.

"No! They look perfect," Hannah assured her with a kind smile and a squeeze of the hand. As they approached the first table, Hannah murmured in her ear. "And now you will meet the biggest gossip in San Antonio, Mrs. Lydia Middleworth. She is *brutal.* Just smile and say as little as possible and concentrate on her unsightly mole if you get perturbed. Let's get her over with first." Bailey wondered briefly why they had to speak with her at all if she was such a shrew. She supposed she did not understand anything about these society games, and found herself wishing she was strolling along the river walk in the cool evening air.

Only two steps from Lydia's table, Hannah nudged her again and glanced purposefully at Bailey's fan, which Bailey had quite forgotten she was even holding. With an inward groan, she attempted to flare it and hold it to her shoulder as instructed, but she gave it a bit too much muscle and lost her grip.

The fan went sailing over her shoulder all the way into the garden patio below.

Both women stopped dead in their tracks and turned to watch the fan settle sedately onto a large palm tree. They looked at each other, Hannah horrified, and Bailey on the brink of a most unladylike belly laugh. Hannah's expression changed from one of despair to one of barely-contained hilarity as they stared at each other for another beat, but then Hannah's good breeding took over: she cleared her throat and continued toward Lydia's table, Bailey struggling for composure.

"Good evening, Lydia. May I present Dr. Bailey Rose?" Hannah's voice was smooth and cultured with just a hint of nervous tension. "Bailey, this is Lydia Middleworth. Her husband is the president of the city's largest bank."

Lydia Middleworth glanced up from a feigned conversation with a woman seated beside her, properly pretending not to have witnessed the fantastic flying fan. No doubt that story would be circulating as soon as they left the table: Bailey's impromptu sojourn into the patio and the launching of her fan would be the topic of conversation for weeks to come. "Oh, hello, Hannah," she said in an unpleasant, nasal tone, barely affording Hannah a look. She shifted her eyes to Bailey. "So pleased to make your acquaintance, Bailey." Lydia was a profoundly overweight middle-aged woman with artificially-colored jet-black hair arranged in curls piled atop her head. Her small eyes glittered speculatively, missing nothing. She was dressed in a voluminous blue gown, no doubt created to match her eyes, and each finger was bedecked with a diamond or gold ring. An incredible diamond necklace adorned her neck. Bailey could not help but stare at the wealth so outlandishly displayed. She wondered briefly if Lydia traveled in an armored carriage.

"Dr. Rose is the newest doctor in town," added Hannah inanely. "She just opened her clinic a few weeks ago."

Lydia shifted her eyes back to Hannah and said nothing. There was an acutely uncomfortable pause. Finally she spoke, addressing her remarks to Bailey. "Yes, I have heard all about it, and I do not approve of our Thomas being involved in a clinic for—well, you know." She finished her thought with a dismissive wave of her hand, a delicate crinkle of her nose, and a quick shake of her head as though she had smelled or tasted something disgusting. Bailey felt her face flare, and she opened her mouth for a sharp retort. Hannah beat her to it.

"Well, it's been wildly successful so far, and the congregation has given it full support. Oh! Bailey! I neglected to introduce Mrs. Sarah Miller. She is the wife of Mr. Cornelius Miller, owner of Miller's Mercantile." Bailey forced herself to turn away from the horrible Lydia Middleworth and her prominent mole, located just to the right of her flabby lower lip, and exchange pleasantries with Sarah Miller, who seemed to be embarrassed and regretful about the awkward exchange. Finally, they moved on, and Bailey heaved a sigh of relief.

"She was—" she found herself without adequate words, and Hannah let out a huff of laughter.

"Yes, she is," she agreed. "Don't feel too badly, my dear. She is mean to *everyone*. George won't even talk to her anymore, but he's good friends with her husband, poor man."

"And what did she mean when she said *our* Thomas?" Bailey inquired, daring to glance back over her shoulder. Lydia was watching her steadily, and did not look away when Bailey caught her at it.

"The Middleworths are members of Thomas's congregation. Thomas has been funding your clinic from the general offertory; he was afraid if he continued to take up special collections, the money would dry up. So now he takes a certain percentage of the offertory each Sunday to fund the clinic and the women's shelter." She paused as she noticed Bailey's look of consternation. "He's perfectly up-front about it; all of the funded projects are listed in the bulletin each week. So far no one has complained—to him, anyway, but to be honest with you Bailey, once the women finally start to pay attention to where the money is going, they will make sure their husbands stop tithing. And people like the Middleworths tithe hundreds each month, so Thomas is worried that other outreach programs will begin to suffer." She stopped suddenly as she noticed Bailey's crestfallen expression.

"Oh no, I've said too much. I really thought Thomas would have said something to you. Don't worry, dearie, it will all work out," she finished with her trademark cheer, and pulled Bailey along to the next table.

Bailey met dozens of women that evening, many of them kind, but many of them coolly censorious of Bailey, and a few of them openly hostile. The excitement of the evening—the beautiful patio, the delicious food, the elegant dresses, even the flying fan—all of that faded into the background as Hannah's revelations began to settle on Bailey's conscience: was her clinic causing Thomas's church to fracture? Were her efforts going to fail after so short a time? Her patients certainly could not pay her; the madams would not pay her, either. She had no money of her own. She was lucky to be living free-of-charge at St. Ursuline's: Sister Anna housed her in a private dormitory room, fed her, and reassured Bailey every day that she wanted her to stay as long as she needed to, so she didn't care that she herself was not earning a living; but for the first time in her life, she felt an innate, deeply satisfying sense of purpose as she served the women and children of the Red Light District. She was saving lives, and sometimes even changing lives—she *was* that savior that she had always longed for as a child. How could that all just go away so quickly?

She worked the problem over and over in her mind as she chatted with her new acquaintances about her lovely dress, the lovely flowers on the patio, the lovely weather, Thomas's lovely carriage. She knew she could not shut down the brothels, although of course, that had always been her ultimate goal. Thomas had advised her that if she took that approach, her clinic would be shut down and all would be lost. If the district must thrive, her clinic must thrive, but how could she save it without damaging Thomas's church or jeopardizing his position?

Near the end of the evening Hannah and Bailey had worked their way quite close to the bar, although societal dictates forbid them from approaching it. Hannah attempted to wave at George to give him the signal that they were ready to depart. Bailey took in the scene: the city's most powerful men seated at the rich, highly-polished mahogany bar, puffing on expensive cigars and downing scotch and beer in thick crystal glasses. She overheard snippets of conversation: "Filthy cowmen and sheepmen fighting over land and water again up north…" "She went for $450, can you believe it? Never thought I'd make that much of a profit, but I guess there's one born every minute…" "I'm telling you, John, it's time for a tax increase to fix these infernal roads. Broke another axel today! You use the service; shouldn't you have to pay to keep it in tip-top shape, you cheap bastard?" Uproarious laughter followed as several men agreed.

You use the service; shouldn't you have to pay to keep it in tip-top shape?

Bailey turned and clutched Hannah's arm, interrupting her in mid-sentence with an elderly lady with a ridiculous pink lace collar, who looked scandalized and uttered, "Well, I never!" at Bailey's rudeness.

"Hannah!" Bailey cried. "The city! They sanction the service, right?" Hannah stared at her, mystified, then excused herself with an apologetic murmur and quickly pulled Bailey away from the elderly lady's table.

"Bailey! I was talking to the assistant pastor's wife! That old biddy will never let me hear the end of this. What are you talking about?"

"I figured out how to keep the clinic open!" Bailey executed an excited little hop and could barely keep herself from jumping up and down. "Since the city sanctions the district, they should pay to keep the clinic open! The men who visit the bordellos consider it to be using the services, so shouldn't the city pay to keep those services in tip-top shape?" There was a silence.

"I believe you've had a bit too much excitement tonight," Hannah finally said, her brow crinkled in concern. "The city will never admit it sanctions the districts. If it denies that, why should it pay to keep the clinic open?" She caught George's eye again and waved impatiently. He held up one finger and gave her a nod and a placating smile, and Hannah sighed deeply. "Look, Bailey, we have time to visit one more table before we go. We'll talk about this later, okay?" Bailey nodded, a bit crestfallen, and followed her friend woodenly to pay yet another social visit.

As they were meeting with Wanda Scott, a kind, wealthy widow flanked by her two teenage daughters, Bailey let her eyes roam over to the men's lair once more. She knew she had the beginnings of the answer here; if she could just think about all of the angles! Perhaps Sister Anna could help her; she was a brilliant woman with a clear, logical mind.

Bailey suddenly froze. Sitting at the bar was a man in quarter-profile who looked familiar to her. He had broad shoulders and black hair, and as she watched, he ran one hand through that hair in a gesture well-remembered from her childhood. She could not see his face, but she felt a tingle of awareness. Could it be? Was Jacob Naplava sitting fifteen feet from her? She let his name run through her mind a few more times and her heart beat triple-time. She was suddenly convinced, and undeniably elated.

She didn't know she had been looking for him all evening until that very instant.

Her feet moved of their own accord: she shot from her chair and ran to the bar, shouldering through a few startled men to get there, and grasped the man's arm and swung him around. Her face was wreathed with a smile of expectation, his name already on her lips. "Jacob!" she cried, and then one hand flew to her mouth, aghast.

The man gaped at her, his eyes wide with surprise. He had a handlebar mustache and Bailey judged him to be a full ten years older than Jacob. He finally cleared this throat amidst the sudden silence at the bar and smiled at her. "No, ma'am, but I've never wished more that my name *was* Jacob," he drawled, and the men around him erupted in laughter.

Suddenly Thomas was at her elbow, commandeering her gently through the lobby, Hannah and George close behind. Bailey was mortified, and she worked frantically to fight the threatening tears. That was all she needed; a trail of black smudge down her cheeks! At last they were on the boardwalk, and Bailey was surprised to see that their carriage was ready and waiting.

"Thomas, I'm so sorry," she finally murmured as they approached the driver.

"Oh, no harm done!" he said cheerfully. "It was getting a little stuffy in there, don't you think? I thought we might get back to the Academy in time for a pleasant stroll through the gardens." Bailey braved a glance at him and saw that he did not seem to be too upset by the scene she had made at the bar. She supposed he was resigned to her antics by now. They were all seated and Hannah and George chatted merrily about this person and that, while Thomas covertly held her hand under the voluminous folds of her dress. All was well.

But all was not well. All throughout the ride home, the peaceful stroll through St. Ursuline's tranquil grounds at dusk, and the genuinely affectionate hug with Hannah before she and George departed, Bailey's mind was consumed with visions of an elusive Jacob. *He is like a ghost*, she finally admitted to herself. He was a part of her past—a past she had put firmly behind her eons ago, and memories of the magical two days at the beautiful ranch by Glory Creek in Hill Country must be stored away carefully, perhaps to treasure in her old age. Being in the city again—as much as it had changed since her childhood—brought to mind those days of scrambling in the hot, fragrant, dangerous yet glorious San Antonio streets with Gabriella, her hidey-hole at Fort Allen, her beautiful, distant mother, and finally, the night of utter terror at the Gaslight Hotel. *Put it away*, she ordered herself. *Be happy with your wonderful life now.*

And at the end of the evening as Thomas bid her goodnight at the foot of the stairs in the dormitory, hesitated, then finally took her in his arms and gently kissed her, her heart beat a bit faster. She finally felt as though her new life had begun, and the elusive happiness was within her grasp at last.

CHAPTER THIRTEEN

Monday at the clinic was moving slowly; most of the bordellos were closed on Sundays, and the women chose that day to flood the clinic. Bailey considered for the first time that perhaps she may close the clinic on Mondays and enjoy a day off. She had seen only one patient thus far, and she had already scrubbed and disinfected every inch of the infernal place in an effort to keep busy. She inventoried all of her instruments and supplies, updating her careful records. She sent today's receptionist—a rather loud and abrasive but well-meaning woman with the unlikely name of Betsy Betterly—home for lack of work. She wrote in her journal. She gazed out of the window in her office and thought about Thomas.

The kiss they had shared had been warm and comforting, and she *had* felt her heart beat faster. Is this what love felt like? Her mind had been wandering to him lately at odd times of the day. She drummed her fingers against the windowsill and allowed herself to consider a life with Thomas Eckles. He would take care of her; she would never want for anything. He was proud of her efforts as a full-fledged doctor and would not demand that she give up her career—or would he? Would she have time for her clinic? A pastor's wife had many responsibilities, both social and church-related. He was already forty; no doubt he would want children soon. She wasn't sure she wanted children, at least not yet. Could they hire a nanny? She felt a sudden rush of apprehension at the vision of herself in a resplendent wedding gown, standing with Thomas at the front of the church, uttering vows in front of San Antonio's finest. With her rotten luck, she would probably inadvertently knock over a candle and burn down the church. People would run screaming from the sanctuary; perhaps one of Lydia Middleworth's ridiculous hats would catch on fire.

Bailey abruptly smacked herself on the forehead and laughed out loud, the sound echoing throughout the empty clinic. What was she doing? He had kissed her once and she was already planning their future! But what if he did love her, and was at this very moment thinking about the same things as she was? What if, after an appropriate courtship period—there could be no doubt that he was courting her—he asked for her hand? They would need to talk frankly, and soon, and the thought of that conversation made her bite her lip in consternation. Thomas seemed so vulnerable, not to mention shy. They talked about many things together with ease, but their conversations were never this intensely personal. She found that she wanted to protect him, and she couldn't bear the thought of causing him worry. She supposed she must be in love; why else would she be spending so much time thinking about him?

Her thoughts wandered in a different direction. As they had walked the grounds of St. Ursuline's after Hannah and George's departure the night before, Bailey had broached the subject of clinic funding to Thomas. He was staunchly against her starting a campaign to halt the city from covertly sanctioning the District: he argued that this would only serve to get her clinic shut down, and she reluctantly agreed. But when she suggested a different approach—that since the politicians and wealthy businessmen use the brothels, thanks to the city's underground promotion of it, the least the city could do is fund the clinic—he was willing to listen, while still dubious. He reminded Bailey that an election was looming in November, and perhaps she could meet with the candidates to see if they would put the issue on the platform. She was wildly excited about this idea, and Thomas, with all of his connections, had promised to arrange something. She could tell he did not believe the plan was a viable one, and perhaps he was just humoring her, but she was filled with a sense of purpose and had immediately begun chattering about a possible strategy. And then when she had finally run out of steam, he had delivered her to her dormitory, bent low, and kissed her goodnight, Bailey standing on her tip-toes to reach him. She had wanted to touch the curls on the back of his neck but had refrained, reminding herself to be the lady that she sensed he desired her to be.

Bailey was so lost in her thoughts that she failed to hear the bell ring as the front door was opened. Not until there was a discreet knock on the exam room door did she fly to her feet, startled. She realized that a patient must have entered and walked through the reception area and exam room to find her.

"I'm so sorry," she was already apologizing as she flung open the door.

And there stood Gabriella Flores.

Bailey stood gaping at a woman who could be none other than her long-lost childhood friend. *Gabby was standing in front of her!* She was stunningly beautiful, in spite of the fact that her glossy dark hair had been dyed a platinum blond, and was now coarsely textured and cut in an angular, shoulder-length bob. But here was the same flawless dusky skin, full, sensuous lips and startling aqua-colored eyes. She was very tall, topping Bailey's five and a half feet by at least five inches. She was wearing a low-cut white peasant blouse with a bright, multi-colored skirt. She stood with a quiet poise, hands clasped serenely at her waist, staring back at Bailey. Bailey knew, by virtue of the mode of dress, hair style, and the familiar hard expression in her eyes, that Gabriella was a working girl, and no doubt very highly-paid.

"*Dios mío*," Bailey finally squealed, and flung herself at Gabby. Gabriella, startled, was forced back a few paces and was suddenly reminded of Bailey's child-like exuberance and displays of affection. She had forgotten that. Bailey was forever hugging her and grabbing her hand when they were childhood friends, so different from Gabby's own quiet reserve. She had supposed Bailey had no one else with whom to show affection, so she had never discouraged it. But now she stood stiffly, unable to return Bailey's embrace. Weeks ago she had heard about the little girl-turned-doctor whose mother used to be a Fort Allen girl, and she had known immediately that it was Bailey Rose. She couldn't quite believe it: Bailey, whom she thought was dead or whoring in horrible circumstances, had achieved everything she had dreamed of. And she was heart-achingly, naturally beautiful, not a speck of makeup or artifice, her bright copper hair in a simple braid with wild corkscrews escaping here and there, her huge familiar eyes, darker than brown, sparkling with intelligence and humor, no longer soulless and vacant. They stood, Bailey hugging her tightly while Gabby's arms remained stiffly at her sides.

"Oh, Gabby," she finally gasped, pulling away. "How I've missed you! I always wondered what became of you!" They stood looking each other over, and Bailey suddenly wished she could take those words back. It was obvious what had become of Gabby: she was a prostitute. She watched as Gabby's expression changed from one of delight to one of self-loathing.

"*Hola, mi amiga*," she said softly. Her voice was richly toned, accented, and as sensuous as the rest of her. "I'm afraid that now that you can plainly see what became of me, I cannot bear to be in your presence." She gave a tremulous smile and abruptly turned and moved quickly to the clinic door.

Bailey, too stunned to move for an instant, suddenly came to life and lunged after her, catching her at the door and grabbing her from behind around the waist, holding her tightly in place. They stood in this fantastic pose for a full minute, Gabriella clutching Bailey's hands, eyes squeezed shut, Bailey's head buried in Gabby's neck, her tears falling onto Gabby's bare skin
.

"Don't you ever think you are anything less than perfect," Bailey finally choked, not knowing what else to say, and Gabby finally broke down with a sob, turning and enveloping Bailey in a fierce hug. The women rocked back and forth, stroking each other's hair, sisters reunited.

They finally pulled apart. "I'm so proud of you, little Bailey," Gabby smiled. "I will call you Dr. Rose from now on."

"You better not!" Bailey returned, wiping away her stray tears. "You are just as beautiful as your mother ever was, even more. The most beautiful woman in San Antonio."

"The most beautiful woman for sale, you mean," Gabby replied gently.

"Gabby! Tell me about your life, please?" Bailey led her back to her private office and guided her into a chair.

"Only if you tell me about *your* life first," Gabby ordered.

The two friends spent the next several hours recounting their lives, Bailey confessing to everything but refusing to divulge details about the night at the Gaslight Hotel, only relenting to say that she had found her mother dead there and had run from Senator Hawk to the refuge of St. Ursuline's, which was the partial truth. Gabby's story was shorter: she had spent years working and saving, hoping for a better life. Her mother was dead, her brother in prison. She worked at the Purple Pansy. She did not elaborate, and Bailey did not push her; she simply held her hands and squeezed tightly.

"Bailey, I have to ask: one night, a few days before you disappeared, a boy was looking all over the city for you," Gabriella suddenly interjected. Bailey stiffened and stared at Gabby. "He looked to be my age, very handsome, black hair. He was looking in all of the saloons and my mother actually propositioned him!" She stopped and laughed as she described how the boy had sprinted from the establishment and how she had to chase him down.

"He asked me where you were and I wasn't going to give you up, but I could see that he really cared for you. He had been looking all night," she added, her voice beginning to trail off as she noted Bailey's stained cheeks and the wistful look in her eyes. "Who was he, dearie?"

Bailey shifted her gaze to the window and there was a long pause. "He was wonderful," she said at last. Gabby waited as Bailey remembered. "Remember how that day I wanted to go to the German school? One of the boys threw potatoes at me during lunch, and then ripped the collar from my dress and—well, he tried to make me…." She stopped, unable to put words to what Otto had tried to make her do.

"I can guess," commiserated Gabby, a knowing, empathetic look on her face.

Bailey's hand moved to her throat to touch her collar as she relived the degradation of that moment. "I got away, and later I found out that Jacob beat him up and then came looking for me. He found me under my porch at Fort Allen and talked me into going to his sheep ranch in the Hill Country to spend a few days with his family."

Gabriella stared at her. "Yes, I remember now. He said he wanted you to be his sister."

Bailey blushed again as she remembered the most un-sister-like kiss they had shared in the wagon on the way back to the city. "Oh, Gabby, it was Paradise there. I loved his family. I was going to stay; I was going to run away and live there." And the whole story poured from her, even the part about the *tecolé* fight. She omitted the parts about the Vodnik and Jacob rescuing her from the creek and taking her to his secret meadow; those were sacred memories and she found that she could not give them a voice, not yet. And speaking of the Vodnik, and how she had vanquished it at the Gaslight Hotel, was something she had promised herself she must never, ever do. Who would believe her, after all? She wasn't sure she believed it herself; it all seemed to be a hazy childhood nightmare, perhaps distorted by the passing years.

"I cannot even tell you how many times I've regretted not staying with Jacob and his father that day. I should have just run away from Ft. Allen and never went back, but I couldn't bear to leave without saying goodbye to Mother. I knew she couldn't care for me properly anymore, but I knew she loved me, and in the end, she died trying to save me." Her voice broke with emotion and Gabby moved closer to envelop her again.

"Shhh, it is all done, Bailey. It's done now, there is no going back, just forward. Let's move forward, yes?" Bailey nodded and straightened her shoulders.

"Yes, no regrets!" she stated firmly, but in the back of her mind, the ghost of a beloved boy lingered.

The women were interrupted three times that afternoon as patients trickled in, and the first time, Gabriella watched with interest from the reception area through the covert little peek-a-boo door as Bailey took the patient's medical history and proceeded with the examination. The second patient arrived as Bailey was tidying up from the first patient, and Bailey was pleasantly surprised to overhear Gabby greet her and begin to take her medical history, remembering every question without error. She led the patient into the exam area and winked at Bailey's quizzical expression.

There was no time for discussion about it, as the third patient arrived while the second was still being examined. Gabriella again took the woman's medical history, seated her, and accompanied her into the exam area when Bailey was ready.

"Hello, Miss Grandell," Bailey greeted the patient, a painfully thin brunette. "This is Miss Flores, my medical assistant," she added, suddenly inspired by a brilliant and obvious idea. Gabby's head snapped around comically, her usual poised demeanor replaced by an incredulous expression. She quickly recovered, walked over to the supply cabinet and, much to Bailey's surprise, removed a gown.

"Miss Grandell," Gabriella began, "based on your medical history, you will probably need to be examined, but we will let Dr. Rose make that decision." She placed the gown neatly on the exam table, quickly entered the office to retrieve a notebook and writing utensil, and seated herself inconspicuously in the corner, ready to take notes. Bailey just stared at her.

"Dr. Rose?" Gabby prompted quietly.

"Oh! Yes! Well, Miss Grandell, I see that you have been experiencing pain in your abdomen."

The exam continued, Gabby taking copious notes and Bailey marveling at the possibilities. *Truly, God must have had a hand in this one*, she mused happily. She remembered with clarity how Gabby had assisted Midwife Martinez many times during their childhood, her calm, composed conduct balancing Bailey's energetic inquisitiveness. Where Bailey would question, offer unsolicited suggestions for improvements, and beg to try this and that, Gabby would quietly and efficiently carry out orders, a trait much appreciated by the kindly, harried midwife.

After the third patient had departed, Bailey whirled and threw a towel into the air, whooping excitedly. "Gabby! Oh, Gabby! Would you possibly consider being my assistant? I mean, for a *job*? I can pay you, I'm sure I can! It won't be much, but it would be enough for you to be able to stop…" here she stopped, tongue-tied. "I mean, if you want to…"

Gabby picked up the towel and sighed. "Bailey, I would love to stop working at the Pansy." There was a pause as Bailey waited patiently, hoping that Gabby would at last reveal the details of her life. When had she started working for Madam Kendra? How old had she been? Was the first time horrible? How many men did she sleep with each night? Had she ever been abused? Had she ever fallen in love? Had any of the men fallen in love with her? Did she abuse drugs and alcohol, like Bailey's mother had? Bailey wanted to ask these questions with a surprising intensity, partly to know more about Gabby's life, but mostly, she admitted, to hear about the kind of life that she herself had so narrowly escaped. But Gabby found herself unable to speak of it; the emotions were locked securely behind a door in her mind, perhaps never to be opened. It was so much easier that way.

"Well, if you want to stop working there, then work for me!" Bailey implored.

Gabriella suddenly looked uncharacteristically fidgety. She wrung her hands and looked anywhere but at Bailey. "Dammit, Bailey, I think I'm pregnant!" she finally blurted. Her words echoed in the room and she felt a sense of relief. "You can't have a pregnant, unmarried assistant, now, can you?" she laughed bitterly. Bailey looked at her evenly, not too surprised.

"It's time for me to examine you, my dear friend. Let's find out for sure, and if you are pregnant, we will find out how far along you are. There are options," she reassured her, taking her by the arm and leading her gently to the exam table.

Ten minutes later the exam was complete, and the women moved into Bailey's office.

"You are pregnant, Gabriella; about four months along already. I would strongly advise against terminating this pregnancy."

Gabby nodded in agreement. "I knew I was pregnant. I don't want to kill the baby," she added, tears forming in her eyes. "But I don't know what to do." Her chin quivered as she clutched her handkerchief.

"Thomas Eckles is a great friend of mine; he is the reverend at St. Mark's. His congregation sponsors this clinic and a wonderful program for unmarried pregnant women. He houses them in a lovely big home called the Harding House just a block down from St. Mark's, and every one of them is from a background similar to yours. Many of them offer their babies for adoption after delivery, and a few are keeping their babies, but they are all learning trades and will be able to support themselves when they leave the shelter." Bailey went on to describe the efforts in detail, and Gabriella noticed how glowingly she spoke of Thomas.

"And this Thomas," she suddenly interrupted. "Is he someone special to you?"

Bailey colored and laughed. "Well, I don't know yet, but maybe."

There was a silence as Gabby considered all that Bailey had told her. "Bailey, I'm so tired. So very tired; I cannot even begin to describe it." Gabby came perilously close to sharing secrets of her sordid life; the monotonous, mind and body-numbing nights with a horrible, endless parade of johns who used her body in every possible degrading manner, the empty black hole into which she seemed to be falling deeper and deeper, and even her thoughts of suicide, but she stopped herself, digging her nails into her hands. Bailey had been so strong all throughout her young life; she could do the same for herself.

Bailey leaned forward and grasped Gabby's hands. "Leave it. Leave it today, Gabby. Go to the Pansy, clear out your things, and come back here. I'll go with you. Stay with me tonight at St. Ursuline's and we will talk to Thomas tomorrow and arrange a room for you at the shelter. And you can begin work with me this week!"

For the first time in her life, Gabriella felt hope. It was a foreign feeling, leaving her quite literally light-headed with anticipation. Every day of her life had consisted of surviving the day: simple survival, breathing in and out, remembering to eat, pretending to feel emotions when she was sure she had lost all ability to feel the day she turned fifteen. Suddenly, there it was, long-forgotten and dormant but still alive, after all: a sense of elation and excitement and expectation bubbling up and threatening to escape through every pore. She supposed her mind had already been made up to leave her life, one way or another, and Bailey had just offered her the best way possible. The decision was simple.

"Yes! I'll do it! Oh, Bailey, thank you!"

Within moments Bailey had the clinic in order and bustled Gabby out the front door, not wanting to lose any momentum now that the decision had been made. They made their way to the Pansy, the boarding house with the famed mirrored floor that covered the entire foyer, lobby, barroom, and ballroom on the first floor. It always unnerved Bailey to step foot into this grand place: the floor created a dizzying array of reflected images meant to intrigue and entice, but they only served to make her light-headed. She gripped Gabby's hand and made her way steadfastly through the lobby and up the stairs, bypassing the bouncer, a hulking man with a jagged scar across the bridge of his nose, as he nodded deferentially to Gabby.

They reached the top of the stairs and made their way down the hall silently, Bailey respecting the gravity of the moment and Gabby in a stupor of disbelief. Gabby paused before the second door on the right, reached a shaking hand to the knob, and opened the door, stepping through for the last time. Bailey followed and could barely stifle a gasp; the room was the most elegant she had ever seen in a boarding house: understated and exquisite, rather than gaudy and opulent. The boudoir had been decorated in shades of aquamarine—to match Gabby's eyes, Bailey mused. Beautiful hand-woven woolen Mexican rugs adorned the floor; the four-poster bed had been painted a rich cream color and was covered with silk bedding in varying shades of green and blue. There were pearls strung everywhere: over the bedposts; across the French Louis XV painted vanity, and over the Tiffany lamps, whose shades sparkled in hues of dazzling turquoise. An Antoinette fainting couch was supplanted with fat pillows covered in green, blue, and ivory silk, and one particularly large pillow was positioned strategically on the floor in front of it, causing Bailey to blush and turn her head away sharply, hoping Gabby had not noticed.

Gabby had not noticed. She was still moving as if in a silent dream, but there was a determined fire in her eyes now as she began to sweep her meager belongings into her small trunk, leaving most of the exquisite gowns except for a spare few.

One painting adorned the wall, and after staring at it for a full minute, mouth agape, Bailey was certain it was an original Joaquín Clausell, an up-and-coming Mexican artist whose work she had seen displayed in New York City. The canvas featured an otherworldly scene: several tufted evergreen trees with clumps of dirt roots rose up majestically from a pool of water; the rising sun shining splendidly through their branches and casting golden rays upon the blue-green pond. It was at once peaceful and mesmerizing. Gabby followed her gaze and nodded. "That was a gift from a client, Anton Naplava. I mentioned seeing a Clausell piece in an art book, and the next time Anton visited, he brought this as a gift."

Bailey stared at her, astounded to hear the name, and adjusted her memory of the young, brash man who had flirted with her so shamelessly those many years ago.

Madam Kendra interrupted her thoughts: the lady of the house had been alerted and was now watching from the doorway of Gabby's room. She looked angry and incredulous, knowing a runaway when she saw one, although she certainly was a kinder, softer woman than Blanche had ever been. She leaned her spare frame against the door in a pose of exaggerated nonchalance and twirled the tail of her faded blond hair, plaited exquisitely with beads and ribbons. Many years ago she had been a working girl herself, and she just could not comprehend the step Gabby was about to take.

"Are you sure about this, Gabriella? Because there's no coming back once you walk out that door. Jasmine will have her things in there before you're ten feet down the walk, m'lady. I've invested twelve years in you. You are the Mexican Pearl! What else do you know how to do?" At this, Bailey quirked an eyebrow at Gabriella as they worked side by side, folding undergarments.

"Mexican Pearl?" she muttered, and Gabby smiled and rolled her eyes. That accounted for the pearls strewn in endless strands throughout the room. Bailey wondered if the pearls were genuine, and guessed that they were.

"*Sí, amiga.* The shining jewel of the District, a Mexican girl with blond hair. But no longer."

"Gabriella, this is *who you are*," insisted Kendra, but she was losing steam. Her soft Southern drawl was resigned now.

Gabriella seemed to snap out of her daze then, pausing her frenetic packing and whipping around, eyes blazing. "Wrong, Madame! *Wrong!* I'm a medical assistant!" she announced with a flourish, and then resumed gathering her things as Bailey tried mightily to hold in a whoop of joy. She engaged Madam Kendra in conversation about the clinic to distract her, and by the time they were ready to leave, Kendra was teary-eyed. She gave Gabby a quick hug. "You know, you're like a daughter to me. I'm happy for you, sweet girl," she said roughly. She waved in the direction of the painting. "Take it with you."

Gabby gave a little gasp, her eyes filling and murmuring her thanks, and removed the painting from the wall, hands shaking. Bailey took her trunk so Gabby could carry the painting herself.

"Now get out and don't you dare come back, except to visit, of course. You're always welcome to do that. But you shan't ever turn another trick, of that I'm certain."

The evening passed quickly, the old friends giggling like schoolgirls as they huddled on Bailey's bed at St. Ursuline's. Sister Anna and the other nuns, including Mother Superior, had been delighted to meet Gabriella and even offered to let her stay at the Academy throughout her pregnancy, but Gabriella gracefully declined, explaining that she preferred to live with other women in her circumstances at Thomas's shelter. Privately, she was tempted to accept the offer: the convent was incredibly peaceful and beautiful, and she could imagine herself getting quite happily lost in the serene gardens and quiet chapels. She longed to renew her girlhood relationship to her religion; she was a deeply spiritual woman, and so very ready to repent. But she knew that if she stayed, she might want to hide there forever, and she had already spent too much of her life being someone she was not meant to be. Though she had not confessed as much to Bailey, Gabriella was determined to keep her baby, and a single mother did not belong in a convent filled with schoolgirls. She was certain the other women at Thomas's shelter could help her learn to care for a baby and make the transition from working girl to mother.

The next day dawned bright and beautiful, and as the women rose and began to dress, Gabby stared as Bailey tackled her hair, swiping at it viciously with the brush until most of the tangles were gone, then braided it hastily, tying it off with what looked to be a strip of a white rag. Bailey caught her looking and grinned. "I know, I know. It's frightful. I've always wanted to hack it off; it would make life so much simpler."

"No, you're not going to do that," her friend admonished. "It's just right the way it is. Exactly as I remember." She turned to consider her own hair in the tiny mirror fixed to the wall, and her mouth drew down in dismay. The dark roots appeared every week, so Kendra had made her bleach it weekly. Now it was damaged beyond repair, brittle and stiff, despite her attempts to soften it with oils. It hung just past her chin in a severe bob, and she had no irons to make the ends flip in the way she had been styling it every day for years.

"Bailey?" she ventured, turning to watch her friend as she stepped out of her nightgown and begin to pull her indigo dress on.

"Hmmm?" she answered distractedly.

"I want you to shave my head."

Bailey froze in the act of pulling the dress over her head. She finally yanked it down, staring open-mouthed at Gabby.

"What?"

"You heard me."

"You want me to shave your *head*?"

"Yes. I want to get rid of this hair." Her usual calm voice began to break with emotion, and she flung the brush she had been using to the floor. "I hate it!"

Bailey suddenly understood, and felt stupid for having missed it in the first place. "Of course you do. Of course I will! Hang on a minute. I'm going to run and fetch supplies."

Five minutes later she had Gabby seated in the middle of the room, a towel spread under her, with a pair of scissors, basin of water, shaving cream, and a razor at the ready. "Do you want to make the first cut?" she asked gently, offering Gabby the scissors.

Gabby stared at her levelly, nodded, and took the scissors. She grabbed a great hunk of hair over her ear and cut it as close as she could to her scalp, starting with a tentative motion but finishing with a satisfying click of the sharp scissors. She stared at the white hair in her hand and began to laugh, softly at first, and then throwing back her head and hooting with glee, tossing the hair into the air like confetti.

"I'll clean that up," she gasped through her laughter, and Bailey joined her, rejoicing in her friend's liberation.

Bailey finished cutting the hair close to the scalp and then commenced to the shaving, and she had a sudden sharp memory of shearing a sheep all of those years ago. She shared as much with Gabby, which caused the laughter to begin all over again.

When she was finished, she rubbed Gabby's head with almond oil then patted the excess away. She silently handed her friend a mirror, and Gabby gazed at herself, wordless.

"My dear, you are the only woman in this world who makes bald beautiful," Bailey finally sighed. "You are ravishing."

And it was true: with the ugly hair gone, Gabby's features shone forth, and it was a sight to behold.

"I don't have anything proper to wear," she finally admitted after putting the mirror aside. All of Bailey's skirts were too short by six inches, falling somewhere between her ankles and knees, making the women giggle. The nuns had nothing but voluminous habits or schoolgirl dresses, none of which were practical.

"Just put on one of your dresses," Bailey finally said. "We'll get you some proper things for the clinic and for everyday just as soon as we can." Gabriella donned a mustard-colored dress with a sigh; it was the most modest one she owned, but still very provocative with a low-cut bodice trimmed in lace that served to bring attention to very strategic areas. The body of the dress, however, was full and cut much more generously than most of Gabby's other dresses.

"Wow!" Bailey breathed. Gabby truly was stunning.

"It is my only dress without beads," Gabby said apologetically. "And the only one I can wear without a corset."

"Amen to that! Death to corsets!" Bailey shouted, one fist punching the air in defiance, and the two dissolved in laughter. "You know," Bailey added, "corsets are really very dangerous to a woman's health." She spent the next several moments educating Gabby about compressed rib cages and internal organs, and extracted a promise from Gabby that she would not wear a corset during pregnancy.

Gabby gazed again at her bald head in the mirror, her expression a bit dejected. Bailey hugged her from behind and then spent a few seconds rummaging through a trunk. She emerged with a beautiful lace shawl, a gift from Sister Anna upon her graduation. "Here, sweetheart, tie this around your head." Gabby smiled and deftly arranged the lace into a lovely head covering that trailed onto her shoulders.

"Somehow you make even an old lace shawl look exotic and fashionable," muttered Bailey, shaking her head in disbelief. Gabby continued to fuss with it until Bailey finally pulled her by the arm, forever impatient with primping.

"Come on, Thomas is meeting us at noon," she urged, and they made their way through the dormitory and gardens, setting off in the rig that Mother Superior had provided for Bailey's use. Indeed, Thomas had preceded them and already had the clinic open and the receptionist delivered. Bailey stabled her horse and grabbed Gabby's hand, nervous excitement building inside of her. What would Thomas think about her new assistant?

They entered the clinic, and Bailey was surprised to see a patient already waiting. Thomas looked up from his conversation with Bailey's favorite receptionist, Rachel, smiled kindly, and approached the women. "Hello, Bailey!" He took both of her hands and squeezed them, smiling down into her eyes. Gabby saw at once how he adored her.

Bailey returned his smile a bit self-consciously and removed her hands gently from his grip. "Good afternoon, Thomas. I want you meet Gabriella Flores! She is a dear childhood friend of mine!" She turned and laid a hand on Gabby's sleeve, beaming.

Thomas finally turned his full attention to Gabby and gulped, his Adam's apple bobbing furiously. The dark, striking young woman before him was exotic and alluring, and clearly a girl from the bordellos. "Hel—hello, Miss Flores," he finally managed, his kind brown eyes locked onto her strange blue-green ones. "So nice to make your acquaintance." Gabby gracefully offered her hand, and Thomas had no choice but to take it and give a brief bow over it. She noticed that his hand was shaking a bit, and she felt a giggle bubbling to the surface. She would have fun with this one.

"Dr. Bailey," Rachel interrupted softly. "Could you see Miss Jones now? She's in some pain with a moderate burn." Bailey snapped her attention to the patient, who was holding her arm with a grimace of pain.

"Of course! Won't you excuse me, Thomas and Gabby? Get to know each other, won't you?" She hurried away, bustling the patient into the exam room, and Thomas was left alone and terrified.

He cleared his throat a few times and began pulling on his earlobe before he could stop himself. Gabby gazed at him levelly, amused and silent. "So, Miss Flores, are you a patient of Dr. Rose's as well as a friend?" He couldn't think of a better way to ask what on earth she was doing in the clinic.

"*Sí*," she said simply, and waited for the next question.

"I see," he said gravely, and stared at the floor, nodding stupidly. Her English must be very limited. Finally he looked up and found his eyes riveted on the lace at her scantily-concealed, generous bosom. She watched as his face turned scarlet.

"Errrr…won't you have a seat? Dr. Rose will be with you in a moment." He dragged his eyes to her face and found her grinning. She was *tall*; Thomas was so accustomed to towering over women that conversing with a female only a few scant inches shorter than he, as opposed to a full foot shorter, like Bailey, was disconcerting. He wondered if she was wearing high-heeled slippers, and sure enough, his eyes were drawn down to her feet. Her gown covered them, of course.

"*Gracias*," she purred, her voice smooth like honey. She crossed the room, seeming to float, and sank into a chair next to Rachel, who was watching the exchange with great interest. Gabby struck up a lively conversation in English with Rachel, much to the astonishment of Thomas. He felt irritation rising to the surface.

He grabbed his leather-bound notebook and pen from the corner of Rachel's desk, removed himself to a chair nearest the door, and pretended to make a list of supplies needed for Harding House. He stole covert glances at the strange woman across the room, and was abashed to be caught every single time, her mocking smile growing wider each time their eyes met. She even waggled her fingers at him once! By the time Bailey emerged from the room with a bandaged patient, he was completely flustered. He jumped to his feet and accompanied the patient to the door, and Gabby was surprised to see the solicitation and genuine kindness he displayed toward the woman. She had judged him to be a bit of an elitist, but she could see now that she was perhaps mistaken.

Bailey tugged him over to Gabby excitedly. "So, did Gabby tell you all about our plans?" she asked, her dark eyes animated. Thomas dared a look at Gabriella, suspicious.

"No, I'm afraid not," he finally said.

"I have found an assistant at last!" Bailey announced. "Gabby helped me out yesterday and did a fantastic job. She's going to be my assistant, and Thomas, we have something else to discuss. Rachel, won't you excuse us? Thomas, please bring a chair." Bailey, with her usual rush of enthusiasm, left no time for anyone to respond, and tugged both of her friends through the clinic and into her small private office. Thomas arranged his chair and Gabby's, and the three of them sat almost knee-to-knee in the cramped space. Bailey's face was wreathed with anticipation, Gabby looked simply amused, and Thomas was completely ill at ease.

"What did you need to discuss, Bailey?" he finally asked, looking anywhere but at the intimidating woman at his left.

"Gabby, is it all right?" Bailey asked, her voice suddenly low. Gabby simply nodded, the serene expression never leaving her face.

"Well, Thomas, Gabby worked at the Purple Pansy until yesterday,"

Bailey began. Thomas nodded, waiting. "She came into the clinic and got reacquainted, and I talked her into quitting the Pansy and working with me." Thomas just stared at Bailey, and both women could feel the disapproval emanating from him in palpable waves. He said nothing.

Bailey hesitated, disheartened by Thomas's lack of response. Whatever was wrong with him? Thus far in their friendship, he had supported her in every decision she had made; she had always found it very easy to bend him to her will. "There's more," she finally admitted. She stopped as Gabby held up a hand, palm out, and shook her head slightly at Bailey.

"Reverend Eckles," Gabby began in a soft, level tone. "I am expecting a baby in five months. Dr. Rose has told me about your church's program for unwed mothers. I need a place to stay, and I would be honored to participate."

Thomas straightened in surprise and stared at Gabriella, then at Bailey, then back to Gabby, as though watching a tennis match. "Oh! I had no idea! I just don't know." He opened and closed his mouth again, not knowing what else to say. There was a long, unnerving silence. Gabriella waited patiently, hands folded in her lap, while beside her Bailey began to fume.

"Thomas!" she finally blurted. "Can I talk to you privately?" He began to rise, but Gabby beat him to it.

"I will go visit with Rachel," she said quietly. "She is delightful!" She was gone, her gown swishing behind her, followed by the soft click of the exam room door.

Bailey turned to Thomas, cheeks blazing. "Whatever is the matter?" she spit. "Do you understand what courage it took her to walk away from the only life she's ever known? Oh, Thomas, you should have seen the joy on her face when I offered this job and told her about your shelter. And now you are being most unwelcoming!" It was the first time she had ever been angry with him, and Bailey's hot temper was a sight to behold. Her hair seemed to blaze a brighter red and her black eyes snapped. Her hands were balled into fists and she sat on the edge of her chair, as if to pounce. Thomas was taken aback; Bailey had always been so easy-going and level-headed. He wasn't sure he completely appreciated this side of her; she resembled a tiger.

"Look, Bailey, if you had introduced her as your friend, and told me straightaway about her—condition—I would have immediately invited her to the shelter, of course!" He leaned forward beseechingly, troubled to see Bailey so angry at him. "But how can you employ a—what I mean to say is, I do not think that my congregation would approve of…"

"Of a *pregnant ex-prostitute* working as my assistant?" Bailey finished for him, gratified to see him blush at the two words he never used. "Are you really that hypocritical, Thomas? I thought this clinic was opened to save these women! To do God's work right here in the District!"

Thomas flushed with anger at being called a hypocrite, feeling the unfairness of the word. "Of course it is, Bailey. Of course! We are serving these women and their children; that is our mission, and it is a righteous and proper one. And the church is so pleased to have a licensed doctor working here in the clinic. I do *not* believe they would be as pleased if her assistant was not a trained professional as well," he finished miserably. He rubbed his hands across his face, thoroughly distressed. He did not enjoy fighting with Bailey. "And to be honest with you, I do not approve either. If you are ever ill or called away to an emergency, there should be a trained nurse in your absence." He stopped again, finally giving up.

Bailey sat back, considering his words. She could not ask him to fund her choice if he did not approve; for this to work—for the church to continue supporting her clinic—she must have his full espousal. This would all be so much simpler if her funding came from elsewhere.

"How about this," she said after a deep pause. "Let's hire Gabby in a temporary position while we are seeking a nurse. I will advertise immediately. I know it's unlikely that a nurse will want to work here, but I'm getting to know the doctors in the city and making some connections; I think I can find a suitable assistant. But in the meantime, I need help, Thomas." She gestured toward the front of the clinic, and even now, they could both hear the door chiming as patients entered. Bailey had no doubt the reception area would be full when she emerged from this infernal meeting. "Surely you can convince the congregation to support my choice of an assistant just until we find a suitable nurse."

Privately, Bailey knew that no high-quality nurse would ever apply to work at the clinic. The wages she could pay would be paltry, and by dictates of society, a nurse would be a single woman. The social price a single woman would pay for working in a clinic for prostitutes would be fatal. Bailey herself would have to train a young woman to be a nurse, and there was no one she would rather have at her side than the calm, quick-witted Gabby.

She could detect the exact moment Thomas acquiesced. He relaxed back into his chair and gazed at her over steepled fingers, carefully considering everything she had said. He would allow her to hire Gabby; he could see that she was not going to take "no" for an answer, anyway. She was the most stubborn woman he had ever met. But he would not bring the matter to his congregation; there were already discontented rumbles about the clinic and shelter, and he was not going to rock the boat further by asking them to tithe to support a former working girl who was expecting. His thoughts wandered to the mysterious woman in the reception room. She was all wrong, in so many ways, and he dreaded future encounters with her.

"All right, Bailey, you have my word that Miss Flores will be funded. We will pay her ten dollars a week, starting next week, and she may stay in the shelter, and she may room with…." He was cut off as Bailey whooped with excitement and lunged into his arms, rocking his chair back against the wall.

He hugged her briefly, laughing, and then quickly set her on her feet.

"Oh Thomas, thank you so much!" she gave his arm a final squeeze and escaped from the room before he could change his mind. Thomas stood looking after her, wondering what on earth he had gotten himself into.

Gabriella proved herself that day: after Thomas departed, daring to look her way briefly, uttering "Good day, Miss Flores," and giving her a slight bow, Gabby was met with a giddy Bailey, who explained that everything had been settled: Gabby would have a home and a job. The two worked together side by side, Gabby a quick learner and efficient assistant. Bailey noticed that the women seemed to be much more at ease in the clinic with "one of their own" assisting, and she made a mental note to speak about this with Thomas. Then again, maybe she wouldn't: he seemed perturbed and anxious around Gabriella, and perhaps she better leave well enough alone.

Late in the day, just as Bailey had sent Rachel home and the women were putting the clinic in order, a stable boy came crashing in, clearly in a state of panic. His muddy boots tracked across the newly-bleached floor, and Bailey stifled an inner groan. "Are you Dr. Rose?" he inquired, *sans* greeting. He barely remembered to snatch the hat from his head.

"Yes," she replied, a knot beginning to form in the pit of her stomach. Whatever was wrong? Was it Thomas? Sister Anna? Gabriella approached and laid a comforting hand on Bailey's arm.

"Come quick to the Lily. A girl is in bad shape and we were afraid to move her." Without further elaboration he turned and fled, and Bailey suddenly snapped into action.

"Get the rig ready," she barked to Gabby. She rushed to the exam room and grabbed her doctor's bag, throwing in some additional splints, bandages, and medication, not knowing what to expect. Gabby obeyed without a word, and the little carriage was waiting at the front door.

They arrived at the Gilded Lily in record time, Gabby dropping Bailey at the door before she drove on to the stables in the rear. The Lily was one of the high-end parlors and boasted a French theme, decorated to resemble one of the infamous *maisons closes*, or "shuttered houses." The grand ballroom was designed to mimic the Pompeiian Room of *Le Chabanais*, the most luxurious of all Parisian brothels. Large, detailed panels of aroused Centaurs in various positions with pale white maidens adorned the walls; the images always made Bailey queasy, and she studiously avoided looking at them now. Red velvet curtains dimmed the light in the lavishly-furnished room, and the lounge was nearly empty on a Tuesday evening; just a few johns sunk deep into soft leather chairs with girls draped across their laps. Bailey glanced their way briefly and did a double-take: one of the men was very familiar, but she had no time to place him; Madame Princess emerged from a back room and tugged on her arm. "This way, doc," she growled. She was an older woman with a strong build, sleek gray hair twisted high on her head and encircled with, of all things, a diamond tiara; hence her nickname. She always wore royal purple, and tonight was no exception: she was draped in an elaborately embellished purple silk robe, and it swished and whispered around her as she hurried Bailey to a distant back room.

Stretched out on a fainting sofa was a small girl, no more than seventeen, and most likely younger, judged Bailey with her first quick glance. Her face was pulpy: both eyes blackened, a bloody mouth, and a rather deep gash on one cheek.

"Any other wounds?" she demanded without preamble, kneeling and opening her bag. She was gratified to see Gabby enter and kneel beside her, ready to assist.

"My stomach," groaned the girl, her words distorted by her swollen lips. "He punched me in the stomach. It hurts to breathe." Madame Princess suddenly spun from the room, and Bailey was relieved; the girl was more likely to talk freely without her in the room.

"A john did this to you?" asked Bailey quietly.

"Yes. He's still upstairs, I think." She paused for a few beats, clearly experiencing pain with every word uttered. "He paid for two hours and he wanted—he wanted the Pinkey's Special and I don't do that; I'm straight up. He was powerful angry and tried it anyway, and I kicked him right in the balls, but he caught me when I ran to the door." She stopped and closed her eyes, wincing horribly.

Bailey released a sigh, unable to help herself. There was no point in calling the police; they would not arrest a man for beating a whore, and most likely the man in question was a man of means, seeing as he paid for two hours, which was in the vicinity of $60, in Bailey's estimation. No doubt Madame Princess had scurried away to soothe his ruffled feathers, hoping not to lose his valuable business, and likely offering him free libation and a girl who would perform whatever perverted act the man wanted.

"Hold this to her cheek until I can stitch it," she ordered Gabby, handing her some gauze. Bailey gently probed the girl's abdomen and found a broken rib, and she hoped there were no other serious internal injuries. She listened to the girl's heart and lungs carefully with a stethoscope. "She's in pain when she breathes, but she's pulling good, deep breaths," she murmured to Gabby. "That's a good sign." She bound her ribcage tightly and turned her attention to the girl's face, cleaning, numbing, and stitching the wound on the cheek while Gabby silently handed her supplies and engaged the girl in conversation. Bailey discovered her name was Mayflower, and she claimed to be eighteen. She was a petite girl with a curvy figure, her soft, short brown curls adorned with a tiny blue bow on one side, and enormous, despairing dark blue eyes.

Bailey finally sat back on her heels. "You have a broken rib; I have bound it and you must wait for it to heal. If you still have trouble breathing tomorrow morning, if there is blood in your urine, if you start to vomit or you get dizzy, or if anything new starts to hurt, send for me right away. Can you breathe better now?"

The girl nodded her head. "Yes, it's better already. Nothing else hurts."

"Leave the binding on for a week or more; just wash around it. Then come and see me for a check-up; I'll decide if we need to cast it. Gabby, will you clean her mouth and check for cuts or broken teeth? I'm going to find ice and water and towels." Gabby nodded and began tending to the moaning girl at once as Bailey ventured back out into the lounge, uncertain of the location of the kitchen. She noticed the man in the chair again, and this time their eyes met. Bailey felt a shock of recognition. Could it be? She hoped not, *oh*, how she hoped she wasn't looking at Anton Naplava!

The man rose from his deep chair, setting the girl on her feet with an apologetic murmur, and moved toward Bailey. The girl glared at Bailey, flinging a few choice words her way, the heavy lines of kohl around her eyes and her bright, sticky red lips making her look even more menacing. Bailey gave her no more than a glance. Even in this dim light she could see that her initial supposition had been correct: it was Anton, even more handsome than he had been fifteen years ago. His wavy, honey-colored hair was combed back neatly, accentuating his stunning, amber-colored eyes. A double-breasted promenade frock coat had been flung carelessly over the back of the chair, yet he still looked immaculate in a crisp white shirt with a high collar and many pearl buttons, a mint-green tie, dark gray vest of the finest fabric, and dapper checkered trousers that bore just a hint of mint green in the thread. His shoes were expensive and polished to perfection. Bailey supposed his face looked much like the sculptures of the Greek gods she had seen in New York, and decided that Anton must have broken many hearts over the years. He did not wear a wedding ring, but Bailey knew that did not mean he wasn't married. He was smiling widely at Bailey and reached out both hands for her. She was surprised to find herself intimidated by him and hesitated before extending her own.

"Anton Naplava, if I'm not mistaken," she said in a low voice. His smile grew wider.

"You remember me! I heard the girls talking about the red-haired Dr. Rose whose Mama used to be a whore, and I knew it had to be the Bailey who visited us for a few spring days! Is it really you?" His voice oozed with charm and he squeezed her hands, looking deeply into her eyes, and Bailey almost found herself falling under his spell, until his words finally registered. Did he just call her Mama a *whore*? She opened her mouth to reply, closed it again, and tried to think of something to say. She was torn: she was simultaneously longing to ask about Jacob and desperate to be free of this man's grasp. How could the two of them possibly be brothers?

Finally she spoke. "Yes, I am Bailey Rose." She succeeded in extracting her hands from his persistent grip. He immediately moved one hand to her arm, stroking it.

"Bailey, I remember you well. What a beauty you were then; I knew you would be a stunner when you were full-grown!" He nodded in a self-congratulatory way and allowed his gaze to roam over her figure, from head to toe. "And to become a doctor! Beauty and intelligence, too; what a combination!" Bailey began to feel like an exhibit in a zoo.

"I really must be going, Anton. A patient is waiting." She hesitated and tried to muster the nerve to ask about Jacob. "So, does your brother Jacob still live in the Hill Country?" she finally added before she lost courage. She held her breath, waiting for an answer as Anton continued to massage her arm and gaze into her eyes.

"Hmmm? Oh, Jacob, yes, he's still working the ranch, if you can believe it. Still lives with Mama and Papa, too, since the old man is getting on in years and needs help. I escaped, though! I work as a banker here in the city; doing quite well, I might add. And I'm not married," he added with a suggestive grin. "I mean I was going to be, years ago, but it didn't work out." His smiled dimmed a bit.

Bailey successfully freed herself and took two steps away. Anton moved with her. "Dr. Rose, would you be so kind as to join me for a dinner this Saturday evening? I would love the chance to get to know a woman of your caliber a bit better." He gazed adoringly into her eyes, smiling at her with perfect, straight, white teeth, and she tried not to laugh aloud. He was the most persistent flirt she had ever encountered, and just too pretty for her taste.

"I truly am sorry, Anton, but I have plans. Please give my regards to Jacob, won't you? Will you be seeing him soon?" She took another two steps and he followed.

"Oh, he'll be in town later this week, I suppose. Forget about him. Marry me," he laughed, bowing deeply over her hand, actually *kissing* it. Bailey swore she felt a bit of tongue, and she finally laughed in spite of herself. She was amused and flattered, and even though she knew better to encourage this merry scoundrel in any way, she was unable to resist a bit of teasing, remembering his family's proclivity for friendly banter.

"Perhaps another time," she said coquettishly, batting her eyelashes, giving her hips a tiny wiggle, and tilting her head, doing her best imitation of a flirt. Then she rolled her eyes, and they both laughed. "You're much too debonair for a poor city girl like me, Anton. But can you point me toward the kitchen?"

"I will assist you, m'lady, even though you have broken my heart!" he announced dramatically, and tucked her arm into his and led her to the kitchen, ignoring her protests. He chopped ice for her, filled a bucket with water, and searched for towels, then insisted on carrying the whole collection to the back room, where the sight of the battered young woman on the fainting sofa finally stopped his cheerful chatter. "Oh…" he breathed, and his face paled. "Oh, Bailey, I had no idea." He rushed to the young woman's side, obviously acquainted very well with her. "Mayflower! You poor baby!" He cradled her in his arms and she burst into sobs.

Gabby and Bailey shared an incredulous look and moved discreetly away, giving Mayflower a few moments of privacy.

"I know that man," whispered Gabby. "I know him very well. He's the man who gave me the painting, Anton Naplava. He was always very charming and never shuts up! Loves women, he does. Lots and lots of women. But a kind man with a good heart, always gentle and considerate."

Bailey smirked. "You'll never believe this, Gabby, but that's Jacob's brother!" she confessed. Gabby's eyes widened.

"*Your* Jacob?" Gabby gasped. Bailey laughed self-consciously.

"Not *my* Jacob, but yes, Jacob Naplava, the boy from the sheep ranch."

Gabby looked at Bailey, wide-eyed. "Do you suppose Jacob looks like *that* now?" she whispered, gesturing to the princely-looking man kneeling with Mayflower, and Bailey snickered.

But then she sobered as she gazed at Anton, remembering his and Jacob's heads bobbing in and out of the enormous sheep-packing bag on that hot, sweltering day. How Anton had gotten under Jacob's skin! Anton had always been a womanizer; he had even flirted with *her,* a skinny, scraggly girl, many times that day, much to Jacob's annoyance. "No, Jacob has blue, blue eyes and black hair," she mused quietly. "He probably looks like his father now: big build, muscular, that big smile with one dimple. Anton resembles his sister and mother." She suddenly snapped out of her reverie, noticing Gabby looking at her strangely.

She really must stop reliving those few precious days.

"Anton, I'm afraid we must continue with the patient; you can have her back in a few minutes," said Bailey gently, and Anton complied, bowing to Gabriella and greeting her by name, conversing with her quietly, then hovering in the background as Bailey applied ice and finished bathing Mayflower's wounds. She finally joined Anton by the door as Gabby held ice to the girl's mouth.

"You are friends with Mayflower?" she inquired gently.

Anton nodded miserably. "Yes, this poor girl has only been here for a few weeks. I've never—I wouldn't be with a girl that young," he hastened, and Bailey believed him. "She's barely sixteen. I made her acquaintance in the lounge the day she arrived here; she's so funny and witty; we talked for hours. I tried to talk her into taking a job back home, maybe cleaning or minding children, but she wouldn't listen." Bailey finally detected the compassion that was such an integral part of the Naplavas. Anton was clearly distressed. "She's been working the streets since she was eleven. *Eleven*, Bailey! Her mother made her turn tricks to support them both. Now her mother's dead—a rotten drunk—and she doesn't even have family. She has no one." He shook his head mournfully, but Bailey remained expressionless. This was a story she heard every week; it was almost her own story.

"You know, Anton, I can work with Reverend Thomas Eckles to rescue her," she began. Anton shook his head.

"It won't work. She won't listen to you; she's too proud. But I'm going to do it, Bailey. I'm getting her out of here and sending her to Lindy, Johann's wife." He looked at her earnestly, all flirtatiousness absent. "I actually already talked to Lindy about it, and she's all for it. But I haven't talked to Mayflower because she's so stubborn, not wanting any charity. She's so different, Bailey. She's like you: she doesn't belong here." He gestured widely.

"Nobody belongs here," Bailey returned quietly.

Anton had the decency to flush. "I need to get her out."

"Now might be your time," Bailey murmured. "Ask her now, while she's in pain. And good luck, Anton." He turned and nodded at her, giving her elbow a brief squeeze.

"Thanks, Bailey. And you've a fine helper there in Gabriella. The Mexican Pearl; what a…." He cut himself off, coloring a bit, then gave her a rueful smile before rejoining Mayflower on the sofa.

Bailey and Gabby collected their supplies and took their leave, leaving Anton behind to pamper the young girl. Bailey shook her head in disbelief. "What a small world," she finally muttered.

"What a small *strange* world!" Gabby murmured in agreement, and they boarded the rig.

Throughout the ride home her thoughts returned again and again to the Naplavas. Jacob would be in town next week, and she had asked Anton to give him her regards. She should not have done that. Jacob did not need to be reminded of the girl who vanished so many years ago.

Leave it, she thought to herself. *Just like you told Gabby to do. Leave it behind: Jake and the Bluebonnet Ranch, and Feather Hill, and Glory Creek—it was just a fantastical dream. Move forward.*

CHAPTER FOURTEEN

Jacob Naplava was sunk deep into soft leather in a dim booth at the Silver King, nursing an oversized mug of cold beer and staring gloomily at a piece of paper on the table before him. Was he really going to do this? How in the name of everything good and sacred had he gotten himself into this? The hand-blown green and white glass stylus in his hand felt foreign; at home they used turkey feather quills and an inkpot. He felt a momentary pang for the simple comforts of the ranch as he gazed around the swank establishment. Very little had changed in the Silver King in the past fifteen years, and even though he had assiduously avoided this place, it seemed unsettlingly familiar. The walls were still a glossy white, still adorned by an impressive array of enormous oil paintings featuring scenes of the Southwest. The same chandeliers cast points of light about the room; the marble bar with the ornate mirror running its length was still occupied by the very same patrons of soldiers, businessmen, and the occasional wealthy cowman and sheepman. Only the faces had changed. Now he and Johann occupied one of the plush booths that he had coveted in his youth with his own mug of beer resting on the finely polished mahogany table. Everything was exactly as he remembered.

"Jacob! Don't turn around! But turn around and look over your left shoulder. Blond hair. Big smile, looks friendly. Oh, mercy, here she comes! Now do it!" Jacob sighed and gazed at his brother Johann, who, having been faithfully married for the past fifteen years, was as inept as he at flirting with barmaids.

"Get him away from the house and wife for one day and he goes stark-raving wild," muttered Jacob, kicking his brother under the table just before the pretty barmaid arrived. Johann winced in pain.

"My brother here *needs* something," he managed to say before Jacob could open his mouth. Jacob aimed another kick, but Johann suddenly spun from the table and waved to an acquaintance. "Charles Newsome! It's been ages, good sir!" He called happily, and winked at Jacob as he rushed from the table. Jacob groaned inwardly and looked up at the comely barmaid, smiling sheepishly.

"Good day," he managed. She batted her eyelashes and leaned in close.

"How do you do, Mr. Naplava?" she purred. "What can I bring you boys to eat?"

Jacob blundered his way through the order, shooting daggers at Johann, who was watching with a big smile a few tables away. The barmaid eased herself into the booth and leaned forward provocatively, and Jacob found to his surprise that he was sad. *Sad!* Johann was his favorite brother, but his never-ending match-making attempts—often with hilarious and unfortunate results—were growing tiresome and beginning to make the usual cheerful Jacob glum. Just last week he had set Jacob up with one of his wife's friends, a chubby, bubbly little woman named Virginia who was five years older than himself and who never, ever stopped talking. Most of her conversation was about her prize-winning flock of hens. She laughed ceaselessly, and every time she did so, she punched Jacob on the arm in precisely the same spot. By the end of the evening Jacob was sure he had a sizable bruise. They had all drunk too much homemade wine, and poor Virginia vomited on Jacob's boots as Johann and his amazingly funny and clever wife Lindy fell off their chairs laughing.

A few months before that, Johann had introduced Jacob to Greta, a thin, attractive brunette his age from the Old Country, and he had called on her a few times after the initial pleasant date. He had actually thought something might come of it; there were certainly no fireworks, but Greta was the perfect sort of soothing, average woman he thought he might need in his life: average intelligence, average looks, average personality. At the close of their third date, he had tried to kiss her for the second time, wondering if this kiss would ignite a small spark, and she had burst into tears, confessing her love affair with her father's stable boy, six years her junior. During her emotional catharsis, Jacob watched her transform from a proper, somewhat boring lady into a passionate woman, brown eyes blazing, hair falling from her tight bun. She was unexpectedly beautiful as she sobbed about her forbidden love, and Jacob felt a tug at his heartstrings as he dried her tears, suddenly understanding how true love begets true beauty. He had driven her straight to the young man that night, urging her to stop wasting time and marry the lad already. And that was the end of that, although he had developed a lovely friendship with her and her beau.

Greta and Virginia had been preceded by various other eligible single women from the Hill Country, all blurring together with the passing of the last seven years or so since he had come home from his stint in Boston. Jacob remained the most eligible bachelor in Boerne; already wealthy at barely twenty-nine, and a sheepman with a law degree had the potential to be a very important man in San Antonio. The pretty young single women—especially those with Moravian roots—buzzed around him like bees to honey, whispering to each other about his handsome face, blue eyes, and his strong physique. If Jacob could have heard them, he would have died of mortification; he put little stock in outward appearances, and longed to find a genuine woman with whom he could talk and laugh and be happy, just like Johann had. Watching Johann and Lindy together was a sight to behold.

He was lonely, dammit. He never imagined that he would not be a husband or father, but that dismal future loomed larger with each passing day. It was the kind of loneliness that could not be satisfied with his large, boisterous, loving family; he supposed he wanted to be in love. He just hadn't known it until he witnessed Greta's revelation. Maybe it was, indeed, time to stop being so selective; many couples experienced love after marriage, after all. But the sultry blond barmaid only deepened his gloom, and he was relieved when she finally left.

Johann rejoined Jacob a few moments later. "How did it go?" he asked, excitement lighting up his eyes. "She fancied you, I could tell!"

Jacob leveled a steady look at his brother. "It went quite well. She was a woman of substance, and I asked her for her hand. We will be married soon, with the proper number of offspring to follow." Johann sighed and slouched back in his seat.

"I know you're not going to *marry* her," he grumbled. "But you have to start somewhere. You know; practice your technique, man! Oh, hell. I'm not the right brother to teach you this stuff. Where's Anton when we need him?"

Jacob turned and glanced over his shoulder to consult the beautifully-carved German regulator clock that hung near the bar. "Let's see; it's six o'clock. Anton is no doubt through the second course of a meal with some gorgeous woman he just met, having brilliant conversation and charming the stockings off of her."

"Among other articles of clothing," added Johann with a smirk. "Probably not a woman of substance though, Jacob. Anton loves the ladies of the evening." Jacob shrugged in agreement, trying to put the comment from his mind, but irresistibly his eyes were drawn to the portion of the bar he had been vigilantly avoiding all evening. There it stood, the same bar stool, unchanged in fifteen years. There he sat, a fourteen-year-old boy still wet behind the ears, searching for an ephemeral girl, and meeting instead a stunning lady of the evening, one who stroked his cheek and then touched him intimately. As though time had been rewound, he once again felt confusion, arousal, and shame quiver through his body.

And suddenly he was there again, drawn inexorably back to that time and place that he thought he had packed securely away. He experienced it all again in one painful flash, the sounds of the club receding. He was searching the city, finally finding the girl he sought at the end of a horrible night; she was slashing him and then healing him; they were lying stiffly beside each other under that infernal porch, then she was curled next to him as she slumbered, a welcoming warmth. The horses were meandering toward home; there was the heady smell of those sweet flowers; the girl was snatching the hat from his head and taking the reins as he laughed; he was finding her terrified in the sheep pen and cradling her in his arms. Then they were eating dinner as she met his family, she was forming a sweet connection to Wenzel and Jacob was once again beholding the look on his brother's face when she asked him to teach her how to fish; he was hearing the gasps of disbelief when she emerged from the barn holding an exquisitely-shorn sheep. He was hearing their screeches of hysterical laughter as they plastered each other with *tecolé*; they were bathing in Glory Creek, his heart was stopping the moment when he heard her scream his name like a dying animal. He was supporting her lifeless body as he kicked her to shore; he was feeling the touch of her cold lips on his; her small form was jerking as he forced water from her lungs; then the two of them were lying by the creek, catching their breath, feeling life return, and with it, a terrible and wonderful awareness. He was showing her the secret meadow and together they were creating a stone cottage with their imaginations; they were with Wenzel under the tree, on their backs with the world spinning, gazes locked; they were riding back to San Antonio in the wagon; he was feeling her hand in his hair as he awakened. And the kiss. The coalescence of two children into something unknowable; the utter bliss of that moment; the feeling that he never wanted it to end.

All of it returned with such a powerful rush of bittersweet emotion that Jacob lost his breath for a moment. Johann was chattering away, the food arrived and Jacob began to eat, but his mind was adrift in the past now. After he had discovered who Bailey was and understood that she was gone forever, the rest of that day had passed in a wretched, painful blur. The ride home was torturous; he sat up front with his father in complete silence, for the first time in his young life refusing to speak when his father spoke to him. Franticek had finally given up, and Jacob sat stiffly on his side of the wagon seat, facing forward, arms crossed tightly across his chest, his face a stony mask. Burning tears were wiped away quickly, but Franticek saw them and wondered and worried about what had transpired between his son and the girl.

Jacob had been in a funk for weeks; angry, depressed, and uncommunicative. Every day he disappeared for a few hours; no one in the family knew where he went, but Gacenka forbid his siblings to follow him, understanding that he needed time and space for his young broken heart to heal. And heal it did: gradually Jacob returned to them, with his infectious smile, sparkling eyes, and kind voice, but there was a new gravity to him, innocence supplanted with experience. He still disappeared for a few hours every day, a habit that persisted into adulthood. He found that though he tried with all of his young soul, he could not forget or forgive the girl who had deceived him and his family. Every memory was tainted: the creek, the meadow, the ride to San Antonio in the back of the wagon. She had been a liar, even when he told her it didn't matter to him if she was a working girl. Over the years as he matured, his anger was mostly replaced with sadness and regret for her; surely she must have met a bitter end or was experiencing a depraved life in some corner of the Southwest. He had never seen or heard of her in San Antonio; she had simply vanished, like so many other children of the street.

The memory faded as his life filled: he was a gifted student and had been persuaded by his father to attend law school in Boston. For the first time, the hard physical labor which had defined his young life was replaced with schooling and, eventually, socializing. Jacob's popular roommate, a jocular and rambunctious young man named Freddy Grindle, had introduced him to Boston nightlife for young singles. They would begin every free evening at the Red House, a pub in Harvard Square, before they moved on to the newly-constructed Hotel Brunswick at the corner of Boylston and Clarendon Streets. The massive six-story brick and sandstone building boasted 350 rooms, but it was the two large dining halls to which Jacob and Freddie gravitated—or rather; Freddie gravitated and Jacob went along reluctantly. The halls were opulently adorned and lavishly furnished with Pompeian-themed walls and white marble floors, accessed via a luxuriant medieval parlor. The wealthy Boston society girls dined here with their frowning, cigar-smoking fathers and bejeweled, bored-looking mothers, and Freddie's favorite strategy was to commandeer a table near to a family with two beautiful daughters and make eyes at them throughout the meal. The women were drawn to Freddie's high-spirited personality and Jacob's quiet good looks, and more often than not, the young men would find themselves escorting the women home with a younger sibling tagging along for propriety's sake, or perhaps even taking an un-chaperoned stroll and ducking in an alley to steal a quick kiss.

Freddie initiated him into the seedier side of Boston as well. On Jacob's twentieth birthday, after several hours at the Red House, Freddie and a small group of co-conspirators surrounded him, lifting him bodily from his bar stool. "Time to descend into the Black Sea!" Freddie had roared, and Jacob had no idea to what he was referring. A short time later they were sauntering down North Street, popping into taverns and jilt shops, and finally goading Jacob into a brothel. The rest of the night was a hazy, erotic dream, but he woke up the next day in the bed of a voluptuous prostitute named Lillian, realizing that he had broken his vow to himself. But before he left, Lillian, who had the whitest skin and reddest lips he had ever seen, endeavored to teach him a few more tricks, and he was a willing participant, much to his chagrin. He had felt sullied for a full week, and that was his first and final foray into the Red Light District of Boston. Freddie, however, was a frequent visitor and described, in detail, his exploits to Jacob, who would always strive to change the subject as quickly as possible.

Jacob much preferred Young's Hotel on Washington Street, another colossal sandstone structure that extended to Court Square and Court Street. He, Freddie, and other Harvard men often dined in the main hall, mixing with the intelligent, wealthy Wellesley girls under the sometimes not-so-watchful eye of the den mother chaperone. On the Court Street side was the entrance to the ladies' restaurant, a highly-ornamented dining hall that possessed the unique feature of an ornate open fireplace at one end adorned with Chelsea tile, the focal point of a truly stunning room. On one occasion Freddie convinced a not-entirely sober Jacob to slip in and pursue an enchanting young woman who was standing by the fireplace alone. And that is how he met Laura Louise Baldwin. Jacob would never forget her first words to him.

"You are the ugliest lady I have ever seen," she had said with a straight face as he approached her, and he had laughed out loud in surprise, attracting the attention of the hall manager who quickly directed him to take his leave of the ladies' dining room. He had smiled and tipped his hat to Laura, not yet knowing her name, and she smiled back with an identical dimple in her right cheek. Later she appeared in the main dining hall, and he was nudged toward her by an ecstatic Freddie, who was already surrounded by three adoring women.

"Hello," he had said simply.

"I do apologize for getting you booted from the ladies' hall," she smiled. Her voice was cultured Bostonian and her words were precise. He noted that her hands were white and soft, her nails immaculately polished and fingers bejeweled.

"Well, I've never been accused of being an ugly lady before, so I was a little off my game," Jacob returned.

They talked for a solid two hours that evening, Jacob finally finding the courage to ask her to spend the next evening with him as well. And so began the most pleasant interlude in his time in Boston: they explored the city together, taking strolls in the West End in the Common with picnics at the Frog Pond; watching Gilbert and Sullivan's *Iolanthe* from the box seats at the petite yet elegant Bijou Theatre, even wading at Nantasket Beach under the vigilant eye of Mrs. Frances Baldwin, who was charmed by Jacob in spite of herself.

The months flew by, and Jacob found himself drifting into an easy relationship with Laura. There was soothing simplicity about their relationship; they never fought or even disagreed. Freddie alternated between referring to her as "that rich dame" and "your sister," referring to Laura's uncanny resemblance to Jacob, with her black hair and matching dimples. "It's really wrong in so many ways, looking at you two," he said once. "You must be long-lost siblings, and really, Miss Baldwin, a woman of your background could do so much better than a sheep farmer from Texas." Laura had only laughed and murmured something about liking sheep for the time being, and squeezed Jacob's hand.

On one occasion, Jacob had paid a surprise visit to the Baldwin's sprawling Beacon Hill brownstone, and after being admitted by a frosty butler, had been met with an ecstatic Laura. Her mother was out for the day, having taken her younger siblings with her, and Laura quickly ushered him to the quiet, spacious library and dismissed the servant. They talked and laughed, and then Jacob had gazed into her long-lashed, dark brown-green eyes, precisely the color of the pond in Grandmother Naplava's back yard, and realized that something momentous was going to happen. It began innocently enough, tender kisses evolving into passionate ones, and then, to his astonishment, she stood and presented her back to him, lifting her wavy black hair. Without a word he had fumbled with endless hooks and buttons and layer upon layer of garments, and when she was naked before him, she proceeded to disrobe him—he couldn't help but notice that she seemed very self-assured and somewhat knowledgeable of men's attire—and for only the second time in his life, he had made love to a woman. It had been a somewhat anxious, hurried experience on his part, due to the fact that he was terrified of the formidable Mrs. Baldwin appearing in the doorway at any moment; in spite of this and perhaps because of it, the experience was fantastically exciting.

Afterward, as they lay together on the richly-carpeted floor, Jacob mustered the courage to ask the question that had been on his mind. "Laura?"

"Mmmm?"

"Please don't answer if you don't want to, but I was just wondering...I mean, it's kind of important to me to know if...was this your first time? I don't care if it wasn't, but if I was your first, I just want to know." He stopped, feeling immensely foolish. She turned in his arms and gazed up at him.

"No, Jacob. My friends and I are modern women, and we do have love affairs. Everybody does it in our circle, they just don't talk about it much in mixed company." She giggled. "Does that shock you? I'm twenty-two and will no doubt marry soon, and I want to experience life before that day happens." She smiled and waited for him to reply, but he found that he had nothing to say. She spoke of marriage as the end of life, love, and passion, a perplexing and tremendously depressing concept to him, and frankly, he *was* a bit shocked at her admission. Their relationship had been ruled by strict propriety up to this point, and he had assumed she was as inexperienced as he, as he was only two years her junior. Then he thought of Lillian.

There was a pause and Laura's brow crinkled a bit. "You *are* scandalized. I'm sorry, Jacob. I guess I'm not who you thought I was." She had turned from him and made an effort to rise, but he came to his senses, realizing his hypocrisy, and pulled her back down in a firm embrace.

"You know, marriage doesn't have to be a death sentence," he murmured, and they had made love again on the plush burgundy carpet. This time he found that he did not give one thought to the return of her mother.

From that day forward they found three more occasions to be alone, and Jacob suspected that he was in love. Laura was perfect: pretty, funny, smart, and passionate, although every time they made love Jacob couldn't help but feel that a part of her was absent, removed to some distant sphere. She was so damn *precise*, as if she had an ordered plan for every move she made and every reaction she gave, and she did not deviate from that plan. Nevertheless, they got along famously, never a cross word between them. She was the most agreeable woman he had ever met, almost exasperatingly so at times.

"I love you," he finally told her as they sprawled on her bed one afternoon.

She didn't hesitate to agree. "Oh, Jacob, that's sweet. I love you too, of course." He had glanced at her sharply: she seemed so casual about it, while his own heart was beating out of his chest. He had just declared his love for a woman for the first time, and he couldn't help but notice that the object of his affection was now yawning and stretching like a languorous cat and then examining her fingernails with a focused concentration. He had imagined this moment so differently!

Do you? Really? he wanted to say, but pride kept him from doing so, although he was annoyed that he felt he had to goad emotion from her.

Then she kissed him and let her hands roam over him, and he had quickly forgotten his disquietude.

And so, a few months before his graduation, Jacob had wiped out a good portion of his savings and purchased a six-prong solitaire diamond betrothal ring from Tiffany and Company, much to the mortification of Freddie, who spent hours trying to talk Jacob out of it.

"It's all wrong, Nappie. All wrong. Listen to the voice of experience, man!"

"Freddie, someday you will be in love and you will understand," Jacob had countered.

"Yes, and you, too, my friend," Freddie had muttered cryptically, finally giving up.

It was a Sunday afternoon in the Public Garden in the West End, and Jacob had rented a swan boat for the occasion. The ingenious boats were lovely catamarans that were operated by a foot-propelled paddle wheel; the captain sat at the back of the boat, partially concealed by a majestic white iron swan. Three benches seating eight were covered with a cheerful, green-striped canopy. Jacob purchased all eight tickets for privacy, and he and Laura sat close, stealing kisses and enjoying the natural splendor of the serene, tree-lined Public Garden as they glided along the pond. He was insanely nervous, and Laura had asked him repeatedly what was wrong. He finally mustered his courage and turned to her, awkwardly dropping to one knee.

"Marry me," he said simply, and presented the ice-blue ring box from Tiffany's, opening it to reveal the diamond.

He knew instantly that he had made a grave error, and a rogue image of Freddie admonishing him popped into his mind. Laura's face was frozen in surprise, and then it folded into an expression of regret. She looked at Jacob, tears forming in her eyes, and just shook her head ever so slightly. There was a long pause, and Jacob quietly closed the box, returned it to his pocket, and took his seat once more. He turned and stared at the passing trees, aware that the captain must have witnessed the entire fiasco. His jaw clenched and he felt a terrible urge to fling the ring box into the pond.

"Jacob," Laura finally said softly. She reached for his hand, but he withdrew it. "Jacob, look at me, please." He turned to her.

"I thought you understood; we have a beautiful friendship, a wonderful love affair," she said evenly, ever graceful and poised. "But I simply cannot marry outside of my social circle. It is not permitted." She gripped his hand tightly again, urging him to understand.

"You can't or won't?"

"I cannot, and I will not." She looked at him steadily, color high in her cheeks.

"Do you love me?" he finally asked, his voice low and intense.

"Of course I do. But that is naïve. I have loved many men." Jacob gaped at her, truly astonished at her insensitivity, and this time it was Laura who withdrew her hand, her face suddenly flaring as she got a glimpse her true self—perhaps for the first time—reflected in the expression in Jacob's eyes.

"You know, you were right the first time we made love, Laura. You're not who I thought you were at all," he finally said softly, signaling the captain to navigate back to shore.

The remainder of the boat ride was spent in silence, and when they disembarked, Laura thanked him coolly and took her leave in their carriage, leaving him stranded.

He discovered, much to his surprise, that after a few days of humiliation and self-loathing, he did not miss Laura nearly as much as thought he would, or suspected he should. Freddie was a welcome source of comfort and comic relief. Jacob returned the ring, put the money back where it belonged, and devoted himself to his studies and then preparing for the bar, which he passed with high honors. He returned home within the year to his beloved ranch as Jacob F. Naplava, Esq.

He hadn't realized how much he missed home until he returned: he spent hours each day toiling with his father and brothers in the Texas sun, and the ranch grew and prospered as the years stretched by. He did not care to practice law, although occasions did arise that called for his legal skills: he much preferred the feeling of the hot wind on his face, the sheep struggling in his arms, the feel of his beloved horses Samson and Frenzy beneath him. Siblings married and Jacob became an uncle many times over; he attended betrothal parties, weddings, funerals, and birthday parties; his family hosted the famous Naplava barn dances twice a month, where he was forever pursued by a flock of admiring young women who longed to dance with him and perhaps even disappear with him into one of the spacious Naplava barns. He found himself leery and distrustful of women, although he knew in his heart that the young Moravian girls were most likely innocent and pure of heart, not hard and jaded like a wealthy Boston socialite or duplicitous like a debased child of the brothels.

It was at one of these barn dances that he became reacquainted with Darla Keller, the sister of Hans, his German friend with whom he had attended school and explored San Antonio so many years ago. Darla was a tall woman, only an inch or so shy of his own six foot frame, and powerfully built. She was a superb horsewoman; respected as the best "gentler" in the community. At twenty-three—his own age at the time—she wasn't yet an old maid, but she had no suitors, and he had heard some of the men gossiping that Darla preferred women. Jacob noticed that she was given wide berth at the dances; she was many times left awkwardly standing alone and often took her leave early after chatting with Hans and the old folks and making the obligatory appearance. He felt sorry for her, recognizing the strained smile on her pleasant, round face. He made the effort to renew their friendship and engage her in conversation at the next gathering, and he found that he thoroughly enjoyed her straightforward, genuine personality and deadpan sense of humor. She was a welcome change from the simpering girls who stood in tight, terrifying packs, giggling behind their hands and making eyes at Jacob until one of them mustered the courage to approach him, inevitably inspiring in him the urge to flee.

He and Darla spent hours discussing horses, and gradually their conversation turned to more personal issues as their friendship deepened. One night they had both imbibed a bit too much and found themselves alone in a dark corner of the stable, stretched out on the soft hay and talking the night away. In the meager lantern-light, Darla was suddenly pretty, her strawberry-blond hair gathered in a no-nonsense bun, her apple cheeks red and round, and her clear eyes steady and unblinking. He leaned forward and kissed her, and she kissed him back. When they parted, Darla sighed.

"Jacob, you've probably heard the rumors that I don't like men, but that's not true. I'm actually in love." Jacob felt his heart plunge; he liked Darla, and he had enjoyed kissing her, but he wasn't in love with her, and knew he never would be.

"Darla, I…" he began, but she stopped his words with a gesture of her hand.

"No, it's not you," she smiled. "I'm in love with my brother-in-law's brother. You know Hilda married and moved to Colorado?" Jacob nodded. "When she married here last year, I met her husband's brother, Frank. There was this moment when we danced together at her wedding; I could hardly breathe! Neither one of us said anything. We just danced and stared into each other's eyes. We've been corresponding through the mail ever since, but he never says a word about how he feels." She sighed again, tipped her head back, and closed her eyes. "He is powerfully awkward and bashful, but maybe I imagined the whole thing. Do you ever get that feeling? That something bright and shining and wonderful happened that turned your world inside out, but it seems like a dream and you'll never get that moment back again? And nothing else in your life ever lives up to it?" She turned to him and pinned him with her familiar direct gaze.

Jacob could only stare at her and nod, his heart pounding. Darla's poignant words had pretty much summed up his life thus far.

She paused as her eyes focused inward. "I dream of that moment every night. Every night I dance with him. Maybe someday I'll get the courage to tell him how I feel, but I have to admit to myself that it may never happen. I mean look at me, after all. I'm built like a man, break horses like a man, shake hands like a man. Frank probably felt sorry for me, just like you did." She finished her confession matter-of-factly, without a trace of self-pity, shrugged and smiled at Jacob.

Without a word, Jacob stood and offered her his hand. She rose with athletic grace, and together they danced, swaying in the moonlight from the open door. And after they danced, he laid her carefully down into the soft hay and made love to her, and it was a fine and tender moment.

Afterwards she had turned in his arms and searched his face carefully. "Jacob, I've never done that before, and you know I don't love you in that way, but I've been so lonely."

And so they took comfort from each other now and again over the next five years whenever they found themselves lonesome. Darla never ceased writing to her love and received two or three letters in return every week; sometimes she even shared them with Jacob. Jacob continued to be matched with one eligible young girl after another, meeting their families, going on picnics, taking carriage rides in the moonlight, kissing at doorways, waiting for the feeling that never came.

One night Jacob noticed that Darla was absent from her third barn dance in a row; he hadn't seen in her over a month. He finally was able to corner Hans.

"Where the hell is Darla?" he asked without preamble. Was his dear friend sick and nobody was talking about it? Was she pregnant? She had told him that she knew when it was safe to make love, and he had trusted her. Was she in trouble now? If so, he would marry her, of course. His alarm grew as he saw the evasive look on Hans's face. Hans grabbed his arm and tugged him to a private spot behind a sprawling oak tree.

"Look, Jacob, I know about you and Darla," he began, avoiding Jacob's eyes. Jacob felt intensely awkward but was determined to pry the whole story from his reluctant friend.

"Where is she? Is something wrong with her?" Jacob demanded, and Hans finally looked at him.

"She's gone, Jacob. She left you this." He thrust a note toward him. "I'm sorry, man." Hans clasped Jacob on the shoulder, increasing his dread tenfold, and turned to walk back to the party. Jacob stood rooted to the spot, gazing after him, wondering what crisis had precipitated this letter so carefully folded and sealed into an envelope. He finally sat down, back against the trunk, and opened the letter. It was brief, funny, and to the point, so like its author:

Dearest Jacob,

He loves me. He finally 'fessed up, the rotten bastard. He sent for me—he cannot live one more day without me, apparently, and the feeling is mutual. By the time you read this I will be in Denver in his arms, and probably married. I had no time to meet with you to tell you, so this is goodbye for now, although we will be home at Christmas. My time with you is a beautiful memory I will cherish always. I forever remain,

Your dearest friend,

Darla

P.S. He knows about you and I, and all is well. He had a similar experience, so he and I will not be each other's first, but we will be each other's last.

Jacob folded the letter and carefully placed it back in the envelope, and a huge smile spread across his face. He pictured Darla and her man riding horses across the vast Denver ranch, her thick strawberry hair escaping from her bun and her cheeks flaming with excitement. He decided then and there that he would personally see to it that Frank treated her like the princess she was, but when he met the man at Christmas he realized that such intervention would be not be necessary: Frank had eyes only for Darla; he could not stop touching her, always holding her hand or stroking her hair, and he was clearly as deeply in love as was Darla. And he was secure enough in that love to shake Jacob's hand warmly, smile genuinely, and strike up a friendship, even knowing what had passed between Jacob and Darla.

Jacob, on the other hand, descended into a dark loneliness unlike one he had ever known. He missed Darla not only for the physical companionship but for her common-sense, cheerful friendship. He began to suspect that perhaps he was looking for something he knew was unattainable, a form of self-sabotage, or perhaps self-defense. No woman was perfect, he chided himself. It wasn't in his nature to be a bachelor for the rest of his life; it was time to get down to business and just *choose* already. *Maybe I'll put names in a hat and draw one out*, he thought crazily.

"So are you going to sign it or just keep staring at it all night, man?" Johann's voice interrupted Jacob's meanderings and he snapped to attention, realizing that he had finished his meal and probably carried on a lengthy conversation with his brother without remembering one damn word of it. He glanced down at the paper in front of him and sighed.

I, the undersigned, do hereby declare my candidacy for mayor of the city of San Antonio, Texas, dated this ____ day of____.

It was a simple document, really, detailing the duties and responsibilities of the office. All he needed to do was date it and sign it: everyone that he loved wanted him to: his parents, brothers, sisters, friends, community, and fellow sheep ranchers. To have a sheep man in the office of mayor would be stunning victory; he could push hard for equitable water and grazing rights. The way things stood now, tempers were at a violent boiling point among the sheep men, cow men, and farmers; men had already died protecting water and grass.

But four years! Four years of his life in this very public office; four years of meetings and fist-pumping and speeches and endless fighting and negotiating. Four years away from the ranch he so dearly cherished, four years of his youth. By the time he finished his office he would be thirty-two, and that age sounded ancient to him. Where had the years gone?

"Jacob? Am I losing you again? Where *are* you tonight, brother?" Johann sat back, crossed his arms and studied his younger sibling. "What's eating at you?"

Jacob stared back at his brother, suddenly tempted to share his doubts and fears and feelings of loneliness, but in the end he just shrugged. "I'm okay. Just give me the damned pen." Johann let out a whoop, drawing several amused looks from the nearby tables, and pushed the pen across the table to Jacob.

I, Jacob Franticek Naplava, do hereby declare my candidacy for mayor on this 18th day of April, 1891.

CHAPTER FIFTEEN

The wretched itchy suit was the worst part, although there was so much to hate about this ordeal that Jacob wasn't sure which misery to curse the most. The seemingly endless glasses of warm sugary lemonade thrust into his hand? The everlasting queue of wealthy, prominent citizens waiting to bend his ear to their causes? The single young women gazing at him coquettishly when their mothers turned away, each thinking that she was the only one sending him ridiculously transparent come-hither messages with her eyes? Or perhaps the question he was to hear for the next seven months: "What's your platform, Mr. Naplava? Why should I vote for you?" This question came from the wealthy businessmen who had attended this fundraiser with money in their pockets, examining him as though he were horseflesh on display, ready to fund his rise to office if only he gave the correct response. Jacob felt as though he were for sale. *Vote for whomever you damn well please,* he felt overpowering urge to growl. *In fact, vote for one of the other candidates, because I'm in hell right now.*

Hell was actually quite pleasant, aesthetically speaking. The luxuriant grounds of a wealthy textile businessman—one who possessed an invested interest in the well-being of wool industry—was the setting for Jacob's first fundraiser, a garden party event he had been dreading for days. A huge brightly-painted banner erected between two mature live oak trees pronounced Jacob's ridiculous campaign slogan, one that Johann and Lindy had dreamed up, no doubt while laughing uproariously in anticipation of Jacob's reaction: "Jake Won't Break" And underneath in smaller lettering: "Jacob Naplava, Esq. for Mayor." White gravel had been laid to create a perfect walk bordered by blossoming rose vines, and this path led directly to a Bird of Paradise flower garden containing every color imaginable of the stunning flower. As guests made their way through the magnificent garden, they exited onto an expansive lawn; placed strategically around the lush green yard were small, lovely tables covered with white damask cloth, porcelain dishes, shiny silver flatware, and crystal goblets. Each table was tastefully finished with a white vase and a single red tulip. Servants in all white scurried around the lawn, serving champagne and directing the exquisitely dressed ladies and gentleman to the enormous red-striped tent for further refreshments.

Johann immediately guided Jacob toward the canvas tent, both of them nodding, smiling and waving at constituents all the while, and when they entered the pleasantly shaded area they both stopped short in wonder. "Close your mouth; you look like a rube," muttered Jacob. Dozens of tables were laden with the dizzying array of food, most of which Jacob could not identify: cold patties of some sort, cold birds, lobster salad, ham, *pâté de foie gras*, ("It's really fatty liver," Johann explained, and Jacob shuddered), salmon dressed with green sauce, jellies of many colors and flavors, Bavarian cream charlottes, ices served in small paper cups on iced plates, cakes of every kind, and pink, frothy punch. Two tables were devoted to an elaborate tea and coffee spread, complete with biscuits, bread and butter, sandwiches, and lemonade. The fruit tables boasted melons, peaches, grapes, and strawberries and cream. One particularly popular area under the tent offered a fine selection of spirits: claret, champagne, brandy, soda water, old Madeira, sherry, and port, with servants ready to replenish the decanters and pitchers and supply fresh goblets, tumblers, and wine glasses as they were snatched up by the gentlemen guests.

"Don't mind if I do," muttered Johann, and made his way to the spirits table, but Jacob found that he had no appetite, and in fact, was having trouble swallowing at all. He was *nervous*. He gulped audibly and pulled at his collar as he glanced outside toward the podium where he would meet his doom all too soon. He understood the need to court the bigwigs, but he felt like a fish out of water, and longed for a good old-fashioned Naplava party with home-made beer and dancing until dawn.

Johann procured his drink and they commenced to mingling with the movers and shakers of San Antonio in the hot April sun: the ladies in their fine bonnets and long silk dresses of every color created a lovely landscape as they lounged on sofas and armchairs or sat in chatty groups on Turkish rugs while the dandy gentlemen in white and cream-colored suits talked business and politics. Jacob was expected to converse with all of the guests—after all, they were paying good money to meet him—and the only relief was Johann by his side, who kept him entertained with witty, caustic comments.

"Watch out, brother. Ten o'clock, there, that one in the pink dimity. She has a pretty face until she opens her mouth. Holy mother, I bet she uses a tree branch as a tooth pick."

"This way, Jake. Howard Brimauld has been spiking his lemonade; ask him about the monkey and a chili queen named Juana. That man is the funniest son-of-a-bitch alive."

"Veer! Veer! Mother with baby to your immediate left! And it smells funny!" This warning came too late: a squalling baby was thrust into his arms with a request to kiss it, and Jacob politely handed his lemonade to Johann and held the infant securely against his shoulder, rubbing his back and whispering in his ear until he calmed and fell asleep. The red-faced, harried mother gave a whoop of delight.

"My husband is voting for you, Mr. Naplava!" she declared. Jacob smiled and tried mightily not to roll his eyes.

And so the day progressed, with Jacob frantically trying to remember names, listen politely, nod at the suitable times, and avoid sounding like a jackass. All the while he just longed to strip off his white club collar shirt with a black bow-tie that was a bit too tight, gray and white striped trousers and vest in which he was sure he looked ludicrous, ankle-high black kid-leather lace-up boots which actually looked quite fine but were squeezing his toes numb, and a straw hat with a bold red-striped band that he suspected made him look like he was about to break into song and dance. He just wanted to leave the whole mess behind and dive into the San Antonio River in his skivvies and float away, preferably with a whisky shot and a large, frosty mug of beer chaser waiting for him at the other end.

His discomfort was accompanied by two bands playing on opposite ends of the lawn: one making merry and one offering more formal fare. The competing musicians added to the surrealism of the experience: he didn't know whether to dance a jig with the fellows while chugging ale or bow to a lady and ask her to waltz. A lively game of lawn tennis caught his attention—he hadn't played tennis since he lived in Boston—but when he moved to join them, Johann laid a restraining hand on his arm. "Can't have you getting all sweaty, little brother. Play after your speech." Short of joining the ladies in croquet, Jacob found himself with little to do but shake hands and spread the Gospel of Jacob Naplava, and he found, to his dismay, that he actively hated it. He had to repeat the same political agenda *ad nauseum,* he had to be almost rude in his refusal to engage in negative dialogue about his opponents, and he quickly discovered that he had to be careful not to be maneuvered into promises he could not keep.

After an interminable two hours—*two hours!*—Johann directed him to the podium, which was elegantly set up in a beautiful gazebo covered with climbing ivy and morning glories. Time seemed to shift into slow motion as he stumbled his way up the podium stairs to the lectern and then fumbled his way through his speech, speaking about the need for grazing and water rights for sheep farmers (loud applause), equity and peace among farmers, cowmen, and sheep men (decidedly more muted applause), and a crackdown on city vice (barely any detectable applause). He glanced at Johann, who was looking a bit let-down, and decided he needed to end on a high note. The changes he may be able to make someday…it was worth feeling foolish, wasn't it? And maybe he could finally get rid of some of these god-awful clothes! He groaned inwardly and steeled himself.

"And finally, let me just say that after earning my law degree, there was nothing more I wanted to do than strip off my coat" (he shrugged out of his detested jacket, released the bow tie, and loosened the top few buttons of his shirt, causing a few female mouths to hang open), "roll up my sleeves" (he paused and did just that, revealing the knotted muscles of his working man's arms), "take off my party hat" (he sailed the straw hat over the audience like a Frisbie pie tin, gaining rather more yardage than he had bargained for, and a tall young woman in the back of the crowd who caught it actually *squealed*, as if she had caught the bride's bouquet), "and feel that wool again, and the sun on my back. That's what we're fighting for: the right to take care of our families and the businesses that our fathers and grandfathers have spent lifetimes building." He raised his arm in victory, then brought it down mightily and pounded his fist on the podium for effect, causing the ubiquitous vase with the single red tulip to teeter precariously. He grabbed it and settled it gently back into place amidst deafening silence, and realized he may have over-done it.

Many of the young women—and quite a few of the older women—seemed to be in a bit of a trance, lips open, fans moving frantically. And then the applause commenced, and Jacob received his first standing ovation.

Finally, after a seemingly ceaseless number of congratulatory handshakes and insistent mothers introducing their eligible daughters, it was time to take his leave. The party was winding down, he had successfully given his speech, and Johann and Charles were tremendously satisfied with the money collected and promised.

"Wait! One more family, brother." Jacob groaned as Johann tried to tug him in the opposite direction of their carriage.

"No! Not one more! Let's just get out of here, dammit," he growled. "I've played Mr. Mayoral Candidate for long enough today."

"C'mon. You have to greet them; they're from the old country and they have loads of money." Jacob sighed, massaged the back of his neck, and turned, walking with Johann to a family of three who was just preparing to board their carriage. "The name is Vogler," Johann whispered. The man, short of stature and dark-haired with a keen, darting gaze, greeted them warmly.

"Well, hello there, Johann and Jacob Naplava, after all of these years! We were hoping to get a chance to speak to Jacob, but can you believe the crowd today? So proud of you, young man!" He extended his hand for a shake, his grip surprisingly powerful. "You know, I first met you when you were a boy, maybe ten years old or so. We attended one of the famous Naplava barn dances, yes, we did. You and Caroline became quite the little pals." Jacob searched his memory, but for the life of him could remember nothing about this family. He laughed and shrugged helplessly, palms up.

"I'm sorry, Mr. Vogler. I have a bad memory," he lied. His memory was actually quite keen, but he didn't want to hurt the older man's feelings. He had many brothers and cousins and Vogler was probably mistaking him for one of them.

"Well, Caroline sure remembers it, don't you, baby?" Mr. Vogler smiled affectionately at his daughter, a petite young woman with lovely, platinum hair gathered in an elaborate braided bun and remarkable grass-green eyes. She glared at him and then glanced at Jacob, her face flaming.

"I'm so sorry, Jacob," she said, forcing a laugh. "Father has been spending too much time with Mr. Brimauld and his funny lemonade." Jacob laughed with her, feeling a bit sorry for her. He detected not one bit of artifice or flirtation; she seemed genuinely embarrassed at her father's antics.

"Oh, I beg your pardon, this is Caroline, of course, our daughter, and you must remember my wife, Mrs. Aloisie Vogler." Jacob took each of their hands in turn, bowing over them formally. Mrs. Vogler was a beautiful woman, diminutive like her daughter, with faded blond hair gathered in a fashionable, puffy bun and sparkling, green eyes.

"So pleased to make your acquaintance once again," Jacob muttered, feeling awkward at the formality. He had no idea why, but he felt as though he were meeting royalty. "I'm wondering, why haven't I seen you since we were children?" He directed this comment to Caroline, who seemed approachable. "I don't know of any Moravian who can stay away from dancing and homemade beer!" He realized that he may have sounded impudent, but a quick glance at the Voglers reassured him that they were not offended; Mr. Vogler laughed and nodded, then turned to Johann to strike up a conversation about the campaign.

"Oh, Father is a businessman here in the city," Caroline replied. She was remarkably soft-spoken, and Jacob was compelled to lean close to her to hear her clearly. "Father and Mama are Moravian. Not that that explains anything," she smiled. "We live in town and I've always had tutors here." Jacob suddenly took note of the elegant and very expensive jewelry gracing her fingers, wrists and neck and that of her mother's. *Not another wealthy socialite*, he groaned inwardly.

Caroline sighed and fanned herself, apparently unaware of the awkward pause. "It is unseasonably warm today. I wish I could jump in that river and go for a swim." Jacob looked at her sharply, taken aback that her thoughts so closely mirrored his own. Caroline was gazing longingly at the water, a playful smile on her lips. "Now that's not very ladylike, is it? But you know what? I don't care." She suddenly began to stride toward the riverbank, and Jacob felt a swell of laughter building. Caroline was no run-of-the-mill prissy socialite!

He watched as she sat on the lush grass and commenced to unbutton her white leather high-top shoes, peel off her stockings, hike up her dress to her knees, and stick her legs in the cool water. She tilted her head back, a look of ecstasy on her face, and Jacob felt a pull of attraction. He dared a quick peek at Mr. and Mrs. Vogler: Mr. Vogler was still deep in conversation with Johann, who was gaping, mouth open, at Caroline, while Mrs. Vogler was laughing gently behind her hand. "Please excuse my daughter," she finally said. "She is a bit impulsive."

Jacob took a deep breath and joined Caroline by the river, stripping off his own shoes and socks and sticking his legs in the water. "Do you think we dare to jump in?" he finally asked.

"Well, no, maybe not *today*," she replied, smiling widely at him with a wink. They sat by the river in companionable silence for a few minutes longer before he mustered the courage to ask the next question.

"Miss Vogler, I would be honored if you and your family would join me for dinner tonight." He glanced at her, nervous. He could not shake the feeling that he was requesting permission to court a princess.

"Why yes, Mr. Naplava, I would be delighted, and I accept on their behalf," she said ever so softly.

Jacob cleared his throat. "Would McClanahan's be acceptable?" McClanahan's was the city's premier steak establishment, and had a quiet, intimate feel, perfect for getting to know someone.

Caroline considered for a moment. "I do believe I would prefer Pacelli's, if you don't mind," she confessed. "That man makes wonderful meatballs." Jacob found himself pleasantly surprised that she didn't automatically consent to his first choice: Laura's habit of constant acquiescence and her unwillingness to voice an opinion had irritated him to no end. On the other hand, Pacelli's was a large, noisy, tremendously popular eating establishment, and would most likely be full to capacity with many of the city's finest—folks he had just been rubbing elbows with for the past three hours.

"Pacelli's it is," he smiled, and so he found himself less than thirty minutes later wedged between Johann and Caroline across a red checkered cloth-covered table from Mr. and Mrs. Vogler, drinking Italian wine and being interrupted every five minutes with campaign supporters. Amidst the chaos Caroline and he spoke easily about a variety of topics, but she was so soft-spoken that he found himself leaning down, her mouth practically to his ear, and enjoying that predicament much more than was appropriate in front of her parents.

"Where did you study law?" she would whisper, and he would lean toward her, cupping his hand to his ear. "Where did you study law?" she would repeat, her lips a scant half inch from his ear.

"Oh! I studied at…"

"Mr. Naplava, our next mayor! Well done, my son, well done! You've got my vote, young man!" a voice would boom, accompanied by a tremendous thump on the back.

"Thank you..." Jacob would kick Johann under the table.

"*Mr. Settle,*" Johann would mouth.

"Thank you so much, Mr. Settle!" Jacob would pivot and shake the man's hand and find himself obliged to engage in conversation for the next five minutes.

All the while Caroline sat patiently, smiling, green eyes sparkling, oozing gentility, poise, and there was no doubt about it, a certain type of sensuality that Jacob had never encountered. There was a stillness, a watchfulness about her that he couldn't quite put his finger on. Eventually Jacob would wrangle free from the well-wisher and she would speak to him again, and he would be compelled to lean close. By the end of the evening he found himself well-acquainted with her flowery perfume and quite enjoying the occasional brush of her lips against his ear. During the carriage ride back to her parents' estate, nestled close to her with their thighs pressed together, he felt more at ease with her than he had with a woman since his time with Darla, although in an entirely different way. *Maybe, finally, this could be the one*, he thought, and then mentally kicked himself. *Don't jinx it!* He decided to take things *very* slowly.

And yet Caroline Vogler was a subtle, accomplished flirt. As Jacob spent more and more time with her, he could not for the life of him decide if he was pursuing Caroline or she was pursuing him. She did not seem to have any designs on him whatsoever: marriage was never mentioned, nor were children or any other inkling of a possible future together. But she somehow was on his arm at every political and social event, smiling graciously, greeting supporters and friends by name, mingling with others easily, referring to herself and Jacob as "we." Somehow, without any deliberate intent on his part, they were a couple. She never asked about meeting his parents or the rest of his large family, even after they had been seeing each other for several weeks. Jacob experienced an odd reluctance to take this step, and was gratified that Caroline did not seem to mind in the least. He was a regular guest at her parents' well-appointed estate, and this was enough for the time being, he supposed.

He had to admit to himself that he had no idea what he was doing when it came to a successful relationship. Johann was not around to talk to; he had returned home to the Hill Country weeks ago while Jacob had been forced to lease a room in the city—one of the sacrifices that he had made was to spend part of his life close to the campaign office, away from his beloved ranch. He couldn't imagine talking to Johann about Caroline, anyway; Johann professed an overt dislike of her, wrinkling his nose and pursing his lips as if he'd bitten into a very sour lemon every time Jacob mentioned her name. Jacob was mystified and irritated by his reaction, especially since

Johann's favorite hobby was to play matchmaker. He suspected that Johann was afraid that this new relationship would interfere with the campaign.

The only way in which Caroline was interfering with the campaign, however, was through her incredible sensuality. Jacob had to admit that he was distracted. Although he suspected she did not possess the sexual proclivity of Laura, their conversations became laced with innuendo more and more frequently, and often while spending time with her family he would catch her staring at him with what could only be described as hunger. Jacob was amazed that her parents never seemed to be the wiser. And yet they had never even so much as kissed; every time he tried, she pulled away and laughed, an apology in her lovely light-green eyes.

It was after one of these dinners, several weeks into their relationship, when Caroline invited him for a stroll around the Vogler's stunning swimming bath that stretched across the vast lawn behind the mansion. He had never seen anything like it, although he had read about large swimming pools with boards for diving in London. The "Vogler Bath" was quite the rage in San Antonio. The pool had been built especially for Caroline and her older brother Henry; they both had loved to swim, taught by their mother from an early age. The waters were clear and clean, devoid of life and the accompanying messy refuse, the bottom maintained with tiny green and blue pebbles, the sides constructed of the smoothest marble. On the lawn around the perimeter of the pool about every ten feet stood an ornate pole with a small, elegant gaslight, and sleek wooden deck chairs were placed strategically around small tables with umbrellas, which were folded every evening in the late-May dusk. Jacob shook his head in disbelief.

"It's heated, too," Caroline said, pointing out the path of the brick flue that led to a steam engine at the back of the house.

"It's amazing!" he finally said. "You and Henry must have been the luckiest brats on the block."

Caroline laughed and nodded in agreement. "You have no idea! Mama was an incredible swimmer; she still is." She gazed at him, as if deciding how much to divulge. "She lived by the Morava River; her family was very poor, and she dove for shells to sell at market and learned to catch fish by swimming with them." Caroline's eyes glimmered. "When we were younger she used to throw things in this pool; you know, like coins and shells, and Hank and I would dive for them. It gets really deep in the middle." A soft smile played about her lips as she remembered, and Jacob was touched by the intimate story, trying to imagine the very wealthy, very beautiful Mrs. Vogler as a destitute child, diving for shells so the family would have enough to eat. They meandered around the pool in silence, and Jacob found himself somewhat mesmerized by the rippling water and the reflection of the gaslights.

"Where is Hank now?" Jacob ventured. Caroline didn't talk much about her older brother, but the few things she had shared made it obvious that she adored and idolized him.

A shadow passed across her face. "Oh, he's studying at Oxford now. He loves it there. I hope he'll stay."

"You do? Won't you miss him, clear across the ocean?"

Caroline reached for his hand suddenly and pulled him down onto the grass. "I have a surprise for you," she confessed sheepishly. "I made mother and father be quiet about it, but it's my birthday today. I'm twenty-seven. I'm an old maid, God help me. But I don't care, because it means that you and I are here now, together." She sat forward on her feet, her expression expectant and anxious.

"What? You should have told me!" Jacob leaned forward and enveloped her in a hug. He was touched by her confession of her age, but was not surprised: he had judged her to be close to his own age and often wondered how such a pretty and wealthy woman could remain single. He decided that, *dang it*, this was the moment. He had waited long enough. He kissed her, and she stayed perfectly still; her lips were so soft she seemed to melt in his mouth. It was like kissing a cloud. He leaned back and looked into her eyes, and they were shining with excitement. He kissed her again and he felt her nails in his back and her teeth sharp on his lips, and he pulled back, surprised, tasting blood.

"Oh, Jacob, I'm sorry," she said, coloring. "This is all completely new to me. Please be patient. I'm a little nervous."

He sucked his lower lip and gazed at her, realizing that he had much to learn, too. Caroline Vogler was full of surprises. He smiled gently and took her hand. "Happy birthday, Caroline."

She shifted away after a beat and withdrew a rather large flask from her skirt. "Do you mind if we drink to my happiness? This is a special drink from the home country. I have no idea what it is, but Mama says it's delicious! I bet your parents have had it. I want to share it with you. But you drink first; tell me if it's vile!"

Jacob took the flask from her and ceremoniously tipped it, then tipped it again. And again. Caroline laughed and grabbed it from him. "I guess it must good," she teased, and enjoyed a lengthy drink, her eyes opening wide with pleasure.

It was the most delicious liquor he had ever tasted. He absolutely could not describe it; the flavor was nutty with hints of honey, ginger, cinnamon, chocolate, and other beguiling flavors he could not begin to identify, but it reminded him of something he had tasted in his childhood, probably a pastry his mother had made. It was incredibly smooth and did not seem to be strong at all. "Are you sure this is liquor?" he laughed. She shrugged.

"Honestly, I don't know. I think we are drinking a little girl's harmless punch! Oh well! I guess we can enjoy it anyway; I'm so thirsty after that meal." She took another long drink and passed the flask back to him. He could not get enough; neither could she. The flask was empty in the space of five minutes.

"Do you have any more?" he tried to ask her, but the words seemed to wrap themselves into a shape of a pretzel. He touched his lips experimentally with his fingers, and his mouth seemed to have grown. "Oh, blah, sorry about that," he muttered, shaking his head a bit. At least those words seemed to come out all right, although it seemed to take an awful long time to say them. Caroline burst out laughing and fell over in the grass, holding her stomach.

"Oh, Jacob, I guess it was liquor after all," she gasped, but all Jacob heard was muffled nonsense. Caroline seemed to be a blur; her white dress, platinum hair, the green grass and the dark shadows were amalgamating into a swirl of sweet, delicious taffy. He leaned down to look at her more closely, and she grabbed him and pulled him on top of her. Time seemed to shift from a linear, predictably-paced experience to a looping, whirling joyride, somehow simultaneously as slow as molasses and explosive as fireworks.

"Kiss me again; I'll get it right this time," she begged. He found that he was all too eager to kiss her, and did so. She wrapped her legs around him and began to move against him, and he froze in surprise.

Suddenly, his clothes didn't feel right at all. They were constricting him terribly. He couldn't breathe.

"Caroline, take them off," he rasped, panicking. She began to claw at his jacket and shirt and he finally struggled out of them, then ripped off his belt and loosened the top few buttons on his pants. Finally, he could breathe again! He lay back down, gulping in huge lungsful of air with relief, the panic slowly subsiding. What the hell was going on? He contemplated the stars and was amazed to see them begin to expand. They were growing! And changing color!

And then the unimaginable happened: Caroline suddenly rolled toward him and slipped her hand inside his trousers, stroking him. Jacob was jolted as if from a deep sleep, and he pulled away, aroused and terrified at the same time.

"Oh, my God. What is happening?" he muttered. Caroline sat up, a confused, fuzzy expression on her face, tears gathering in her eyes.

"I don't know! I'm so sorry!" She shook her head, trying to clear it, clearly mortified.

"It's okay," he slurred, clumsily capturing her hand. "But we shouldn't do that for the first time when we're drunk."

She nodded, relieved. "Jacob, let's go swimming. The liquor will wear off that way."

It seemed like the perfect plan, but as the two staggered to the edge of the pool, Jacob suddenly stopped. Instead of his head clearing, he seemed to be getting more and more disoriented.

"We don't have, you know, whatevers," he slurred. "You know. Something to swim in."

"Just slip a few things off," Caroline managed. "Don't worry, we'll behave. We won't even kiss again. Let's just bathe and get our senses back." All of this seemed to be uttered in a rapid-fire garble, and Jacob stared at her, perplexed.

"Whatcha say?" The world was moving slowly now in luscious great sweeping arcs, first one way, then the other, as if he were on a giant swing.

Caroline laughed and unbuttoned her dress and removed layer upon layer of clothing; the process seemed to take hours. Finally she stood naked before him, her soft, pale body an array of curves. *She's a bit chunkier than I thought*, Jacob thought wildly. She held out her arms to him, and he stepped forward and cupped her generous breasts in his hands. One last sober thought crossed his mind: *I have no control over myself right now*, and it was almost a cry for help.

The next morning Jacob awoke naked on the grass, shivering. It was dawn, and Caroline was beside him; he could feel her back pressed lightly against his. He turned his head; a pain shot through it and the earth tipped sharply. He fought through the nausea and looked at Caroline; she was dressed only in a white chemise, and the two of them were wrapped in her dress. He closed his eyes and tried mightily to remember, but only bits and pieces came to him: the warm water caressing his bare skin, a chase across the pool and back—had he been chasing Caroline or was she chasing him? He remembered the hard, cold marble pressing against his back and the soft, slippery Caroline pressing him from the front. Hardness, softness. Coolness, warmth. Caroline moaning his name. Caroline shimmering, dazzling in the gas lights. He remembered the feeling of being immobilized and the taste of salty tears. Whose tears? Had they made love?

He felt overwhelming regret followed quickly by an overpowering panic. What if her father found them out here like this? Why hadn't he come to investigate? Had her parents just assumed they had made their way back inside last night? That must be the case. They had to get in the house before anyone awoke! God almighty, this was the tightest spot he had ever been in, and he suddenly hated every minute of it. He looked at Caroline again and prayed that he hadn't taken advantage of her, prayed that they hadn't done what he suspected. He cared for her, but he wasn't ready for this, and she certainly wasn't, either.

"Caroline?" he whispered. She groaned and shifted.

"Caroline? We have to get in the house. It's morning."

She sat up suddenly and turned to the side, retching. He held her shoulders and waited it out. "Oh my God," she whispered. She finally turned to look at him, her blond hair loosened from its tight braids and her face puffy with sleep. She clutched her dress away from him, covering herself as best as she could. "Jacob, what happened?"

Jacob buried his face in his hands. "We drank all of that liquor. It must have been absinthe or something, or some drug."

"Yes, I remember we were absolutely pickled," she mumbled. "I should have listened to Mama's advice about only drinking a thimble full."

That would have been good to know, thought Jacob angrily, but he bit his tongue. She looked as miserable as he felt.

"Caroline," he began, and reached for her arm. She allowed him to take her hand. "Do you remember anything? I think we went swimming, but I don't know if we, well, did anything else." She bent her head and shrugged forlornly, and Jacob felt like the biggest ass in the known world.

"I don't know either," she admitted. "I'm—*pure*, Jacob, so I have no idea. How would I know?" She looked up at him beseechingly, and although he could sense that she was in distress, she remained dry-eyed. He wondered fleetingly if she were in shock, and decided that this was officially the second worst day of his life.

"Err, well, I think you will be able to tell if you feel…sore…down *there*, and maybe there will be some, oh God, stickiness, although we were in the pool." Jacob stopped, completely abashed, but determined to see this through.

Caroline studied him silently, and the moment seemed to stretch on interminably.

"Let's go inside," she said abruptly. She arose and began dressing in one quick movement, and Jacob did the same, although he had to admit that he was clearly feeling much worse than she was. He felt as though he were going to retch and pass out, simultaneously, perhaps, and very soon. He struggled into his clothes and staggered after her, making his way across the lawn and into the house a good five paces behind her hurrying form.

"Come on, hurry, Jacob. Take one of the guest rooms in this wing. Just get in bed and the servant will find you there. Mother and Father are still sleeping," she whispered as they climbed the winding marble staircase. "I'll see you in a bit at breakfast!" She smiled, winked, and kissed him quickly on the cheek, spinning the opposite way, heading to her own quarters. She seemed downright perky now, he thought crankily. He would never understand women. Maybe nothing had happened after all: they got smashed, engaged in some petting, went swimming in their altogether, and passed out. Yes, that must be the way it had worked out.

Jacob drank a pitcher-full of water, splashed more water on his face, relieved himself for what seemed like an eternity, washed himself with lavender-scented soap until he was shivering and clean, and climbed into the massive four-poster bed, feeling his body relaxing. Everything would be fine, he reasoned.

Those sentiments were dashed after an intensely awkward breakfast with her parents; her father spent a full sixty minutes pinning him with a murderous gaze and said very little. After they excused themselves, Caroline accompanied him to the stable to fetch his rig, and they walked without speaking or touching.

"Jacob, I think I know a little more about what happened last night," she finally said, breaking the uncomfortable silence as they reached the stable. She pulled him inside and they sat together on a bale of hay, out of view of the gardener and stable boy. She peeled a piece of hay into three perfect strands with her fingernail and began braiding them. She took a deep breath. "You were right. I am, well, *sore*, and there are other indications that we consummated our relationship. There was blood on my dress; I think we may have been lying on it." She delivered the news without looking at him, and her cheeks were stained a deep pink. Jacob felt his world collapse a bit.

He took both of her hands. "Caroline, I'm so very sorry—" he began, but she shook her head.

"I'm the one who gave you that awful stuff. It's my fault, too. And Jacob, for what it's worth, I'm sure it was a beautiful moment." She finally looked him in the eye. "But now we have to talk about the consequences."

The incongruity of the word "consequences" superimposed over "beautiful moment" seemed to hang in the air like a noose above their heads. Jacob gulped and let the gravity of the situation settle around him. He suddenly realized, with startling clarity, that the words he was going to say next would probably irrevocably change the course of his life.

"You could be pregnant," he finally said in a low voice. "And if you are, I will marry you, Caroline." She stared at him, unblinking, her hands limp in his. He didn't know what reaction he had expected, but it wasn't this. She was absolutely still and the air was heavy with disapproval.

"I could be with child, Jacob; that much is true. So am I to wait to find out if I am, and then ask my parents to prepare a shotgun wedding?" Her voice was soft as ever, but her face was distorted by anger: green eyes blazing, lips a thin line, eyebrows shaped into a deep frown. For the first time Jacob detected a steely resolve in this small woman—a razor-sharp edge he had never observed before. Just as quickly, her face seemed to soften and her hands were warm in his. "I'm sorry, love," she amended. "I'm just so very frightened." Her mouth was downturned and she, indeed, look scared out of her wits.

"I'm sorry, too," he choked out, and gripped her hands tightly, his own fear constricting his breathing.

"The daughter of a very prominent citizen and the future mayor of our great city cannot have a scandal such as this; can't you see that? The race will be lost for you, and my parents will be lost to me." At this, her voice broke.

"My father; he is very—protective—of me. He is so very strict. I think he already suspects something, and if he finds out that I'm with child before being married, he'll kill you."

Jacob stared at her, his skin crawling. He dearly hoped that she was using the phrase "he'll kill you" figuratively, but he had his doubts.

"I was going to ask you anyway," he lied. There was nothing left to think about now, was there? He awkwardly sunk to one knee beside the bale of hay. "Will you marry me?" he said simply, finding that he had no grander words at his disposal.

She gazed at him for a long moment. "But what if I say yes, and we find that I am not expecting a child? Will you leave me, Jacob? And then what do I tell my family and friends?"

Jacob flushed; he had not realized it until she vocalized it, but she had put her finger on his thoughts very precisely. Nonetheless, he intuitively understood that he was being manipulated. This was all happening too fast.

Think, man! Be logical! Jacob made one last effort at an alternative plan.

"Caroline, you should know in a few weeks, a month perhaps, if you are likely to be carrying a child. Why don't we wait until then to decide?" He was still perched before her on one knee and found that he could not move.

Caroline rolled her eyes and gave a joyless laugh. "I may not know for two or three months. My—monthly—is not regular like clockwork. And I know women who have had their monthlies for a few months after becoming pregnant! It's all in the timing, Jacob. If we announce our engagement now, the very soonest we could be married would be four weeks from now, and that would be a tremendous rush as it is; oh yes, eyebrows will be raised. People will whisper, 'Why must they rush so?' We can just say we are in love. Then if I am expecting, we can announce it shortly after we're married. Even then, with all that rush, the baby will be a month early, arriving eight months into our marriage or even seven, but babies do come early sometimes, don't they?" Jacob felt her rush of words weave around him like filaments of a web. "The truth is if I am going to have a baby, even if we get married within a month, everyone will suspect the child was conceived out of wedlock. People tend to forgive that when they see how devoted a couple is to each other, and that they have done the right thing. But I would prefer not be married in a maternity gown," she attempted to laugh, and Jacob's heart softened as he saw the effort she was making to accept the situation.

They stayed in their fantastic positions, immobilized; Jacob on one knee, Caroline perched on a bale of hay, clutching her dress for dear life.

"It comes down to this: I love you, Jacob. I don't want to be alone anymore. I'm so ready to be married and start a family. Do you feel the same way? Yes or no?"

The words could have been his own. It was all so simple, really.

"I do," he whispered. "Marry me."

She nodded and sobbed, and this time, there were tears.

CHAPTER SIXTEEN

The ride through Hill Country was spent in silence. Caroline wore a huge bonnet to protect her white skin, and she read a book of poetry for the duration of the arduous two day trip. Every once in a while she would look at Jacob and smile, read him a few stanzas, and take his arm and snuggle close. She loved the feel of his strong arm against the side of her breast. She adored listening to his musical voice as he described the flowers, although she wasn't the least bit interested in flowers, to be honest. In fact, she was vaguely aware that the country they were traveling through was probably quite scenic and maybe even beautiful, with its rolling hills and whatnot. But she wondered if they would stop for a picnic lunch soon, and when they did, if he would kiss her, or perhaps touch her intimately. Or perhaps even more; she closed her eyes and imagined the weight of him on top of her. She couldn't quite believe that she was betrothed to this fine-looking man.

But she absolutely abhorred the thought of meeting his crude, obscenely large and no doubt noisy Moravian family. She detested the notion of being lifted down from this god-forsaken cart he called a "rig" when they could have—*should* have—taken the train, a trip which would have taken exactly one hour and twenty minutes. But he had wanted to go by horse in order to introduce her to the marvels of the countryside, and she was obligated to demonstrate her delight. They had already stayed one night at a horrid little house on a creek; Jacob had taken her for a walk through a bee-filled orchard, and she had gotten stung twice on her arm. And when they finally arrived at his home, she most likely would be forced to tromp through steaming piles of sheep shit to reach a ramshackle cottage or shack or whatever it was that his family lived in. She had gone over this again and again in her mind—how could she keep the man and get rid of the coarse family?—but she had come to realize, after listening to everlasting stories from Jacob—that it was a package deal. Very well, she would take the package, but she wouldn't compromise her standards, thank you very much. She drew his arm closer to her breast and laced her hands with his.

"Let's stop for a—nibble—Jacob," she purred.

Jacob shifted on the hard seat and invented a need to lean forward to adjust a rein, shrugging away gently from her firm grasp. His stomach was in knots; his mind whirling. What in the *hell* had he gotten himself into? Since the day of their betrothal—one week ago today, as a matter of fact—Caroline had been nothing but, well, very *aggressive*. She took every opportunity to caress him, and when they were in privacy or even semi-privacy, she made it very well known that she was willing to do any goddam thing Jacob wanted to do. On a memorable evening several days ago, with servants milling about as she bade him goodbye at her door, he leaned forward to kiss her and she took both of his hands and placed them on her breasts. "Touch me, Jacob. Don't you want to?" she had breathed, and he had found to his dismay that no, he *didn't* want to.

At dinner with her parents a few nights later, she had begun to rub his thigh out of sight under the table; he had glanced at her, a little alarmed, but she had just winked and smiled at him, and so he tried to relax and enjoy the mild seduction. Then her hand wandered north and began stroking him, causing both of his knees to strike the table and overturn a glass of wine. He was angry, and he was, truth be told, a little concerned at his own reaction. Shouldn't he be enjoying these little sexual interludes? He was engaged to this woman: they had professed their love for each other. What was wrong with him? If he so desired, she was his for the taking; she had made that clear. So why wasn't he taking, for God's sake? Any other man would be enjoying this as an early honeymoon, perhaps multiple times per day.

He had to admit that his reticence could be attributed to that fact that since the day they had become betrothed, Caroline had seemed to morph into a different person altogether. Gone was the cool, serene, quietly intelligent Caroline; in her place was what he suspected at times was a nymphomaniac. It was not that she wasn't desirable—she was—or that he didn't care for her—he did—but her sudden advances seemed desperate and oddly out of character. They no longer had conversations about politics, religion, art, literature, or just mundane everyday things. Their conversations had always been so pleasant and effortless, if somewhat dull, but with just the right undertone of sexual tension. Now, Caroline directed their interactions one of two ways: endless plans for the wedding, or attempts to seduce him—to find time and space to be alone with him; not so they could connect on a deeper level and let things evolve naturally, but so she could grind up against him or begin disrobing until he stopped her.

And he was beginning to wonder if perhaps she knew she was not pregnant, and was actively trying to remedy that situation.

He tried to imagine standing up in front of his parents and his family today and announcing his engagement, and found that the thought of it made him queasy. They had already announced their betrothal to Caroline's parents, amidst tears of joy and congratulatory hugs from Mrs. Vogler. Mr. Vogler had been more reserved, and, to Caroline's chagrin, he absolutely forbade her from marrying before September. "We must have my family here, you *know* that. They must travel all the way from the homeland; it will take months for them to prepare and sail. You *cannot* be married next month! That's not a problem, is it, Jacob?" He had glowered at Jacob, and Jacob had the distinct impression that Mr. Vogler was testing a theory. If Caroline was indeed pregnant, she would never agree to wait four months to be married. Before Jacob could even form a coherent argument for an immediate wedding, Mrs. Vogler grabbed Caroline's arm and steered her away.

"You must have the grandest wedding this pokey city has ever seen; it will be the event of the decade! The gown alone will take months to create, not to mention the decorations, the invitations..." She had rushed Caroline away to the parlor to commence planning, but not before Caroline threw Jacob a despairing look. He knew what she was thinking: if she was pregnant, she would be a full four months along by the time of her wedding. She could, perhaps, still hide her condition, but she wouldn't be able to explain away delivering a child five months after they were married. He hoped she was right and that people would be forgiving, for her sake. For his own reputation or even the election, he cared not a whit.

But it seemed ludicrous to introduce her to his family as his fiancé when he had only mentioned her name in one letter—he had simply written, "I'm bringing home a girl I'm courting to meet you all. Her name is Caroline Vogler." And why hadn't he told them? Was he, after all, waiting to see if this was a step he was going to take? And why wait? Didn't he *want* to get married? He glanced at her suddenly, wishing with all of his heart that she would transform back into the woman she was just a week ago. Maybe she was just scared, dammit; scared of losing him, her reputation, scared of possibly becoming a mother. He felt his heart soften a bit, and he turned to her and offered a smile. She returned it, face glowing.

"Caroline?" he ventured.

"Mmmmm?"

"Would you mind if we didn't make our announcement today?" Her smile seemed to freeze into place, and Jacob felt himself break into a sweat. "I mean, your parents and I already knew each other so well, but my folks have never even met you; can we just make this a getting-to-know-you weekend?"

There was an icy silence as she continued to stare at him, the bright smile dying by degrees from her lips. Jacob swallowed convulsively. "What I meant to say was, I can't imagine saying 'Ma, Pa, this is Caroline Vogler, and oh, we're getting married in September.'"

"How long would you like to wait?" she finally said after a pause, her voice unnaturally cool. *Until you find out if I'm pregnant? Well, we can fix that very quickly.*

Rich, handsome, properly-pedigreed Jacob Naplava was poised to be the next mayor of San Antonio—and with her father's connections, he could make it happen—and she wasn't about to lose him on a technicality.

"Well, um, how about, I don't know, another month or so?" He glanced at her again, stomach churning.

She forced herself to tilt her head, nod with understanding, and allow a sweet, loving smile to cross her lovely features. It was exactly as she feared: she was losing him. She knew damn well she wasn't pregnant, and apparently Jacob was not willing to help that process along, judging by his prudish behavior this past week. She had tried too hard, and now he looked at her as if she were some kind of over-sexed freak in a traveling circus. *Time to take a step back, Caroline.*

"Sweetheart, I totally understand how you feel. Let's wait a month and then let your family in on the good news." She watched as a look of astonishment flashed across his face, and then one of relief, and she felt a slow burn begin.

They arrived at midday, and Caroline was flabbergasted at the size of the ranch: there were numerous, massive white barns—she counted seven that she could see—and vast rolling hills of new spring grass dotted with gigantic live oak trees. And sheep. *Everywhere.* Her mind quickly filtered out the natural beauty of the place and zeroed in on the house. Tucked into a valley was a very large, sprawling ranch house, one that had been haphazardly built onto over the years as the family had increased in size. She hadn't visited this ranch since she was a very young girl, and the magnitude of the wealth that was now here was nothing short of damned impressive. "It's lovely," she murmured as Jacob swept his arm expansively, and she almost meant it. He droned on and on about the function of this barn and that barn and this pasture and that fence and this breed and numbers of sheep and that quality of wool, but she tuned it all out and just concentrated on his magnificent jaw line, and she was very pleased. Their children would be divine-looking.

Eventually they made their way to the house, and they were greeted by no less than thirty family members standing on the massive porch, and probably more than that, had she cared to count: Mr. and Mrs. Naplava, who wore strained smiles and ugly homespun clothing, much to Caroline's amusement; a man who looked a bit like Jacob but was obviously an imbecile; Johann, whom she had met before and instantly disliked; a plain-looking, unsmiling woman who must be his wife; Johann's four clinging brats, all under the age of six, it seemed; two girls and a boy who must be Jacob's youngest siblings, a collection of older siblings and spouses and children who all just ran together in a great blur, and...and...

The most handsome man Caroline had ever laid eyes on.

He was standing in the shadows, leaning against the door frame, watching the introductions and hugs and handshakes with a sardonic smile on his incredible lips. He was about the same height as Jacob, but slimmer with not so much obvious muscle; he was clearly a gentleman, not a laborer. His hands were smooth and without calluses, his nails perfectly manicured. His expensive, tailored trousers clung to his thighs, she noticed.

"And you must be Anton," Caroline breathed softly, finally approaching him after meeting most of the others and suffering through the obligatory hugs and questions and niceties from Jacob's parents, who were positively provincial: she cringed to imagine them conversing with her own parents in their ornately-furnished parlor back home. Jacob was engaged in an animated conversation with them now, speaking in a Moravian dialect she had never bothered to learn, although her parents used to speak it to each other when she was a young girl. Now it was considered gauche, and rightly so. She held out her hand and Anton bent over it, his lips lingering and kissing it no less than three times. Up close, he was even more incredible: a perfectly chiseled face, soulful wide-set hazel eyes, rich, light-brown hair with natural blond highlights, not a strand out of place.

"And you must be Caroline," he returned, bestowing her with his brightest smile. "At last I meet Jacob's new lady friend. I must say, I didn't think he had it in him. He's always been a bit backward, my little brother has. But look what a stunning young lady he has ensnared."

Caroline laughed and left her hand in his. He was stroking her palm with his long fingers, concealed from the others by her own hand, and she felt a thrill of excitement. "Anton Naplava, be forewarned that I have heard plenty about your—hobbies. Shall we just say that your reputation precedes you?" Her pink tongue briefly touched her top lip, her thin, perfectly arched eyebrows lifted ever so slightly, and her green eyes sent him an unmistakably bold message. She let those eyes wander over him, pausing here and there without apology, and Anton felt a thrill of his own—and a warning bell.

He removed his hand gently. "Well, we won't get into the particulars right *now*," he laughed and winked, suddenly feeling uncharacteristically awkward. He squeezed her arm and moved away to greet Jacob, and Caroline reluctantly turned to speak with Johann's wife, Lucy or Lizzy or some such dull name.

No. Not yet, thought Caroline, her eyes straying to Anton. *We won't get into the particulars right now. But soon.* The young women in her circle loved to gossip; their parents would be utterly scandalized to hear the stories that were whispered in the ladies-only swimming parties that Caroline regularly hosted.

Letting Anton Naplava make love to you was a bit of a rite of passage among her elite set, although Caroline had never even met him—no doubt her father had seen to that. Make no mistake: she had enjoyed her fair share of lovers over the years since the age of eighteen. Her "confession" of virginity made to Jacob was laughable. Mother and Father were forever hosting families in one of the guest wings, and late at night, away from their watchful, trusting eyes, she had spent many a late hour in her bedchambers entertaining these men, fathers and sons alike. But in short, they were boring and predictable, and Caroline marveled at her luck now: engaged to one magnificent man and soon to be sister-in-law to Anton Naplava! Anton Naplava, it was said, was a Don Juan of epic proportions: the most exciting, skilled lover in the southwest. Many of her contemporaries had reputedly been bedded by this Adonis, and they loved to give intimate details of the experiences. The stories were always titillating: lovemaking in a dark corner of a public library; lovemaking outdoors in one of the city's most exclusive public gardens; lovemaking in the carriage with the driver a few feet away. She felt her body flush just thinking about it. No, she would never marry a cad like this, but oh, the fun they could have!

"…so we were—interested—to finally meet you," Johann's dumpy wife finished. Caroline looked at her blankly; lost in her fantasies about Anton, she had not heard a word the woman had said.

She smiled sweetly and tilted her head. "I'm sorry, could your repeat that, dear? I'm just so tired from the ride, I'm afraid I drifted off there for a moment." Johann's wife—what on earth was her name again? Lindy! That was it! Lindy was pinning her in a disconcertingly direct fashion with her nondescript brown eyes.

"I was just saying that our matchmaking efforts with Jacob have failed miserably over the years. Tell me; what's your secret?" Lindy crossed her arms over her chest and waited. Caroline snapped to attention.

"Secret?" she repeated. What exactly did this woman know? "I'm sure I don't know what you mean." She attempted to return Lindy's unwavering regard, but found she could not. She cleared her throat nervously and gazed around, desperate for a distraction.

A few more awkward beats passed, and Lindy suddenly broke the tension. "Have you met Wenzel yet?" she asked, and pulled Caroline, none too gently, toward a tall, pudgy, quiet man sitting in a rocking chair, tending to a baby. Caroline groaned to herself. *I'd much rather spend more time getting to know the other brother*, she wanted to say, but bit her lip and forced a smile. "I don't know if Jacob's told you about Wenzel. Wen speaks slowly, but don't let that fool you; he's very keen. He's just marvelous with children," Lindy whispered to her. Caroline suppressed a snort of derision. Lindy was beaming and Caroline tried to conjure something positive to say, but she dreaded the thought of making conversation with an idiot, even one who looked vaguely like Jacob.

"Wen? This is Caroline, Jacob's—lady friend," Lindy said brightly. Caroline stiffly held out her hand to Wenzel, the forced smile still pasted on her face. Wenzel kept his eyes trained on the baby until Lindy finally reached down and took the child. He slowly rose to his full height—he really was gargantuan—and without looking at her, took Caroline's hand gingerly, as if he were handling something distasteful.

"How do you do?" he said softly to his shoes.

"Fine, thank you," Caroline returned quickly, longing to get this meeting over with. Wenzel finally looked up, and his hand, which had been limp in her own, suddenly tightened into a vise-like grip. As his faded blue eyes met her green ones, a sluice of fear shot through him. He was afraid of strange women in general, being intensely shy, but this was different: he had been watching her talk to Anton; he watched her lick her lips and let her eyes roam over Anton's body; he noticed Anton stroking her palm. He noticed things that other people didn't. He had been watching Caroline from the moment his beloved brother Jacob had lifted her down from the wagon; he had watched her approach the porch—watched her gaze at Anton and watched Anton return the close regard. He could see that Anton liked her an awful lot. Maybe that was it. He supposed she was beautiful; maybe he was just scared of that. Yes, that must be it. She was beautiful and men liked to look at her, and she liked to look at men. He hoped she wouldn't look at him that way. He was sure he would die if she looked at him that way.

Lately he had been getting kind of lost in the color of things. He liked to think about colors. They seemed to hold still for him and let him dive in, like diving into a pond. Sometimes he would recreate them on canvas with the paints and brushes that Jacob bought him. He never showed anyone his paintings, not even Jacob. But he thought he might try to paint Caroline's eyes, and if he got it just right, maybe he would show Jacob. He was sure that he had never seen eyes the color of new spring grass. No, that wasn't quite right: more like brand new light green spring grass touched with dew in the morning sun. He swam around in the color of her eyes and felt himself getting lost. It was cold and sad. *She* was cold and sad. He felt repelled by her and sorry for her at the same time.

Caroline tried to pull her hand away. "Nice to meet you," she said inanely. "I need to meet Jacob's younger siblings now." She took two steps back, but Wenzel did not let go of her hand, which was becoming numb.

"Here, Wen, can you take care of Mary again?" Lindy handed the baby to him and he finally released Caroline, who couldn't get across the porch fast enough. She involuntarily wiped her hand on her skirt and mentally chided herself for doing so as she noticed Lindy glaring at her. Damn that Lindy for putting her in that awkward situation! And what was with Wenzel the Idiot Boy? He positively scared her with that creepy glare and the painful hand-squeezing routine. She moved toward Jacob and took possession of his arm, gesturing for him to lean down so she could complain sweetly into his ear, but before she had a chance, Gacenka herded them into the spacious home for dinner.

They entered into a hallway foyer and were instructed to hang their hats and leave their baggage on a rustic, beautifully-carved tiger oak hall tree; Caroline took one look and declined; there was just *no way* she was going to hang her expensive steamer hat on one of those ancient-looking pegs! They made their way through an exceedingly odd, wide hallway, Caroline's head swiveling right and left, utterly confused at the labyrinth of adjacent hallways that seemed to erupt randomly. "Jacob, where on earth do all of these hallways go?" she murmured, keeping her voice light.

"Oh, we've added onto the house so many times; every time we need a new room or two we knock out a wall, build a hallway, and tack on a few more bedrooms." He was smiling jovially, clearly expecting her to be delighted, and so she smiled back brightly, thinking to herself that she had never seen such an incongruous, ugly home in her life. The walls of the hallway were un-papered, of all things! They could have at least painted! But no, instead, they had covered the plaster with the plain, wide planks of wood.

"And why—why are the walls covered with wood?" she asked sweetly. "Does that provide better insulation?" she hastened to add, hoping the question was a smart one.

Jacob laughed. "No, you don't need to insulate these interior walls! Ma has so many paintings and portraits; we figured out pretty quick that it was easier to hang 'em up on wood. Plaster is a bitch to drive a nail into."

Caroline winced at the rustic vernacular he seemed to have lapsed into instantly upon stepping foot onto the ranch. She nodded wisely and gave the appropriate inspection to the aforementioned décor: it was beyond hideous, all of it. All of the children's portraits had been painted in some sort of provincial, naïve, rural fashion. Caroline and her brother had traveled to Springfield, Massachusetts in their earlier youth to have their portraits painted by none other than Irene E. Parmelee, and the result was certainly better than this embarrassing mess! Why, Jacob had been painted next to some dirty old sheep!

They eventually veered into one of the hallways and she found herself in a large dining room; at least, she supposed it was a dining room. She could see at a glance that it was connected to the kitchen, of all things. She could actually *see* into the kitchen! It was almost beyond comprehension. There was absolutely no décor or furniture other than an enormous table over which hung an austere lighting fixture—you couldn't possibly even call it a chandelier—a huge, ancient-looking sideboard, and one mirror on the wall. The walls, at the very least, were papered with a Canterbury pattern featuring pink tulips on a sage background; it was actually rather lovely, she had to admit. It was the only lovely thing in the room, however. The many-leaved oak table was a monstrosity! It was at least twenty feet long, and Caroline counted twenty-four chairs. Jacob followed her line of vision and noticed her lips moving.

"I built that," he muttered, sensing that she was displeased. "It has eight leaves to it, believe it or not. That's as big as it gets; even so, when we have a big crowd in here, the kids eat in the kitchen." He jutted his chin in the direction of the kitchen and abruptly turned away to talk to Johann, and Caroline flushed. She needed to be very, very careful, and she smiled brilliantly at no one in particular, counting the hours until they could take their leave.

Anton lagged behind the crowd of Naplavas moving noisily through the house, attempting to stay out of Caroline's line of vision as much as possible. What in God's name was that woman trying to do? He was frequently on the receiving end of such blatant sexual signals from beautiful women, but he had never been as unhappy about it as he was today. He would never do anything to hurt his little brother, but *damn*, he was going to be sorely tested trying to keep his hands off of that luscious little woman. He covertly watched her from behind: she was possessive of Jacob; that much anyone could see. It was easy to see what she prized in his younger sibling: Jacob was incredibly bright—the smartest of any of the Naplava children, hands-down—and quite wealthy: the ranch he had built with Papa was thriving and growing larger with each passing season. He was masculine and naturally handsome, just like Papa, and Anton supposed that women loved his bright eyes and labor-hewn physique. He was also the kindest individual Anton had ever met: patient, genuinely concerned with the welfare of others, and fair to all, characteristics Anton knew he himself would never possess. And Jacob laughed easily and often. But Anton suspected that all of those attributes paled in comparison to the very real possibility that Jacob would become a ridiculously young mayor of a booming southwest city very soon. Yes, it was simple to understand why Caroline—and no doubt many of her contemporaries—would be lining up to marry Jacob Naplava, who was reputed to be a man who wanted to marry but just could never find the right woman.

What confounded Anton was this: what on earth was Jacob doing courting Caroline Vogler? She was rich and beautiful, but Jacob had never put much stock into those attributes. In fact, ever since he was thrown over by that Boston socialite, he seemed to prefer plainer women like Darla Keller and that plain-Jane woman he had dated a while back, the one who was having an affair with the family's teenage stable boy, of all hilarious things. Anton doubted that Jacob was in love with Caroline: he seemed to enjoy being around her and they had an ease with each other, but his eyes weren't *shining*. Anton didn't know a lot about a lot of things, but he knew love. He had been in love once as a very young man, barely out of his teen years, and she had broken his heart irreparably. From that point forward he had made a conscious effort to avoid love at all costs; unencumbered lust was so much easier to satisfy. He suspected he had witnessed Jacob in love, years ago—how his eyes had shone for that little red-haired girl! He *must* remember to mention Dr. Rose to Jacob if he got the chance. He frowned and reconsidered—Jacob had been horribly hurt by that incident, and he seemed happy now. His little brother was longing for a family, and that must be the answer: he had finally decided to stop looking for the real thing and just settle for *this* thing.

And what a thing it was. Caroline oozed sensuality. Jacob probably could not begin to fathom the wildcat that waited patiently under all of those layers of expensive clothing and gentility and cool Victorian propriety. His poor trusting brother probably thought he was marrying a virgin. Anton, on the other hand, had understood within seconds of meeting her that she was an essentially carnal woman. He had also understood that he would like to carry her away to his home in the city where a gigantic, custom-made claw-foot bath was waiting for the two of them, along with expensive Indian oils that they could smooth over every inch of each other's bodies.

He cleared his throat and gave himself a mental shake, looking around desperately, and seeing Johann whispering into Lindy's ear, approached them quickly.

"So is Caroline a man-eater or what?" he hissed without preamble. Lindy raised her eyebrows and then dissolved into her familiar laughter. She had always appreciated Anton's unconventional antics.

Johann glanced around at the woman in question, making sure his words would be concealed under the layer of chatter. "I don't know, my good man, but she's not for Jacob. She's all wrong." He shook his head forlornly and tightened his grip around his beloved Lindy's waist.

Lindy snorted. "What do you mean, you don't know? She's got more notches in her belt than Rachel Fay." Rachel Fay was an itinerant chuck wagon driver who freely offered her services to just about any lonely sheepherder who was game. "Well, can you blame him for courting her?" she finally sighed. "We've been playing matchmaker for years, and he's got it in his head that he needs to find a woman, and fast. You know he's always wanted a family." She looked at Jacob wistfully, thanking God for the millionth time that she had found her dream man in Johann and wanting the same happiness for the fine young man across the room.

"Look, we've got to do something," Johann finally said. "I saw the way she looked at you, Anton; Jacob must be blind, or else she's very clever with her timing." Anton flushed and examined his impeccable nails.

"I didn't mean—" he began, but Johann waved away his words with an impatient hand.

"You never *mean* to do it, Anton, but for some inexplicable reason, women can't seem to resist you. And vice versa." At this, Lindy snorted.

"He's never shown any interest in me. C'mon, Anton, give it your best shot," she said playfully, running a hand down his chest and smiling coyly, her brown eyes sparkling. Johann smacked her hand away from his brother's chest and she smacked back, and the two engaged in a brief wrestling match while Anton watched, bemused and more than a little jealous. Lindy was dead wrong: even though she was not a beauty, she had qualities that Anton adored: she was earthy, smart, funny, utterly fearless, comfortable in her own skin, and a wonderful mother. He had always been very drawn to her. He flushed: there was definitely a pattern here. It was time to stop coveting his brothers' women!

"Johann…Johann!" Anton tried to break in. His brother finally captured his wife's hands, holding them tightly in place. She laughed and gave up the fight, and they turned to him. "I'll make sure I'm never alone with Caroline. I'll avoid her like the plague. If she's what I think she may be, Jacob will see it soon enough."

"No! That's exactly what I *don't* want you to do!" Johann exclaimed, and Lindy nodded in agreement.

"I'm not following you," returned Anton, brow crinkled.

"Don't be dense, Tony Boy," Lindy chided. "It's time for you to put that perfect face to good use," she pinched his cheek affectionately and Anton wished again that he would have found her before Johann did, although he admitted to himself that he probably wouldn't have given her a second look, being the shallow jerk that he was.

"I still don't follow," he returned, smiling down at her.

Johann groaned. "Seduce her, Anton. See how far you can take it. Better yet, just be friendly and let her seduce you. We have to find out how far she'll go. She thinks you're a lecherous scoundrel and would never tell Jacob about your *indulgences*, but we know otherwise. You're lecherous, but you're no scoundrel. Right?"

Lindy frowned at this as she realized that Johann's remarks cut a bit too deep. Anton stared at the floor, wondering how he had come to this point in his life.

"He's not a rogue, Johann. There's much more to Tony than meets the eye." She was serious for once and flashed Anton a genuine smile. "Johann's just trying to say that Jacob is blinded by—well, not love, I don't think; maybe infatuation, or desperation, or boredom, whatever the case may be—and needs a wake-up call. Obviously Johann is too ugly to be the bait."

Anton laughed. "Well, we all know that's true. But so what if I pursue Caroline, or she pursues me? What if something happens; what am I to do then? Tell Jacob? That'll be a pretty scene: 'Jacob, I seduced your girl to find out if she was faithful. Turns out she's not.' Or how about 'Jacob, your woman won't leave me alone: she's on me like a kitten on milk, and I took it all the way just to prove that she's not the girl for you.' I wonder what would happen? Oh, I know: he would beat me black and blue. Either that, or he wouldn't believe me."

Johann nodded. "You're right, we will need a witness. Ideally, it would be Jacob himself, but I'm not quite sure how to work that. I could be the witness! Or Lindy here." Lindy made a gagging noise at the suggestion.

"No, really, thanks, but no." She watched as Caroline caught a glimpse of herself in a large, gold-framed mirror mounted on a nearby wall. She smoothed her hair and then, with a quick look to make sure Jacob wasn't watching, pouted her lips as if kissing herself. It happened so quickly that Lindy didn't quite believe what she had seen. *"Každá liška svůj ocas chválí,"* she murmured. *Every fox praises its own tail.* Johann snorted his approval.

There was a silence as all three of them turned to look at Caroline and Jacob. He bent low as she whispered into his ear, his arm properly and lightly resting around her upper back. As they watched, Caroline's arm crept around Jacob's front and rubbed slow, sensuous circles on his belly just north of his belt, her little finger dipping lower and lower, a bit *below* belt-level. Her other hand rubbed his back and strayed down ever so briefly to his upper thigh, which she squeezed quickly before she returned both hands to a proper place.

"Rub me like that, Lin. Right now," whispered Johann, eyes bugging.

"Don't worry, love, I know exactly where and how to rub you," she muttered back. "But I have to admit, she seems—shall we say—a bit *charged.* Jacob might not stand a chance."

Anton witnessed the scene, cleared his throat several times, and thought for a bad moment that he might have to excuse himself. Caroline was an incredibly desirable temptress; she oozed sexuality, and he knew he must stay as far away from her as he could he possibly could. He could not—*would* not—be the bait.

"I can't do it," he finally said, and Johann sighed heavily. Lindy just nodded and smiled.

"It's okay, Tony," she murmured. "We're not being fair to you at all." She grabbed his hand and squeezed it.

Anton suddenly decided that the time was right. "Hey Lindy, I actually have something else I need to talk to you about. Privately," he said with a pointed look at Johann.

"Really? You're excusing me? Oh, well, now I've heard it all," the older brother grumbled good-naturedly, moving away to pluck an errant toddler from climbing the massive sideboard.

"What is it?" said Lindy, her fingers still entwined with his.

"There's this girl," he began uncertainly, and waited, by habit, for the inevitable teasing. How many times in his life had he begun a sentence that way? Lindy stood patiently, pinning him with her level gaze.

"She's a—she works in a bawdy house," he continued, his face coloring. He cleared his throat. "She's a friend of mine. I never—we never—she's just a kid, only sixteen. But she's so funny and smart and she speaks her mind; she reminds me a lot of you, actually." At this he looked up and smiled fondly at Lindy, and she returned his smile, still silent. A beat passed.

"Anyway, well, she was beaten by a customer not long ago, and I'm trying to convince her leave the life." Lindy nodded in approval. At Anton's continued silence, she finally spoke.

"You care deeply for her, young or not; I can tell. I can see it in your eyes." Anton's mouth dropped open and closed again, startled. Until this moment, he had never thought of Mayflower in that way, but as he conjured her image, he suddenly felt a sharp longing and a peculiar protectiveness. Lindy watched the emotions parade across his face: surprise, denial, wonder. She laughed and pulled him into a hug. "Oh, Tony, I'm so happy for you. I truly do hope this all works out."

Anton pulled away. "That's kind of where you come in, actually," he muttered sheepishly. "I was hoping you and Johann could—she needs a safe haven; she needs to learn how to do things like cook and keep a house or just time to figure out what she wants to do. Her mother was a waste; she sold Mayflower to a pimp when she was only eleven. She has no idea what normal is, but she's so smart; she could be a teacher or a lawyer or whatever she puts her mind to!" He paused as Lindy absorbed the gravity of his request.

"So you are asking me to take her in, to care for her and train her. To raise her." It was a statement, not a question, and so Anton remained silent, realizing for the first time how preposterous this whole idea really was. What had he been thinking?

"Oh Lindy, I'm sorry. This is possibly the dumbest idea I've ever had, and I've had some dumb ones," he finally managed. "You are just...you are my ideal, and there's no one else I would even think about asking."

Lindy stared at him, eyebrows raised, honestly speechless, which was a rarity for her. "Your ideal *what?*" she said at last.

"My ideal woman. Wife. Sister. Lover. Mother. Everything."

Lindy's jaw had dropped, but when she recovered she rewarded him with a dazzling, genuine smile. "Tony, you have made me a very happy woman," she pronounced. "You know Johann is the love of my life, but I shall cherish what you have said, and you have my permission to flirt with me as much as you like. In front of Johann, too, if you don't mind." Anton breathed a sigh of relief and leaned forward to kiss her lingeringly on her cheek.

"We'll just start with that," he said with a wink, and they both laughed.

"You know I am honored that you would entrust your Mayflower's care to us," she finally continued. "I would love to bring her into our crazy Naplava fold, that is, if she doesn't mind sleeping on a cot, at least at first, until Jacob can build her a proper bed. Johann is a hopeless carpenter." At this she looked over her shoulder at her dear lover, catching his eye, and they shared an intimate look. "Let's go talk to him, okay?"

Anton could only nod, overcome with gratitude.

As dinner commenced, Anton seated himself as far as possible from Caroline as he could, not looking her way even one time.

Caroline suffered the meal in a quiet frenzy. To her left sat Jacob, a virile, handsome man with incredible eyes who would soon be her husband, and whom she *must* stop assaulting. She was determined to be the proper lady from this point forward. She balled her hand into a fist.

And all the way down the interminably long plank table sat Anton, who refused to even glance her way. She wondered if he was trying to drive her wild on purpose—she wouldn't put it past him! Perhaps tonight, after the household was soundly sleeping, she would sneak into his bedchambers—did he have his own room? Oh God, she hoped so—and wake him with a kiss in a most unexpected spot. Her entire body positively sizzled just thinking about it. But he may tell Jacob; she could see that he adored his brother. She must let Anton come to her, all in good time, perhaps after she was securely Mrs. Jacob Naplava.

And to her right sat none other than Gacenka Naplava, whom she had to admit was a beautiful woman who bore a disconcerting resemblance to Anton. Correction: her face was beautiful, although aging, but her attire and demeanor were homespun and plain, and her honey brown hair, gathered into traditional Moravian braids—Caroline actually admired these—was fading. And how many children had she borne? It was some horribly repulsive number, and clearly apparent in her wide hips and back end. She really couldn't blame her too much, though: her husband was obviously virile and very handsome, now that Caroline had a chance to look more closely. He was a mirror image of Jacob, plus thirty years or so. He had aged quite well. *Very* well. Every time she caught his eye, Mr. Naplava would nod stiffly and reach for his wife, holding her hand or pulling her into a little hug. Caroline smirked to herself; she could have a bit of fun making this one squirm. But for another day.

"Are you a bit overwhelmed, Caroline?" Gacenka suddenly turned to her and smiled sweetly, and Caroline felt a prick of annoyance. She was never overwhelmed, and certainly not by these country hayseeds. She was used to feeling different; to being the outsider, as her parents had at least attempted, mightily, to shelter her. This whole experience was easy as pie.

"No, ma'am, I am enjoying meeting you all so very much," Caroline returned softly, and was gratified to see that Gacenka clearly had not heard everything she had said. Gacenka nodded and smiled uncertainly, and societal rules dictated that Caroline should broach a conversation topic next, but Caroline simply turned and placed a small forkful of something disgusting—she hoped it wasn't mutton—into her mouth. Gacenka tried twice more to strike up a dialogue, asking about Caroline's parents and schooling, but Caroline always answered so softly and so succinctly that Gacenka soon retreated, conversing animatedly with Jacob instead.

For the remainder of the meal, Caroline suffered the covert stares of every Naplava except two, and she couldn't wait until this ordeal was finished. Wenzel's eyes in particular were tracking her every move, she was sure, and she had a fleeting and horrible notion that he could read her mind. To test her theory, she looked directly at him and thought, *Hey Wenzel, I think you are a creepy, dumb creature*, all the while smiling. Wenzel smiled back uncertainly and looked away, putting Caroline's mind at ease.

After dinner the clan made their way back to the porch, where the men produced homemade wine, an ice cream churn, and musical instruments, and began *singing*, of all crude things. Caroline couldn't understand a word of it: they sang in their native tongue, Jacob included. And the women danced! Lindy made a move to pull Caroline into the fray; Caroline had to laugh and grab Jacob's arm, feigning shyness. There was just *no way* that was going to happen. Anton kept busy with one young brat or another, avoiding her gaze, and Caroline decided it was time to act. Jacob was churning ice cream, getting drunk, and singing at the top of his lungs, and she was bored out of her mind.

She slipped easily through the crowd and zoned in on Anton: he was dancing with a small girl with blond pigtails, who was taking the ride on his feet. Caroline stopped for a moment to admire him from the rear before she announced her presence. "May I cut in?" she said softly, very sweetly, and was gratified to see Anton's head whip around at the sound of her voice.

"Oh, I don't know; Betsy here is a mighty fine dancer…"

"It's okay, Uncle Tony," Betsy said solemnly. She stared at Caroline as she moved away, looking back over her shoulder to get one last look. Caroline gave her a genuine smile; she actually had a soft spot for little girls, and this one resembled Caroline as a small child. She dearly hoped to have one of her own someday. She was absolutely certain that Jacob would be a perfect father.

Caroline turned and inserted herself into Anton's arms all in one precise movement, and the two began to dance, Anton looking a bit thunderstruck. Finally he laughed. "You are some piece of work," he muttered.

"You have no idea, Uncle Tony," she purred back.

The two danced for a few moments in silence, Caroline keeping her proper distance with nothing more than a polite smile on her face while

Anton gulped and tried to breathe properly. He had never felt such simultaneous dislike and desire for a woman. He closed his eyes and was startled that an image of Mayflower popped into his mind, with her brown sausage curls, enormous, sad, sparkling eyes, and her lovely, cupid lips, causing him to miss a beat and tread on one of Caroline's tiny feet. She kicked him playfully and tightened her grip. Anton sent a silent appeal to Lindy, who was watching from the far side of the porch with an eyebrow cocked in amusement. "Save me," he finally mouthed to her. *Save me from myself.* He watched as Lindy pulled Wenzel down to her and whispered something in his ear, and Wenzel began to make his way over. Caroline noticed and groaned.

"Anton, let's go for a walk," she whispered quickly. "Show me the barns." It sounded asinine and she realized she was playing her cards much, much too soon, but she was downright repelled and somewhat frightened of Wenzel the Idiot Boy.

"Let's see what Wen wants first," Anton said smoothly, regaining some of his usual finesse. "Then maybe we can take a walk." *Wen, please get me out of this, dear little brother.*

Wenzel lumbered across the porch and stood stiffly in front of Anton, looking somewhat confused. "Tony. Lindy said you need to take your turn at the damn churn now or the deal's off. And she said she's ready for another kiss." Anton struggled mightily to suppress his laugher—Lindy was not one to mince words or play it safe—and he smiled tenderly at Wenzel.

"Thanks, Wen. Lindy's weird and funny, isn't she?"

Wenzel visibly relaxed as he realized that he was helping them to joke around. "You bet, Tony. She's a daffy one." He laughed and pulled Anton away from Caroline without so much as an "Excuse me," and Caroline was left gaping after them, wondering what on earth Lindy meant by their "deal" and about the fact that she was ready for another *kiss.* Her eyes swerved to the woman in question, and she found to her dismay that Lindy was staring at her with a smirk on her ugly plain face. Caroline reached a boiling point as Anton approached his sister-in-law, leaned down, and brushed his lips across hers.

The rest of the evening was a dreadful blur, and Caroline finally excused herself with a headache. Jacob was solicitous and kissed her in front of everyone, to her great gratification, offering to walk her to her room, but Caroline remembered her vow—*hands off!*—and insisted she could find it on her own. One of Jacob's annoying twin sisters—Marianna, who had a married a *Mexican* of all horrible things—showed Caroline to a room on the opposite end of the sprawling home, and after trying and failing miserably to make polite conversation with Caroline, quickly left to rejoin the party.

Caroline surveyed her surroundings: a small dreary bed, made up with some obscenely brightly-colored countrified quilt, and an ancient wardrobe, no doubt from the "homeland," were the focal points. The wooden floor was bare and scuffed—was that *writing* scratched in one corner? No doubt one of those unruly unsupervised brats had taken a knife to the floor—and atop a small commode stand was a pitcher and bowl for washing. Did they not have an indoor bathroom yet? Was she going to have to do her business in an *outhouse*? She laughed aloud, one humorous bark that hung rudely for a beat in the serene room. She looked closely; there was a sizable chip in the pitcher. The wardrobe wore its age and groaned when she opened it, and she wrinkled her nose as she caught a glimpse and the musty smell of horribly prehistoric dresses. She shut the door quickly. The walls were not papered, but left as raw wood, with a child's sampler hung above the bed serving as the only "art" in the dreadful room. The window was large and dressed with calico curtains, but as she glanced out, she saw only barns and sheep and hills. And more sheep. She felt an oppressive weight in her heart.

And it was then and there that Caroline decided that she would never, *ever*, not for any amount of money or social status, sink to the depths of living in this house as she knew Jacob expected her to do. He didn't need to know that yet—but she had it all planned, and she almost always got what she wanted. After serving as mayor for four years, Jacob was going to be a political climber: they were headed for Washington, and she could not wait to get there. She would be a wife of a senator, and then, years from now, once their two children (a strapping boy and a delicate girl who looked just like her mother) were grown, she would be the First Lady of the United States. The dream wasn't preposterous: her father had the connections, and Jacob had the intelligence and charisma, to make it happen. She collapsed on the bed and closed her eyes and dreamed of the perfect future while the party on the porch wore on into the night.

Two days later—two long days filled with awkward conversations with her future in-laws and stultifying activities that included baking bread with Gacenka and touring sheep barns with Franticek—they were finally taking their leave. Caroline smiled sweetly and made sure that she was the first to move in for the farewell hugs; she made certain that she expressed her thanks to her hostess, and gushed over every drooling baby and ankle-biting toddler, and proclaimed how she would miss the peaceful beauty of the ranch.

All the long ride home Caroline fantasized about Anton. Uncle Tony's apparent disinterest was gnawing away at her and increasing her desire tenfold. Did he want her or not? It was horribly frustrating and wildly exciting. She closed her eyes and pretended to nap, her head resting on her fiancé's shoulder, but all the while she was removing Anton's clothing, piece by piece, and constructing delightfully wicked scenarios in her mind.

Jacob was deep in thought, especially during the second leg of their trip. It had been obvious to him that his family was ambivalent about Caroline.

Anton seemed to like her well enough, but he liked all women, and Jacob knew he wouldn't cross a line. Johann and Lindy did not care for her at all, but Jacob was willing to attribute that to their never-ending quest to find him the perfect woman. The reactions of the rest of his family seemed to be guarded; no one had approached in private to say "Well, done, Jake! She's a keeper!" Then again, no one had asked him what the *hell* he was thinking, either, even though that was a question he had continued to ask himself.

He glanced down at her then. Her bright blond head was bumping on his shoulder, and as he gazed at the back of her delicate white neck she suddenly seemed so incredibly vulnerable. Here she was, a woman of great wealth and social connections, abruptly engaged to a sheep farmer to whom she had given her virginity, and she was, quite possibly, with child. She was quiet and reserved around people she didn't know; had he endeavored to make it easier for her these past few days? Had she been frightened and worried? If she was pregnant, how sick was she feeling right now, and had his attitude made it impossible for her to confide even that to him? He felt a surge of tenderness and regret, and he shifted to pull her closer to him.

And yet not five minutes later his mind wandered helplessly in a different direction. They were nearing *the spot.* Fifteen years ago he kissed a girl here, sitting in the back of a wool wagon, his hands in her warm, fragrant hair. If he closed his eyes, he could still feel her small, strong hands clutching him around his waist, pulling him closer, closer. He could still taste her lips and smell her skin. He could still feel that rush that filled every part of his body. He closed his eyes, indulging himself, and lived the most precious and profound moment of his life all over again.

Later that month, when June was old and the San Antonio sun was bright and searing hot, Caroline invited Jacob on a picnic. She took his face in her hands, and it only took two words to change his life. "I'm pregnant," she had choked out, tears streaming down her frightened face. And Jacob had felt that peculiar breath-robbing sensation that one feels when something of great magnitude is irrevocably over, and something else is about to begin, ready or not.

EPILOGUE

She was dreaming of him again. Always. They were deep in Glory Creek, and they were children again. But it was all different: she wasn't bare, and she wasn't drowning: she was just simply drifting through the dark blue-green water in her fancy, ridiculous red dress. And then he was swimming toward her, pulling her close, the dragon wing wet and sleek on his chest, and his gaze was so intense that she had to close her eyes or she would shatter.

When she awoke she could still feel him in her arms, as solid and real as anything in her life.

PREVIEW OF ROSIE'S CASTLE, BOOK 2 BAILEY ROSE, M.D. SERIES

CHAPTER ONE

She was trussed up like a turkey in her gray traveling suit again, and she was reasonably certain that at some point during the course of the afternoon she would expire from heat stroke or perhaps just spontaneously combust in a spectacular puff of fire and smoke. Bailey Rose sighed miserably and turned stiffly to her left to gain a breeze from the small "window" of the barouche. She tried in vain to filter out the voices of her two closest friends as they engaged in their customary never-ending game of bickering.

"Miss Flores, I just don't understand—"

"Oh, for Christ's sake, call me Gabby or Gabriella like everyone else."

"Please, if you don't mind, would you not take the Lord's name in vain?"

A snort. "Oh for Chr—oh *criminy*!"

"Miss *Gabriella*, as I was trying to say, I don't understand why you felt the urge to join us today. Maybe you haven't noticed, but it's July in southern Texas, and it's well over one hundred degrees, and you are in no condition—"

"I have."

A confused pause. "Pardon?"

"I have. I *have* noticed the temperature, Tommy; I'm not a moron. It's hotter than a whore house on nickel night." Bailey squelched a huff of laughter. Nobody called the esteemed Reverend Thomas Eckles *Tommy*, or even "Tom," for that matter. In fact, everyone called him "Reverend" except for Bailey herself, who called him Thomas. And Gabby's quaint little sayings always added an interesting dimension to these discussions. She must really be in an ornery mood today. Bailey felt a bit sorry for Thomas; he would never win this game. Gabby, a childhood friend whom she had rescued from a high-priced brothel, was never one to censure her words.

"I beg your pardon, *Miss Flores*. Those crude references do not—they don't represent who you—" Thomas stuttered to a halt, and Bailey snuck a look. If he pulled on his earlobe any harder, it would pop right off. A vein was standing out in his forehead. Gabby was wearing her usual serene, slightly amused expression, looking stunning as she always did. Her hair, once dyed a platinum blond in her days as the Mexican Pearl, was growing in, but it was still so short and close to the scalp that she had it covered with a wrap; a beautiful yellow scarf with tiny golden beads that caught the sun. Her face, naked of any artifice, glowed with health, and her eyes sparkled with mischief.

"Oh Tommy, lighten up, baby. Let's play Quaker's Meeting the rest of the way—for Bailey's sake, all right? She's obviously nervous." At this she flashed a smile at her friend and leaned forward to squeeze her hand, and Bailey smiled gratefully in return. Gabby had morphed back into exactly the girl Bailey remembered from her childhood, and she loved her like a sister.

"Oh, no, I'm feeling just fine!" she squeaked. She *was* nervous. The three of them were on their way to the first official mayoral debate, and Thomas was going to introduce her to the candidates! Bailey Rose, child of the bordellos, was going to shake hands with powerful political officials and suggest to them they pony up money to fund her clinics for prostitutes. Was she crazy? She began to feel panic creep around the edges of her bravado.

"So you are sure you will be able to introduce me, Thomas? Before the debate, if only for a moment?" This was important to her plan; she wanted the candidates to ponder her idea while they were debating each other; she wanted them to remember her face, so that perhaps they would feel compelled to call on her when the discussion was thrown open to the audience.

"Yes, yes, I know at least one of them quite well, a Mr. Harris, and I've met two of the other three candidates. I'm sure they will be delighted to meet *you*." He smiled at her reassuringly, and Bailey was reminded yet again of how lucky she was to have him in her life. He had paved every step of her way, putting his own position in his congregation at risk while doing so. And that was precisely why she wanted to gain this funding; so Thomas could quietly step out of the business of funding the clinic with offertories and other undisclosed funds, which he would not, despite her best efforts, reveal.

"How will you introduce her?" Gabby asked suddenly. Thomas just stared at her.

"What?"

She leaned forward until her face was two inches from his. "HOW WILL YOU INTRODUCE HER?" she repeated quite loudly, as if speaking to someone hard-of-hearing. "What, exactly, are you going to say? Because if you start it out on the wrong foot, she's screwed."

Bailey groaned and slouched down into her seat. "What happened to the Quaker Meeting?" she grumbled.

"Well, Miss Flores, not that it's any of your business, but I will introduce her as Dr. Bailey Rose, obviously."

"Well, Tommy, that is stupid, obviously."

"I beg your—"

"You can't just waltz her up there and say 'Hey, meet Dr. Bailey Rose; she runs a clinic for harlots. Will you pay for it? You should, because you use the services.'"

Thomas's face grew redder by the second. "Give me some credit! I'm not going to—I know how to be subtle!"

"Okay, then, pretend I'm a mayoral candidate. I'm Mr. Big Trousers. Introduce me to Bailey." She waited as Thomas fumed.

"I'm not going to play your games," he finally managed.

Bailey sat up straighter. "Actually, Thomas, that's not such a bad idea. Let's practice, because I'm not sure what you're going to say and I sure as heck don't know what *I'm* going to say. Please?" She tilted her head, smiled charmingly, and watched as his features softened. She caught Gabby rolling her eyes and making a gagging motion in her peripheral vision.

"Well, if you think it would be helpful," he agreed kindly. He cleared his throat and gave his ear a few preliminary tugs. "Miss Flores, are you ready?"

"I was born ready," she growled, and punched him on the arm, hard. He opened his mouth to chastise her but closed it again with a look from Bailey, sighed, and took a deep breath.

"Mr.—Mr. Big Trousers," he began, pausing as Bailey giggled. "Allow me to introduce you to Dr. Bailey Rose. Dr. Rose, here finally is the man I've been telling you about! My parishioners tell me he has more to offer every citizen of this city than any other candidate. A true champion of the common man and woman."

"Oh! Um, hello, so pleased to make your acquaintance, Mr. Big Trousers," Bailey managed; Gabby had puffed her cheeks, stuck out her chest, and wore the self-satisfied expression of an important man. Bailey offered her hand for a shake.

Gabby took her hand delicately and turned it, palm down, then leaned over and kissed it. "So pleased to meet you, *Miss* Rose," she boomed. "What's this about *Dr.* Rose? No woman of your beauty could be in that sort of profession. Shouldn't you be at home tending to your young ones and *servicing* your husband?" she smirked.

"Well, I never!" gasped Bailey, thoroughly enjoying herself. "You will apologize for that outrageous sentiment, you oversexed pompous ass!" Thomas groaned and slouched in his seat.

"Oh! Wait a minute, there, missy! You aren't married, are you? How about you and I sneak in a back room of the Lucky Strike over there and—"

"Okay! Thank you, ladies! I believe today's play is concluded!" said Thomas loudly as the women dissolved in laughter. "You know, that could have been quite a useful exercise, Miss Flores, if you wouldn't have made a mockery of it." He frowned at her and crossed his arms.

"*That could have been quite a useful exercise, Miss Flores,*" Gabby imitated in a stuffy professorial voice, crossing her arms over her chest and frowning, executing a remarkable impression of Thomas. "Honestly, Tommy, couldn't you see I was just trying to get her to relax?"

They both looked at Bailey, who, at the moment, was biting her fingernails to the quick.

"Yes, I see your point. Well done," Thomas muttered wryly.

"That was actually a smart approach," Bailey mused. "Butter him up, get him to admit he is the champion of the common man, and then I move in to explain how my idea takes care of those very people." She was nodding, suddenly seeing how this could all work.

"No Bailey, *those people*, the Jezebels, are *not* the common man. The common man is the humble farmer, housewife, shop worker. Not someone who's involved in vice." Gabby looked disgusted with the whole conversation. "You're only chance is to spring it on them in front of everyone after the debate."

"Miss Flores, I hardly think that you are the expert on how to—" Thomas began.

"Oh, put a sock in it, Tommy. You know I'm right, and so does she."

There was silence as the two of them stopped squabbling for a moment and looked at Bailey. She bit her lips in consternation. How on earth was she going to make this work? This whole thing, now that it had been set in motion, was possibly a colossally stupid idea.

Finally she sighed. "Gabby's right."

Gabby smiled brilliantly and reached over to give Thomas's earlobe a quick tug. "She said I'm right. That means you're wrong," she clarified in a stage whisper.

Thomas closed his eyes as if praying for strength from the Almighty God. "Criminy!" he uttered under his breath, much to the amusement of Gabby. "What do you want me to say, Bailey?" he finally asked.

"Just introduce me as a friend—Dr. Bailey Rose—and we'll let them wonder about that. Then I'll bring the whole issue up after the debate, like Gabby said. That is, if they'll call on me." Gabby nodded in approval and Thomas opened his mouth as if to argue some more, but he didn't have a chance. The driver had entered the Main Plaza and the carriage slowed to a halt, unable to make progress forward.

"You folks will need to hop out here, I can't go no further," he called cheerfully. He swung his bulk off the seat, gestured to a passing boy and handed him a few coins and the reins, and opened the door to the cab. Thomas jumped out nimbly and immediately turned to help Bailey, who suddenly froze in place as she looked out over the bustling crowd. A sizable platform draped with American flags had been erected at the foot of the brand new Bexar County Courthouse, whose construction had just been completed. It was a massive, grand Romanesque Revival-style masterpiece of native Texan granite and red sandstone, roofed in distinctive green and red tiles. Her eyes were drawn to the nearby towering San Fernando Cathedral, and she experienced a fleeting urge to run inside and hide away in a corner of its quiet, cool interior. She had not expected the crowd: there were *thousands* of people milling about: men, women, and children from all walks of life, some in their Sunday best, some in simple homespun. Farmers, cowboys, sheep men, businessmen. Wealthy ladies, poorer simple folk, chili queens and numerous other vendors, even soubrette girls and prostitutes. White, Negro, Mexican, Indian. Carriages and horses crowded the streets of the Plaza, and the garden in the middle of it all—a sizable area filled with trees, fountains and benches—was utterly packed with people. Everyone looked to be jockeying for a spot from which to watch the debate; many of them had chairs or blankets and were snatching a piece of ground as quickly as they could, facing the courthouse and waiting for the show to begin.

Bailey sat right back down again.

"What are you doing?" questioned Gabby. "Get out, Dr. Rose. You won't get anything accomplished sitting in here." She prodded Bailey's rear end with the pointy end of her parasol.

"Did you see how many people are here?" whispered Bailey.

"No, I didn't," whispered Gabby back. "You won't let me out."

Bailey took a deep breath and stood again, allowing Thomas to hand her down from the carriage.

"Everything okay?" he asked.

"I just didn't expect all the people. I thought, maybe a few hundred, but there's twenty times that number." She looked at him beseechingly, hoping he would talk her out of this crazy plan.

He just nodded. "Yes, that sounds about right. I'd say there could be about four, maybe five thousand. Maybe not, though. It's hard to count when they won't stand still."

Gabby gave an astonished laugh from the carriage as Thomas handed her out. "Did Tommy make a *joke*?" He made a face at her and released her hand quickly.

The driver conferred with Thomas and then gestured to the boy to park the rig. "Shall we proceed, ladies?" the reverend asked, and offered an elbow to each. They made their way through the garden, Thomas nodding and greeting several people along the way, and it occurred to Bailey that Thomas himself would make a very fine mayor. He seemed to know everyone, and he was clearly a revered figure in this city. She saw more than a few young ladies following him with their eyes, admiring his tall, boyish good-looks. They had to step around countless sprawling families, and by the time they neared the debate platform, Bailey was positively sweltering. She glanced at Gabby and noticed that she was swaying a bit.

"Gabby!" she cried, alarmed. She automatically reached for her wrist and felt for her pulse, which was strong and steady. Her skin was warm, not cold and clammy, and when Bailey pinched the back of her hand, the skin rebounded nicely.

"Oh, I'm fine, Dr. Silly," she murmured. "Just a little dizzy. It's to be expected."

Bailey noticed an expression of acute worry flit across Thomas's face. He glanced around and then took Gabby by the arm. "I'm getting her settled in the shade with a very large cup of water and ice," he pronounced. "And I won't take 'no' for an answer." Gabby shared a look of amazement with Bailey, who was gratified to see the relationship between the two of them finally starting to thaw. She suspected Thomas was making a Herculean effort to be friendly to Gabby for Bailey's sake.

"Bailey, I'll be back in time to introduce you to Mr. Harris and the other candidates." She nodded her assent, already turning back to the courthouse with growing anxiety, her mind racing.

"Really, Tommy, you are my knight in shining armor," murmured Gabby with her usual undertone of sarcasm, and the two of them moved away, quarreling the whole way.

The debate was scheduled to begin in ten minutes, and for the first time she noticed men milling about on the courthouse steps. There were what appeared to be four men utterly surrounded by reporters, and she felt her stomach churn again. These were the candidates. If she spoke after the debate, would she be reported in the *San Antonio Express*? She dreaded that thought: in the back of her mind was always the possibility that she would be recognized by that Gaslight Hotel porter as the little girl who went to Senator Hawk's room the night her mother and the Senator had died. She had even told him her name! There was no statute of limitations on murder, she knew, and that thought alone caused her to be very wary of putting herself into the public eye. But she simply couldn't hide under a rock forever: if she wanted to make a change in the district, she had to fight for it, tooth and nail; no one else except Thomas seemed to care a whit for the welfare of these women and their occasional, unfortunate offspring.

The candidates soon separated from the pack and made their way to the platform, heading for the four chairs set up behind the podium, which was festooned in banners and balloons of red, white, and blue, left over from the Independence Day celebration the day before. She noticed they were stopped frequently by well-wishers and those seeking favor, and the pack of people was getting thicker by the second. This was her chance! She glanced around for Thomas, but he was nowhere to be found. She took a deep breath, used a handkerchief to blot the sweat from her forehead and neck, and pushed through the tightly-packed crowd. Standing on her tiptoes, she could barely see what was transpiring. She had to get onto that platform! If she had to introduce herself, she would do it. Finally, after being jostled and scolded and—she was sure of it—groped on her backside, she arrived at the stairs to the left of the stage. From this vantage point she could get her first good look.

And then the earth spun crazily on its axis. She groped for the railing, struggling to stay on her feet. She saw black dots before her eyes. All noise ceased; all was silent except the sound of her own heart pounding. She found herself completely unable to draw a breath—it was as if much of her body had simply stopped functioning.

She was looking straight into the bluest eyes she had ever seen.

ABOUT THE AUTHOR

Jenny Haley is the author of the *Bailey Rose, M.D.* series. As a writer, she was shaped by the works of LaVyrle Spencer, immersing herself in compelling stories of strong women in authentic and relatable situations within rich historical settings. Jenny's genre is tricky to define: historical magical realism paranormal romance, perhaps. You will not find bodice-ripping stories with helpless, flawless protagonists in her books, but stories that deeply resonate, featuring courageous, imperfect women and the men who love them.

Jenny makes her home in the American Upper Midwest where she lives with her husband, teenage daughter, her young adult son close by, and two retired racing greyhounds. In her spare time, she works as a college administrator and writing instructor at a public university.

Jenny loves to hear from her readers! Visit her website at www.jennyhaley.com, where you can watch the latest book trailer, read her blog, and connect via email. If you enjoyed this novel, the nicest way to say "thank you" is to leave a favorable review online!

Made in the USA
Middletown, DE
05 December 2021